The Quest of Eight

Part Two:

In Search of the Alchemist

Richard Reda

ISBN: 0985192607
ISBN-13: 978-0-9851926-0-0

Dedication

This book is dedicated to our first eight grandchildren:

Summer

Lochen

Solveig

Sean

Natalie

Stella

Quinn

Liam

ACKNOWLEDGMENTS

A special thanks to my wife, Karren for her editing and support, and to my daughter, Jill Fox, for her editing. And a special thanks to Sean for asking, "Papa, when are you gong to write another book?"

Cover art: Mike Reda and Richard Reda

Chapter one

It was the first day of spring. Even so, the days were still short this far north. But Quinn didn't care. Any chance to get outside and explore the Ice Kingdom filled him with excitement. The sky was a bright blue, at least for now. The weather could change very quickly any time of year. But with the onset of spring and longer days, storms could appear without a moment's notice, and on rare occasions, melting ice and snow could bring with it sudden flash floods. That almost never happened, but one couldn't be too careful. Quinn had been taught well, and he never went far without a fully equipped sled and his faithful companions: Rover and Kelsey.

The dogs, too, were excited to be outside for more than just a minute or two. The temperatures were still on the low side, although it seldom got above freezing anywhere in the Ice Kingdom. In spite of this, the winds had been calm and no storms had flared up for at least a week. Quinn was ready to blaze a new trail and the dogs were more than anxious.

He took his role as a Guardian very seriously, as did everyone who held this title. It was his job not only to protect his people from invaders (although, truth be told, no one had invaded the Ice Kingdom ever in their recorded history), he was responsible for making sure that the mountains, valleys, ice bergs and seas were safe and clean and that the wild animals were protected. It was difficult to do this in the winter months, although not impossible. For the weeks in which his land was in total darkness, he rarely ventured out for more than a few days. Traveling in the dark was just too dangerous.

In order to make up for his limited exploration during winter months, he would often go on excursions during the rest of the year that lasted for several days or even weeks. This trip was no different. He expected to be gone for about a week and a half and his sled was well packed with supplies for himself, as well as Rover and Kelsey – tent, sleeping bag, rope, pick-ax, and plenty of food. After all, they would be pulling the sled most of the time and he had to keep them in good condition and well fed. Because it was such a bright day and he loved the feel of the sun on his face, he headed east.

The first day out was fairly uneventful. They saw flocks of snow hawks overhead and signs of a passing herd of ice deer. On the second day, they reached a steep incline well before midday. Quinn was helping the dogs push the sled up the long mountainside. They had to stop every few minutes to catch their breath and to rest. The air was getting thin and the winds were picking up. He surveyed the horizon. Even though the skies were still clear, he knew that a storm was approaching and he needed to find some kind of shelter – not immediately, but soon.

Even a small outcropping of rock would help – something that would shield him enough to get his tent set up. They weren't close enough to an ice shelf that would allow him to cut blocks of ice and construct an igloo. That would be the best shelter. Right now, they just needed something to help shield a tent from the wind. Rover and Kelsey knew that the storm was getting worse, but, as tired as they were, they kept struggling to pull the sled and Quinn to a safe place.

Kelsey was the first to see it: a dark spot on the mountainside off to the right. She started barking loudly, looking over her shoulder to see if

Quinn spotted the same thing. Within seconds, Rover spotted the slight projection, too and joined in the barking. It was clear that they both wanted to stop.

"Good girl," he yelled over the roaring wind. "You too, Rover. Let's see what it is. I hope it's enough to block this wind, even just a little."

They pushed ahead towards the patch of black. The storm hadn't arrived, yet, but the wind was blowing the ground snow around, making visibility worse. Quinn lowered his head and ran alongside the sled. The dogs would have less weight to pull with him running, and they could make a little bit faster time. Quinn just wasn't able to run as far or as long as the dogs, and had to jump back on every once in a while.

As they got closer to the black spot on the side of the mountain, Quinn could see that it was a small opening. That was even better than he could hope for. In a few minutes they reached what looked like a shallow cave. Better, yet, he thought. He brought the sled to a stop and got off. He left the dogs in their harness while he checked it out.

The entrance was somewhat narrow, but it was just large enough for Quinn to squeeze into. He stuck his head into the opening just far enough to see if he'd fit. A little tight, he said to himself, but it'll work. He then unloaded a few supplies and tossed them into the opening. Then he retied the cargo, drove some long spikes into the snow and ice, and secured the sled. They'd be in a really difficult position if the wind blew the sled away.

Once everything was secured, he gave Rover a push towards the cave entrance. To Quinn's surprise, Rover dug in his feet and began to growl. The hairs on the back of his neck stood on end and almost immediately Kelsey began to bark and growl, too. Quinn looked around to see if some predator had suddenly appeared. There was nothing in sight.

"What's the matter with you two?" asked Quinn. "We nearly busted our butts to get here and now you're afraid to go in? Get out of the way."

He pushed past them and, before they could stop him, he dove head first through the opening. The narrow entryway dropped down steeply for a few feet. Quinn slid on his belly to the bottom, where it widened out. It was deeper than he expected, but not high enough for him to stand. He was able to sit upright and he wiggled further into the interior to make room for the dogs, pushing his supplies ahead of him into the darkness. He was about to find something to light up the darkness when he heard a low snarling sound.

"Oh, poop," he thought. "This is what those two were growling about. There's something already in here."

He stopped moving further into the cave and stayed completely still for a few seconds. The growling continued, but closer to him. It sounded as if it was coming from the top of the cave. "Oh, poop," he thought again. "Whatever it is must be really big." He knew he couldn't stay where he was, especially in the darkness.

He slowly began to wiggle back towards the opening and quickly bumped his head. The opening was so narrow, the only way he'd fit through was to extend his legs back into the cave so he could crawl out head first. He had come into the cave like a diver; that would be the only way he could get out. He was afraid of getting too close to whatever was in there with him. He needed to see what was in here with him. In spite of the potential danger, he reached inside his coat pocket and pulled out a light stick. He hesitated for a second, wondering if this was the right thing to do. Realizing he didn't have much choice, he tapped it against the side of the cave and the crystals inside slowly swirled around lighting up the inside of the cave.

The light began to expand, and Quinn could see that the entire inside of the cave was not much bigger than his tent, and that was barely big enough for him and the two dogs. He bent his head down and tried to wiggle closer to the opening, as the growling echoed in the chamber. As the light level rose he could see two large red dots less than an arm's length from him.

"Oh, poop," he said out loud this time, but barely above a whisper; his throat was as dry as cotton. "Whatever you are, you're really close."

The crystals in the light stick began to swirl faster and the light became brighter. Quinn could now see that below the two large red dots were two rows of very large and very sharp teeth. He was quickly regretting lighting up the inside of the cave. Not seeing those teeth was much, much better than seeing them.

The large red dots were two piercing eyes, which, along with the teeth, belonged to a very large arctic wolf. It was snow white with a large bushy head, which was crouched just beneath the ceiling of the cave. The only color visible was its bright red eyes. As far as Quinn could guess, it appeared to be about four or five feet high to its shoulder and nearly six feet long. It was lean, having gone through the winter, but even still, it must have weighed almost four hundred pounds. These animals were huge and very mean, but Quinn had never seen one this large.

Quinn could see that the wolf was backed up against the far wall of the cave, about as far as it could go. He probably feels trapped, thought Quinn. He forced his eyes to move from the wolf's teeth to it muscles, which were tensed, ready to pounce at a moment's notice. His eyes moved back to the wolf's mouth and those enormous teeth, which were bared, ready to chomp – also at a minute's notice. Except for his shaking hand, which made the light from the light stick bounce up and down and back and forth, and his eyes, which shot from the tensed muscles to the enormous teeth and back again, Quinn didn't move an inch. He just looked at the wolf and smiled nervously.

"Nice, wolfy, wolfy," he said in as soothing a voice as he could muster.

He slowly brought his free hand up to his mouth to pull off his glove. He slid the hand out of the glove and even more slowly reached in his pocket and pulled out a piece of meat. He kept several in his pocket as treats for Rover and Kelsey. He slowly extended his hand with the piece of meat in it and offered it to the wolf.

"Easy, boy," he said. "I'm not going to hurt you, so please, don't hurt me. And please don't eat my hand. I really like my hand."

The wolf kept his eyes glued on Quinn, all the time still growling deeply. Quinn kept the meat within the wolf's reach. He had one eye closed, because he was afraid to look and he was squinting through the other eye, because he was afraid to not look. His arm was getting tired stretched out with the chunk of meat in it. After what seemed like forever, the wolf shot a quick glance at the meat and then slowly, keeping his eyes on Quinn, waiting for some trickery, leaned his head slightly forward and sniffed the meat. Quick as a flash the wolf snatched the meat from Quinn's hand and nearly swallowed it whole.

"Okay," said Quinn, looking at his empty hand and counting the fingers to make sure they were all there. "Does that mean we're friends?"

The wolf growled again.

"I guess not yet," said Quinn. "OK, let's try this once more, and maybe you'll decide not to eat me."

He slowly reached back in his pocket for another piece of meat and again very slowly extended it towards the wolf. This time the wolf seemed to relax a bit and gently took the meat from Quinn's hand, instead of quickly snatching it. That was better, thought Quinn. In spite of the cold, Quinn found that he was sweating. He only hoped the wolf didn't mistake his sweat for flavoring. He reached into his pocket a little bit more confidently and extracted another piece of meat.

After about three more pieces of meat, the wolf stopped growling and lay flat on the cave floor. He extended his legs and dropped his head down on them, still watching Quinn. When he did this, Quinn could see dried blood caked on the wolf's right front paw. The paw had been pierced and badly sliced by a long, splinter of what looked like glass. Whatever the wolf had tangled with had left a long wide gash down the front of its leg to the paw where the shard of glass was imbedded. The bleeding had stopped, but with any movement, the glass cut deeper and the wound would start to bleed again.

"I'll bet that really hurts," said Quinn, as he placed the light stick on the floor of the cave and removed the glove from that hand. The wolf watched him closely, but didn't begin growling again. So far, so good, Quinn said to himself. He slowly inched closer to the wolf. The wolf just watched. He offered one more piece of meat as he reached for the injured paw. The wolf slowly chewed the meat as he very closely watched Quinn. Quinn gently picked up the paw and carefully examined the glass.

"What on earth did you get yourself into?" Quinn asked, more to himself than the wolf. He slowly and gently removed the glass. The wound bled slightly and Quinn glanced nervously at the wolf. The animal stared at Quinn, but made no sound. Quinn held the object over the light stick and then up towards the cave opening to get some more light on it. What he had pulled from the wolf's paw was about six inches long and glittered like a prism.

"It's a crystal," said Quinn in surprise. "Where _were_ you?" He looked at the wolf who just stared blankly back at him.

"You probably should have that stitched up," Quinn added as he placed the crystal in his pocket.

"Right," he continued after seeing no reaction from the wolf. "I don't see you letting me do that, not that I'd try. You're going to have a nasty scar, but I don't think there's anything I can do about that. Besides, you'll probably attract a lot of girl wolves. Chics really dig scars," he said laughingly to the wolf. The wolf still offered no reaction.

"OK, maybe they don't. What are you, a lone wolf?" he said making another feeble attempt at humor. "Well at least I can wrap it. That might keep it from getting infected."

When he saw that the wolf had not pulled his paw away from Quinn's hand, he dug around in an inside pocket and found a large handkerchief.

"This is going to have to do," he said, as he slowly wrapped the paw and tore the end of the handkerchief and tied it off with a knot.

"I know it looks kind of ratty, but I promise it's clean. I haven't blown my nose in it at all. Really." He told the wolf. When he was done, he stroked the wolf's head tentatively and was a bit relieved when the wolf sniffed the makeshift bandage, licked Quinn's hand and then laid his head on Quinn's lap.

"You're not so tough, after all," Quinn told the wolf.

As soon as those words were out of his mouth, the wolf sprang to his feet, hunched his back, bared his teeth and snarled ominously. Quinn sat bolt upright, banging his head on the back wall of the cave and stared at the wolf in shock, wondering what had happened. Things were going so well, he thought. Then he turned towards where the wolf was facing, and noticed Rover's and Kelsey's heads both squeezed into the cave opening, both growling at the wolf.

"No, Rover; no, Kelsey," Quinn shouted. "Down!"

The two dogs had their heads still jammed into the entryway, neither one able to squeeze past the other to gain entry. They both looked at Quinn with puzzled expressions as they dropped down to the ground, heads still side by side. Quinn reached a tentative hand up to the wolf's head and stroked his ear. The wolf calmed down just enough to let Quinn wiggle sideways towards the cave opening to position himself between the wolf and the dogs.

"Easy, you two," he said. "Rover, get your head out of the opening. Kelsey, come in here – slowly. No, Rover. Stay put. Kelsey, come!"

After some confusion between the two dogs, Kelsey low crawled up to Quinn, her head down low. She stopped a few inches away from Quinn's legs, staring at the wolf who had lowered his head, but had not put it back on Quinn's lap. Quinn then made the introductions.

"Wolf, this is Kelsey. She's pretty easy going and she won't hurt you as long as you don't get crazy. Of course if you get crazy, I think you're way too big for her to do any serious damage. Kelsey, this is Wolf. You be nice to him; you hear me? He's wounded, but even wounded, I think he can take you in a fight. Let's not find out. OK?"

Once it was clear that hostilities between the wolf and Kelsey were on hold, Quinn brought Rover in and did the same thing. In the confined space Quinn managed to place himself between the wolf and the dogs and all of them eventually settled into an uneasy peace. Quinn chattered on incessantly, in part due to nervousness about the three animals in a confined space, and in part because it helped to pass the time. The animals didn't seem to be bothered.

With all the excitement, Quinn hadn't been able to put any kind of barrier over the opening to the cave. The wind periodically blew gusts of icy air and snow into the opening, but neither got very far down the entryway. Quinn unwrapped the meager supplies he had taken from the sled. There was a large blanket, some water and more food. The odd quartet ate well; he poured water into a small container and the animals eagerly lapped it up.

With the blanket and the body heat from the four of them, they were all quite warm and comfortable. Night fell quickly and the storm raged on. No other visitors arrived at the cave, and eventually all parties drifted off to sleep. The next morning, the storm had blown itself out, the sun peeked through the cave opening, and the wolf was mysteriously gone.

Quinn wondered how the wolf had managed to get out of the small enclosure without waking or disturbing the other occupants. He pushed Kelsey and Rover out of the way, mumbling about what terrible watchdogs they were, and clambered out of the cave. The sled was undisturbed, still staked and tied down to the ground, with a layer of snow covering it. He looked around the outside of the entryway and didn't even see any prints or other marks in the snow. Of course, the storm could have blown them away, he said to no one in particular, but he expected to see some indication as to which way the wolf had gone. It was like he disappeared into thin air.

Still mystified, Quinn shouted down for the dogs to wake up. It was time to get going. He cleared off the sled, reloaded the supplies from the cave, hitched the dogs and continued on his way. By midday they had crested the small mountain they had been climbing the day before, and the vista ahead of them was wide open.

The threesome traveled four more days, continuously heading east, and never saw another living thing. The weather cooperated and there were no more storms. By the morning of the fifth day, they saw the eastern sea approaching. Off in the distance, it was a deep blue-gray in color with a few large pieces of ice floating off in the distance. The land sloped gently down to a wide shore of volcanic rock and to the bay beneath. There was a huge misty cloud hanging over the water and the coastline was covered with seals.

"That's odd," said Quinn. "Why aren't they in the water? Why aren't _any_ of them in the water," he said on closer inspection.

As Quinn, Rover, and Kelsey approached, the dogs began barking and whimpering, sensing danger. Quinn slowed the sled down; and stopped about a hundred yards away from the shore. He secured the sled with a stake he drove into the snow, and traveled the rest of the way on foot. It was unusual to see so many seals on the beach at any time, but especially at this time of year. As he got closer he could hear their plaintive bellowing. None of them ran off as he got even closer. Normally, some of the smaller or younger ones would run away from him or at least skitter off, but instead, they all stayed in place, barely moving as he walked among them. They just looked up at him with listless eyes and barked pitifully at him. The barks were not warnings or threats so much as pleas. Something was terribly wrong.

As he zig-zagged his way through hundreds of seals he noticed that their fur seemed to have clumps missing and the skin underneath looked tender and raw. He stopped and pulling off his glove, he reached down to touch one of them. Some of the larger ones barked at him and made feeble attempts to scare him away, but soon gave up. He gently touched the fur and moved it aside to see what looked like a burn mark on a large portion of the seal's body.

"What did this," he asked, not really expecting an answer. He was surprised that the seal allowed him to touch it. This was really weird, he thought.

He stood up, put his glove back on and moved further through the giant herd. After a few more steps he noticed an odd odor in the air. At first he just assumed it was the seals, but it didn't smell like the normal odors created by seals. He sniffed the air again and then he realized it was coming from the water. It smelled of sulfur. He walked up to the shoreline where the smell was the strongest, and discovered that the mist that covered the sea wasn't fog, it was steam. And here the water wasn't the normal blue gray. It was an ugly murky brown. He had never seen it this color before. He took off his glove again and reached into the water. In addition to smelling bad, it was hot and burned his fingertips.

"What the what?" he said out loud to no one in particular. "That water is hot."

He jerked his hand out and shook the water off. The burning in his fingers didn't stop when he pulled his hand from the water, though. In fact, it got even worse. His fingertips began to blister as he stared at them and blew on them. He was about to shove his fingers into his mouth to cool them off, but at the last minute thought that might not be a good idea. The burning continued to get worse and he began to dance around in circles.

"Ow, ow, ow," he shouted, "That hurts, that really hurts."

He shook his hand in the air, trying to cool the burning sensation, looking for something to cool it off. He ran around in circles for a few seconds and then bolted from the rock shore to a nearby ice ledge where a small snowdrift was piled and shoved his burning hand into the mound.

"Holy blubber on a biscuit," he shouted, sighing in relief as the burning finally subsided. "There's something <u>in</u> that water!"

He was hit with a sudden realization. He spun quickly around and looked again at the seals. The clumps of missing fur and the rawness on the skin was because of the water. Something – whatever it was in the water - had burned them, he concluded. As he was trying to figure out what had happened, he heard a muffled cracking sound. The snow and ice beneath his feet began to give way. A large chunk broke off and began to float out to sea, carrying him with it. He teetered, waving his arms to keep his balance, and jumped at the last second. He managed to get back to shore, slipping and splashing into the water at the broken edge of the shelf.

"Holy blubber on a biscuit," he shouted again as he scrambled to his feet and moved away from the shore. "What's going on?"

The water hissed and a cloud of new steam rose. Quinn thought for a minute or two, and then decided he first needed to get the seals further up the shore and away from the water.

"Come on, you two," he shouted to Rover and Kelsey. "Let's get these seals herded up the hill."

It was slow work, since the seals weren't used to Quinn or the dogs, or to being herded; but they eventually moved away from the toxic water, a little more than a hundred yards inland, up over the crest of the hill and past where his sled was anchored. Once the seals were in a safer location Quinn decided he needed to see if he could find the source of whatever was polluting the water and if there was anything he could do about it.

He began unpacking the sled and removed the collapsible kayak. He thought a minute, and then decided he needed to pack some supplies, since he wasn't sure where he would end up. He constructed the kayak, pulling the outer skin as tight as he could. He was pretty sure it would withstand whatever in the water had burned the seals, but to make sure, he put a second skin on. Then he put a container of food and water and a few other odds and ends in the nose of the tiny craft.

He didn't have to tell the dogs anything. If he didn't order them to go home, they would stay there and wait for him to return. He wasn't sure how long he'd be gone this time, but he made a mental note not to stay away too long. When everything was ready, he put the kayak into the water and waited to see if it sprung a leak. It looked fine and he carefully got in. Rover and Kelsey watched him as he paddled off, disappearing into the mist.

The bay was shaped like a backwards question mark. The northern part was a large half circle and the southern part went straight for several miles following a long land mass. The circular part of the bay was mostly ice and snow. It was an enormous shelf of glacial ice that came down from the nearby mountains into the sea. At this time of year, it should be fairly stable. Instead, it appeared to be melting at an alarming rate. Fortunately, the straight part was a long shelf of granite. In the winter it was often covered with several feet of ice and snow, but the snow and ice that covered the top now was also melting away, and the granite base was clearly visible.

Quinn started off by sailing straight out into the bay, and then he paddled to the northern end, following the shoreline, as best he could through the fog. Once he reached the peak and the coastline doubled back to the northwest, he headed due east out to the open sea. He only had to go about a mile and a half before the steam was completely gone, and the sulfuric smell disappeared. He took off the glove on his unburned hand and tentatively touched the water. It was cold – just about the way it should be – he was relieved to discover.

He then turned the small craft around and headed due south towards the bottom part of the bay's circle. About halfway across a fine mist started to appear. It soon became a much thicker steam and the sulfur smell reappeared with it. He looked to the sky and took the positions of the suns to mark his location, and then he turned east again, out to sea. This time he only had to go about a half mile before the mist and the smell disappeared, and he was able to turn back south towards the granite shelf.

By the time he reached land again it was nightfall. He was quite a ways from his starting point – too far for him to walk back. He would have to make camp here. He pulled the kayak on shore and pulled out some of the supplies he had packed. After a quick meal, he spread a blanket on the ground, tipped the kayak over onto the blanket and crawled underneath where he could keep warm and sleep for the night.

The next morning he had a breakfast of walrus jerky – not his favorite, but it was easy to carry and seemed to keep forever. He walked inland for about a half a mile to rise where he could see more of the bay. From there he was able to get a better fix on his location and the shape and size of the pollution, although he still couldn't detect the source. The water was slightly discolored in a long patch – at least as much as he could see through the mist that still hung there.

He estimated that the area of pollution was oval in shape with one side following the shoreline and the other side sort of like a long arc running from the northern peak of the bay to about two miles down the shelf. The part along the shore could have continued under the ice or under the granite. He couldn't tell, but the water was a murky brown instead of the deep blue that it normally was all along the shoreline as far as the mist ran.

He put the kayak back into the water and paddled to where he thought the middle of the pollution was. Before setting off, he picked up a few small rocks. He had pondered a way to determine how deep the pollution went; assuming that whatever was heating the water was the reason for the pollution. An idea struck him and he would need the rocks to help with his experiment. When he was ready, he reached into his pocket for a chunk of the meat he used as treats for the dogs. These pieces were not preerved like the walrus jerky he was still trying to digest from breakfast.

He tied a piece of meat to a line, weighed the line down with one of the rocks he had brought along and threw it all over the side. He let out about fifteen feet of line, counted to ten and pulled the meat back onto the kayak. In just the ten seconds he counted, the meat had already started to cook. It was hot to the touch and it looked like it was nearly burned to a crisp.

"This is not good," he muttered. "At that depth, seals and turtles are going to cook."

He tied a second piece of meat to the line with the rock and this time he dropped it down about twenty-five feet. He let the line out as fast as he could, again counted to ten. As he pulled the line back up, there were waves of heat emanating from the line itself. The piece of meat was nearly charred.

"Oh, poop," he said. "The walruses and dolphins will get cooked if it's that hot that far down. How bad can this be?"

Once more, he decided. This time he added the other rocks he had picked up. He wanted to make sure the line dropped down quickly and that the burning of the meat wasn't just because it was passing through a hot layer. He threw the meat and sinker over and it plummeted down. This time he let out nearly forty feet. He didn't count to ten. This time as soon as the line was played out, he began yanking it back in. When he pulled it up, the meat was gone, and the end of the line was burned.

"What the what?" he said, "the water's hotter the further down. It's supposed to get colder, not hotter. Whatever is polluting the water is coming from underneath. What do I do now?"

He started paddling back to where he started, but he noticed a change in the smell. It wasn't so much a different smell, but an additional, strong odor. It reminded him of when the skins for the kayaks were being cured. He leaned over the side and saw several tendrils of smoke rising from the parts of the skins of his kayak that were pulled tightest across the framework.

"Oh, double poop," he nearly shouted. "This is really not good. I don't want to even think about how quickly I can get cooked."

He turned around and headed for the deeper water, where it was clear the pollution hadn't extended. From there he headed back to the granite line where he pulled his boat ashore and disassembled it. He tightly wrapped the pieces into a pack he threw over his back and began walking to where Kelsey and Rover were waiting for him. It would take him almost two days to get to them. Wondering what he would eat, he reached into his pocket and wished he had packed something more than walrus jerky.

Chapter two

Quinn hiked back to his sled, arriving just past midday two days after he began. He was exhausted, but took the time to transfer his backpack to the sled, and attach Rover and Kelsey. He was as happy to see them as they were to see him, but he didn't waste any time. It was going to be a long trek home. He drove them hard for several hours before making camp and treating himself to something besides walrus jerky.

As he crawled into his tent and situated himself between the two dogs, he tried to understand what he had seen. He knew that he didn't have the answers to this problem. He wasn't even sure what the problem was. On top of that, he wasn't sure where to look. As he drifted off to sleep, he thought that the ancient writings might give him a clue. He drove himself as hard as he drove the dogs hard. They were fortunate to have good weather and a full moon, so they traveled even after sunset. They cut the time almost in half, but by the time they got back, all three were exhausted.

Kelsey and Rover barely made it into the Ice Kingdom where they just dropped. Quinn picked them up one at a time and moved them to his room, setting out a small feast for them when they woke up. He changed his clothes and freshened up before climbing into his own bed. As tired as he was, Quinn couldn't rest.

He jumped out of bed, threw on some clothes and ran off to the Chamber of Chronicles, where the history of the Ice Kingdom people was stored. This Chamber was deep in the cavern and much of the history had originally been captured in drawings on the walls. Over time those images had been transcribed and added to other ancient writings on scrolls, parchment, various animal skins and in tapestry drawings. He wasn't sure what he was looking for but he was hoping that these writings would provide a clue.

He was overwhelmed at first by the amount of information. I should have paid more attention in school, he thought. At first he shuffled randomly through one reference after another. Then he told himself to get organized. He started with the earliest accounts. After hours of searching, he couldn't fight his need to sleep. The low light in the Chamber only intensified his fatigue.

He started his search at one of the tables, and then because some of the documents were so large and unwieldy, he moved them to the floor. He had been on his hands and knees reading over stories of ancient myths when he put his head down for just a minute to rest his eyes. He immediately collapsed across the scrolls and fell fast asleep, scattering the parchments and skins across the floor. The next thing he knew, he was being shaken.

"Just ten more minutes, Mom," he mumbled. "I promise I'll be on time."

His mumbling was met with a toe prodding him in his ribs. He never recalled his mother nudging him with her toe. He struggled to open at least one eye. A blurry image began to take shape in front of him. He saw the bottom of an old black robe. He didn't remember his mother ever having a robe like that. He twisted his head back as his one open eye traveled up to the thin, wiry figure that was bent over him. A gnarled hand was reaching for him to shake him once more. As he brought his head up, he saw that he was face to face with the Sage.

She was said to be the oldest member of the Ice Kingdom people. Her features were exaggerated by the blackness of the robe that covered her from her neck to her foot, which, Quinn was glad, she had stopped jamming into his side. Her long white hair was as light and airy as spiders' webs. Her skin, nearly translucent, was as white as the ice and snow of their surroundings and as wrinkled as the parchment on which many of the ancient myths were written, but her eyes were bright blue. It wasn't just her irises that were blue. Her entire eyes were blue. She was also blind.

In spite of her spindly frame, her voice was clear and commanding.

"Get up, you lump. You're drooling on the Ancient Allegories of Dubb Alyoo. It doesn't matter that it's filled with spelling and grammatical errors, or that most enlightened thinkers believe he was simply a puppet monarch led by radical extremists that helped him steal the throne, and that he nearly ruined the Kingdom. It's a history that needs to be preserved, such as it is. Otherwise we may be led astray and allow another like him to take us to the edge of ruin. Besides, your snoring is disturbing the balance."

He jerked his head up as he struggled to get his feet to work. How did she know I was drooling, wondered Quinn. She can't see a thing. She's blind as a...

"I could hear it as it hit the papers," she interrupted his thoughts, answering the question he was certain he hadn't voiced.

Holy blubber on a biscuit, he thought, I better be careful what I think. He stumbled trying to stand and fell back on his butt.

"Yes, you should" she said as she reached down and unerringly took hold of his elbow and helped him to his feet. "Now what exactly are you looking for?"

"Ah, well, um, yes, your highness, I mean, your Excellency, I mean, your, ah, um, your sageness," Quinn stammered on, trying desperately to rub the sleep from his eyes and to clear his mind. He had never directly met the Sage, although he had seen her often enough. He had never been this close to her. He had never once spoken to her and certainly never alone with her. He wasn't sure how to act.

"Since you're much taller than I am, calling me 'your highness' seems a bit ridiculous, doesn't it?" she said to him.

She didn't wait for an answer. Putting her hand on his arm, she continued, "You can just call me Sage. There must be something important going on someplace to cause the Guardian to spend so much time in the Chamber of Chronicles. This is foreign territory to you, isn't it?"

How does she know who I am, wondered Quinn. He looked around to see if there was someone else in the Chamber somehow giving her this information. He felt like he was the brunt of some colossal practical joke. He couldn't resist the temptation to wave his hand in front of her eyes to make sure she was really blind.

To only add to his confusion she smiled at him and said, as she reached up and patted his cheek, "Yes, I'm quite blind."

She stepped over the parchment on the floor as if she could see it, linked her arm in his and explained, "It's a condition that every Sage is born with. No one knows why. It doesn't seem to be planned, and none of us know how we're chosen. That's just the way it is. We make up for our lack of vision in our eyes with what some may call a 'second sight.' I can feel your presence and tell who you are. I can even get an image of what you look like. But that doesn't tell me why you're here."

When he didn't say anything, she added, "So, why are you here?"

"Oh," said Quinn. He told her he was trying to find out about what caused severe changes in the water on the eastern edge of the Ice Kingdom.

"This sounds like it will take some time to explain. Start from the beginning."

She led Quinn over to a bench against the wall and they both sat down. Even though she was holding his arm, she had taken the lead and walked effortlessly across the room. She moved so confidently and directly, it was hard to believe she couldn't see. In spite of the commanding tone of her voice, it also carried with it a calming quality. Quinn almost immediately got over his nervousness. He forgot that he had never spoken to her before, and felt like he was sharing something with his oldest and best friend. The Sage let him talk without interruption until he had finished his story.

"So, I guess I don't really know what I'm looking for, but I thought I might find an answer here. I don't know where else to look," he told her. "I just figured this was a good place to start at least."

She took a few seconds before answering. She hadn't moved or changed position throughout most of Quinn's story. He began to think that maybe she had fallen asleep.

"No," she said. "I'm not asleep, and I'm afraid I don't have an answer for you," she replied, much to his dismay. Sensing his disappointment, she quickly continued, "but I may know in what direction to point you."

She stood up, grasped his arm and pulled him along. She walked quickly through a maze of corridors deeper into the Chamber. As unfamiliar as Quinn was with the main Chamber, he was totally lost in the maze. He was afraid to think about where he was or if she knew where she was going. She might read his thoughts. Then he realized he was already thinking these things, and that he couldn't stop. His mental confusion came to an abrupt end when she stopped in a small alcove and started shuffling through rolls of manuscripts.

"I seem to recall something about an Alchemist who lived a long, long time ago."

"An Alchemist?" asked Quinn. "I thought they turned metal into gold. How will that help?"

"Yes, that's always been the belief. But it's wrong. Pay attention, now."

His eyes had been wandering in every direction looking at the shelves stuffed with books, scrolls and parchment. He snapped his head back in her direction, again wondering if she was really blind.

"I think ancient Alchemists made that up just to keep from being burned at the stake for being witches or wizards" she continued when he was again giving her his undivided attention. "You know, of course, that they had all sorts of secret talents, but they mostly used herbs and elixirs for healing. They got so good at curing diseases that people believed they could develop potions that would give eternal youth. Another pile of rubbish."

"Right," he said to show he was paying attention. "Rubbish."

She was flipping through piles of parchment and moving scrolls around as if she could see what she was doing. Quinn was becoming more and more certain someone was playing a practical joke on him.

"No one is playing a joke on you, so quit thinking about that," she said in mid thought, and then continued with her commentary on Alchemists. "In their search for knowledge, though, they often discovered ways to cure other kinds of problems. Some of them could create rain in areas of drought. Others could calm rough seas; and still others were said to be able to tame lightening. I knew of one who was a spagyric."

"What's a spaghettic?" Quinn asked.

"Spagyric," laughed the Sage. "That's someone who can transmute plants. A really good one can transmute them into just about anything."

"Anything?" asked Quinn. "Even gold?"

"Yes, just about anything; and no, – just not gold. I told you that was a myth. Haven't you been listening?"

"Of course I've been listening, I just thought…never mind. So what, an Alchemist is supposed to change something into something and something happens." Quinn cleared his throat a bit nervously, "I don't mean any disrespect but I think this problem is too big for someone who just changes things into other things. I just don't see how an Alchemist can help."

She stopped rummaging through the documents and turned to face him. She smiled at him and patiently continued, as if speaking to one of the little ones.

"They deal with the balances in nature. Everything that happens has a consequence. If we take something away from nature, it has an impact on something else. What you described to me seems to be some kind of imbalance. It only makes sense, then, that an Alchemist could help you to regain the balance. Or do you have a better idea?"

Quinn thought about what she had said, and had to admit that he didn't have a better idea. After all, here was the Sage herself telling him what he needed to do. Who was he to question her wisdom?

"OK, so I guess I need to find an Alchemist."

Just as he was about to ask her where he had to go look to find one of these Alchemists, he remembered hearing about the ancient Alchemist who ministered to plague victims in some far off land. Where had he heard that story, he wondered. Then it hit him. He knew where he had to go.

"I've got it!" he shouted.

He gave her a big hug and then realized what he had done.

"Oh! I'm sorry your sageness. I didn't mean to...I have to go."

He let go of her arms and ran down the nearest hallway.

"Wait," she called. "Don't you want to know..."

"No," he interrupted when he ran back into the alcove, having taken the wrong hallway out. "I need to get going. Thanks. You've been a great help."

He looked over her shoulder to another hallway and ran in that direction.

"But," she said, completely mystified by his sudden reaction. His thoughts were such a jumble, that she was unable to read them.

"No, seriously," he shouted again, returning from yet another wrong hallway. "I have to get going. It's going to be a long trip. I have to go now."

"That way," she pointed to the correct exit. As he ran off she added to his disappearing figure, "I just thought you'd like to know where he is."

He was in a frenzy. He spent the rest of that day securing provisions and loading and reloading his sled. His excitement overran his better judgment and he packed the wrong kinds of supplies only to unpack and then repack again – several times. He was up through the night, packing, unpacking and repacking, too excited to sleep.

Early the next morning he put the harnesses on Rover and Kelsey, jumped on his sled and headed south. It was a long way to the Venomous Swamp. He said goodbye to his family and friends and his journey began before the first light. He used the stars to guide him until the first sun rose. Along the way he saw a few arctic terns fly overhead, but other than them, he and the two dogs were the only living creatures for miles.

In three days of hard running they came to the edge of a large, long glacier. The ocean below was almost 300 feet down. He could have traveled to the west and stayed on land the entire way, but that would take several days, and maybe even weeks more than going across the bay. As he stared down the edge of the glacier, he wasn't so sure.

"Holy blubber on a biscuit," said Quinn, as he stared at the sheer drop off. "This isn't going to be easy – or fun."

After convincing him that he could make the crossing here, he unharnessed the dogs and told them to return home. They sat and stared at him quizzically.

"No, seriously. You two have to go home. It's going to be hard enough for me to get myself down to the water and across that sea. There's no way I can take you two with me. Besides you two don't really like water. Sort of reminds me of someone else. Go on – get going." With that they reluctantly turned back and started their return run to home.

Quinn unpacked the sled and assembled the makeshift kayak. He nudged the kayak to the edge of the cliff and then turned his attention back to the supplies he had packed and repacked several times on the sled. He put the bare essential provisions in a pack that he strapped to his back. He debated about some of the other items, and decided he would have to take his chances that he wouldn't need them.

Then he took a deep breath and pushed the kayak over the side and watched as it drifted downward to the water. It seemed to take forever as it turned to the right and then back to the left, then rose up on a brief updraft of wind before the nose dropped and it shot like a sea bird hunting prey towards the ocean. It cut the water cleanly with a small splash and bobbed immediately upright, floating serenely on the surface of the black sea.

"All right!" he shouted. "That part worked."

Quinn unfurled the sail, connected a series of strings to a harness around his chest and made sure the lines were clear of each other, with no snags in them. He move about 100 feet back away from the edge of the glacier and then turned back towards the sea. He took another deep breath, closed his eyes for a second and said to himself, "Here goes nothing." He then opened his eyes, focused on the edge of the glacier, gathered the sail in his arms, keeping the lines from the sail to his harness untangled, and started running.

He picked up as much speed as he could and, planting one foot on the front edge of the glacier, pushed off with all his strength and jumped out as far as he could. He kicked his feet to increase the distance between himself and the face of the glacier. At the same time he let go of the sail, tossing it up above his head, hoping it would fill with air behind him.

He felt like he was dropping too far and too fast, but within seconds the sail ballooned out and the cords attached to his harness gave a jerk, slowing his descent. He looked for the kayak, and for a few frightening seconds, he couldn't see it. He managed to turn himself to the left and caught sight of the tiny boat. It was farther off to one side than he had expected.

"Oh, poop," he thought, "this is going to be like threading a needle in a blizzard. Maybe this wasn't such a good idea."

He was floating downward faster than he had hoped, spiraling along the way. Although the small opening in the kayak was coming at him quickly, it didn't seem to be getting any bigger. He forced himself to stay calm and focused. He pulled on a cord on the right and then readjusted to the left, keeping his feet pointed at the opening. At the same time the sea swells moved the kayak up and down, forward and backward. Quinn was having difficulty matching his descending movement with the shifting kayak.

Then his time ran out. Before he could even think about it, his feet slid quickly and easily into the opening, he landed on his butt with a hard thump and the sail dropped over his head. He started laughing almost uncontrollably.

"I did it! I did it! Holy blubber on a biscuit, I did it!" He was laughing so hard he was almost capsized by a huge wave that hit the side of his kayak.

"Oh, poop," he said still laughing, "I guess I better pay attention to what I'm doing."

He quickly pulled the sail off of his head, folded it as neatly as he could and tucked it into the space in front of his feet for the time being. He then pulled three poles out from the back of the kayak. He fitted one into the other to make it longer and then seated it into a base that he had installed into the flooring between his legs, forming a mast. This had been his own invention, and now would be the first opportunity to see how well it worked. He only wished that he had been able to test it out under less dire circumstances. Then he lashed the third pole across the mast, retrieved the sail, and tying it to the cross piece, raised it up. Within seconds, the wind filled the sail and the kayak was racing forward.

He then reached back and pulled two paddles from the back, which he attached together to form a long oar with blades at both ends and began paddling and steering further south. Fortunately, the sky was clear and the twin suns overhead were bright. The waves were not too bad and he was able to see the icebergs well in advance so he could avoid hitting them. For nearly an hour he was running on pure adrenalin.

As the day began to darken, he came upon a large, flat sheet of ice. He lowered his makeshift sail, and disassembled the mast and crosspiece. He climbed out of the kayak onto the ice sheet and then pulled the kayak after him. He used some of the cords from the sail to tie the kayak down and then created a small lean-to with the sail and curled up for the night. At first he was worried that he would be too excited to sleep. That was not the case. After the lack of sleep from the previous night, and the subsiding of his adrenalin rush, he was out like a light in seconds, and slept soundly through the night.

The next morning he was again lucky enough to have clear weather as he started out. He reassembled his sail and set off. Between the power from the sail and his paddling, he felt he was making good time. However, his good luck didn't last. By mid-morning the sky clouded over and the winds picked up. They were getting so strong, that he had to lower the sail. That got trickier than he had expected, as the waters got rougher and rougher. He nearly lost both the sail and the mast, and then he nearly lost his paddle.

"Oh, brother," he mumbled once he had finally managed to secure everything and get back on course. "I'm going to have to work on that maneuver."

At first the waves weren't too bad, but soon they reached 30 to 40 feet. It was like riding a roller coaster. It was even making his stomach lurch as if he was riding a roller coaster, except Quinn had never been on a roller coaster. He didn't even know what a roller coaster was, but he knew what the ocean in a storm was: a place he didn't want to be. He looked around frantically for some kind of safe haven.

Pieces of ice were still floating this far south. The problem was that none of them were big enough to land on and ride out the storm. He knew that he'd just roll off of them into the sea. But they were big enough to crush him and his kayak. When he was riding at the top of a large wave he shot a quick glance to his right and left to see if any ice bergs were nearby. Then, he dropped like a stone to the bottom of the swell where the water towered above him on all sides and he hoped and prayed that no massive pieces of ice and rock would squash him like a bug.

Just when he thought it couldn't get any worse, the rain started. Only it wasn't just rain. It was sleet and hail. He was being pelted with ice balls nearly as big as his fist at the same time the sleet felt like arrows being shot at him. The sleet hitting the unprotected parts of his face stung like bees. He was also having a hard time seeing much further than the end of his boat.

His coat and the fabric of the kayak were made of seal skin, which was very tough, but he wasn't sure either the boat or he could withstand much more of a beating. Besides, the hood on his coat didn't keep his head from getting beaned by the hail stones. His rowing was becoming more erratic, every time he raised an arm to shield his face. As if the waves and the storm weren't bad enough, nightfall turned everything black.

The cloud cover was so dense that the stars and the moon were completely blotted out. He had no way to establish any sense of direction. He was doing everything he could just to stay afloat. He was being bounced like a cork by the waves that seemed to be getting higher and higher, and being hit with hail stone rocks and sleet as sharp as arrows, and now he was sailing blind. He only hoped that he wouldn't be tossed into the path of any ice bergs or ice flow.

"Oh, poop," he shouted over the storm to no one at all. "This is really getting bad. I'M NOT HAVING FUN!!!"

He eventually gave up rowing shortly after it was clear that the storm wasn't going to let up any time soon. His paddling wasn't having any effect anyway, and it was only exhausting him. By what he guessed was close to midnight, he just leaned his head forward to keep as much water out of the kayak as possible, and hunkered down until daybreak. He thought about pulling out the sail to cover him up completely, but he was afraid of losing it in the wind.

Instead, he rested his arms on the front edge of the opening in which he sat and spread his hood as widely as he could. In spite of the beating downpour and the massive waves, he gradually nodded off. There was nothing he could do about his circumstances, but to ride it out. He just figured he could ride it out asleep as easily as he could by trying to stay awake. Once he got over his fear of capsizing, it was like he was in a large cradle, being rocked to sleep.

He was in this condition when the storm finally wore itself out. He hadn't noticed the gradual change in the weather or the motion of his small boat. When he woke up, he poked an eye out from under the hood of his coat and was greeted by a sea hawk perched on the front of his kayak. He raised his head, and shook off the residual rainwater and ice from his hood. He scanned the horizon in every direction. Aside from his unusual visitor, nothing else seemed out of the ordinary. The sky was clear, the sun was low on the early morning horizon and the sea was smooth as glass and littered with ice flow and ice bergs. As far as he could see in any direction there was nothing but ocean, him and the bird. And then the bird flew off.

"Was it something I said," he shouted after the bird. "Well good riddance. You probably don't have any better idea than I do as to where I am."

He got a fix on the sun and then sat back, opened his backpack and took out something to eat. More walrus jerky, he thought, bleakly. He thought about dropping a line to see if he could catch some fish, but the thought of eating it raw made the walrus jerky a bit more appealing.

As he had his meager breakfast, he watched to see what direction the twin suns were moving and then from that, figured out which way to start paddling. He got himself headed back in the right direction and after a while set up the sail and let the mild wind do more of the work for him. He traveled in this manner for two more days before he saw any other signs of life.

By mid-morning of the third day after the storm, he noticed some movement low on the horizon. A few minutes later, off in the distance ahead of him he saw the first flocks of birds. After about two or three more hours he started seeing signs of vegetation – seaweed and kelp in the clear water below him. If he looked closely, he could see sea life darting in and out of the plants.

The temperature had started to climb as well, and he wiggled out of his heavy clothing, stowing his coat and leggings in the front of the kayak. As the dusk began to settle in, he saw the beginnings of a marsh. He still didn't see any real landmass, but he was coming across large reeds and other marsh plants. He could tell by the change in the color of the water, first from black, then to blue, and now to brown, that it was getting shallower and shallower. He scooped up a handful of the water and tasted it, knowing enough not to swallow it. It was brackish – a mixture of salt water from the sea and fresh water from inland rivers.

He knew that he was approaching the outer edges of the Venomous Swamp and thought it might be better to stop here for the night rather than to get himself stuck somewhere within the dangers of the Swamp. He recalled with a slight shiver the stories Liam had told of the treacherous plants and animals that called this place home.

He stopped rowing, and tested the water depth with his paddle. The clear water he crossed several hours ago had changed considerably. Now it was so murky he couldn't see the bottom and had no idea of its depth. The paddle was just over six feet long, and he tentatively pushed it straight down. It hit a sand bar about four feet down.

"Perfect," thought Quinn. He pushed harder, shoving it into the sand about a foot down, and tested how well it was holding. He pushed a little harder, just to make sure, and then tied the kayak off to the length of the paddle that remained above the surface of the water. Satisfied that he was well anchored, he again surveyed his surroundings. Even though he was several hundred yards away from the outer edges of the reeds and cattails that marked the beginning of the Swamp, he could hear the faint buzzing of insects. They hadn't discovered him – yet.

"Better safe than sorry," Quinn said to himself as he spread the sail out over the top of the kayak covering himself in the process. He would be a bit warmer than was normally comfortable for him, but at least he would be protected from any pesky mosquitoes or whatever other creepy-crawly-flying vermin the Swamp had to offer. He stuck his gloves in between the edge of the sail and his kayak to create small openings near the bottom, just to let in some fresh air, and then settled back.

As he drifted off to sleep, the tide gently began to rise. In doing so, the water level rose above the top of the paddle wedged into the sand. As the kayak rose, it pulled taut the cord securing it to the kayak. As the tiny boat rocked back and forth with the gentle motion of the water, the paddle moved back and forth in the sand. Before long, it came loose and floated to the surface. The knot holding it to the kayak loosened, and the paddle floated off.

The rising tide softly nudged the kayak and its sleeping passenger past the reeds and cattails and deep into the giant delta that formed the entrance to the Venomous Swamp. The kayak quickly became lost in among the labyrinth of thousands of tiny islands and sandbars. Before long and well before the sun would rise the next morning, Quinn and his small craft were surrounded by tall grasses, rushes, reeds, and overarching trees covered with hanging moss – and a variety of reptiles and other predators who watched as this odd looking creature in his odd looking craft floated beneath them.

Chapter three

In another part of the Swamp, far on the other side, while Quinn was still asleep – and still floating aimlessly through the delta – a tall thin young man was traveling around in an odd looking ship, checking various traps that had been set at seemingly random locations.

The locations were not really random, though they were well hidden. They coincided with small openings in the few "dry" spots in the Swamp. The openings were portals to the nearly defunct underworld caverns that had been occupied by gargoyles and fire lizards. The former leader of the gargoyles had been defeated in another battle at another time long ago. The gargoyles, though, still existed and still used the portals to make forays into the Swamp to launch attacks or set ambushes for the person who was hunting them.

They were not very well organized and their leadership was often inefficient and predictable, but they still made life in the Swamp hazardous. They were destructive and ruthless, undermining at every turn any efforts to clean up the pollution and poisons that were pervasive in the surrounding lands. The person hunting them was called The Pathfinder. To his friends, he was known as Liam.

Liam had set the traps to capture wandering gargoyles. Some of them he released to distant lands where they could do no harm. Others he did not. The ones who refused to give up their destructive ways did not have a pleasant future. Those that weren't trapped and who engaged the Pathfinder in battle usually paid for this error with their lives. From these unfortunates, Liam scavenged several useful items. From their skin, for example, he was able to make protective fabric that covered his odd looking ship and served as the clothing he wore. The fabric was scaly and frequently shifted coloring to match its surroundings. It was strong enough to withstand almost anything — except blades forged from wizard's steel, of which Liam had several. Or the fangs of other gargoyles – another item he scavenged.

Almost a year ago, their leadership had been under the mystical influence of an ancient sorcerer who had been banished to an icy prison far to the north. Liam and his friends had been key to eliminating that influence, and the leadership of the gargoyles quickly fell apart.

Over the last year or so since the demise of the leader of the gargoyles, Liam had worked diligently and had transformed several pockets of the Venomous Swamp. Plants that were beneficial and beautiful rather than lethal and threatening had begun to be cultivated. He needed to get this kind of vegetation established so that he could encourage less dangerous animal life to move back into the Swamp.

The gargoyles would often venture up from their underground hiding places to destroy these plants and ravage Liam's supplies. He had made several attempts to coexist with the gargoyles and to live in peace, but they were unyielding and intractable. They had vowed to destroy him, giving him no alternatives. So in addition to replenishing his need for the fabric made from their skin, he discovered ways to keep them from reversing the transformation of the Swamp he had undertaken and to protect himself and his home.

He had made significant progress in the transformation, but it was slow and the Swamp was very large. It was still necessary for him to be well protected when he ventured out and to establish and maintain sanctuaries at strategic locations. His ship was covered with the same scaly protection as his clothing, and was also armed quite extensively. He needed to be ready for any threat. He had lived in the Swamp all his life and knew it very well. He had mapped out the entire Swamp over several years, and had developed a variety of localized charts to identify where the more dangerous areas were. However, it was still a swamp and, as such, the geography changed constantly. He had to update his information regularly and in doing so, reestablish and replenish his safe havens.

In these sanctuaries he created supply caches. The caches were well hidden, and armored with the same material made from gargoyle skin and contained food, first aid materials. Weapons and materials to repair the odd assortment of vehicles he invented to travel throughout the Swamp. In case Liam somehow got separated from his ship and otherwise stranded, he wouldn't have far to go to find a secure place to get additional supplies. He could hold off an attack for a considerable length of time, and then could easily make it back to his home.

In conjunction with these safe havens he had also created an early warning system. He developed this with the assistance of some friends he had made not too long ago and it involved a little bit of magic and faerie dust.

On this particular day Liam was checking traps in one of the western quadrants of the Swamp. He had set more than twenty traps over a five mile area and was puzzled to find that none of them had been tripped. He almost always found at least four or five gargoyles had been caught. They were very mean and aggressive, but generally stupid and greedy. He used some of the most ridiculous things as bait. Sometimes he used broken glass; other times he used rotting meat; and other times he just used empty bags or boxes he had around his fortress. It almost didn't matter. What also didn't matter was hiding or camouflaging the traps.

When he first began setting these traps he had gone to great lengths to hide them. On a couple of occasions, he either didn't have time or the resources nearby to disguise the traps to the extent he preferred. He was somewhat surprised to find that they had been sprung and several gargoyles had been captured. Eventually, he stopped trying to hide them, and just set them out in the open. This made it easier for him to check on them.

The gargoyles knew what the traps were and what would happen to them if they got caught in the traps; but, as Liam well knew, they were so stupid and greedy that, if they saw something inside the trap, they couldn't resist the urge to try to steal it, even if it was worthless junk, which it almost always was. And they couldn't be at all stealthy about the attempted theft. They were so aggressive they just walked into the trap (knowing what it was) and grabbed the bait. Even after the trap was sprung, they puzzled over the bait for several seconds and, sometimes even minutes, before realizing that they were trapped.

And to make matters worse for them, if the gargoyles were traveling in groups, which they almost always did, the ones who did not get trapped either couldn't figure out how to release their captured comrade, or just didn't care. On a number of occasions, Liam came upon three or four shouting and banging on a trap that held one of them. Instead of simply releasing the catch, they simply ran off.

This time, though, none of the traps had been sprung, and the bait remained undisturbed. Liam finished checking all the traps on this particular circuit, making sure they were properly set and that the bait was still there. Just as he was finishing, the monitor inside his ship went off. He looked around to make sure no danger was approaching and then climbed back on board. Once inside, he reset the protective covering and went below to check the monitor.

One of his other friends had improved his on-board systems. The sorcerer, Lochen, had designed the basic system, and the Enchantress, Stella, had cast the spells that made it work. It helped to have friends with some magical powers. Now he had several holographic platforms on which he could summon three-dimensional displays of whatever area of the Swamp he wanted to see and a vision of the incoming communication that was being received.

The system was still getting calibrated, so the image quality was better when he was closer to the item being transmitted. Lochen and Stella had told him that the spells that had been cast to protect and hide the gargoyle caverns could sometimes block or interfere with the images on his monitor. Those spells could not be broken by either of them, but they were able to counteract them enough to ensure that he would at least get an early warning. In this case, the transmission was from a distant part of the Swamp and was not at all clear.

He checked the sensors in areas closer to his present location. All he could see was some general movement of a few of the larger animal life forms. They seemed to be heading in a direction generally north and east of where he was. At first Liam thought it was just as well that some of the poisonous snakes and other reptiles were clearing out of the area. His initial reaction was to ignore the alarm and keep on his schedule of checking traps. He then reconsidered, and thought about leaving his traps and going to see what the image might be. He came to the conclusion that he needed to explore this bizarre reading and the movement of so many animals to the north a little more. He hadn't lived his whole life in the Swamp without being suspicious of unusual changes in the behavior of the plants and animals.

He climbed aboard his ship and headed into some of the channels where he knew large nests of snakes and poisonous lizards were located. He was protected well enough that he had no concerns about traveling in these areas. He also thought it was better to know where the dangers existed and where they were the worst, than to ignore or avoid them. Besides, he needed to know if they were being vacated.

His presence attracted some attention and a few of the local inhabitants approached him cautiously, maintaining a safe distance, but getting close enough to check him out. Once they seemed to recognize the ship, they quickly darted away. For the most part, though, the nests were either deserted or occupied by smaller, younger animals not yet ready for going out on hunting adventures. He came to the conclusion that there seemed to be a general movement to the northeast. In fact, the more Liam studied the creatures, the more it looked to him like they were forming hunting parties.

"They're after something," he muttered. "But what?"

He rarely if ever had visitors to the Swamp, and certainly not from that direction. He couldn't think of anyone or anything that would come across the sea from the north, except, maybe an arctic seal or a bear or wolf that might have gotten lost or stranded on a drifting iceberg. But that almost never happened. By the time any ice got to the northern edge of the delta, the waters were far too warm and any ice quickly melted. Any animals trapped on those ice flows seldom survived the sea to make it into the Swamp. Also, the storms in the sea between the Venomous Swamp and the Ice Kingdom could flare up at a moment's notice and make the seas even more impassable.

Then it hit him. The only person he knew who would attempt to make that kind of crossing was Quinn. As soon as the thought entered his mind, he dismissed it.

"What could possibly bring Quinn south?" he asked out loud.

And even if Quinn did come south, he surely wouldn't take the direct route by sea. There was a land connection, although it was far to the west. Of course coming by sea, if a traveler could even survive that journey, would cut days and maybe even weeks off the trip.

"He's a nutty guy," thought Liam, "but I can't believe he would be that nutty."

Liam was growing apprehensive. He was not completely certain that Quinn wouldn't dare to attempt such a passage, and something in the back of his mind couldn't let that thought go. He decided he needed to check out a few other areas prior to coming to any conclusions and making a decision to go north in search of whatever had popped up on his monitor. Before he moved out of this area, he took some readings on the direction in which the hunting parties appeared to be moving. He knew that the readings wouldn't be exact, since these creatures would keep to the waterways and none of the waterways went straight in any direction. They all wound in, out and around, which made navigating them so difficult. Still, it would be better than nothing.

"It looks like the general direction of movement from this area is the same," he said to himself. "Pretty much north or north east."

When he was done, he turned his ship due east and put it into high gear. He wanted to gather one more piece of information before deciding what to do. There was an active gargoyle portal in that direction. If there were fresh prey somewhere to the north, the gargoyles would most certainly be on the move, too. This would be a little out of his way, but it would help him to avoid making a wasted trip. It was after midday by the time Liam reached the area of the portal.

He slowed down only slightly as he passed the gateway. It wasn't hidden very well, so he didn't have to stop to examine it. He examined it closely and noted several tracks leading from the tightly closed hatch. There's a party on the move, he thought, and began pedaling faster. As he rounded a bend in the marsh still looking back at the portal, he almost ran over the hunting party. His head jerked around just quick enough to see a group of seven gargoyles. It happened so fast that he wasn't able to prepare his ship for a fight. Fortunately, his unexpected and sudden presence caught them equally off guard.

"Oh, poop, to quote a friend of mine," he shouted and he held on tightly to the controls.

Before he could stop his ship, Liam had literally run over the rear echelon of the hunting party. The craft came to a bumpy and sudden halt. Two of the gargoyles were trapped under the hull of the ship and pinned to the sandy bottom of the marsh. They wouldn't be going any place soon, Liam thought, and he locked the gears down, securing the ship in place where it had stopped. He reached to his right and grabbed a crossbow and a handful of arrows. Running to the front of his ship he loaded the crossbow and fired off two quick but very accurate arrows, which brought the number in the hunting party down to three.

Those three, though, were better prepared and hurled their spears at Liam. They had their bows armed with arrows before the spears landed. Two of the spears flew over Liam's head and off into the Swamp ineffectually, but the third struck him in the shoulder. His armor protected him from injury, but the force of the blow knocked him off his feet. He was a little surprised that they had stood and fought at all. They usually only did that when they were certain they outnumbered their enemy. He lost sight of all three of them when he fell to the deck.

As he scrambled to his hands and knees, he figured that the gargoyles would think he would run away to the back of the ship. They usually assumed their enemies would behave the way they did, so instead he crawled quickly and quietly to the front, keeping below the bulwark. He reloaded his crossbow and listened intently for signs that would tell him which way the gargoyles were advancing. He could hear one of them making more noise than necessary on the starboard side of the ship. It was sloshing in the water and grunting. It was much too loud for a veteran hunter, and judging from the speed with which they had shot those arrows after throwing their spears, these were clearly veteran hunters. Liam concluded that the noisy one was trying to create a distraction. That meant the other two were sneaking up on the port side.

"They must think I'm as stupid as they are," he thought to himself.

Liam crawled up as far as he could to the front of the ship, getting as far behind the three of them as he could, and poked his head slowly and quietly over the port side. Sure enough, there were two creeping slowly towards the back of the ship. They were hugging the side with one of them about four feet in front of the other. He could hear the third one moving noisily up the right side of the boat.

"They're veteran hunters, all right," thought Liam.

He checked the arrow he had loaded into his crossbow and then set out a second arrow to be close at hand. Inching up above the bulwark, he took careful aim and released the first arrow. Without looking to see the results of that shot, he picked up the other arrow, loaded it and fired all in a flash of motion.

His first arrow had struck home and dropped the number of gargoyles to two. The other gargoyle had been alert and reacted to the attack. Liam's second arrow just grazed the front gargoyle, who turned immediately and fired as soon as he saw Liam's head appear. His shot caught the edge of Liam's crossbow and tore it from his hand. He and Liam simultaneously reached for and prepared another shot. Before the gargoyle could load a second arrow, Liam drew a long narrow blade from a scabbard at his side and flicked the knife at the enemy as he ducked his head to the left.

The gargoyle had been just as fast in loading his bow. His shot and Liam's knife passed each other in mid flight, but his arrow flew past Liam's head as he ducked it to his left. It was close enough for Liam to feel the rush of air as the feathers brushed his ear. Liam's knife was more accurate, finding its target and leaving only one remaining gargoyle. That one seemed to sense the shift in the numbers and quickly ran off. Liam thought about going after him, but then heard thumping from beneath the ship. He had forgotten about the two he had pinned in the sand.

He sat back down behind the controls of the boat and pulled some levers. Large knobby wheels – made just for maneuvering through the marshy sand – dropped down from the hull, raising the craft slightly into the air. Liam began pedaling and the boat shot forward.

"You got off lucky this time," he shouted back to the two that were pulling themselves free of the muck. "I'll give you a rain check."

By the time they could collect themselves and fire at him, he was too far gone. His ship flew off the sand bar and into a wider section of the stream. He retracted the wheels and shot across the reed-covered water.

Liam was now convinced that something real had been picked up on his monitors in the northwest and that it was in serious trouble. He didn't really care who or what it was. The fact that the predatory animals and reptiles of the Swamp, as well as the gargoyles, were after it was enough for him to consider it important to save. He scanned the transmissions again, trying to pick up a clearer image, while at the same time trying to keep his ship from running into something it couldn't handle.

The waterways twisted and turned, making his progress slow. It was even slower because he was shifting his attention from steering the craft to scanning his monitor. He knew he didn't have much daylight left and traveling in the dark would be even more treacherous, but he didn't have any choice. He decided to take a more direct approach. He'd cut straight across the streams, marshes, sand bars and land, and sail straight for whatever it was that his monitor had picked up.

He pulled a series of levers and several blades extended from both sides of his ship. A large long and spiraled arrowhead projected from the front. He then re-extended the large wheels from the hull. He knew the wheels would drag and slow him down in water, but would be necessary whenever he hit stretches of land, and especially the sand. The blades spun like the blades of a lawn mower and cut through the reeds and rushes, while the arrowhead on the front continued to spiral, digging through whatever met the boat head-on.

Without warning, the ship bucked and jolted, nearly tossing him out of his seat. He had come upon solid ground. He pushed hard on the pedals while he checked his maps and charts to recalculate his position. He saw that he was on a long narrow tract of ground. That was the good news.

The bad news was that for far longer than he had hoped, he would be traveling through some very thick sections of razor grass that grew in this area of the Swamp. This grass was nearly 15 feet tall and was impassable without the armor that covered his ship. Even with their natural coating as protection, the gargoyles avoided this vegetation. As strong as that armor was, the razor grass could eventually cut through it.

Liam had triple-covered the front of his ship, and hoped that the spinning blades would cut through the razor grass before it could do damage to the sides. The blades would get most of the tall rushes, but not all of them, especially the newer shoots that were below the level of the cutters. As the blades did their work, strands of the grass flew in all directions. Before he knew it, they were raining down on top of him. It was like being showered with shards of glass. He quickly deployed the canopy cover, but not before a number of the clipped blades of grass sliced across his face and arms.

"That was close," he said to himself, as he wiped blood from his face.

He pulled a wide flat machete from his belt looked at his reflection in the blade. He saw that the cuts were not severe – just a few scratches.

"That was also careless," he admonished himself.

He judged that he could stay on this course for a little while longer, but would then be on softer ground. At least he'd be out of the razor grass, but the sand meant slower going.

Sooner than he thought, the ship lurched and slowed down. The razor grass faded away and was replaced by a lower growing sand vine. He knew he needed to keep his speed up in this stuff. If he slowed down too much, the vines would quickly start wrapping themselves around his ship and engulf it. Once that happened he and his ship would become dinner for the Swamp. He normally avoided this stuff by keeping to the waterways. He was beginning to wonder if this so-called short cut was really going to save him time or if it would be the end of him and whatever or whomever he was racing to meet.

The growth was becoming thicker and he could feel the ship slowing down. The vines were already trying to work their way into the wheel wells and around the axels. He checked his maps to see if there was a nearby alternate route he could move to, but he found nothing. By now he was too far away from water deep enough and open enough to make any difference.

"Looks like this is as good as it gets," he said. "All right, then. Let's see what we can do."

Liam had developed an additional set of wheels just for this kind of terrain. Now was as good a time as any for a test run, he thought. The tricky part would be that he'd have to slow down enough to disengage the current wheels and replace them with the new ones. He had several different kinds of wheels stored inside the hull for the different kinds of terrain he traversed. They were on separate axel systems, but all the wheels were attached to the same set of gears that were propelled by his pedaling. He would have to stop pedaling and run in "neutral" any time he shifted wheels. He'd have to do that now. If his coasting slowed down too much, though, the vines would get a firm hold and he'd never be able to escape their grasp.

"I'll have to make another modification to the wheel system," he thought. "That's if I'm around to design it."

He dug down deep and pedaled like a maniac, gaining as much speed as he could, trying at the same time to keep the ship from slipping and sliding. The vines were being torn of their sandy hold, roots and all. Some of them were sticking to the wheels and trying to take hold. When he was going as fast as he could, he dropped into neutral, pulled a set of levers and the wheels retracted. The ship's hull slid across the sand and the vines, slowing much too quickly, Liam thought. As soon as the wheels were fully disengaged, he switched levers and the new wheels dropped into place. These were studded like football cleats.

Initially, as the new wheels took hold, the ship lurched almost to a stop. Then Liam started pedaling frantically, and the ship slowly regained speed. It was like trying to run through a knee deep river of molasses at first, but then, slowly, the ship picked up more speed. The scraping of the hull had pulled the loose vines from the ship, and the bits that still clung to the previous set of wheels were too fragmented to take root.

"It worked!" shouted Liam. "I can't believe it myself."

His excitement gave him a shot of extra energy and he gained even more velocity. The cleats of the wheels dug into the sand and the vines and the ship whizzed across the surface. Liam was nearly flying now. Bits of torn vines were shooting into the air in his wake.

He checked his charts again, made a minor course correction and kept an eye out for the local wild life and large trees. His armor would protect against a lot of things, but it wouldn't move a tree. He saw a small group of alligators off to his left. They, too, were headed in a northerly direction and seemed to be in a hunting formation. He assumed they had the same objective he did and he again adjusted his course to match theirs. He'd be able to move ahead of them while on land, but once they hit the water, they'd have the speed advantage.

After a while, the sand gave way to more water and a different area of the Swamp. Here the water flowed in streams bordered by more solid ground, but the ground was more rock-like and impassable. From this point forward, Liam would have no choice but to follow the winding waterways. The shores were choked with Poison Oaks. Even if he could traverse the rock, he couldn't get through the growth. These trees grew close together and their branches twisted and turned, intertwining. The lattice formed by the interwoven branches made trying to climb through them uninviting to say the least.

What made such a thought even more unwise was that the bark and the leaves of these trees were extremely poisonous. Contact with either would cause a person's skin to blister in minutes. If those blisters weren't treated soon, the blisters would blister and soon the skin would just start falling away from the body. The poison would complete its work within two days – tops.

Even the protective clothing Liam wore was not a certain safeguard against these trees. The bark and leaves excreted a thin, clear oil that was extremely sticky. It wouldn't penetrate the gargoyle skin, but it could take days or even weeks for it to wear off. Until it did, it was still venomous, and could transfer itself to any unprotected surface. Liam avoided having his ship make contact with this stuff. If it did, he'd be better off just burning it. Cleaning the skin or replacing it was just too dangerous.

To make matters worse the trees were covered with Medusa's Moss. This particular type of moss penetrated the skin and attacked the veins and arteries. It caused them to swell up and harden within hours. Blood stopped flowing within a day. The victim didn't really turn to stone, but the effect was the same. As a result, Liam would keep his ship as close to the center of the stream as possible. He even slowed down a bit to maintain better control. The twists and turns could happen suddenly. This area of the Swamp was one of the worst.

Night was beginning to close in. Dusk had already settled in, and Liam had passed up two havens, either one of which he would have put into by now under any other circumstances. Even though Liam never liked being out or traveling through the Swamp at night, he was compelled to go as far as he could. Whatever was out there that was being hunted wouldn't survive long. He didn't want to think about the possibility that it might be Quinn. He knew Quinn wouldn't last a minute after dark.

Once again checking his charts, he saw another cache that was only a few hours away. He'd have to stop. He couldn't chance trying to go any further. He would put in there and get a couple of hours rest and set off again before first light. As much as he wanted to keep going, he knew he wasn't safe. It would do no good for him to just become another target for the beasts of the Swamp.

He had been traveling in darkness for nearly two hours. There were far too many nocturnal predators for his tastes. The noises alone had been nerve wracking. He supposed that whatever was out there was equally frightened by the strange craft that never appeared in the night. Probably not, but it made him feel a little better to think so.

Shortly before midnight, Liam arrived at the cache. This one was well protected and had a narrow launch into which his ship neatly fit, allowing him to transfer from the ship and into the cache without being exposed. He didn't bother getting off the ship. He stretched out on the deck and drifted off to sleep almost immediately. But it wasn't a sound sleep.

He was worried that he wouldn't get to whatever was being stalked in time to be of any help. A few hours later he was restocking his ship and easing out of the launch. He grabbed some food to eat along the way, made sure his weapons were at the ready, and was back in the waterway before the first sun rose in the sky.

He wasn't sure how close he was or in what specific direction to travel. The gargoyles, alligators, snakes and other predators were doing their best to stay out of his sight. It was as if they knew he was headed to the same destination. There were enough of them to fight over whatever prey was out there. They had no intention of sharing it with him. However, the buzzards high in the sky were less concerned and pointed the way. He maneuvered through the crisscrossing waterways with one eye on the trails and one on the buzzards. As long as they stayed airborne there was still a chance.

After what seemed like forever, he was positioned almost directly under the circling birds. He had slowed down so as not to be taken by surprise by anyone or anything that might ambush him. As he poked the nose of the ship around a large clump of bulrushes, he stopped short. In front of him was a battered kayak drifting back and forth in the current. He could see someone huddled under a ragged white sealskin.

The only thing showing was one arm holding a piece of bone like a club. Every couple of seconds the kayaker would blindly swing the club on either side of the kayak in an attempt to keep any unseen predator at bay and to paddle the kayak forward. The tiny boat would move forward a few feet, propelled by the club splashing through the water, and then would drift back with the current just about the same distance. It didn't seem to be making any progress whatsoever. Liam wondered how long it had been stuck in this location.

"Quinn?" shouted Liam.

Quinn's head popped out from under the sealskin, his face beet red and covered in sweat.

"Liam! Boy am I glad to see you. It was really getting hot under that sealskin, and there were a bunch of things trying to bite me. This is NOT a nice place!"

Chapter four

Amazingly, Quinn had managed to keep any and all predators at a distance with his blind flailing of the bone. He told Liam he had no idea of how long he had been drifting through the delta.

"You're not anywhere near the delta," Liam informed him. "In fact, you're miles from the delta. How long have you been adrift?"

"I wasn't adrift," Quinn shot back defensively. "I'm an excellent sailor and navigator. I just didn't know where I was going."

"You have no sail," Liam pointed out. "You have no idea where you are. You don't know how long you've been where you don't know you are…"

"I was paddling," he snapped back. "I was steering my kayak and I was coming to find you."

"Paddling?" asked Liam. "With a bone?"

"A bone?" he wailed incredulously.

He held the bone up above his head to examine it more closely, and then started waving it back and forth, not sure if he should throw it away or keep in, since he had no idea where his paddle was.

"What kind of bone?" he wailed some more, finally deciding that holding it was becoming increasingly uncomfortable. "Whose bone; where did I get this thing; who would leave a bone just laying out in the open; where's the rest of this...this...whatever it is; what kind of place is this?"

He was rambling on excitedly and beginning to hyperventilate. Liam knew Quinn's reaction was a combination of relief and the high level of adrenalin. The bone went sailing into the air back upstream from where Quinn had floated. Before it hit the water, the giant jaws of a very large alligator shot out of the water and clamped shut, snapping it into several pieces.

"Oh poop," shouted Quinn, scrambling frantically to get out of the kayak. "What kind of place is this?"

"Come on," said Liam. "Climb onto my ship and let's get you some place safe."

Once he got Quinn safely secured inside his ship, he hauled the kayak on board, then turned his boat around and headed for home. Along the way, he just sat back pedaling, listening and watching Quinn vent – and vent – and vent. In between each rant, he would peel off one layer of arctic clothing after another. It was like watching an onion peel itself down to almost nothing.

"How many layers of clothing are you wearing, exactly?" asked Liam.

The question went unanswered, having been unheard as Quinn continued his tirade. Finally, he was down to just about nothing but his underwear, and piles of clothing were strewn about the floor near his feet. At the same time, he also seemed to be just about done with his rant. His hair stuck out wildly in every direction, he was bathed in sweat and his cheeks were flushed.

He took a deep breath, announced, "I'm a little tired. I think I need to take a nap."

He sat down with a thud onto a bench before which he had been standing all the time he had been venting. Before he could drop to his side and rest his head, he was fast asleep and snoring softly.

Liam just shook his head in wonder. He headed for the nearest haven and pulled in. The first thing he did was to pick up the discarded clothes, and find suitable substitutes. He didn't really have anything in Quinn's size and had to patch some things together. He assumed Quinn would be out for some time, so he didn't feel too rushed. Even so, he didn't want to be away from his base for too long.

Liam had a large supply of gargoyle skins. These were among the supplies he kept in his numerous sanctuaries. He made some guesses at the size Quinn would need, and then began piecing together the requisite clothing. He knew he would never make a living as a tailor, and hoped that Quinn wasn't too fashion conscious. As soon as he was done, he added a few more supplies onto his ship, left the sanctuary and set a course to return to his fortress.

On the return trip, Liam stuck to the main waterways with which he was familiar, and ones he was more confident were safe to travel through. He made good time, not running into any obstacles. As darkness began to settle in, he docked the ship in another one of his caches for the night. He thought about trying to move Quinn, but knew that would be futile. He decided Quinn would be safe enough where he was and that it was probably best to let him rest. Liam restocked his ship, spent a restful night and headed out again after the first sun had risen. All the while Quinn remained motionless on the bench just where he had fallen.

He finally stirred back to life just as Liam was arriving home. He rolled onto his back and rubbed his face, somewhat oblivious to his surroundings, not fully alert. His eyes were still closed as he stretched, and shook himself.

"Wow, Mom!" he said through a wide yawn. "I had a really strange dream. There were these things..." he stopped midsentence as his eyes focused on his surroundings and he became fully aware of where he was.

"Holy blubber on a biscuit – that wasn't a dream."

He looked around and saw Liam watching him.

"And you're not my Mom!"

"No, Sweetie, I'm not," answered Liam, smiling.

"Hey, Little Guy," Quinn said excitedly and smiling broadly, the perils of the last several days quickly forgotten.

Little Guy was a nickname he had given Liam the last time they were together. In fact Liam was not much shorter than Quinn, but was only about half his girth. He crossed the ship in two long strides, wrapped his arms around Liam and, lifting him off the deck, gave him a huge hug.

Liam just shook his head as Quinn lowered him back to the deck and said, "It's about time you woke up. I didn't want to think how I was going to haul your big butt out of this ship and into the fortress." They both laughed.

Quinn yawned, roughly rubbed his head and face, and stretched again, "I'm so hungry I could eat a walrus."

"Well," said Liam, "I don't have any walruses, but this should do the trick."

He had anticipated that, after nearly two days sleeping and who knows how many days wandering lost in the Swamp and at sea before that, Quinn would be famished. He had a tray set with food on a table next to the bench where Quinn had slept. Quinn didn't waste any time and started wolfing down almost everything in sight.

"Mmpff – this is really good," he said between mouthfuls. "What is it?"

"Uhhh - You probably don't want to know," answered Liam, quickly adding, "but it tastes just like chicken."

"Great," said Quinn. "What's chicken?"

Liam thought about it a minute and then decided it was probably still better that he didn't know, and he quickly changed the subject.

"So can you tell me now, what, exactly, were you doing out there in the Swamp?"

"I came to find you."

"And so you did. Why exactly?"

In between stuffing his mouth with whatever it was that tasted like chicken, Quinn filled Liam in on the boiling and acidic water in the bay, the burned fur on the seals, the smell of the water, his experiment with the meat over the side of his kayak, his study of the ancient myths, his meeting with the Sage, and his resulting search for the Alchemist.

Then he told about his adventure to the southern shore, the jump to the kayak, his adventure during the storm, and how he ended up in the Swamp- at least as far as he could recall. He left out the part about the wolf. He knew how dangerous that had been and didn't want Liam to think he was foolhardy. Of course, Liam had come to that conclusion just about the time Quinn was describing how he tossed the kayak over the edge of the glacier. Had Quinn included the part about the wolf, Liam couldn't have thought him any more foolhardy,

Liam thought a minute once Quinn had finished and then said, "Yeah, I remember those stories about an Alchemist…"

"I knew it," shouted Quinn, interrupting. "I knew you could help. Woo-hoo! We're going to fix the water and the bay, and everything will be the way it's supposed to be, and the animals will be safe."

Liam cut him off. "Hold on there, big guy. I said I recall the stories. I have no idea if they're true or not. No one has ever found that village the so-called Alchemist supposedly saved from the plague. Even the stories about him and the Thumpers are just that – stories. No one knows if they're really true. I know all sorts of stories like that one. I used to think they were only made up stories told to children to keep them from getting into trouble. Although, I have to admit, they didn't keep me from getting into my share of..."

"No, no," protested Quinn, interrupting Liam. "They have to be true. The Sage wouldn't make something like this up. She just wouldn't. Not about the Alchemist. After all she's...well, she's...The Sage."

Liam knew better than to challenge Quinn about the Sage. He thought some more about what Quinn had told him about the bay, the water and the animals. He went over to a large table in the stern of his boat where he had a number of charts and maps. He rifled through them until he found what he was looking for.

"I came across this about a month ago, when I was showing Natalie these maps," he said, referring to the Princess of the Sea Sprites. "At the time I didn't think anything of it."

He spread the map out for Quinn to see. Quinn stood behind Liam, peering over his shoulder.

"This is an area near the eastern end of the Swamp." He ran his finger along the map.

"The shore runs nearly parallel to a long fault line that drops sharply off deep beneath the ocean. Natalie told me that this same fault line runs all the way up to your bay, and is not far from an old, inactive underwater volcano. About a mile in from this fault line I was mapping out an old waterway in the marsh and came across a stretch of dead and dying razor grass. The ground that this grass had been growing in was mushier than normal and smelled like sulfur. I also saw a few dead swamp rats and one or two scorpion lizard bodies that were dead and bloated. I just thought some gargoyles had been hunting them, or that something else had gotten to them. But after hearing about your bay, I wonder if whatever is happening up there is happening down here, too."

"It looks like that whatever is ruining my bay is the same thing that's ruining your Swamp," said Quinn. "Maybe we should check it out, just to make sure. How far away is it?"

"We can make it in a day."

"Let's do it then."

Quinn was standing next to Liam eager to leave that minute. He was still wearing just his underwear. Liam looked him up and down.

"I think you need something," he said.

Quinn wrinkled his brow, wondering what it could be as Liam pulled a package from behind the breakfast table.

"Here," he said, tossing the package to Quinn. "These are for you. I can't have you running off on an adventure in your underwear."

Quinn opened up the package and found the clothing Liam had put together for him.

"Oh, WOW!" he exclaimed. He was as excited as if it was his birthday. "These are really neat."

He pulled the clothing on. Liam had been pretty accurate in guessing the size. Everything fit just about right, except for the pants. They came halfway between his ankles and his knees, and one pant leg was slightly longer than the other. Quinn didn't seem to notice, or if he did, he didn't care.

"Pockets, too," he said, still marveling at the outfit. "Just like yours."

"Yeah," said Liam, just shaking his head, unable to stop looking at the uneven and too short pant legs. "Neat."

The next morning they boarded Liam's ship and followed a passage eastward along one of the larger streams that eventually emptied out into the Cerulean Sea. By late afternoon, they arrived at the place Liam had pointed out on his chart the day before. They were in a section of the waterway that had turned northward and paralleled the shore, which was less than a mile further east. The eastern side of the waterway – between the Swamp and the Cerulean Sea - was covered with razor grass. Normally this grass rose up 15 to 20 feet, was mottled green and brown, and stood stiffly upright. The blades were usually two or three inches wide and thin as a razor. Now, though, as far as they could see, the grasses had turned gray to black and hung limply, just as Liam had described earlier.

The other side of the waterway was crowded with Poison Oaks.

"Those limbs are normally rock hard," said Liam, pointing to the trees. "Look at them now. They looked spongy and soft."

The Medusa Moss that hung from the branches was brittle and broke off, evaporating into dust, with the slightest breeze. Liam looked down into the water. It was the same murky brown, but there was an oily sheen to it and a light mist above the surface. It looked like steam and had a faint odor of sulfur.

"The water around here never looked good," said Liam, "but even this doesn't look right. And it stinks – differently than it normally stinks."

A subtle rustling in the reeds caught Liam's attention. He bolted upright and motioned to Quinn to remain quiet. Off to his right he could see the dead reeds of razor grass swaying gently and then stopping. There was no breeze blowing through them. Something was slowly making its way through the reeds. The only thing Liam knew of that moved easily in razor grass was a blue dybbuk, which wasn't really blue. At least it had never been blue as long as Liam was aware.

It was a long thin creature. Its gray-green in color normally enabled it to blend quite well into the surrounding grass. It moved on three very long, skinny legs and stood about ten feet tall. Its head was long and narrow, too, so its shape as well as its color served to camouflage it. Its eyes were low on the sides of its head, and its four arms weren't really arms, but were more like tentacles. The ends of each tentacle had two long hook-like appendages that were very sharp, and curved like the talons of a giant bird. It lived near the edges of stretches of razor grass, near the water where it fed on snakes and lizards and anything else that floated by.

Liam and Quinn waited patiently, as the rustling in the reeds got closer and closer to the shore. Finally, they saw its head slowly appear over the tops of the reeds. Since these plants normally stood much higher, the dybbuk's head would be hidden. But whatever was killing the plants, reduced the normal protective foliage, and the dybbuk was easily visible.

It edged closely to the water, watching for some unsuspecting prey to float past. But, instead, it got too close to the water. The sandy ground along the edge of the razor grass was usually much firmer, and would normally support its front leg. Whatever was polluting this stream – even more than normal – was turning that sand into a mush that was much softer. As the dybbuk planted its foot, the ground quickly gave way.

The dybbuk lost its balance and began to topple forward. One long tentacle reached up to latch onto some overhanging Medusa Moss, but the Moss, which was as dead as the razor grass, just crumpled into dust. Without this stabilizing hold, the dybbuk lurched forward and its arms began to flail like a windmill. When it started to lose control of its balance, its second leg splashed into the water and the rest of his body was carried forward, out of the reeds and into the stream.

There was an almost immediate hissing sound and a burst of steam billowed up around the dybbuk's legs. Another tentacle shot across the water and latched onto one of the Poison Oak branches. The branch was so soft that the sharp edge of the tentacle merely cut through it, lopping it from the rest of the tree and causing the dybbuk to sink deeper into the water. The branch toppled down on top of the creature and then fell into the water, quickly dissolving in another burst of steam, splashing the acidic water on the creature.

The hissing continued but was soon lost in the ear-piercing screech that came out of the dybbuk. The splashed water was burning the animal. It shot another tentacle at the Poison Oak, but this time around a trunk where it attached to something more solid. It tried to pull itself free from the muck at the bottom of the waterway, but didn't have enough leverage. It was screeching louder now as it sank deeper and deeper, moving its legs more and more quickly – both to free them from the burning water and to try to extricate itself from the mire.

A third tentacle looped around a neighboring oak and the dybbuk pulled harder trying to free itself. But it was now off balance and its third leg reflexively dropped into the water to keep it from falling over. By now it was hopelessly stuck in the middle of the stream. No sooner did that leg enter than another loud hiss sounded and a billow of steam emerged. The screeching of the dybbuk got even worse. It was clearly in pain and shock. Something in the water was burning the animal's skin. As it thrashed it splashed more water onto its body and blisters began to form. Its tentacles thrashed in agony only jostling it more.

Liam pulled a small "V" shaped blade from his belt and gave it a quick flick towards the dybbuk. In the blink of an eye, the blade whizzed past the dybbuk and the screeching immediately stopped. The blade spun around and headed back towards Liam, who snatched it out of the air and returned it to his belt in one smooth motion.

Quinn stood awkwardly staring at the creature, not sure of what was happening or of what had just happened. He had been backing away from the front of the boat, step by step, as the drama played out – to avoid getting splashed, but also in horror as the wretched animal's suffering increased.

"What happened?" he asked. "How did you make it stop screeching?"

Before he finished his sentence, he watched the dybbuk's head drop from its body as the body sank slowly into the water. The head bobbed as the water bubbled around it, and it slowly sank, following the body, which had already disappeared from sight.

"OH! OH! Oh, no," shouted Quinn in absolute shock, "you cut off its head. OH! OH! Oh, yuk!"

"It was going to die," said Liam, "I couldn't just let it suffer like that. Something was burning it alive."

"Yeah, but you cut off its head," Quinn kept shouting.

"I know," said Liam. "I was right here when it happened."

Quinn stopped shouting, and it took a while before he brought his breathing back under control. He watched as Liam grabbed a long pole with a blunt hook on the end and snagged the remains of the dybbuk before it sank below the water or burned completely. He pulled the body closer to the side of the ship, careful not to touch it or to let the water splash up on him.

"Smell the sulfur?" he asked Quinn, who was still staring with his eyes wide open and his mouth in a large round "O."

Liam looked more closely at the water. He bent down over the side of the boat, keeping the remains of the dybbuk far enough away from him to avoid any contact with it while he sniffed the odor coming off the stream. He could also see small bubbles churning from the bottom.

"There's something under the water that's causing this," he said.

When Quinn didn't answer, Liam turned to look back at him. He was still staring in shock, his eyes riveted on the dead animal hanging from the pole in Liam's hand. Liam tossed the corpse into the water and secured the pole. He then walked over and snapped his fingers between Quinn's eyes.

"Snap out of it," he shouted. "Don't feel sorry for this creature. It would peck your eyes out in a second if you got close enough to it, and take its time eating you while you were still alive."

He could see he wasn't getting through to Quinn. He took a minute to think of a different approach. He had to remind himself that all this was very foreign to his friend and that Quinn had gone through a very harrowing experience just to get here. It wasn't going to help matters for Liam to be curt with him.

He lowered his voice and asked, "Are there any animals in your Kingdom that you have learned to stay away from – ones that would hurt you if they had a chance?"

The mention of the Ice Kingdom got Quinn's attention. The startled look in his eyes began to fade and he was able to pull them away from the body that was floating in the stream. He took a deep breath which helped clear his mind, and he thought about the question as he started to calm down.

"Yes," he said as he thought about the wolf in the cave. "Of course. Wolves."

That had seemed like ages ago. What would his father have said to him if he found out about that wolf? He didn't want to think about that. For as long as he could remember, he had been taught to stay clear of wolves, especially arctic wolves, and especially wounded arctic wolves. What had he been thinking? Sitting in that cave with a wounded predator? Was he nuts?

"Did you ever have to kill one?"

"No," Quinn answered, "but my uncle did. It was mad with hunger and had been cast out of its pack. It attacked a hunting party. I hated it – not the wolf – the fact that my uncle had to kill it."

He finally took his eyes off the carcass that had finally sunk out of sight, and he turned to look at Liam.

"Are you okay now?" asked Liam. He could see the tenseness in Quinn's body slowly evaporate.

"Yeah, I guess," said Quinn. He shot one last glance at the water. "Next time just let me know you're going to do something like that, will you?"

"I'll see what I can do," answered Liam. That is, if I have enough time to consult with you first, he thought, but didn't say.

Liam had seen all he needed. He turned the ship and set course back the way they had come. As they returned to Liam's sanctuary, they talked about what to do next. Liam wanted to search other areas of the Swamp and gather more information to see if this was an isolated situation or if there were other similar pockets. Quinn reminded Liam that he was searching for the Alchemist. It was important that he be found, but Quinn had no idea where to look for him.

"That's why I came to you. I understand that you want to check out your own ...ah...land...uh...home...uh"

"Swamp?" offered Liam.

"Yeah. Swamp. I knew that. But...and I don't mean any disrespect, but how can you tell if the water and the land is being poisoned. Isn't it all poisoned?"

Before Liam could take offense, Quinn quickly continued, "I know, I know. It's not all poisoned, but you have to admit, a lot of it is. But in my homeland, none of it is. So what's going on there is really, really bad. But here it's only a little bit bad – maybe not even really bad at all. So even if you find another place that's like the place we just were, it doesn't really help, does it?"

He knew he was making a mess of this, but he didn't know how to stop himself. Liam had already made up his mind that Quinn was right, but was having some fun watching him try to squirm his way out of the hole he was digging. He just stood and watched him, not making any further comments.

Knowing he was beyond salvaging his argument about the worth and status of their respective homes, he quickly changed strategy, "Besides," he said, "I know you can find your way anywhere, even blindfolded and in the dark. I mean I can do that sort of, but nothing like you. You're really, really good at that, which is why it's so important that you find the Alchemist. I'm positive you can do this."

"I could," said Liam, cutting him off. "If I knew what I was looking for. But you don't have any idea where this Alchemist could be, or if he's even alive, or if he's even a he. He could be a she, couldn't he?"

Quinn was getting confused. "But if you can't find him...or her...or...whatever; what are we going to do?" he asked in a near panic.

"If you give me a destination, I can get you there," Liam commiserated. "The problem is, we don't have a destination. Neither one of us has any idea where to start. We need someone who can tell us where to find an Alchemist."

At almost the same instant they turned to each other and said, "Lochen!"

Quinn smiled broadly recalling their sorcerer friend. "All right! Now we have a destination, so you can lead us there."

"No," corrected Liam, "we have a person, which is a start, I'll admit, but we don't know where Lochen is. I'm not sure anyone ever knows where Lochen is at any given time. Remember, he likes to commune with the planets. He could be anywhere. Who knows if he's even on earth?"

"Solveig will know," said Quinn, refusing to give up. "All we have to do is find Solveig. She's his sister. She'll know."

"Right, Solveig," said Liam. "She's more likely to know where he is than anyone else - or at least how to get in contact with him. At least she keeps her feet on the ground – most of the time - sort of."

He recalled hearing about the castle in which the mountain princess and her sorcerer brother lived - up in the clouds. At least that was a real live destination. He'd never been there before, but he knew he could find it. It was going to be a long journey, though. He only hoped she would be there when they arrived.

"All right then," he said when he could think of no other options. "We'll need to get an early start, and we should probably try to avoid the desert, if that's all right with you."

"I suppose," said Quinn.

"It may take us a day or two longer, but I think it will be safer for us to go towards the western edge of the Swamp and travel south from there."

Liam was talking more animatedly than he normally did, running through a mental checklist of provisions they would need and the terrain they would encounter. Quinn had spent his life in the Ice Kingdom and this was all foreign to him. All he knew was that he didn't like the Swamp at all. It was much too hot, much too humid, and much too unfriendly.

"I'd feel more comfortable traveling through the fields and forests. What about you?" Liam asked, returning to the subject of their itinerary.

Quinn bobbed his head left and right, thinking the question over. He had no idea what a desert was, but if Liam wanted to avoid it, he knew it must be really bad. So going through the desert was definitely out. Fields and forests? What could be hard about strolling across some fields and through a forest? Whatever they were. Isn't there any ice around this part of the world, wondered Quinn? He thought about the words - desert, fields and forest. Like deserts, he had no idea what a forest was. The only fields he knew about were ice fields, but he was pretty sure the fields Liam was talking about weren't ice fields.

"Fields and forest. Sounds good to me," answered Quinn definitively, as he daydreamed about ice fields that seemed much too far away. "This ought to be fun."

Chapter five

The next morning by the time Quinn woke up, Liam had provisioned the ship with additional supplies and weapons. Everything was ready, including Quinn, who had slept in his new clothes.

Liam was showing Quinn a map of the route he planned to take. Quinn was pretending to understand what Liam was talking about. He was still marveling at his new clothes, especially all the pockets.

"I've been all over the Swamp at one time or another," Liam was explaining, "so I know how long it will take us to get to the southwestern edge. After that it's only a guess."

He had a general idea as to where Solveig's castle was located, but getting there was another story. She had described it at length the last time he had spoken with her. It was nestled in among the highest peaks of the mountain range that separated the Swamp from – Liam didn't really know what it separated the Swamp from, since he'd never been south of the mountains.

All he knew was that her castle was high in the clouds and nearly impenetrable, although he recalled that Summer and Sean had managed to scale the southern side of the mountain on which it was perched. But Summer was a faerie and she could fly, so he didn't know if that really counted. Sean, on the other hand, was a forest creature, and while excellent climbers, the mountainside had been granite, and it had taken more than one day to scale. And he did it by hand. Liam would like to have seen that. Anyway, he and Quinn would be coming at it from the north, so they shouldn't encounter the same obstacles. Still, it would take time and, he expected, a lot of effort.

As Quinn climbed on board the ship he couldn't help but notice all the knives, spears, axes, swords and arrows.

"Holy blubber on a biscuit," he exclaimed. "What kind of neighbors do you have around here?"

"Not very nice ones," answered Liam. "You've already seen a couple, remember?"

Quinn nodded silently, but kept staring at the hardware. He had never seen so many weapons in one place.

"There's so much of it, though," he said. He gave a worried look towards Liam and added, "Is there something about this trip that you're not telling me?"

"We probably won't need most of this stuff,' explained Liam, "but we're going to an area of the Swamp that I normally tend to avoid, and besides that, with the changes to the water and marshes around here, anything is possible. I've already noticed some migration of a few of the nastier Swamp residents to areas they usually stayed away from. It seems like all the old 'territories' are changing. It wouldn't be wise to be caught in the middle of turf wars without the right armament."

He moved a few pieces around until he found a narrow dagger in a scabbard with a belt.

"Here," he said, tossing the weapon to Quinn. "Strap this on."

Quinn caught the item awkwardly, and fumbled with it. He dropped it once or twice trying to handle it only with his fingertips, before finally clasping the belt around his waist. He was clearly uncomfortable with the blade.

"You probably won't need it," said Liam, trying to ease his friend's anxiety. "But just in case you need to cut something – like rope – or something."

"Yeah," said Quinn, resigning himself to being armed, but seeing a way out, so to speak. "Cutting rope. I could do that."

Quinn was beginning to wonder if his search for the Alchemist was such a good idea. He hadn't thought through all the ramifications. When he set out, he thought it would be a simple matter of reaching Liam and then finding this Alchemist. It was becoming more complicated than he had imagined. But he also knew he couldn't just let bad things happen to his home – or even Liam's - without trying to fix them. He pushed any misgivings he had out of his mind and focused on what needed to be done.

"Okay," he said. "Let's get moving."

And with that Liam maneuvered the ship into the adjacent waterway and set off. Over the next few days, he zig-zagged through marshes and bogs, avoiding some of the more treacherous areas, but also limiting his travel to the smaller and slower passages. He believed that avoiding trouble would save them time in the long run.

It all looked the same to Quinn. Once or twice he was sure they were passing an area they had already been through. Liam had not yet raised the sail, since it wouldn't do much good in the close quarters through which they were presently traveling. For the time being their means of propulsion was limited to his pedaling, and because the streams were so narrow and twisted in every direction, their progress was slow.

Quinn tried to occupy himself with watching out for dangerous animals, but he hadn't seen anything so far. He would spell Liam at the pedals periodically during the day, but that was pretty monotonous, too. After nearly three days Quinn finally had to ask about the so-called dangerous animals and things that Liam was always warning him about.

"I thought you said there were dangerous animals around. I haven't seen anything, and I've got pretty good eyes."

"The animals and reptiles of the Swamp are all familiar with this boat, or the other ones I have that are a lot like it," he explained. "They know enough to stay out of my line of sight. Don't worry, though, they're around and they're keeping close watch on us."

And that they were; just waiting for a moment when Liam might be distracted, or make a mistake. They also kept an eye on his large traveling companion, who looked very much out of place in the Swamp. They were certain that one would do something wrong very quickly.

Liam could sense the presence of a number of predators. He was a little frustrated that he wasn't able to see them but he was satisfied that there were other signs that he and Quinn were being followed. Smaller creatures were noticeably absent and the Swamp was almost too quiet. There was not much he could do other than stay alert. He thought about warning Quinn, but he didn't know what to warn him about, and he didn't want to worry him needlessly.

For three days Quinn had scanned the shoreline constantly, looking for dangerous predators that Liam was always talking about, but had never really described. He never saw a single one. In fact, he never saw anything, except for a fish splashing in the stream or a bird overhead. Every once in a while he spotted a turtle. They were pretty small, and didn't look at all dangerous. Heck, he thought, we have fish and birds at home. We don't have turtles, though, but the fish and birds we have are a whole lot bigger than anything here. He was beginning to wonder if Liam wasn't having fun with him and just telling stories.

One thing that did amaze him, though, was the amount of plant life. He had never seen so much all squished together. When he first entered the Swamp he had covered his head most of the time and didn't really get to see all the vegetation. He was truly amazed by the amount as well as the variety.

Every time he reached out to touch one, Liam would stop him. Just about every plant or tree they passed, Liam told him looked harmless but was far from it. Just like all the imaginary animals, Quinn asked himself. But, instead of helping Quinn to keep alert, it seemed to just remind him of how foreign this land was from his own.

After three days of traveling and being told to be careful and don't touch this or that, and don't drag your fingers in the water, the boredom was wearing on Quinn. And three days of having to keep close watch on potential threats, making sure they didn't take a wrong turn, and watching Quinn to keep him from doing or touching something harmful was wearing on Liam. They were both getting a bit short with one another.

When Quinn said for about the tenth time, "Isn't there anything around here that won't hurt you?" Liam thought that maybe pointing out all the dangers wasn't the right approach to take.

"Actually, yes," he finally said, trying hard to keep his tone civil. "Since the last time I saw you, I've been able to develop a strain of flower that can withstand all the toxins in the grounds and waters. It is very hardy and has a pleasant aroma. The petals of the flower also have some interesting medicinal properties."

He thought Liam was starting to sound like some peddler trying to sell home and gardening supplies.

Quinn just looked at him. "Flower? Only one?" he asked.

"Yes," Liam gave an exasperated sigh. "Only one. How many kinds of flowers do you have in the Ice Kingdom, then?"

"It's an ICE KINGDOM!" answered Quinn a bit too defensively. "We don't have any flowers. We have some arctic moss, and there's sea weed and kelp in the ocean, but at least it's not poisonous."

"Moss?" asked Liam in a tone that bordered on mocking. "Moss? And seaweed, and kelp? That's all that grows up there?"

Quinn stood up straight and puffed out his chest. "Yeah. We can use the moss for a bunch of things. And we don't have to worry that it will eat us or poison us or burn us or...whatever. It's just moss. And the seaweed..."

"Well, the plants here in the Swamp may be dangerous, but at least I can make them useful," Liam snapped back, interrupting Quinn, and getting indignant. "I can use the razor grass as a slicing tool; I can use the wood from the Poison Oaks for the wheels and gears in this ship; I can use the vines for cords and ropes."

"Yeah," countered Quinn, standing up as his voice started to rise, "if it doesn't cut you, burn you, choke you, scratch you, or eat you first."

He stomped off in a huff to the front of the ship before Liam could offer any rebuttal, getting as far away from him as he could, and mumbling to himself, "I didn't even get to tell him what we can use the sea weed and kelp for, Mr. Smarty pants – like one flower is something to brag about."

As Quinn marched off in a huff, Liam kicked at the pedals, climbed off his seat and moved to the stern – as far away from Quinn as he could get, and sat next to the tiller.

"Moss," he mumbled. "Like that's the greatest thing known to man. What can you use moss for? A doormat? Wipe your feet on the moss so you don't track any snow into the Ice Kingdom," he muttered in a mocking voice, which he didn't care if Quinn heard.

The heat, the boredom and the tension had finally gotten to the both of them. They had both lost their tempers and were sitting on opposite ends of the ship mumbling and sulking. Quinn sat down on the forward bulkhead, arms crossed, staring at the murky water, and the stubby, twisted bushes on either side of the stream.

What kind of place is this, he asked himself. Who in their right mind would want to live here? You can't go anywhere without taking stuff to defend yourself, and not just a little stuff – a whole bunch of stuff – a whole arsenal. I'm surprised this boat doesn't sink, we're carrying so many weapons on it. He looked back and saw Liam glance in his direction. He jerked around and faced forward.

And you need shelter just about everywhere, he continued to complain; in case you get stranded, and food in case you can't get back home. As he kept listing everything Liam needed to travel anywhere he went in the Swamp, it slowly dawned on him that he did exactly the same thing when he traveled around the Ice Kingdom.

But it's not the same, he attempted to rationalize. The weather in the Kingdom could change at a moment's notice, leaving an unprepared traveler at the mercy of the elements. The weather here is always the same: stifling. It goes from hot to really hot. He looked up at the sky, which was blocked almost completely by the overhanging branches and moss. I'll bet a storm in this place would be really bad, he thought.

But we don't have snakes and lizards and all sorts of poisonous stuff. Although there were wolves, bears, walruses and seals that would easily make a meal out of any unsuspecting or unprotected prey. He felt a bit guilty when he recalled the wolf he spent the night with in that cave. It was beginning to dawn on him that there were more similarities in their respective worlds than there were differences.

Even when he sailed in his kayak, the sea was filled with danger. He always had a spear and a knife with him. He reflexively felt the dagger Liam had given him and couldn't recall where he had lost his own knife –

73

somewhere in the ocean on his trip here. Maybe the Swamp wasn't really much more dangerous than his own homeland. Maybe he was being unfair. How could he have been so rude to Liam? After all, Liam had saved his life. Liam hadn't asked him to enter the Swamp; he never scolded Quinn for getting lost; he even risked his life to come to Quinn's rescue.

Quinn was beginning to feel really guilty for having said such disrespectful things about Liam's home. He began to chastise himself for being so self-centered. He didn't deserve a friend as good as Liam. I'm such a poop, he said to himself

At the other end of the ship, Liam sat with his back towards Quinn, staring out at the direction from which they had just come. He had his hand on the tiller and only glanced forward when he absolutely had to in order to keep the boat on course. He didn't want Quinn to think he was looking at him. He saw that Quinn had glanced back at him at one time when he had been looking forward to check their course. They had briefly made eye contact and then he, too, jerked around to stare at the water behind them as he sat with his arms crossed, scowling.

Who was Quinn to belittle Liam's Swamp? This is my home, he thought. I know there are a lot of dangerous things here, but it wasn't always like this, and it will change – eventually. He thought about the new gardens he had planted. It didn't matter that most of them were quickly overrun or destroyed by the poisons, the pollution, the predators, or the gargoyles. Fixing that would take time. He reflected on how even the most dangerous things in the Swamp had good uses to which they could be put. There were a lot of areas that were beautiful and enjoyable. Better than that old Ice Kingdom – a bunch of snow, ice, and rock. Who could live there?

What was so great about the Ice Kingdom? Then he remembered Quinn describing the ice mountains that soared so high in the sky, the clouds hanging majestically over their peaks; the enormous ice formations that were created from huge glaciers calving and dropping into the sea; how the seals would play in the water and flop around on large sheets of ice.

He also thought about how Quinn had risked his life to find help. He left his home and sailed alone across a stormy ocean at night because something threatened his home. Liam wasn't sure he had the courage to do that. He was on that ocean for days and nights in that tiny kayak. The only thing separating him from the sea and all the dangerous creatures in it was a thin layer of skin. And he made that trip to find me – so I could help him. I'm an idiot, he chastised himself. The more he thought, the more he felt guilty about being impatient with Quinn.

"What am I doing?" Liam asked himself. He stood up and started towards the front of the ship to apologize to Quinn.

"I'm lucky to have him as a friend, and my friend needs my help," he muttered to himself. "You need to get over yourself," he told himself. "You need to make things right, no matter what."

He looked up and saw Quinn leaning far over the side of the ship. What's he doing, Liam asked himself.

As Liam had been thinking about Quinn's description of the Ice Kingdom, and Quinn was thinking about Liam's efforts to fix his home, something just below the water's surface had attracted Quinn's attention. He turned to get a better look and leaned his head slightly over the side.

At first he thought it was just his imagination, but then something glimmered and he started seeing what looked like a small face. What IS that, he asked himself. A face? Quinn knew from his own experience that there were people of all shapes and sizes in the world, and they lived just about everywhere. This one had what looked like a head that was about the size of a grapefruit. Although he had never seen a grapefruit, he remembered Solveig had described them.

He sat back, momentarily distracted, thinking about grapefruits and wondering what they looked and tasted like. Then the face moved and faded out of sight, sinking lower into the water, and then glided just as slowly upward again. The movement recaptured Quinn's attention and he turned back towards it. The image was so faint, Quinn wasn't really sure what he had seen. He leaned a little forward to get a better look.

"That's definitely a face," he said to himself, "I think."

Just as he thought he could make out the features on the face, it again drifted deeper into the water, this time not quite completely disappearing from sight. Quinn leaned forward a little more, waiting for it to float upward again.

"Come back," he whispered. "I won't hurt you."

In a few seconds, it rose up, but not quite as high as it had the time before. It was just enough so that he thought he could see more clearly what exactly it was. He leaned a little more forward. He frowned, thinking that this time it didn't look quite as much like a face as it did the first time. He wasn't sure what it looked like.

As it faded from sight, Quinn leaned over a little more to get a better look. Nearly half his body was hanging over the side and his face was about a foot above the surface. He could see the object better now. He thought he could see it moving. The water was just too muddy to get a really good look. He wanted to get as close as he could so that the next time it neared the surface, he would be able to tell if it was a face or not. It seemed to be rocking softly a little to the left and then back to the right. Quinn was holding on to the bulkhead, staring intently, when he was suddenly and almost violently jerked back.

"What...hey!" he shouted.

Before he could finish the sentence, the object below the water shot up into the air. Large snapping jaws filled with glistening pointed teeth crashed shut like a steel trap in the space where Quinn's head had been only seconds before. The long thick body behind the teeth thrashed violently before dropping back into the water and disappearing from sight – not that Quinn was looking to see where it went.

"That was a dragon eel," said Liam, as the giant snake-like creature splashed back into the water.

Quinn was too stunned to talk. He stood there with his mouth open, his eyes darting back and forth from Liam to where the eel had been.

"That was a small one," said Liam. "They can grow to nearly fifteen feet long and a foot and a half in diameter. They can open their jaws wide enough to fit a saber boar in them and swallow it whole."

Liam noticed the look on Quinn's face hadn't changed and thought a second, assuming correctly that Quinn had no idea how big a saber boar could get. He needed to put this into a context Quinn would understand.

"They could eat a walrus," he clarified.

He didn't know how big a walrus could get, but he made an educated guess based on stories Quinn had told him, and figured that he had guessed about right, judging by Quinn's wide-eyed reaction.

"A walrus?" sputtered Quinn. "Holy blubber on a biscuit. How could it get its mouth around something that big?"

"Its jaws are hinged and its teeth fold back inside its mouth. When it attacks there are three or four rows of fangs that spring forward and act like hooks, pulling whatever has been caught into the mouth and down the throat of the eel. The fangs also have venom in them. The venom doesn't kill the prey. It just paralyzes them. That way it can't fight while the eel digests it."

"You mean if that thing had grabbed me, I'd be eaten alive? And I'd know I was being eaten alive?"

"Yeah, I suppose so. I've never been eaten by one, so I don't know for sure," Liam added, trying to lighten the mood a bit. "But from what I've seen, yes, whatever an eel catches can't move, but it knows what's happening."

Liam was getting more self conscious as he talked. Maybe Quinn was right. Why would anyone live in a place with so many dangerous plants and animals? Had he gotten so used to the dangers and the violence that he just took it for granted? He had been born and raised here, but it hadn't always been this unsafe. Maybe his efforts to try to change the Swamp back into what it used to be were all a waste of time. Maybe he needed to find someplace else to live before he became as nasty and vicious as the other inhabitants of the Swamp.

"Look," he said to Quinn, "you're right about this place. It's the pits."

"No," interrupted Quinn, "I mean, yeah, it is – but not everywhere – just in some places. But you got me thinking. The Swamp isn't all that different from where I live. The Ice Kingdom isn't always the nicest place to be."

"Look," said Liam.

"Wait," said Quinn. "Let me finish. Yeah, we don't have all the plants you have here, but if you're not careful, you won't last a day out on the ice. You can get caught in a storm or an avalanche and get buried alive; you can freeze to death; you can fall into a crevasse or some other giant hole covered with soft snow; you can get attacked by just about anything – even the arctic rabbits can get nasty if...uh...if...ah... if they're hungry enough!"

"Arctic rabbits?" asked Liam, skeptically.

"Oh, yeah," said Quinn. He was on a roll. "Let me tell you they can be really vicious, especially if you're attacked by a herd of them...or a pack of them...or ...well a bunch of them. And squirrels, too. Arctic squirrels."

"Gee," said Liam, who was beginning to think Quinn was making stuff up, "you make it sound like such a wonderful place to visit."

"Yeah," he said, "it's just like here – only different."

They looked at each other and started laughing.

"You know what I mean," Quinn gave a gentle push at Liam.

"Yeah, I do. We both live in places that are dangerous, but for better or worse, they're our homes. We get used to where we live. Just do me a favor."

"Sure," said Quinn. "Whatever you want."

"Don't lean over the side of the boat like that again. If you want a close up look at a dragon eel, let me know. I'll catch one for you."

Quinn took a deep breath, "Don't worry, I'm staying put. And, no, I hope I never see one of those things again."

"Well, I'm sorry to disappoint you. Where we're going, we're going to see a lot of them; and a bunch of other stuff that will make them look tame."

"You mean these things live in places besides the Swamp?"

"Not that I know of," Liam answered. "We're going to be in the Swamp a while longer.

He saw a look of confusion on Quinn's face. He needed to show Quinn where they were and where they had to go. Liam took Quinn below deck and showed him some charts.

"This is where we are now," he said.

Liam's finger was on a spot near the top right section of the map. The whole thing was a maze of criss-crossing waterways and everything was colored green. He moved his hand about an inch or two to the right.

"This is where we started."

Then he pointed to the bottom left side of the map.

"This is where we need to go."

Quinn's spirits dropped. He wondered if he'd ever get out of this Swamp.

Sensing Quinn's dismay Liam quickly added, "It's not as bad as it looks. In about a day we'll reach the Wetlands." Liam's finger moved closer to the center of the map. "This is where a lot of these small tributaries all feed into. The currents move faster and the plants are all a lot smaller. We should be able to set sail there and make up a lot of time."

His fingers had flown over several different parts of the map, and Quinn hadn't been able to follow him. All he could think about was how long it had taken them to go not very far.

"The only problem is," Liam had continued, "that after the Wetlands we hit the Sludge Shelf. We have to pedal through that. The Shelf is the real reason I put in those studded wheels. With both of us taking turns pedaling, it won't be so bad – only a couple of days. But the Sludge Shelf is also where we can run into trolls. That won't be fun. But after that we will be at the end of the Swamp."

Quinn had stopped paying attention right after Liam had told them where they had to go. He knew that Liam was trying to downplay how long their travel through the Swamp would take as well as the dangers they faced. But he also knew that in spite of any spin that Liam put on it, the going would be rough, and that this was just the beginning. And the worst part was that they were making this long trip, not to find the Alchemist, as he had hoped, but to find Lochen. They were going all this way just to find Lochen!

And then he realized that wasn't even true. They were going all this way to find Solveig, whom they hoped knew where Lochen was. And they weren't even sure if they'd find Solveig whenever they reached wherever they were going. He was trying not to feel overwhelmed, but the news was depressing.

He watched Liam as he described the journey ahead of them without any apparent concern for the dangers. He's going all this way to help me, he thought. He never even gave it a second thought. He is just doing it. He reminded himself of what a good friend he had and the good friends he was going to find. There was no question things would be tough, but he was confident that with his friends, he'd be able to face anything. His spirits began to rise again and he realized he was hungry.

"Hey," he said to Liam, "I'm not worried about what's down the road. As long as we have enough to eat. What's for lunch?"

Liam stopped talking and looked at Quinn. A sly smile crept onto his face. "I can drop a net over the side and catch some great tasting dragon eel."

Quinn thought about the snakey-looking thing that had tried to swallow him. He wasn't too sure about trying to catch one of those things. He thought Liam was putting him on, and smiled widely.

"It tasks just like chicken," Liam added, encouraged by Quinn's reaction.

Quinn's smile faltered just a little. Now he was really confused. Was Liam really joking or was he serious?

"Great," Quinn said. "But I still don't know what chicken is."

Chapter six

As Liam and Quinn continued their trek across the Venomous Swamp, on a small island much further to the south in a quiet bay along the Cerulean Sea there lived a community of Sea Sprites. For a long, long time the Sea Sprites had lived in a large bubble on the Sea floor. They had sought refuge in this shelter to avoid the wars that raged on the land.

For centuries they had remained separated from the peoples who lived above the surface of the Sea. Their only contact had been periodic visits from a sorcerer who had managed to discover their world and had promised to keep it secret. No one was really sure how he had discovered their refuge or how he had managed to bypass the sea that encompassed the enormous bubble, but he had.

And then one day, he had brought others – his princess sister, a faerie princess and a forest creature. After that a wild adventure had thrown them all together and had forged a lasting friendship.

Not long after that adventure, the leader of the Sea Sprites, a Princess named Natalie, decided the time had come, and that it was now safe, to move to the surface. It was not only safe for them to move, she believed it was essential. They needed to return to life on the surface.

She discovered, with the help of some friends, the island on which they now resided. It was near the shore where the faerie village existed and not far from the forest creatures' lodge. Her enchantress, Stella, had come across a large transport stone that was able to move large numbers of the Sea Sprites at one time. With the help of the sorcerer, the transition began. When they had all been moved, along with their houses and belongings, Stella relocated her Sanctorum.

The Sanctorum was a large circular room that now sat several floors below the main floor of Natalie's castle. In spite of being below ground, it had a domed roof that gave the appearance of opening up to the sky. It was an illusion, of course, but Stella claimed that it made her less claustrophobic. She had designed and constructed it herself. Natalie thought she was just showing off, but never gave voice to those thoughts. She knew it wouldn't do to offend the Enchantress.

Natalie had spent much of her time over the several months since relocating her community to getting life back to normal. The Sea Sprites had lived for quite some time in the bubble on the floor of the Cerulean Sea. Many of them had been born there and knew no other life. They had to adjust to so many things that were a part of everyday life on land. Simple things like day and night. The bubble had always been illuminated. Natalie's people had never experienced the darkness of night.

She had to calm the fears of several of the Sprites the first time it rained. Even living under the water with it surrounding them on all sides but the sandy floor, they had never experienced rain or even the concept of rain. The idea of water falling from the sky led them to believe their bubble had sprung several leaks and near panic had set in. The whole incident caused Natalie to recall an ancient myth about a chicken that had been struck on the head by an acorn and claimed that the sky was falling. The first time she heard that story, she thought the whole idea was completely ridiculous, but now it seemed to make much more sense.

At times, the adjustment to living on the surface had been difficult for the Sprites, but eventually, things settled into a routine and many of them adapted quite well. Most of them enjoyed their new surroundings and the new experiences of days and nights and variations in the weather. Natalie knew, though, that they really had no idea of how much different life could be.

She recalled her adventure not long ago of traveling through jungles and deserts, across swamps and ice fields. The changes on her island were minimal compared to her journeys. She knew there was the potential for her people to encounter adversities they had never experienced before, and probably couldn't even imagine. However, she felt they had been cut off too long from the rest of the world. It was important for them to realize they were only a part of a larger environment.

The Sea Sprites were exposed gradually to the other residents around the bay. Natalie had maintained her contact with Summer and the faeries, and Sean and the forest creatures. The Sea Sprites had lived in their underwater bubble for more than five hundred years. Adapting to life on an island had been quite challenging. Meeting the faeries and the forest creatures was upsetting at first until Natalie assured the Sprites that these new people were their friends. There were some Sprites, though who wanted to go back to the bubble.

"That's not possible," Natalie told them. "That life is gone. We must create a new life on this island and begin to look to the future." She never really said they couldn't go back. As the Princess of the Sea Sprites, she couldn't lie. But that didn't mean she couldn't be a little deceptive. In reality, the bubble still existed. When Stella moved the village to the surface, she asked Natalie if the bubble should be destroyed.

"No," she replied. "There may come a time when we will need it as a refuge."

Stella studied the Princess before commenting, "Which way is it? Either we can go back or we can't. If you've decided to commit our people to live on the surface, why are you, yourself, holding on to the past?"

"I'm just keeping our options open," she answered. "Be assured. I have committed to having the Sea Sprites become a part of the larger community. You know as well as I that there are forces that would threaten our friends and threaten our world. If we live divided from them, who can we turn to should we need help? By the same token, it's not my goal to leave us no security whatsoever."

"So," said Stella, "we're keeping the bubble – just in case of what? Global disaster?"

Natalie smiled. "Nothing as dire as that. I'm keeping it to give you something to check on in your spare time."

Stella laughed at that. "You know, some of our people would just as soon return."

"That's why we're not going to tell them that it's still there."

"You mean you're going to lie to them?" Stella asked, disbelievingly.

"No," answered Natalie, "not exactly. I'm just not going to tell them it's still there."

"And what if circumstances should arise where we need to return? Won't they then know you held the truth from them?"

"I'll just tell everyone that you constructed another bubble – as if by magic."

Stella just shook her head, but agreed to keep Natalie's secret.

She and the Princess let the rest of the Sprites believe the bubble no longer existed, without specifically saying it had been destroyed. They convinced the Sprites that they needed to adapt to life on the island.

However, Natalie had Stella construct a long, sturdy tube from a place near the Sanctorum that could serve as an escape hatch to the bubble if a hasty retreat was needed. Because the Enchantress often would disappear for days on end and no one really noticed, Natalie asked Stella to periodically return to the bubble to make sure it remained intact and well supplied.

"You were serious about that?" asked Stella.

"Of course," said Natalie. "Would I lie to you?"

The return of the Sea Sprites was a cause of celebration in the faerie world and for the forest creatures. The Sea Sprites were invited to take part in the festivities and there were parties and events that ran day and night for several days. Even though Stella's comings and goings were generally not noticed, she felt confident that her absences during these festivals would be even less observed. She took advantage of this time to construct the passageway from the Sanctorum to the bubble.

Once it was complete, she established a fairly regular inspection schedule. She took her time whenever she conducted these inspections, and actually began to look forward to these periods of solitude. Her Sanctorum had always been a place of quiet for her, but it was easily accessible to anyone who came looking for her. There were just times when she wanted to be alone so she could think. Before long, she started looking forward to her inspection tours.

The bubble was quite large and covered miles across the floor of the Sea. It wasn't a bubble in the way most people understand. It wasn't a thin layer that could be easily punctured. It was actually more of a force field that had been constructed by one of Stella's predecessors. When the Sea Sprites fled to avoid the wars between the faeries, the forest creatures and the mountain people, the Enchantress at the time (one of Stella's ancestors, named Virginia) had generated the giant pocket of air and shielded it with several magic spells.

Over time the population of the Sea Sprites grew and the bubble had to be expanded. Whenever that happened, the spells would weaken and whoever the Enchantress was at the time would have to cast new spells. However, no two Enchantresses cast spells in exactly the same manner. As a result, the repairs on the bubble were a patchwork of mystery and magic. In spite of this, the structure had held for over five hundred years.

In all the years it had stood, there had never been any leaks, but where the spells had weakened, the surface of the bubble would start to cloud. When the Sprites lived there, everyone took part in making sure there were no breaches, and any inspections could be done easily and quickly. It was a matter of routine. Everyone had an assigned section and keeping the bubble intact was just a part of everyday living.

In spite of her mystical powers, Stella could only cover a portion of the bubble in the limited time she had. She prepared a chart so that she could systematically conduct her examinations. Last month she had come across something that was a bit out of the ordinary. Normally the spells weakened in the upper regions of the covering. This time, the clouding appeared along an area where the bubble came in contact with the Sea floor.

Like most magic spells, the bubble didn't really have an "edge" or an end. It went as deep into the ground as it needed. If anyone started digging to try to get under the bubble, it would just keeping growing and extending into the sand to keep the air in and the water out. If the digging went on for miles, the side of the bubble would continue to grow as far as necessary. And if that wasn't enough, the bubble itself was extremely flexible. It was impossible to poke a hole in the side. It was also impossible to "crash" into it. Objects tended to either glance off to one side or another, or to be gently caught as if in a spider's web, and redirected. Since it was a force field, it would move, soften, or harden as necessary.

What caught Stella's attention was not only the clouding up on a portion of the side, but there was a leak. It wasn't much of a leak, but it was definitely a leak. Impossible, she thought. There wasn't a particular spot where water was squirting it. Instead, there was a dampness in the sand several feet from the wall of the bubble. It seemed to run the length of the haziness. The clouding itself ran for almost a mile and was worse along the part that came in contact with the sand on the Sea floor. It faded away and cleared up about three or four feet up.

As she got closer, Stella saw that the wall was not only clouded, but the bottom four or five inches of the bubble was turning brown. The leak seemed to be coming through this brown section. It wasn't serious, yet, but water was definitely seeping in. The sand inside the bubble was mushy and the water was beginning to pool. Stella also noticed one more thing. The sand close to the side of the bubble was hot. She reached forward and pressed her hand against the bubble. It was hot, too.

"What on earth?" she said as she pulled her hand away.

She quickly cast a new spell and the clouding slowly began to disappear. Too slowly. Stella tried another spell and the brown part faded a little more quickly, first to a milky white and then gradually began to clear as well. A few minutes later, the sand inside the bubble began to dry out. Everything was back to normal, but Stella wasn't sure how long it would last. She cut her inspection short and returned immediately to the surface to find Princess Natalie.

She found her speaking with a small group. Rather than interrupt her, she stood apart and meditated on sending a mental image. Natalie received the message without changing her expression. She excused herself and joined Stella.

"I'm not sure what that image was that you sent me," said Natalie when they were alone. "It looked like an edge to the bubble."

"It was," answered Stella. "You need to see this for yourself."

She escorted the Princess to the Sanctorum and the transport tube to the bubble. Once they arrived, Stella took her to the exact spot she had shown Natalie in the mental image she had transmitted. The bottom edge was already slowly beginning to cloud again, and the sand was slowly getting warmer, just as Stella had described.

Natalie reached down and picked up a handful of sand next to the clouding wall. There was a slight smell of sulfur. She spun her hand in a small circle above the ground and created a mini-tornado. The sand whirled around and a hole appeared. She kept spinning her hand and pointed her finger down into the widening hole. In a few seconds, the hole was almost fifteen feet down. The sulfur smell was stronger. A puff of steam rose as the cooler air met the heated wall and sand. The sand itself was a darker brown color, but it was sparkling. It was almost like it had been burned.

Natalie pointed to a small cluster of the whirling sand, turned her other hand palm upward. She crooked the finger that had generated the swirling and motioned like she was motioning for the sand to "come here." In fact, that was exactly what she was doing. She pointed to her open hand and the mini-twister moved across the air. The cluster was about an inch or two in diameter, and was still swirling around. It looked like an even smaller version of the mini-tornado. The swirl of sand floated towards her and landed on her opened palm. As it continued to spin on her palm, Natalie could feel the heat intensify. She quickly snapped her fingers and the two inch tornado stopped – frozen in the air. Natalie moved it closer to get a better look.

The sparkling parts looked like bits of broken glass.

"It is glass!" she said to herself. "The sand has been heated so much it's been melted into glass and then broken up again."

She showed Stella the particles.

"It would take much more heat than what we are feeling to have melted the sand," said Stella. "But what would cause that much heat?"

Stella could feel the heat radiating off the motionless swirl of sand. Something was terribly wrong. Although Natalie had moved her people out of the bubble, and hoped it was permanent, she was worried about two things: first, she didn't want the bubble to be damaged and a potential safe haven lost to the Sea Sprites; and second, regardless of what happened to the bubble, the entire Cerulean Sea and maybe even the planet as a whole, was being threatened.

She returned to the island and sat with Stella in the Sanctorum trying to sort out what they had seen. Neither of them had encountered anything like this before and could find nothing in their recorded history. They spent the next few days examining the ancient Sea Scrolls. Between the two of them, they made daily returns to the bubble to check on the damaged edge and to mark the speed with which it deteriorated.

"It's getting worse, and the deterioration seems to be happening faster each day," Stella reported.

"I thought so, too," agreed Natalie.

"We're running out of time and we need to find another solution. Recasting spells isn't going to be a permanent fix to this problem."

"We aren't even sure what the problem is. How are we going to arrive at a solution?" Natalie asked.

"I think we need to take a short cut. We have a wealth of information at our hands."

"You want to resurrect the memories, don't you?" asked Natalie.

"I think that would be best."

In the Sanctorum, Stella was able to resurrect memories stored by Enchantresses from the very beginnings of the Sea Sprites. These memories were imprinted on mystical filaments and fused into the construct of the Sanctorum at the moment each Enchantress passed from the world of the Sea Sprites. They could be shared only with the current

Enchantress. But even these memories couldn't explain what was going on. It was clear, though, that there was some kind of imbalance that needed to be corrected. In the end, they felt that they were no further along than they had been when they started.

"Haven't you found anything, even the remotest clue?" Natalie asked Stella.

"I may have found two things that might help," she answered. "One is a recollection from one of the earliest memories recorded. It comes from the Seventeenth Enchantress and happened almost two thousand years ago. At first I wasn't sure it meant anything, but the flash from the memory was persistent."

When an Enchantress sought answers to mysteries by resurrecting the memories in the Sanctorum, she first would go into a trance-like state and totally clear her mind of everything but the problem that needed to be solved. And then things would start to happen. The walls and ceiling of the Sanctorum would look like nothing had changed to anyone but the Enchantress, but what she saw was completely different.

In her vision, the walls expanded and collapsed and the ceiling floated skyward until it was out of sight. It was like being awake in the middle of a dream. The Enchantress would see herself floating through another dimension, surrounded by brilliant colors, shifting from one color of the rainbow to the next in no particular arrangement. Clouds would appear, growing from nothing into huge billowing shapes, changing from white to gray and sometimes almost black. Through the clouds and across the sky flashes of lightening would appear, but without any sound of thunder. These flashes were the memories of earlier Enchantresses – or at least those that seemed to apply most to the problem that needed to be solved. It was like researching in a library of thoughts.

Sometimes the flashes were bold and brilliant, streaking across the entire field of vision. Other times, the flashes seemed to be miles away and barely flickering. Most of the time several flashes would appear at once or one right after the other. There was never any predictable pattern. They would shoot in different directions and at different intensities and for different spans of time. The Enchantress reading these memories would recall them as if they were her own; and like her own memories, some were stronger than others. It wasn't like watching a movie or reading a book. It was reliving the memory as if it were your own.

"You know what it's like when you know that you know something," Stella asked, "but you just can't remember exactly what it was? That's what this one memory was like. I knew it was key, but it was so old and so hard to bring to the surface, I almost gave up. In the end, though, I recalled a time when the islands on the other side of the land, far into the Viridian Ocean were first being formed. Deep under the surface of the Ocean, the soul of the earth broke free and exploded. Great geysers rose thousands of feet into the air, spewing rock and sand. The waters around the explosion boiled and gave way to the escaping soul which finally cooled off and formed the islands."

"I don't understand," said Natalie. "What do you mean, 'the soul of the earth?' What is that?"

"Molten lava," answered Stella. "The early islands were volcanoes that were formed by lava from the earth's core erupting through to the surface."

"But there were no eruptions along the edge of the bubble. The bubble is nowhere near a volcano – above or below the surface."

"That's right," replied Stella. "But the heat along the edge of the bubble is the same kind of heat that caused the eruptions thousands of years ago. That heat must be coming from somewhere below the ground and judging by the degree to which the sand had melted, it can't be too far down."

"But if this heat is the same, then why isn't anything erupting?" asked Natalie.

"I think that's because the lava isn't being forced through a small channel as it is in a volcano. From what we've seen along the edge of the bubble, it doesn't appear like there's a single eruption."

"That would be good, then, wouldn't it?" asked Natalie.

"No," said Stella. "The discoloration of the side of the bubble and the heat in the sand extended for almost a mile. That means it's not a volcano, but a split in the earth's core. A single eruption would be devastating to our bubble and to our island; but a breach in the earth's core that long could poison the entire Cerulean Sea. There's no telling what it could do to the land."

"It can't possibly be as bad as you think," Natalie said.

Contrary to her own words, she knew there was a very real danger that Stella was not only right, but maybe even underestimating the potential hazard. She knew that gargoyles lived in underground caverns in the Venomous Swamp. Who knew how far those caverns criss-crossed beneath the earth, or how deep?

"Yes it can – or even worse," replied Stella. "Depending on the extent of this breach. If it's narrow, the lava could fill it and seal it. The gases and other matter that escape would make the waters immediately around the fissure unlivable for a while, but the bubble would be uninhabitable indefinitely. And worse, we wouldn't be able to destroy the bubble, since that would only release the poison trapped there."

"And what if the break isn't narrow?"

"Then the lava and the gases would just keep emptying into the Sea, poisoning it. The water table under the shoreline would be poisoned as well."

"It would be like the Venomous Swamp."

"Yes, except no plant life would be able to grow in the infected land areas. At least not for a very long time."

"This news is hardly helpful," said Natalie. Cutting Stella off before she could object, she added, "but it's important that we know the worst case scenario. You said you discovered two things that might be helpful. What was the other?" Natalie asked as an afterthought.

"I'm afraid the second memory is more of a mystery than an answer," she answered. "It was more like a simple statement than a complete memory. In fact, in reflecting on it, I'm not sure it means anything at all. I don't want us to waste time on a misleading clue."

"It would be better for me to hear what it is and make a decision on it."

"Search for the Alchemist," said Stella.

"That's it?" asked Natalie. "Nothing more?"

"That was all of it. It was repeated, much like an echo. I tried to learn more, but there was nothing."

"What's an Alchemist?"

"I don't know," said Stella. She was distraught. She felt she had let Natalie down. "I tried to search the memories for an answer, but I could find none," she repeated.

"Did this come to you as a memory flash, like the other one?"

"No, it didn't," admitted Stella.

"Then are you sure it was related to your original inquiry?"

"Yes," Stella answered. "I wouldn't have mentioned this to you at all, except that as I was leaving the trance, the words came to me like a shout. There was no memory flash and I first thought it was a diverted hex, but before I came back fully, the statement came again. This time it was even louder. It was as if all the Enchantresses from the beginning of time were shouting in unison. But it was just the one statement: Search for the Alchemist. I tried to return to the trance, but it was too late. I was already returning."

Natalie was silent; thinking of options.

"I need to go back," insisted Stella. "This time inquire only about the Alchemist."

Resurrecting the memories was extremely taxing on any Enchantress. Going back too soon was dangerous. There was always the potential for losing oneself in a chain of memories, or worse – losing one's mind in a death memory.

A death memory was like a nightmare from which there was no escape. Resurrecting them once and on rare occasions was fairly safe. The Enchantress doing so had a certain amount of control. But each time it was exhausting and each time the Enchantress was more vulnerable. Going back immediately after having just returned was fraught with mortal peril.

"No," said Natalie. "I can't let you do that. The risk is not worth it."

"We have no alternative," argued Stella. "I've learned nothing about this dilemma other than the severe ramifications of sitting back and waiting to let things happen."

"But what if the break is minor and the resulting damage is minimal? You'll have risked your life for that?"

"I don't think that's the case. The message about the Alchemist was too closely connected with this event and too insistent."

After some debate, Natalie reluctantly agreed. She watched closely as her Enchantress returned to resurrect the faint and elusive memory of the Alchemist.

When she returned she was so drained she could hardly speak, but she seemed to be otherwise unharmed. Natalie called for help and had Stella taken to her room to rest. She barely had the energy to object, but once there, she declined to rest. She gathered her strength and reported on her last venture. She was sorry to say that she could discover nothing more than she had originally gathered.

"Maybe it's just a mistake," said Stella, propping a pillow behind her back. "Maybe it was just...I don't know... an echo of some kind? It was distinctive, but not really connected to anything or in any way informative. I don't know what else to tell you."

Natalie thought for a few minutes with Stella just sitting in silence. Stella knew her Princess needed to be undistracted, and waited patiently. Minutes seemed to pass by. Natalie paced around the room, her brow knit deeply in concentration. Finally she turned to Stella.

"No, I don't think the message was a mistake, even though we don't know what it means. I think it's clear that the two memories are linked. There's no other reason why, when you were researching memories of the environmental issues the referral to finding an Alchemist would be so insistent. Your ancestors have given us a direction and we must find a way to understand it."

"But I have been given no indication where to look. Where would we start?" asked Stella.

"We must find someone who can help us find the Alchemist."

Natalie turned to Stella and in the same instant they both said, "Lochen."

"Yes," cried Natalie. "We must find Lochen. Do you know where he is?"

"No," answered Stella. "I will have to return to the Sanctorum."

"Absolutely not," declared Natalie. "I shouldn't have allowed you to attempt that second resurrection."

"It's not what you think," answered Stella as she climbed off her bed and hurried out of the room. She shouted over her shoulder as Natalie watched her run down the hall, "It won't be anything at all dangerous. The last time we met, I gave him a large transporting stone, but I implanted a spell on it. I can track him from the Sanctorum. I'll send someone to get you once I'm able to locate him. At least if he's still on this planet."

Chapter seven

The sun was just emerging from the far side of Capurnica, the beams of light sparkling like millions of gems off the field of ice and rocks that formed the outer edge of its rings. Contrary to the normal laws of physics, these outer rings wove in and out of each other, seldom colliding. On the rare occasion that they did collide, the particles would explode into hundreds and thousands of tiny pieces and eventually blend into one of the several bands that raced around the planet or would float off into space as dust.

The rings stretched from the closest at 60,000 miles to the farthest at over 500,000 miles from the planet's surface. At various intervals there were spaces between sets of rings, many of which were only a few miles wide. Others were separated by mere feet. In a contradiction to the normal laws of physics, some of the inner bands intertwined with one another. In some cases these intertwined rings traveled faster than outer rings. The composition of the inner rings was more like meteors or asteroids and these were generally darker in color.

The bands towards the center were comprised more of minerals and ice with much brighter colors. Rays of light from the distant twin suns at the center of the solar system would pass through these bands and glisten with all the colors of the rainbow. But it was the outer rings that moved like roller coasters, twisting in and out of one another at incredible speeds, and which shimmered in white and bright yellow or were completely clear that attracted Lochen most.

At some point in his last adventure he had promised himself that he would see the rings of Capurnica at least once more, and revel in the mystery of those outer rings. He had managed to keep that promise. This time, though, he was accompanied, albeit a bit reluctantly, by a friend. For Sean, who had only once before in his life ever ventured out of his village, this excursion had been mind-boggling. He had accepted Lochen's invitation mostly because he thought it was a joke. How could anyone travel to the stars, he wondered. When he saw what Lochen proposed they travel in, he was even more certain that it was a joke.

One sunny summer day, Lochen had appeared unannounced and seemingly out of nowhere near the outer edge of Sean's village, deep in the forest. He was ready to plunge ahead and search for his friend, but recalled Sean's cautions. It was not wise to attempt to enter the village itself without an escort. He decided to follow this advice, since he didn't want to raise any alarms. He considered that his presence in the forest would be quickly detected and conveyed to the Lodge's council. As soon as this happened, the council would quickly dispatch the Lodge Dozor to investigate. He also knew that Sean was one such Dozor, and it was logical to assume the chances were fairly good that he would be the one to be sent. So he patiently sat near a Banchu Tree and waited for Sean to show up. He didn't have to wait for long.

"Lochen," shouted Sean. "Someone told me a really strange looking person just appeared out of nowhere. I had a suspicion it was you, from the way you were described, so I offered to come check it out. Oh – no offense meant about the strange looking person comment,"

"None taken," Lochen responded. "In fact, my people would have the same reaction to seeing you if you appeared suddenly in the mountains. In fact, as I recall, they did react exactly the same way."

"Yes," said Sean, "they did."

Lochen was once again wearing his traditional robes, complete with peanut butter and jelly stains on the front. He stood to greet Sean, looking at him without any other explanation for his presence.

"Wow, it's really great to see you," said Sean uncertainly – trying to fill the conversational void. "What brings you here?"

"Have you forgotten?" Lochen asked. "You said you would be interested in joining me when I went to see the rings of Capurnica again."

"Oh, yeah, that's right," Sean answered. "But that was about six months ago, and I didn't think you were serious. I mean, really, go to the stars?"

"The stars? Oh no," he replied. "Well, I'm sorry if I misled you. We won't be going to any stars. Actually, we'd probably burn up if we tried to go to a star. And they are much too distant. Although I suppose the twin suns in our own system are stars that are closer than Capurnica. That's irrelevant though. We'd still have to contend with burning up. But I digress. Capurnica is our destination. It's a planet, not a star. It's the one with the rings. I'm sure I was clear about that."

"No, I mean, yes," said Sean. "You were clear. I just meant it's up in the stars, I mean in the sky, I mean...you know what I mean. Anyway, like I said, that was six months ago."

"Yes, you're correct. Capurnica is up in the sky, and our conversation was six months two weeks and three days ago, to be specific," said Lochen.

"Whatever. I just thought maybe you forgot about it or you were just kidding me."

"I would never kid about something like that," he answered, a bit taken back by what he perceived as a rebuke. "I made a promise and I intend to keep it. I regret that it took me so long to fulfill it, but it took me this long to be able to arrange our transportation. Come on, let me show you."

With that Lochen headed away from the village and towards an open, sandy area not too far from the water's edge. Sean followed.

"We don't have to get in the water, do we?" Sean asked nervously, slowing his pace and coming to a stop.

"Of course not," answered Lochen a bit confused. "Why would we have to get in the water to go into the heavens? That makes no sense at all." He just shook his head. "Sometimes you really puzzle me."

He stopped abruptly and added, "Ah, yes; you were joking. Of course. I understand joking." He chuckled briefly before continuing on his way.

As they entered the clearing Sean saw a tube-like object sitting on the sand. The base was a flat long oval. It looked like some kind of stone; shimmering and milky colored. The rounded sides and top were clear. Moving closer Sean could see inside beneath the clear covering. There appeared to be two cushioned areas, one behind the other, with some kind of an instrument panel in front of the front position, and nothing else. The entire object was about ten feet long, three to four feet wide and about three and a half feet high.

Sean laughed nervously, "What is this?"

"This is our transport," Lochen announced proudly.

This is worse than getting in the water, Sean thought, but didn't say. Instead, he looked closely at Lochen to make sure it wasn't a joke. No, he thought, Lochen never really jokes; in fact, I don't think he knows what a joke is, even if he says he understands joking. I don't think so, he thought to himself.

"I know what you're thinking" pronounced Lochen.

Sean's head jerked up as he turned to face Lochen, looking stunned. Oh, poop. Can he read minds, now, he wondered.

"You're thinking, where did he get so much transport stone material."

"Well, that's not exactly what I was thinking," Sean replied, somewhat relieved, "but OK, where did you get so much transport stone?"

"From the Enchantress of the Sea Sprites," Lochen replied.

"Stella?" asked Sean.

"How many Enchantresses do you know?" asked Lochen. "Of course, Stella. After that adventure we had, I spent some time with Princess Natalie and her. It was very informative. In fact, I helped them move their community to an island not far from here. Anyway, during our time together, Stella showed me where the transporting stones came from and helped me find this one. She also helped with the spells that make it work. Amazing, isn't it?"

Sean walked a little closer to the pod.

"This thing will really fly? Up in the sky?" he asked.

"Of course. Not only will if fly up into the sky," he added, becoming more excited, "but it will carry us into space."

"Into what space?" Sean asked, really getting confused now.

"Outer space," said Lochen.

"Out of what space?"

"No. Out ER space. You know. Up among the planets and the stars. Well not really the stars, but they're in the same general location as the planets. Outer space, that is. And this covering," Lochen said as he poked the transparent shell above the base, "...it's made of the same material as the Sea Sprite's bubble. Look. Isn't it amazing? It's incredibly durable."

Sean walked completely around the small pod, peering at it from every angle. When he was back behind the tube right where he had started, he looked up and saw that Lochen was inside.

"Just walk in," Lochen said. "This material is strong enough to keep out the most invasive objects, but the spell Stella put on it allows us to pass through it. It's as easy as walking through water."

Sean's head popped up at the mention of water.

"I thought you said we weren't going in the water."

"We're not. Trust me. Just get in," said Lochen. "Make sure you keep your mouth shut, though. Whatever this bubble is made of tastes terrible. I regret to say that I've made that mistake more than once myself."

Sean stepped tentatively to the edge of the pod. He put out one hand to brace himself, expecting to meet some level of resistance from the bubble. He took a deep breath and then closed his eyes. He silently counted to three and then took two steps forward. When he didn't feel anything, he was sure he hadn't stepped far enough. He waved his outstretched hand back and forth, and took two more steps forward. When he opened his eyes and let out his breath, the pod had vanished. He spun his head right and left trying to see where it had gone.

"OK. Quit playing games," Lochen said. "I really had no idea you could be such a jokester. No one has ever mentioned it before."

He heard Lochen's voice behind him and whipped around. He had stepped completely through the bubble and was standing in front of it – or in back of it. It was hard to tell. He took another deep breath and held it, but this time he kept his eyes open and stepped into the pod.

"Wow," he said as he let this breath out and stood with his head just inches below the top of the pod. "I didn't feel a thing."

"Now, sit down," Lochen told him. "We can't get to Capurnica in one leap. We will have to do this in stages.

Sean blinked as he sat down, and in just that amount of time, the sky was dark. The forest had vanished.

"What happened?" he asked. "Did something go wrong? Where did all the light go? And where are the trees and stuff?"

"No. Nothing at all has gone wrong. We're halfway to the moon. Just be patient. We'll be there shortly."

Sean knew Lochen almost never joked and certainly not about things like this, but was sure he must be joking this time. Before he said anything though, he leaned over, careful not to put his head through the wall, and looked out the side of the pod. His home planet floated below him and to his right. He could see the green of the forest and the blue of the Sea. He thought he could even see the purple hue of the side of the mountain where Solveig's palace sat.

He was too amazed to be frightened, until he realized how high they were. All of a sudden, his heart started hammering in his chest, beads of perspiration broke out on his forehead, and he leaned forward to grab on to Lochen. At the same time his home planet disappeared in an instant and he was surrounded by almost total blackness, which was broken up by thousands of tiny lights. There was no sound, no feeling of movement, nothing. The surroundings just changed in an instant.

He slowly let go of Lochen and the view changed again. Now there was a large bright orange planet to his left.

"That's Poseidon,"

"Where is the sky?" asked Sean.

Lochen thought for a minute. "I'm not sure what you mean. Where is Poseidon's sky? There really is no sky on Poseidon, not like our planet. There's no atmosphere."

"I mean, why is everything around us all black? Where are the clouds and the suns? Where did the blue sky go?"

"Well," said Lochen, "the larger sun is that star over there to our right, and our smaller sun is just behind it" he said pointing to the right and behind Sean. "The clouds and the blue sky are still on our planet, but they don't rise this high.   It's all black around us because there's no atmosphere."

Lochen could see that Sean still didn't understand.

"It's black because...well, because there's no air," he said, trying to clarify. "We're in a vacuum."

"What?" shouted Sean. "No air? How are we going to breathe?" he cried as he took a deep breath and held it.

"That's a good question. I'm not sure I can explain, since I don't really know how it works. But whatever the bubble material is that Princess Natalie and her Enchantress provided to encase this vehicle is the same as that which enveloped their community for centuries beneath the sea. You recall their bubble, don't you? I would assume that it's some kind of living organism that produces oxygen. I don't recall anything else inside their bubble that would have generated sufficient breathable air.

"It probably works much the same as plants do – absorbing carbon dioxide and converting it into oxygen. It must also be able to regenerate itself. It's funny that you should bring that up. I never really thought to ask, and the question never popped into my head. Imagine if I had been wrong, or the bubble material didn't produce oxygen. We'd be in big trouble then, wouldn't we? Oh, by the way, I think it's safe for you to breathe."

Sean was on the verge of turning a rather dark shade of purple. At Lochen's direction, he let out an enormous gasp and started breathing again. In another blink of the eye Lochen announced they had arrived.

Sean looked up and saw that they were in a completely different location. This time though, they were moving. They were floating slowly towards a spectacular display of multi-colored rings circling a gigantic planet. Nearly the entire sky – or whatever it was – filled the view immediately before them.

"Wow," he said as he stared upward. "Those rings are shimmering. It almost looks like they're moving."

"They are," answered Lochen. "The speeds at which they are moving are incredible. Watch this. We're going to get a little closer."

Lochen moved his hand over the small console in front of where he was seated. The pod moved slowly up towards the rings, heading for a narrow gap between two sets of rings. He positioned the pod directly beneath the rings and slowly ascended in the middle of the path.

"I made a few modifications to the transporter stone. These controls allow me to make more precise movements of the pod. I've always wanted to get a closer look at these rings. Previously I have only been able to observe them through the lenses of a telescope. You can't imagine what a thrill it is to get so close. Oh, yes" he corrected himself. "I imagine you can imagine the thrill, since you're right here with me."

The pod had slowly risen into the space between two sets of rings as the others fanned out to the right and left almost as far as they could see. The end of the pod in which Lochen was seated was facing forward as both sets of rings flew at them head on. The speed was blinding. This particular gap was about a mile wide, so the pod was a fairly safe distance from the debris that was shooting past them. But even still, the edges of the rings were not neatly defined and every once in a while a wayward rock or chunk of ice would sail immediately over their heads or under their feet, or zoom right past them. They floated through thin clouds of space dust that appeared at random locations in the gap, as well. Sean was too engrossed to be afraid, peeking over Lochen's shoulder to look at the amazing sights.

Lochen nudged the pod forward in the circular path between the rings and around the far side of the planet. After a few minutes sunlight began to filter through the rings. It was like looking through the most spectacular and biggest kaleidoscope in the universe. Waves of space dust passed through the rings, swirling from the racing objects that orbited the planet. The movement of the dust and the additional sparkling gave the rings the illusion of undulating motion and the display of light against and through the dust created a variety of images and sights.

Sean was initially startled by the images made by the space dust and by the speed of the passing rings. It looked at times like the rings were moving towards them. He kept ducking his head.

"Relax," said Lochen. "These rings have been revolving around this planet for millions of years. There is almost never any kind of collision."

"Almost never?" asked Sean. "That means the same thing as 'sometimes,'" but he was much too amazed to be really worried.

"Let's have a little fun," suggested Lochen.

Before Sean could respond, Lochen had rotated the pod within the gap. Now it was as if they were flying sideways with one of the sets of rings racing over their heads and the other shooting beneath them. With the curvature of the orbit the path of the rings looked as if it separated to allow them to pass through. The gap was still nearly a mile wide, but the illusion was completely different.

"Whoa," shouted Sean as he reached out and braced his hands on either side of the pod walls, expecting to fall over, and completely unaware that they didn't pass through the bubble material.

"Exhilarating, isn't it?" exclaimed Lochen.

Sean realized after several seconds that he was holding his breath again. He didn't know what to make of the sights flashing before him. He was oblivious to the fact that he wasn't leaning to one side or floating freely. Something in the transporter stone kept the both of them secured to it, and when Lochen flipped the pod on its side, it automatically adjusted so they still felt like they were upright.

"Can you do that again?" asked Sean. He was starting to get over his anxiety and enjoy the experience.

"Sure," answered Lochen as he flipped the pod once more.

Now the giant planet that had been on their left was on their right. Without any additional encouragement, he spun the pod around and the rings were now flying away from them instead of at them.

"We're flying backwards now," he announced.

"I hope no one comes up behind us," Sean laughed.

"We have to go," announced Lochen abruptly.

"We're already going," said Sean, laughing. He was thoroughly enjoying himself. "How much more 'going' can we do?"

"No," said Lochen. "We have to leave. We have to get back home."

"Why?" asked Sean, not taking his eyes off the display. His earlier trepidation had been replaced by awe and curiosity. "We just got here. I'm just getting used to this. Did you forget to go before we left?"

"I don't know why," said Lochen. "Something's happened. We have to leave immediately."

The apprehension in Lochen's voice got Sean's attention. "What's happened? Where? How do you know?"

"I told you. I don't know. We have to go back home," said Lochen as he maneuvered the pod out from between the rings.

"You're starting to freak me out. How do you know?" Sean repeated more insistently.

"Stella told me," he answered, and then realized he needed to clarify. "When I made the modifications to the transporter stone to allow for more precise movements, I had Stella cast an additional spell and added some of my own embellishments to her spell. I thought it would be a good idea to be able to stay connected in some way to home. She can send me telepathic images."

"Tele-fatty images? What is that? How does she do that?" Sean asked. "And what did she just say?"

"Telepathic," corrected Lochen. "It's like a thought wave. She sends them to me from her Sanctorum. I don't know how, exactly. That's another really good question. I should have thought to ask her, but I'm not sure she could explain it herself. I assume her ability is either innate or connected to the Sanctorum, or maybe it's a skill that's taught to all Enchantresses…"

"So what did she think to you?" interrupted Sean, who was getting increasingly impatient.

"I can't be precise. We're too far away for any really clear communication. All I'm getting is more of a sense than an actual message. But it's a very strong sense. Something important is happening. The only feeling or message I'm getting is 'help.' We need to get back. Hold on."

"Hold on?" asked Sean in near panic. "Hold on to what? You didn't put any handles in this thing."

"It's just a figure of speech."

With that brief explanation to Sean, Lochen engaged the transporter stone and the pod disappeared from the rings of Capurnica. In the blink of an eye it reappeared, but not exactly where Lochen had intended. As soon as the pod made the first leap, it was immediately buffeted by hundreds of rocks. The battering threw both Lochen and Sean around the small inside area of the pod. They collided with one another and bounced off the sides of the bubble. The pod had landed in the middle of an asteroid field and was being bombarded.

"I don't remember this on the way out here. I think you made a mistake. Get us out of here," shouted Sean.

"I have to be seated properly at the controls," Lochen shouted back as he tried to pull himself back to the console.

The hits against the underside of the transporter stone were jarring, but the hits to the bubble were worrying both of them. Large rocks struck the bubble and bounced off. The bubble itself gave slightly as it repelled the missiles. It was unnerving to see the amount and the size of the debris being fired at them, especially with only a clear bubble serving as a shield.

"I don't know how much more of a beating this bubble stuff can take," shouted Sean. "Just move us."

Lochen was not completely in the right position, but he had to agree with Sean's concern. The bubble was never meant to take such abuse. He quickly got situated and concentrated. The pod immediately disappeared out of the asteroid field. In another blink of an eye, the buffeting had stopped and the pod was slowly spinning. It was as if one end of the pod had been struck at the moment it was transported, spinning the craft like a top. Lochen regained his equilibrium and adjusted the controls so that the pod stopped moving.

"That's better," said Sean. "I was worried there for a minute that I was going to blow chunks."

"Chunks of what?" asked Lochen.

"You don't want to know," answered Sean as he looked around.

Everything looked the same to him as it had before – except for being blasted by asteroids: a lot of black with millions of stars. But something was different.

"I don't remember this either. Where are we?" he asked.

He was looking at three small moons. The one on the right was such a dark gray it was almost invisible against the black space surrounding it. There were giant craters on the surface that reflected light from a nearby sun, which was the only reason he saw it in the first place. Sun, he thought – only one. Where is the other one?

The second moon was higher in the sky and more towards the center. This one looked like a crescent moon at first glance. Then Sean realized that almost two thirds of it was missing. The last one – down and to the left, looked more like a cloud. It was covered in a mist of gases.

The three moons seemed to be orbiting a very inhospitable planet. Even from this distance, Sean could see multiple volcanic eruptions on the surface. Other areas of the surface contained wide expanses of what appeared to be molten lava. Mountains were engulfed and crumbled. The entire planet looked unstable. Behind their pod was a large swirling funnel-shaped cloud of yellow and blue gas, slowly fading away. Aside from the planet, its moons and the gaseous cloud that was beginning to evaporate, there was nothing else visible.

"I don't know," answered Lochen, hesitantly. "I've never seen anything quite like this."

He looked back at the cloud. Its odd looking color seemed out of place. He focused on the shape as it faded into nothingness. It was very long and twisted, with a widely flared opening. Within seconds it was gone.

"I think we transported into a worm hole."

"I didn't see any worms," said Sean. "So how do we get back?"

"It wasn't that kind of worm hole," answered Lochen as he took stock of their surroundings.

"And I don't know how we get back. I think we're lost."

Chapter eight

After several days Liam and Quinn were finally out of the Venomous Swamp. As Liam had predicted, once they reached the wider waterways, he was able to hoist the sail and make much better time. They arrived at what he referred to as the end of the Swamp around midday. It still looked pretty much all the same to Quinn, but he trusted that Liam knew what he was talking about.

They had come upon a wide expanse of rugged terrain and solid ground, and were no longer able to use Liam's ship for transportation, even with the cleated wheels. He closed and sealed the canopy, and secured the boat to a large rock. Then they stocked up backpacks with supplies and headed out on foot. The first couple of days were slow going.

The ground was made up mostly of large, uneven rocks, many of which were covered with some kind of slippery matter. It was hard to get a sound footing as they made their way across the terrain. Their feet, shins and legs were tired and sore. Quinn actually was able to keep his feet under him better than Liam could. Several times Liam slipped on the scum-covered rocks and fell hard on his butt or his side. Quinn tried to not be so smug whenever he helped Liam to his feet.

"Why aren't you falling," he finally asked as his frustration reached the breaking point.

"I don't know," answered Quinn. "I guess it's like walking on ice at home. We've done it all our lives, so it's no big deal."

The ground was so rough, that there was no place to camp the first night. It was too dark to continue, and they both agreed that it was foolhardy to try to keep going in the dark, so they sat down in the middle of no place. There was nothing with which to make a fire, but luckily the nights were still warm. The worst part was that they couldn't get comfortable trying to sleep. No matter which way they positioned themselves, the ground was covered with rocks.

By the middle of the second day, the rocks gave way to a field of clover and low grass as far as the eye could see, and the traveling was much easier. The lush ground cover also provided a comfortable bed when they made camp at night. There was still nothing around which they could use for a fire, so their dinners were cold.

Two days later other plants started to appear and the countryside began to get hilly. Late one afternoon the two travelers decided to make camp early and get a good night's rest. They had been pushing themselves hard over some inhospitable ground and easily convinced each other that they needed just a little pampering. They had started seeing shrubs and small trees along the way and looked around for some wood to make a fire. As the night settled in, the sky was crystal clear and filled with stars. The roaring fire sent sparks into the air to join the stars. Liam managed to find a number of different kinds of roots and vegetables he threw into a pot with some water. Quinn cut up some jerky he had and added it to the mix. In very short order the aroma of a wonderful smelling stew filled the air. It was the first hot meal they had in almost a week and they savored every mouthful.

The next morning Quinn told Liam he thought he had seen a stream not too far away. He was going to get some water to refill their canteens and he wanted to get cleaned up.

"Hold on and wait for me," said Liam. "I should probably go with you."

"What are you worried about?" asked Quinn. "We haven't heard or seen any other living creature in the last four days. You even said yourself that you didn't feel we were being followed or watched."

"I know," said Liam, "but there are other things around here that could be dangerous. It's probably best not to separate – even for a little while."

"Whatever," answered Quinn, still feeling like Liam was being a bit overprotective. I'm not a baby, he thought to himself.

Liam threw a few items in his backpack and said, "We can leave most of our stuff here, since we'll be coming back this way. You're right. We haven't seen or heard anything for days. It should be all right, but I'm still coming with you. I could use some cleaning up, too."

He was about to douse the fire, but then reconsidered. It was in a hole surrounded by rocks, and all the grass and other burnable items were several feet away. It would be just fine. There was no danger of it spreading, since there wasn't much more left but a few burning embers. Besides, he thought to himself, it would take too much time to restart a fire if they needed it when they returned, only to put it out again. With that they headed off together in search of the stream.

They didn't have to go far. Just over the hill there was a narrow valley and a clear stream ran quietly through it. To the left of their approach was a large field of flowers. Quinn hadn't seen anything like them before, and he thought they were really pretty. They stood on stalks about a foot and a half high. The flowers themselves were white with vivid purple centers like a splash of paint. In the very center of the flower was a bright yellow tube. Quinn assumed that this tube attracted insects, or maybe it held rainwater. Not being very familiar with flowers, as Liam had pointed out earlier, he wasn't sure. They sure were nice to look at, though.

Liam checked out the water and decided it was safe to drink. Quinn filled his canteen and then, downstream from Liam, scooped up some water in his hands and washed his face and neck. He rubbed his face roughly, feeling refreshed by the cool spring water. While Liam was filling his canteen and washing up, Quinn wandered over to the field of flowers. They seemed to have gotten closer to them as they were at the stream washing and filling canteens.

How odd, thought Quinn. I must still be tired. Plants can't walk.

He went over to the nearest cluster of flowers. He could smell a very pleasant and enticing aroma floating up to him. Just as he bent over to pick one, he heard Liam shouting from behind him.

"No. Don't. That's dragon spadix. Get away from there."

But Liam's words were too late. The bright yellow tube from the center of the closest flower literally spit fluid on Quinn's hand. At first he felt a slight warming sensation. He turned back to Liam.

"What?" he asked peevishly. "I just got a little flower juice on me. It's no big...OH!! POOP!! That really burns."

He jumped straight up as the flower's venom sunk into his skin and started to burn. He shook his hand rapidly trying to cool it off and he hopped from one foot to the other. When the burning increased and felt like it was spreading, he ran past Liam, knocking him down as he made his way to the stream.

Liam rolled over onto his stomach, as Quinn bolted past him, and yelled, "No, don't put water on it."

Again, his words came too late. Quinn had run into the stream and plunked his hand into the water up to his elbow. Quinn rested his elbows on his knees and sighed with relief as the burning sensation slowly faded away.

"I never know when you're joking," said Quinn. "The water made the burning stop. Why wouldn't I put water on it?"

"Yes," answered Liam and he got to his feet. "It stops the burning as long as you keep it in the stream. Once you take it out, not only will the burning start again, but it will spread; and fast."

"Oh, you're not just saying that to teach me some kind of lesson are you?" asked Quinn with a look of concern on his face. Without waiting for the answer he knew would be coming, he added, "Blubber on a biscuit. I can't keep my arm in this stream forever. What do we do?"

"Stay put, and DON'T take your arm out of the water," Liam shouted at him. "I have an idea. I'll be right back." And with that Liam turned and ran back towards their camp sight, shouting once more for Quinn not to move.

Quinn was standing in about two feet of water, bent over with his arm sunk to the elbow. His back was beginning to ache. He was getting very uncomfortable. He tried squatting down, but his backside got wet which made him feel even more uncomfortable. He could no longer feel anything burning and started to wonder if Liam was overreacting. He decided to take a quick look at his wrist where the flower's venom had been sprayed. He figured that there would still be water on the spot, so it should be all right to take it out for just a second. He slowly removed his arm and hand from the stream and stood up straight.

He brought his hand up in front of his face. On his hand there were eight or ten pale blue splotches. He didn't feel anything burning and started to go back to the shore. While he was looking at his hand and wading through the water, the splotches quickly merged together and spread up his arm. The pale blue began to turn dark and then turned purple and black. The skin began to look like it was melting or rotting, and the burning sensation returned even more painfully than before.

"Yeowwww!" he screamed as he ran back into the stream and sunk his arm back in the water. The pain immediately subsided. "That was definitely not a good idea," he said out loud.

"No kidding," Liam said as he ran up to the stream carrying a smoldering piece of wood. "I told you not to take it out of the water. Do you ever listen to ANYONE?" Liam was shouting. "Now take it out of the water and give me your hand."

"You just told me NOT to take it out of the water," Quinn shouted back.

"I know. I told you not to take it out of the water until I got back. I'm back now and I want you to take it out of the water and give it to me."

"NO!" shouted Quinn. "It will hurt if I do that. Make up your mind."

"I know it will hurt, but only for a little while. Trust me. After all, didn't I warn you not to put it in the water in the first place?"

"I'm confused now. Put it in; don't put it in. Take it out; don't take it out. OK," said Quinn begrudgingly when he saw the look of impatience on Liam's face. "What are you doing with that piece of wood?"

"I'm going to burn out the venom," answered Liam.

"WHAT?" asked Quinn. "It already burns like fire. How is burning it with fire going to make it stop burning like fire? That doesn't make any sense. You're just talking crazy talk."

And he took a step further into the stream, still bent over holding his arm under water.

"Can't you just make tiny little cut marks and suck the poison out?" he wailed.

"That's what you're supposed to do for snake-bite, and even then that's not really a good idea."

"Snake bite; flower bite. What's the difference?" Quinn called back. "I still don't see why you have to burn me."

"Fine," shouted Liam. "Come here and I'll cut you."

"No way!" Quinn nearly screamed. "I wasn't serious."

Liam was quickly losing his temper.

"I'm NOT going to cut you. I have to burn you. I know how it sounds. But I have to burn out the venom to keep it from spreading. Then I'll put a poultice on it, which will make it heal."

"Is it going to hurt?" Quinn started to whine. "It's going to hurt. I just know it."

"Yes, it's going to hurt," said Liam. "What do you think? I'm going to put a burning hot stick on your arm. Of course it's going to hurt. If I don't though, you'll have to spend the rest of your life with your arm stuck in the water."

Quinn didn't move. It was as if he was weighing the options between getting his arm burned by a smoldering stick and keeping it in the water for the rest of his life. In the end, he decided he couldn't stay here forever. In fact, his back was beginning to ache again and he doubted he could stay there much longer at all. Liam helped him come to a decision.

"I sure hope there are no snakes in that water, or any of those dragon lizards."

"Snakes?" asked Quinn, his voice starting to quiver as he strained to look over his shoulder into the water behind him. "Dragon lizards? OK, you win, what do I have to do?" he asked.

"Stay there. I'll come to you, and you need to just trust me."

Liam waded into the water and stood next to him. He debated with himself about telling Quinn what he was going to do, and decided against it.

"When I say 'go' I want you to pull your arm out of the water and stick it out in front of me. If you do it fast enough, you shouldn't feel the poison start burning again. All right?"

"All right," said Quinn in not much more than a whisper. "Then what?"

"Just look away or close your eyes. It will be over quicker than you know."

He closed his eyes and did as he was instructed. The next thing he heard was a loud hissing sound as Liam pressed the burning stick against the skin of his hand and rolled it back and forth over all the blue splotches. Liam was right: it really, really hurt. Quinn jumped from one foot to the other, but never pulled his arm away as Liam burned out all the venom.

"Now go sit down on the shore and don't move," he ordered Quinn.

He pulled a knife from his belt. Quinn's eyes went wide.

"Wait, I thought you weren't going to cut me! Were you lying to me? What are you going to do with that knife?"

Liam just looked at him as he scraped off ash from the burned stick onto a flat rock next to the stream. Then he went over to the bed of dragon spadix and with a quick swipe of his blade, cut the tops off several flowers along the edge of the bed. He then dug up the roots of some of the closer plants and took them back to the rock with the ashes. He chopped up the roots into very small pieces, and then crushed them with another rock. He mixed the crushed roots with the ashes and some water until he formed a paste. Then he spread the paste over Quinn's burned arm. When he had used up all the paste and spread it as evenly as he could, he wrapped the poultice tightly in a piece of cloth he cut from a spare shirt.

"There," he said. "That should take care of it. Your arm's going to stink really badly, but it should heal in about three or four days. Don't take the bandage off."

He looked a Quinn for a few seconds and said again, "I'm serious. Don't take the bandage off. Are you going to listen this time?" "Yeeeees," said Quinn a bit cantankerously. "I won't take it off." Then under his breath he added, "You're not my mother."

Liam pretended not to hear the last remark, but said to himself, "and you have no idea how happy that makes me. Your poor mother!' He cleaned off his knife, picked up the canteens and began to head back to the campsite. Quinn followed a few steps behind.

"You don't have to treat me like a child," he mumbled to himself while nursing his injured arm. "What kind of crummy place is this where flowers burn you? Maybe that's why we don't have flowers at home."

"Did you say something?" asked Liam.

"No," said Quinn. "I was just saying thanks."

"You're welcome."

The next day as they continued their journey, Liam still took the lead and Quinn, still grumpy, followed a few steps behind. In spite of his complaining, his arm felt much better and he had a hard time resisting the temptation to peek beneath the bandages. It seemed like Liam had eyes in the back of his head. Each time Quinn picked at the bandage, Liam would say, "Don't take it off." He wouldn't even look back. He just seemed to know what Quinn was thinking.

By midday they were in an open expanse with large trees scattered in a hit or miss fashion. The pair stopped to rest and have something to eat, sitting in the shade of one such tree. It felt good to be off their feet and under some shade.

"Do you know where we are?" asked Quinn.

"Not exactly," answered Liam. "I just know we're going in the right direction. I estimate were still at least a week away from Solveig's realm. The passage should be fairly safe, judging from the vegetation we've come across lately." He looked at Quinn and added, "No more dragon spadix for you to pick."

Liam stood up and looked to the distance, raising his hand to his brow to shield his eyes from the suns.

"Over the last few days, we've been getting to a higher elevation. There will be some more hills ahead, but then we should reach some rivers coming down from those mountains off to the right. Once we hit the rivers, we should be able to build a raft and travel a little faster."

As Liam turned back and bent down to gather up his pack, Quinn stood up and looked in the same direction, but had no clue as to what Liam was looking at. Quinn raised his injured hand to his brow in the same manner Liam did to shield his eyes. As he did so, the stench from the poultice floated under his nose. The odor startled him. Worried that the injury might be infected, without thinking, and before Liam could stop him, he lifted the edge of the bandage and took a big whiff.

Liam looked up just as this was happening. He could only watch in horrified fascination, as if everything was happening in slow motion. Quinn's eyes rolled back in his head, he spun slowly around as his legs turned to jelly and his entire body went limp. He dropped to the ground like a bag of wet sand. He was out like a light before he ever hit the ground. As he landed, his head struck the trunk of the tree and his eyelids slowly dropped over his eyes.

Liam just stood there looking at him, shaking his head.

"If he wasn't already unconscious that probably would have hurt," he thought out loud. "Wonderful. What am I going to do with this lump now?"

He knew that the vapors from the poultice, if directly inhaled as Quinn had done, would cause unconsciousness for several days. That could be longer, depending on how much of the vapors Quinn had taken in. He sat down under the tree to go over his options.

They couldn't stay here for very much time. He didn't like sitting in one place so exposed for so long. Even though they hadn't encountered anything dangerous, it was foolish to believe that could last for any length of time. He knew Quinn was too big for him to carry or drag. So that wasn't an option, either. He had to find some way to transport him easily.

He looked around for an idea. Off to his left he saw a small cluster of trees covered in vines. He thought for a minute and decided Quinn wasn't going any place soon. So he left him under the tree and went off to cut some of the vines. When he had cut as much as he thought he would need, he brought them back to where Quinn was spread out and went to work.

He braided them together to increase their strength. Once he was finished he had a very strong "rope" about thirty feet long. He then braided a second one of equal length. He rolled Quinn out from under the tree into a more open area. Once there, he looped the end of one of the vines around Quinn's legs and the other around his upper body, and then intertwined the opposite ends of both vines together.

He then pushed Quinn, rearranging him so that he could be rolled on the ground in the direction they needed to go. As Liam rolled him, the vines wound around Quinn's body. When the vines had wrapped Quinn like a cocoon, Liam gave it a quick pull and Quinn unrolled. As he unrolled, the vine contraption played itself out until it reached the parts looped around Quinn's body, and then it began to re-wrap him. It was like rolling a large yoyo along the ground.

"This might just work," Liam said, smiling.

Liam moved Quinn along in this manner for quite some time. It took a few tries and a couple of errors, but eventually, he fell into a rhythm. For the most part, his system worked. Every once in awhile, though, Quinn's head would encounter a rock or a tree root sticking up from the ground. It happened so quickly that Liam was unable to avoid the collision. Each time this happened, Quinn's head would take a knock, and Liam would wince at first, and say, "Sorry about that;" but then he would chuckle to himself and repeat, "If he wasn't already unconscious, that would really hurt."

By nightfall, they had made considerable progress. Liam propped Quinn up against a tree so he wouldn't roll away and wrapped the vine around his body, tying him to the tree so he wouldn't fall over. Then he lit a campfire and made dinner for himself. He helped himself to Quinn's stash of walrus jerky. He wasn't particularly fond of the taste, but it added some flavor and substance to the stew.

The next morning he started off again shortly after daybreak and had developed a rhythm to rolling Quinn. This worked quite nicely until he came to the hills. He couldn't roll Quinn up the hill, so he had to push him. The first ones weren't too difficult, but as they became increasingly steeper, Liam knew he wouldn't have the strength needed. Quinn was just too heavy. At the top of one particularly tall hill, he stopped to rest and contemplated his next move.

Studying the terrain, it occurred to him that he could probably use Quinn's weight and natural gravity to help. Instead of slowly lowering Quinn down one hill and hauling him up the next, he placed Quinn at the top of the hill and gave the vine a sharp snap. Quinn shot down the hill, with Liam running after him. Once he hit the bottom, momentum carried him up the next hill, again wrapping the vine around him. Liam only had to push the last few feet to get him all the way to the summit.

At the top, Liam congratulated himself on such a wonderful idea. He gave himself a few minutes to catch his breath, and then he repeated the process. Quinn rapidly rolled down one hill and up another. Aside from a few more bumps on the head, things were going great until Quinn got a little too far ahead of Liam. One of the next hills wasn't quite as high and it wasn't necessary for Liam to push Quinn to the top.

As Quinn crested the peak of the next hill, Liam came running up behind and saw to his shock that this hill wasn't like all the earlier ones. It was much steeper on the far side. Quinn had reached the top, but instead of stopping as he had in the past, he only slowed down. He was inching forward; teetered for a second and then slowly began to disappear over the crown of the hill. Before Liam could grab the end of the vine to slow Quinn's descent, the cocoon was rocketing down the much steeper slope and headed downward at an alarming speed.

Liam dove for the trailing vine and skidded across the grass. His fingers latched on to the trailing end, and he clamped down as tightly as he could, but Quinn's momentum yanked it out of Liam's grasp. Quinn was like a runaway log, rolling and bouncing down the hill. He rolled over small shrubs. He struck a tree with his head and spun completely around several times, like a top, but still didn't slow down. He steamrolled over low rises in the ground and shot up into the air, landing with a bone-rattling thud, but never lost momentum.

Liam jumped to his feet and gave chase, running like a mad man, but nothing was stopping Quinn. His body continued to roll faster and faster. Liam was nearly falling over trying to catch up. Finally, Quinn hit the end of the hill – the edge of the cliff – and soared over the top like a ski jumper, and dropped out of sight.

"No," shouted Liam, as if his mere command would stop what was inevitable.

He lunged forward trying to will himself to keep Quinn from flying over the cliff. As he did so, he fell forward, scraping his hands and knees in the dirt. In a single motion he up righted himself and staggered into a run again.

Liam, ignoring the searing pain in his side, ran to the edge, skidding to a stop and leaning over to look down the drop-off. He stood there with his hands on his knees, completely winded. Below him by several hundred feet, was a swiftly flowing river, churning up white water, and winding in and out of boulders and broken tree limbs. Liam was frantic. He couldn't bear the thought of his friend and traveling companion splattered on the rocks below.

Raising both hands to his brow, he shielded his eyes against the sun and searched the area immediately below him. The river was in a wide ravine with the opposite side of the cliff nearly thirty feet away. He examined the rocks and debris on the opposite cliff face for any signs of Quinn's body. Then he lowered his view to the water below and searched among the driftwood. He looked further downstream when he didn't see any signs of him on the rocks or among the branches.

There was nothing there. Quinn couldn't have been swept down the river that fast. His heavy breathing, the blood pounding in his head, and the roar of the rushing water had blocked out all other sound. He was nearly oblivious to his surroundings. He pushed his hat off his head and pulled on his hair in frustration.

"Quinn!" he shouted, not really expecting an answer. "Where did you go?"

His breathing quickly returned to normal and the pounding sound in his head subsided. When it did, he heard another sound. As he became aware of this new sound, a shadow passed over his head. He looked up to see an object silhouetted against the sunlight sky. Liam stepped back from the edge of the cliff to change the angle and get a clearer image. It was Quinn, still wrapped like a cocoon, floating in air about twenty feet from the edge of the cliff. And what was even more unusual was that he was hovering several feet above and almost straight in front of Liam.

The vines wrapped around Quinn's body had blended into the tree line on the other side of the river, obscuring him from Liam's vision. Now he seemed to have risen above the horizon line and was floating in mid air. A wave of relief flooded over him before turning to confusion.

"What are you doing up there," he muttered.

He was distracted by an unusual sound that he hadn't noticed beforehand. Liam was too stunned to wonder what was happening. He staggered backwards a few steps as his eyes moved from Quinn to a position slightly higher in the sky. He could see another object behind and above Quinn. It was a shadow that was now blocking out the sun. He was flooded with a number of conflicting emotions and as the adrenalin rush subsided, he sat down hard on the ground.

"Are you an angel?" Liam whispered.

The unusual sound was the flapping of a pair of enormous wings. As the image moved slightly and became less of a silhouette, he was able to see that the wings didn't belong to an angel. Above both him and Quinn was a winged horse. Astride the horse Liam could see the darkened image of a woman; her long hair fanned out behind her by the wind, one arm outstretched. Over her shoulder was a small bird fluttering back and forth from one of the woman's shoulders to the other.

"No, wait," he thought.

It was a faerie.

Chapter nine

While Quinn was suspended in air above a raging river, Princess Natalie had returned to the Sanctorum to see what progress Stella had made in locating Lochen. The Enchantress had been gone far too long to check on a simple tracking device, and she had not, yet, sent word to Natalie about her efforts. When she arrived she found Stella in a crumpled heap on the floor.

"No," cried Natalie. "I knew I shouldn't have allowed this."

She rushed over to the Enchantress to examine her. Stella's eyelids were fluttering rapidly and she was repeating incomprehensible words. The only thing Natalie could discern was that someone or something was lost. It was apparent that she was in some form of a trance. Natalie knew not to try to awaken her, but instead, straightened her out and found a pillow to place under her head. She called for help and then sat on the floor beside Stella, holding her hand and waiting for the trance to end and for someone to come to their aid.

Almost an hour passed before the Enchantress stopped rambling. During that time, assistants had come and gone, bringing liquids that Stella could not drink, food that she could not eat, or compresses for her head, which seemed to do nothing. Natalie finally noticed the rigidity of her body decrease, along with the end of the rambling. But instead of awakening from her trance, she lapsed into a deep sleep. By now Natalie knew it was safe to move her. Natalie called for attendants to help carry her to her room and put her to bed.

"Whatever visions she had must have really taken a toll on her," Natalie told one of the assistants. "She appears to be all right now and will just need to rest. Please stay with her and then call me as soon as she awakens."

She hated to leave, but she knew there was nothing she could do, and she believed that Stella was past any danger. As she was crossing the promenade, a messenger called out and ran up to her.

"Your Highness," she said, "I have news from Eastern Outpost Five."

When Natalie brought her people to live on this island, caution told her not only to maintain the bubble that had been their home, but to post sentries at strategic positions completely circling the island. She had no reason to suspect any danger, but she knew not to take any chances. Her previous experience with sorcerers gone bad had taught her a valuable lesson.

Since moving her people to the surface, she had formed alliances with the forest creatures, the faerie kingdom, and the mountain people, and hoped these alliances would enhance her island's defenses. But it was wars between these same groups that had forced the Sea Sprites to seek refuge beneath the sea in the first place centuries ago. Regardless of how much she trusted her new friends, she knew she could not place her community in jeopardy. Consequently, due to the potential threat from currently imprisoned evil forces and renewed hostilities among her current allies, she decided it was necessary to send small groups of volunteers to live in isolated areas to serve as her extended eyes and ears.

Eastern Outpost Five was one such isolated area. It was located nearly one hundred miles to the northeast – one of the most remote. It was a small atoll that was considered to be the safest and quietest of all the outposts. The idyllic nature of this outpost greatly offset the disadvantage of its distance from the island and any related support. It was such a peaceful location that this was the last place Princess Natalie thought would report any problems.

"Not here," she told the messenger as she led her to a small room inside the palace. Once they were behind closed doors she listened to the messenger's report without questions or interruptions.

"The village Dryad directed me to tell you that she has received information about instances of large numbers of fish and other sea creatures to our north that have been found dead. It is as if they had been boiled. The Dryad sent scouts to run tests of the water, which they did, approximately fifty miles to their north. The scouts detected high levels of acidity in the water as well as unusually high temperatures, but could find no reason.

"The scouts expanded their inspections at her direction. As a result, they were able to determine that on at least one occasion a long dormant underwater volcano had erupted. They believed this to be the source of the heat and possibly the acidity. The Dryad sent a single scout to the bottom of the Sea to examine the volcano, but the scout never returned. She is fearful of sending another only to be lost. She awaits your direction."

When she had finished, Natalie asked her to repeat the message, and asked a few questions as the messenger did so.

Dead sea creatures? Boiling water? A lost scout? Any one of these was troubling to Natalie, but all three represented something very dangerous. The loss of the scout was especially ominous. Was it an accident, or intentional? An active volcano was unheard of in this area. What caused such a change?

She would have preferred to be able to consult with her Enchantress, but she knew Stella would not be awake for quite some time; maybe even days. This could not wait that long. She would have to address this herself. She decided she must see the Dryad personally.

"Gather whatever provisions you think we will need and to prepare two sea horses," she told the messenger. "I will be returning with you. We will leave as soon as you are ready."

"Yes, your Highness," answered the messenger. "I will await you at the stables," and she left to prepare.

Natalie changed into clothing more suitable for the journey, and then looked in on Stella before she left. The attendant reported that there had been no change. She was still soundly asleep and had not spoken in her dreams. Natalie moved closer to the bed. The Enchantress was so still that she almost looked lifeless. Natalie had seen such deep sleeps rarely and was concerned about leaving Stella.

"Why now?" she asked. "When I need you so much."

She touched the stone in the headband that she wore, and then took an amulet from around her own neck. She waved her hand across it before putting it around Stella's neck. She had cast a simple spell that should let Stella know where she was, once she woke up — assuming Natalie wasn't back before that happened. The spell would also ensure that Stella did not try to follow her. With that she left for the palace stables and joined the messenger who was already waiting for her.

They would travel under water by sea horse. It was not as fast as traveling on the surface of the Sea, but it was likely to be safer. Black Raptors were large predatory birds that were known to be able to fly for hundreds of miles out to sea. There were no known nests anywhere near the Sprites' island, so they weren't much of a danger on land. However, they were very territorial and preyed on anything and everything on the open sea. Traveling on the surface would have to be by traditional means, which meant being exposed for almost three days. That was just too much time to be exposed to the Raptors and two Sea Sprites would make too tempting a target. There were few spells that could ward off Raptors.

Eastern Outpost Five was one of the few outposts that could not be reached in one leap with a transporter stone. And there was no place along the way to stop. I'll have to do something about that, Natalie thought. That ruled out this method of transport. Sea horses could make the trip without stopping to rest, even though it would add a day to the journey. They were also very good at avoiding danger and finding excellent hiding places, if necessary. That made them the logical choice for a trip of this nature, in spite of the longer traveling time.

Although the sea horses could breathe underwater, the Sea Sprites couldn't. They would have to surface every three or four hours, but only for a few seconds. They would be traveling non-stop. At night it would be impossible to see the Black Raptors until it was far too late. The sea horses would know if any predators were above them. At least Natalie hoped they would.

---------------- *** ----------------

It had been almost an hour since Lochen had made his pronouncement that they were lost. Since that time he had barely spoken a word. Sean had waited patiently for an explanation of what they were supposed to do now, but one hadn't been forthcoming. Actually, he had been less than patient. He jumped up and down and wailed, "What do you mean we're lost?" He did this for nearly twenty minutes while Lochen seemingly ignored him and just stared out at the strange planet, the surrounding stars, and the planet's three even stranger moons.

When he had exhausted himself, Sean plopped back down in his seat and waited. Lochen continued to study the planets and stars, apparently making mental calculations. Either that, Sean thought, or he was drawing faces with his finger on the wall of the pod. Finally, he couldn't wait any longer.

"Come on. I can't take this much longer. Have you come to any conclusions?" he asked as Lochen continued to stare.

"Yes, actually, I have," he responded.

"Well," said Sean when no further explanation or information was forthcoming, "would you be so kind as to enlighten me?"

"Of course," said Lochen, somewhat distractedly. "We are most definitely lost."

Sean was stunned. He opened his mouth to say something, but words failed him. His mouth snapped shut in frustration, and then opened again, only to still be devoid of words. After several attempts, he finally found his voice.

"That's it? We're lost? After sitting there for hours on end, that's all you can come up with? We're lost? Brilliant!"

"Thank you," acknowledged Lochen. "But to be more correct, it's only been fifty-seven minutes - not hours on end – since I said that I <u>thought</u> we were lost. I never said that for certain, if you recall. I, myself, wasn't even convinced of that initially. In the interim I've had to do some calculations to verify that assumption, but now I'm certain. I have no doubt at all that we are lost."

"Arrrgggh!" was all that Sean could reply.

"It appears that what I originally perceived to be a nebula – that one behind us that has been dissipating at an increasing rate - was in reality a worm hole that we entered at the time we transported out of the asteroid belt. Although, I'm not entirely convinced that it's not both a nebula and a worm hole. I've never seen a nebula dissipate as that one has. But if you look closely, you can see that it's actually changing shape somewhat and perhaps isn't..."

"Who cares?" interrupted Sean, frustrated by Lochen's frequent tangents. "Is that why we got lost?"

"Not exactly. We made the leap without being properly aligned. I told you that I wasn't properly positioned to conduct a leap. I really can't be held responsible for this."

"So what? Now this is all my fault?" asked Sean, incredulously. "You're blaming ME because we're lost?"

"Of course not," answered Lochen. "I'm not placing all the blame on you. It's only half your fault. The other half, I admit, is mine."

"OH, well that makes it all better, doesn't it?"

"I'm not sure I see how it's all better," answered Lochen as he finally turned back and looked at Sean. "We're still lost."

Sean's sarcasm was clearly lost on Lochen.

"And do you have any thoughts on how to get us out of here?" Sean persisted.

"Certainly," said Lochen. "I have been thinking about how we can get back the entire time since we arrived at this location."

Sean waited again for an explanation. When it appeared that none was coming, he asked," And that would be...?"

"Ah, yes. Well we just have to wait for that nebula to restructure its wormhole, assuming it is as I believe, both a nebula and a wormhole. Once that happens we should be able to transport back to where we came. I'll be properly positioned this time. And I think we also need to reestablish telepathic contact with Stella to provide a frame of reference for such a transport attempt."

"That's all?" asked Sean. He nearly jumped for joy. "That's simple. Why didn't you say so? All right. Great. What do we need to do? When can we get ready? I'm all set."

"Oh, I can't answer that. I would suppose it took about a millennium for that nebula to form a wormhole that could transport objects to something other than a black hole. There's no telling how long it will take to restructure, if ever. As to telepathic contact with Stella, it was broken off at her end. She needs to reestablish it."

As quickly as Sean's spirits had risen, they plummeted.

"How is that a solution? You haven't fixed anything."

"You didn't ask me if I 'fixed' anything," responded Lochen. "You just asked if I had any thoughts on getting out of here. I have to say - sometimes I really don't understand you."

There were times when Lochen's precise answers could make Sean want to bang his head against a wall. This was one of those times, except there was no wall hard enough against which to bang his head. Instead he bellowed out another "Arrrgggh!"

Princess Natalie and the messenger made excellent time. Fortune and good weather were with them the entire way. They encountered no predators or other obstacles under the sea and were even happier about not coming across any Raptors when they surfaced for air – especially at night. In four days they arrived at Eastern Outpost Five. The messenger escorted Natalie to the Dryad.

"Would you like me to stand by to escort you back to the island?" asked the messenger once they met the Dryad.

"No," said Natalie. "You've already made that trip more times than you should have to. Thank you."

She turned to the Dryad, whose name was Marcella, and said, "It must have been something extremely important for you to send your daughter on such a perilous journey by herself."

Marcella was not surprised that the Princess recalled that the messenger was her daughter. She knew the Princess' ability to recall names. Natalie knew the names and relationships of every subject in her community, in spite of the fact that there were several thousand of them.

"Yes, your Highness," replied Marcella. "The scout I sent out earlier was one of the best from this outpost; one of the most resourceful. When he didn't return I knew that could only mean he was killed. I didn't want to put anyone else at risk until I had conferred with you. I didn't expect that you would come, yourself."

"I'm truly sorry," said Natalie. "Please let me know what we can do for his family and friends."

"Thank you. I will."

"How long have there been problems with the water and the sea creatures?" Natalie asked, getting back to the reason for her visit.

"It only recently started, but it happened three times within a very short time. I was prepared at that time to send a messenger, but then I received the reports of another disturbance. I sent scouts to inspect and discovered that it was due to the eruption of the volcano. I thought it would be better to advise you of both events. I had also hoped to have substantial information to provide you along with some recommended solutions, rather than merely problems. That was why I sent the scout to examine the volcano. I should have gone myself."

"You did the right thing," Natalie told her. "Both in directing the further examination and in sending a scout instead of going yourself. Have your most trusted aide be ready to accompany me within the hour."

"Yes, of course, your Highness," replied the Dryad. "But you've just arrived. Are you returning so soon?"

"No." said Natalie. "I plan to find what killed the sea creatures, what poisoned the water and what caused the volcano to erupt. I also want to find what out happened to your scout and to see if we can find him – dead or alive. I'll need an experienced and trusted guide to lead me."

"I'm ready now," said the Dryad.

Natalie knew there would be no way to talk the Dryad out of accompanying her. In truth, she was glad to have someone so experienced with her. They mounted fresh sea horses and traveled first to the area where the dead sea creatures were found. The Dryad pointed out that they had been discovered in an area running from about twenty miles from the Outpost and extending about ten to fifteen miles north from there.

"I thought the boiling was discovered fifty miles north?" asked Natalie. "This is much closer than I was led to believe."

"You were not misled, your Highness" said the Dryad. "Where the deaths of the sea creatures and fish took place appears to have been fifty miles north. The currents brought the creatures closer, where they were discovered. That's what prompted the investigations."

She led Natalie to the area where the scouts believed the boiling occurred. They rode down to the Sea's floor, and moved carefully, closer and closer to the sandy bottom. The sea, which was normally crystal clear, was brown and murky here.

Natalie dismounted and walked around the area. She bent down and picked up a handful of the sand. She noticed the same brownish color and the same sparkling she had seen along the bottom edge of the bubble. There was what looked like an enormous gouge cut into the floor of the sea.

"All right," she said to the Dryad. "Now show me where the volcano is."

They turned to the north, almost following the long gouge in the sea floor. Along the way she could see patches of the brown murky water running parallel to the gouge and every once in a while the light would catch a glass-like sparkling. Before long Natalie could see a giant mountain ahead of them. The top of the mountain was about a hundred yards beneath the surface of the water. Many of the islands in this area of the sea had been formed by ancient volcanoes. But there had been no further formation or eruptions for thousands of years. What was causing that to change now, Natalie wondered.

Both of them had stopped once the volcano was in clearer view. The water was still brown around the base and nearly midway up the sides, but not as murky as around the gouge. Nearer to the top, the water was the normal bright blue. Natalie started to move closer to get a better view.

"Please, your Highness," the Dryad warned her. "It's not safe."

She pointed to an indentation in the side of the volcano. Bubbles were escaping and floating to the surface. It did not appear to be merely air escaping from some underground cavern. There was no plant life near the area and the fish avoided it.

"There's a break in the mountainside where those bubbles are being released," said the Dryad. "The volcano is unstable."

Natalie was stunned. That kind of instability was only evident when volcanoes were active. She was aware that active volcanoes still existed, but not in the Cerulean Sea – at least not anywhere on this side of the Sea or this close to her island. Disregarding the Dryad's caution, she nudged the sea horse closer. Suddenly, there was another burst of bubbles from the break in the side of the volcano, and the sea horse reared, throwing Natalie off. The horse darted for an outcropping of coral as if to hide. Marcella's sea horse began doing the same thing, but seeing what had happened to Natalie, the Dryad was prepared and held tightly to control. She forced the sea horse to where Natalie was and reached out her hand.

"Take hold, your Highness. The horses are spooked. Something dangerous must be near."

She no sooner spoke those words than Natalie detected a nearly overwhelming odor of sulfur. That was almost immediately followed by a thunderous rumbling, and a radical change in the water temperature. It was becoming hot. It appeared that the volcano was getting ready to erupt.

- - - - - - - - - - - - - - - - - *** - - - - - - - - - - - - - - - - -

"I'm hungry," announced Sean.

"I suppose you are," answered Lochen. "Don't you forest creatures eat constantly throughout the day?"

"Noooooooooooo," whined Sean, "we don't eat CONSTANTLY throughout the day. We only have seven meals. Aren't you hungry?"

"No. I ate before we left," said Lochen.

"If I had known we'd be gone forever, I'd have packed some food."

"There really wouldn't have been sufficient room on this small pod for supplies to last forever. And furthermore, you won't live forever, so much of that food would have gone to waste, even assuming we could have stored it."

"It's just a finger of speech," replied Sean.

"Finger?" asked Lochen. "I think you mean 'figure.'"

"Whatever."

Sean was pretty certain that Lochen was purposely trying to drive him insane. He decided to ignore him. They had been sitting for quite some time since their last exchange and the boredom was starting to get to him. He squirmed in his seat and then leaned up against the wall of the pod. He turned outward towards the nebula that had been fading in and out of clarity for quite some time now.

He pressed his face against the side of the bubble and it expanded very slightly outward in the shape of his face. He pressed his lips against the bubble and blew hard. His cheeks expanded, but the bubble didn't move. He pulled his head back and stared at the wall. He reached out and pushed the side with his hand. The wall bent slightly, but didn't give and his hand didn't go through. He pushed harder, but the bubble didn't move any more.

"Hey," he said to Lochen, "how come when we were back on the beach we could walk through this bubble stuff, but now when I push against it, nothing happens?"

Lochen had been watching the nebula and making mental calculations. He began to detect a pattern in the movements and formations of the clouds. For most of the time he had tuned Sean out and gave nonsensical answers to his questions or he would go into lengthy explanations he thought might discourage Sean from interrupting his concentration. He was about to do the same thing this time.

"Because the atmospheric pressure is different. Back on the beach the pressure inside the bubble was the same as outside, so the spells cast on the structural make up of the bubble allowed for us to pass..." he stopped in mid-sentence, turned and looked back at Sean.

"Brilliant," he said, breaking into a smile and reaching back to pinch both of Sean's cheeks. "You're absolutely brilliant."

"It was a simple question," groused Sean, swatting at Lochen's hands. "You don't have to make fun of me."

"I was being serious," answered Lochen. "Of course. Differential pressure. I should have thought of it before."

Sean sat bolt upright. "What? You forgot something? Does that mean you figured out a way to get us back home? You did, didn't you? And it was my idea? Right?"

"Yes, not exactly, and probably," answered Lochen as he looked down at the console and gesturing like he was doing yet another math problem in his head.

"Yes, not exactly and probably?" asked Sean. "What does that mean?"

"Yes, I forgot something; not exactly in that I've not exactly figured a way back home, and probably it was your idea" he answered, his voice displaying a level of excitement. "Now give me a minute to think."

Sean started jumping around the tiny pod and shouting. He stood on his seat, bent over and waved his butt back and forth, smacking each cheek as he did so.

He started singing, "We're going home and it was my idea; we're going home and it was my idea. What was my idea, anyway?"

"When I cast the spell on the transporting stone which amplified Stella's telepathic communication, I included memory threads as well. At the time I thought it was a frivolous addition, but that it might come in handy if Stella sent multiple thought transmissions, and for some reason I hadn't been able to sort them or respond to them at the time. I wasn't really sure they'd be needed. I didn't even bother to discuss this with her, not that I think she would have cared."

Sean just stared at Lochen wondering when he was going to get to the point.

Lochen glanced up, and seeing the rather blank look on Sean's face continued more to the point, "These memory threads, though, aren't limited to Stella's transmissions. They simply record everything from the time I installed them to now. But most importantly for our present purposes is that they should also record the varying atmospheric pressures experienced throughout our journey. Each planet and each place we've stopped during a leap has its own atmospheric pressure, as well as other individual traits and characteristics."

"Blah, blah, blah," said Sean. "Give me the abridged version."

"I WAS giving you the abridged version," Lochen answered. He sighed and then continued a bit more slowly, "I should be able to calculate the atmospheric pressure at the precise point inside the worm hole at the exact moment we leaped into it, and from there calculate the location of the asteroid belt."

"Oh, wonderful," said Sean. "Back to being bombarded by rocks. That's really an improvement. What happens if you're wrong?"

"On which calculation?" asked Lochen.

"Well, duh! Any of them."

"Hmmm." Lochen thought for a second. "I have to have each of the calculations computed before we make any leaps at all. In each calculation there are multiple factors. Add to that the fact that I can't really think of two locations at the same time, so I'll need to have you help, which adds an entire new set of probabilities into the mix. If any one calculation is off, we'd still be lost, but we probably wouldn't have the nebula as a common point of reference any more. Each additional calculation that is off, even by a fraction, increases the error exponentially."

"I'm sorry I asked. What does all that mean?" asked Sean.

Lochen thought again and then replied, "Should that happen – should any one of the calculations be off - we would be lost beyond all hope of ever returning. We would have no point of reference from which to make any further calculations. After that, everything would be only a guess. Worse than that, we could relocate inside solid rock, molten lava, inside a sun, or any number of places where this bubble would no longer protect us."

Sean gaped at Lochen, his mouth wide open. "You could have just said you didn't know."

Chapter ten

Quinn's body was still floating in mid air; hovering silently . The rider with the outstretched arm swung it to the right and made a gentle downward motion. Slowly Quinn was lowered down towards the river and came to rest on the sandy bank on the far side of the rushing water. It was the only level place nearby, and he wouldn't do any more rolling at this location. The giant winged horse and its rider moved towards Liam and landed a few feet from him. With the sun out of his eyes, he recognized the rider. It was Princess Solveig. She was accompanied by the Faerie Princess, Summer.

"I'm not sure I even want to know what the two of you are doing," Solveig said as she climbed down from the horse. Summer was still fluttering over her shoulder. "But maybe you should tell us anyway."

Liam peeked over the edge of the cliff to look down at Quinn. He wanted to make sure Quinn was safe and wouldn't be floating down the river alone.

"Don't worry," said Solveig. "He'll be fine where he is. At least he won't be rolling up and down these hills."

"What are you two doing here?" asked Liam. "How did you find us? And where did you ever find a flying horse?"

"We didn't find you," said Summer. "We weren't really looking for you."

"Oh, no," said Solveig, motioning to Summer to go no further in answering Liam's questions. "You're not going to distract us. I have to hear what you two have been up to first."

She looked down at Quinn and then back at Liam.

"This ought to be good," she said.

Satisfied that Quinn was secure, Liam began to fill Summer and Solveig in on Quinn's story about the water and the poisoned seals near his home, his journey from the Ice Kingdom, their meeting in the Venomous Swamp, Liam's own experiences, their conclusion that they needed to find Lochen who they hoped would lead them to the Alchemist, their journey to this point, including Quinn's current state of unconsciousness and Liam's solution to that problem.

Throughout the tale, Solveig and Summer listened intently without interruption. Every once in a while Liam would peek over the cliff to make sure Quinn hadn't moved or hadn't awakened. When he finally finished, his two friends looked at one another shaking their heads and smiling.

"And he just got away from you?" Summer asked.

"Well, none of this would have happened if he hadn't tried to pick that lousy flower. And everything was going fine until that last hill," said Liam, a bit defensively.

"And the cliff," added Solveig.

"Oh, yeah," answered Liam, "and the cliff. But now that you two are here, you can help get us to Lochen. That's why we were headed to find you. We figured that you would know where Lochen is."

"I have no idea where Lochen is," Solveig told him. "The last time I saw him he said he was going to see Natalie and Stella and was planning a long voyage immediately after that. He wasn't exactly clear on where he was going and how long he'd be gone. For all I know, he's gone someplace where he can get a better view of the stars and planets, but I couldn't even begin to guess how to reach him."

Liam slumped down on the ground and put his head in his hands. "Oh great. We came all this way for nothing. What are we going to do now?"

"No, you didn't come this far for nothing," said Solveig. "It might just take a little longer, that's all. Summer and I can take you to the Sea Sprites. They're on an island near Summer's village. Either Stella or Natalie will probably know where Lochen is. And if not, Stella will likely have a way to contact him."

"OK," said Liam, still a bit dejected at yet another delay. "I guess we don't have much of a choice. Thanks for helping, though."

"No problem," answered Solveig. "For now, let's get down to where Quinn is and figure out what to do next."

As Liam and Solveig climbed on the winged horse, he said, "You never told me where the horse came from. Is it a pet?"

"Yes," said Solveig, "she is. She was a gift from Lochen."

Without any further explanation they flew down to the riverbank below. Summer flew right behind them. Quinn was still out like a light, but was covered with dust and bits of vegetation, not to mention a number of bumps and bruises. Solveig had settled him on a narrow stretch of sand at a bend in the river. The walls of the ravine rose on either side. There was just enough room for the winged horse to land.

"That's quite a contraption he's wrapped in," said Summer as she flitted from one end of Quinn to the other, examining the vines that were now tightly wound around him. "He looks like a giant caterpillar just before becoming a butterfly. Too bad he won't be able to fly once we get him out of there."

"Can't you just make him fly like you did when you caught him when he went over the side of the cliff?" Liam asked Solveig. "Then we could all just fly to where the Sea Sprites are. That would be great."

"No," answered Summer. "That was a team effort — a little bit of Solveig magic with a little bit of faerie dust, but it's not something either of us can do for a long time. Especially not with someone as big as Quinn. He's way too big." Compared to Summer, everyone was a giant.

"This river is a major artery to the Cerulean Sea," said Solveig. "The island where Natalie's people live is not all that far away — a few days, maybe. If we build a raft, we should be able to sail most of the way."

"We?" asked Liam. "Why would we put a flying horse on a raft?"

"We won't," said Solveig, turning to the winged horse and stroking its head.

"You have to go home by yourself, old girl. You can't carry all of us and you can't follow where we're going."

"Wait," said Liam. "I can't ask you to do this. I'm sure Quinn and I will be fine. I'll just need a little help building the raft. You and Summer fly ahead. I'll meet you there."

"Nonsense," said Solveig. "I know you probably can find the island yourself, but we're not leaving friends behind. Don't worry about it. Nothing bad is going to happen. This isn't the Swamp, you know. Besides, it's been a while since we've seen each other, and I'm sure you'd prefer to have some company, wouldn't you?"

"Of course," said Liam. "I'd love the company." He looked down at Quinn. "Especially since he's not going to be much for conversation for the next few days."

Solveig reached in her pocket and pulled out an apple. She opened her hand and gave the treat to her horse as she rubbed its nose. Once the apple had been devoured, the horse shook its head and then leaped skyward and flew off. She watched it soar into the sky and quickly disappear over the horizon.

"Now let's build a raft," she declared with a sigh.

Summer flew over the surrounding forest and located branches and trunks that would make good parts for a raft while Liam pulled them to the bank. When enough had been gathered, Liam cut away the excess branches, knobs and gnarls until he had about a half dozen smooth, straight logs, each of which was nearly ten feet long. He placed the longest logs in the center, giving the raft a pointed front and back. He then took the vines from around Quinn and lashed the timbers together with one of them, securing the logs together. He still had a long section of the other vine left over, which he coiled up and stowed on the raft.

"You never can tell when you need a rope," he said to Summer.

While Liam was constructing the ship, Solveig pulled the hood from the back of her cape and made it into a pouch. She then searched for nuts and berries that were edible and filled the pouch to its brim. When everything was ready, they rolled Quinn onto the raft and Summer used some faerie dust to move the small ship from the sand into the water and they were off.

Initially, the water was flowing fairly fast so the raft moved freely with the course of the river. Liam had built a number of other sailing vessels for excursions along the waterways of the Swamp, but he had never built a raft before. He hadn't been able to figure out how to attach a rudder. As a result, the raft was rudder-less, which made steering it impossible, in spite of the pointed shape he had given it. Consequently, the ship ran into some of the large rocks that stuck up out of the water. Each time the raft hit one, it jolted to a stop before turning to one side or the other and continuing downstream. Each jolt caused the raft and all its passengers to jerk and bounce. Quinn had been tied down to the raft, but even so, he couldn't brace himself for each of these impacts. Every time they happened, his head flew up in the air and landed with a crack and a loud smack on the floor of the raft.

"Ouch," said Solveig holding her own head in sympathy. "If he wasn't already unconscious, that would really hurt."

Liam, having thought the same thing earlier on this trip as Quinn had rolled up and down the hills, kept silent.

Eventually, the river widened and the rushing of the water slowed down. The ravine where they started had given way to a much lower bank, covered with rolling hills and open fields. For the next few hours they coasted along at a leisurely pace. As nightfall crept over the sky, the group decided it was probably safer to stop somewhere along the bank to make camp. The problem was that there was no shore to speak of. Along this stretch of the river, both sides were covered with trees and bushes that leaned from the shore over the water. In other places rocky shores prevented the raft from making a landing.

"I could just tie the raft off to one of the overhanging branches," suggested Liam. "That would work just as well as an anchor, which we don't have."

"We could spend the night on board," said Solveig. "That should work out just fine. That way we don't need to find any kind of beach. Good idea."

Darkness had already settled in by the time Liam found a suitable tree limb — one low enough to easily reach, strong enough to hold the raft in place in the river's current, but not too big as to provide some predatory animal a perch from which to pounce on them. He laced one end of a vine through the lashings around the raft's timbers and tossed the other end of it over the branch as they glided beneath it. Once the vine played out, the bough of the thin tree bent as much as it was going to, and the raft came to a stop, he tied off the loose end and they all settled in for the night

As the suns finally set, the moon rose in the darkened sky, and its light filtered through the branches and leaves. It was enough light for Solveig to dole out nuts and berries for everyone. Liam was glad they had decided to join him. It was such a pleasant night, but it was even better to share it with friends.

"What about Quinn?" Solveig asked. "Exactly how long has he been unconscious and when was the last time he ate?"

"Oh, he'll be all right," said Liam. "He's only been out about a day and a half. But I'm sure he'll be hungry when he wakes up. And a few nuts and berries won't be hardly enough."

"A day and a half," Summer nearly shouted. "How much longer will he be this way?"

"It's hard to say," said Liam. "He had a lot of that poultice on his arm and he took a really big whiff. If I had to guess, I'd say three, maybe four days."

"Three or four days," repeated Solveig incredulously. "And he's already been out a day and a half? We're going to have to haul him around for – what? - a day or two, maybe even three?"

"Oh, no," said Liam as he slid down and pulled his hat over his eyes, in part to be able to drift off to sleep, but also in part because he didn't want to see Solveig's and Summer's reaction. "I meant three or four days from now."

The two were speechless.

As the moon reached its apex, marking midnight, the four travelers had been asleep for a few hours. The all slept soundly, especially Quinn, who wouldn't have been awakened by an explosion. As they slept, two tiny yellow eyes peered down at them from the branch above. When the vine had been tossed over the limb and the raft, being pulled by the river's current, had tugged on the branch, the unusual motion had sent off sensors in hundreds of minute hairs that ran along the legs of the owner of the peering eyes. The unusual motion had also disturbed a nest. A drone had been sent from the nest to investigate.

The drone, and the nest from which it came, belonged to a queen. The queen was a very large and very nasty scorpion spider. She was not happy at being disturbed and especially irate that her territory was being invaded. She commanded the drone to identify the disturbance and to report back. She further commanded the drone to take no action, and the drone well knew the consequences of failing to obey the queen's commands – to the letter. He left the nest as stealthily as possible and inched silently to the end of the vine that was looped around the tree limb. His tiny yellow eyes focused on the sight below. He took note of the bodies sleeping below and immediately returned to his queen.

He scuttled before her, inching closer, and waited until she directed him to speak. As he made his report, he was fully aware of the queen's large and needle sharp stinger poised over his head. He concentrated on keeping his eyes from darting up to her stinger. One inaccuracy in his report, or one factor not considered, and before he could take a quick breath, her stinger would pierce the armor on his back and enter his heart. His body would be wrapped in webbing to preserve him for dinner later on. He finished his report and was still breathing. Apparently she was pleased.

"Take a squadron of attackers to them, but don't kill them. Wrap them carefully so that we can feast on them as we wish. Is that clear?" She directed the drone.

"Yes, your majesty."

As he turned to leave, she tapped him with her stinger lightly on his back. He froze in mid-step, thinking that maybe he hadn't been so lucky, after all. With his head lowered, he turned back towards her, waiting for the strike.

"Well done," she said, and sent him on his way.

"Thank you, your majesty," he said with relief, and he scurried away before she could change her mind.

A swarm of attacker scorpion spiders, once assembled, slowly made its way down the vine, not making a sound. Once it landed on the raft, it paused, and then divided into separate teams, each with specific assignments. Two legionnaires crept towards Liam's head and positioned themselves on either side of his neck. If he awoke and attacked or made any movement at all, they would strike his jugular vein. Their venom was not strong enough to kill, but their strike would instantly paralyze him. Two more made their way towards Solveig's head, and positioned themselves at her neck, while another two moved to Quinn and did the same. Summer had tucked herself under the folds of Solveig's cape and luckily remained out of sight. She remained as unnoticed by the swarm as she had by the drone.

The remaining attackers began spinning webs, starting at the feet of the sleeping victims. There was enough room underneath their feet and legs to completely encase them. Once the wrapping reached the parts of their bodies that rested on the raft, smaller shrew spiders would imperceptibly crawl beneath them and continue the wrapping. The webbing filament was very fine, but contained miniscule barbs. The barbs also contained venom. As the wrapping progressed and tightened, the toxin would seep through outer clothing, into the skin and then to the blood stream. Even Liam's gargoyle skin clothing couldn't keep him protected for long. Eventually, the venom would bleed through the scaly covering and into his skin.

As the swarm began spinning webs, Quinn, who was deep in an unconscious sleep, began to dream. In his dream he was back at home with his dogs. He was entertaining them by making music with his narwhal bone horn. He puckered his lips and blew. In his dream he was blowing into the horn and making a beautiful whale-song sound. In reality, he was just blowing air through his lips and sounded more like whales passing gas than whale songs. The rude noise woke Summer from her sleep. It also attracted the attention of the drone, which was in charge of this operation. He crept to the top of Quinn's head, trying to identify from what direction the sound was coming.

He had ordered the legionnaires to stand by. He didn't want them striking for fear that the sharp pain would cause this prey to make a noise that would alert the others. He would investigate first. He crawled up Quinn's hair to his forehead. As soon as he reached the top of Quinn's head, the sound stopped. Summer drifted back to sleep, and the drone scuttled back to his earlier position. And then it started again. The drone silently moved to the top of Quinn's head and this time determined that the sound was coming from Quinn's mouth. The drone inched his way up Quinn's head, over his forehead and down his nose. He stood poised on the tip of Quinn's nose ready to strike.

Summer rubbed her eyes, wondering who or what was making that awful sound. She poked her head out from under the folds of Solveig's cape, which was almost even with Quinn's elbow. She was blocked from the legionnaires poised at their positions near the jugular veins, and out of sight of the attackers spinning their webs around the feet and ankles of their prey, but could clearly see the drone perched on the point of Quinn's nose. She quickly ducked back out of sight, and then slowly pulled the cape in close around her and peeked out to look. At that particular moment, Quinn imagined he was playing a long loud note on his narwhal bone horn. But such was not the case.

The noise and vibration from the air escaping his flapping lips shook the drone, causing him to slide up Quinn's nose to the bridge right between his eyes. The drone recovered himself and marched back to the tip of Quinn's nose and raised his stinger, ready to strike. At the same instant, Summer flashed a shot of faerie dust at the drone causing him to literally explode, his spider guts splattering over Quinn's cheeks, nose and forehead.

Not sure what had happened, the legionnaires were confused. They left their positions along Quinn's neck looking for the source of the flash. Summer saw the one closest to her and zapped him into oblivion. She assumed, correctly, that another one would be on the other side of Quinn's body. She ran up to the side of Quinn's arm, and staying close to his body, flew over the top of him and zapped the other one. By now, the attackers could sense a disturbance. Before the squadron between Quinn and Solveig could form and launch any kind of offensive, Summer blasted them. Several exploded and the others scattered.

She soared into the air to get a higher vantage point and blasted the legionnaires poised at Solveig's neck, shooting faerie dust in rapid shots from both hand, one right after the other. She spun around in the blink of an eye and took out the ones' covering Liam. She dropped down next to Solveig and hovered next to her ear.

"Wake up," she shouted. "Please, wake up. We're being attacked."

The venom from the webbing that encompassed Solveig's legs had already started to work. She was groggy and disoriented. Summer flew over to Liam and shouted for him to wake up. Fortunately his gargoyle skin clothing had slowed the effect of the webbing venom. He looked down at his legs and saw the filament and then the scorpion spiders scurrying in several directions fleeing Summer's raid.

He kicked his legs free of the webbing, pulled off one of his shoes, and brought it down with several loud cracks on the escaping spiders. He looked over at Quinn and saw that two others had crawled onto his forehead, apparently in search of the decimated drone. Without thinking he brought his shoe down hard on Quinn's head, smashing the two with one blow.

"It's a good thing he's already unconscious; otherwise that would probably really hurt and he'd be really, really mad," he thought.

Summer looked like she was conducting a symphony orchestra, her hands flying to the right and the left, shooting magical bursts one after another with deadly accuracy. Shrews, attackers and legionnaires were sent flying or splattered on the raft, the vines or on Quinn. Liam got Solveig to her feet and then, pulling a long blade from a scabbard on his belt, cut the vine from the overhanging branch in one quick motion, just as reinforcements were making their way down the vine from the nest to the raft.

He quickly slipped his shoe back on his foot and began stomping at the spiders that were not able to retreat. Solveig had now come fully awake and quickly took in what had happened. She clapped her hands and with a wave of her arm a strong wind blew across the floor of the raft, blowing the remaining invaders into the river.

Meanwhile, Quinn, who had been oblivious to it all, continued to blow air out of his lips, dreaming about playing his narwhal bone horn; spider goo still on his forehead and dripping down the side of his face. The raft was flowing gently downstream with the current and gaining a little speed. The travelers were finally well away from the nest of spiders, but they had no idea where they were going. The moon had disappeared behind some clouds. It was nearly pitch black.

"Is everyone all right?" asked Liam.

Each of them checked themselves. No one had been bitten or stung.

"Ugh," said Solveig when she turned her attention to the sounds Quinn was making and saw the remains that were spread out over his face. "That's disgusting"

She pulled a handkerchief from her sleeve and cleaned off the remnants of the drone spider and his two henchmen from Quinn's forehead, cheeks and nose.

"I should have thought about something like that," Liam said. "I've lived too long in the Swamp to have been this careless. I guess I was lulled by the serenity of this place."

"We all should have been more cautious," Summer answered. "It wasn't your fault."

Her comments were interrupted when the raft crashed into a large rock in the middle of the river. The jolt nearly threw Solveig into the water. Liam quickly grabbed her arm to pull her back to the center of the raft. Summer flew into the air and landed ungraciously on her backside. Quinn just bounced up and then down, cracking his head against one of the raft logs. The other three just looked at him and winced.

"Ouch," said Summer, staring at Quinn. "It's a good thing he's already unconscious, because that would really hurt."

Liam and Solveig just lowered their heads, keeping silent on the matter.

"We need some kind of rudder in order to steer this thing," said Solveig.

"You're right," said Liam. "I just couldn't think of how to attach one when I put this thing together. But even with a rudder, without being able to see where we're going we wouldn't know which way to steer."

The raft crashed against another rock to their right and bounced sharply to the left where it struck another rock. It was also gaining more speed. They all sat down and held on to each other to keep from falling off. Solveig clapped her hands and threw her fist skyward. A bolt of light shot up like a flare.

"That won't last long," she said, "but it should help a little."

They could see a few yards ahead as the light slowly began to fade away. The river had narrowed considerably. It was about twenty feet wide at this point and the banks on either side were still either sheer rock or outcroppings of trees and shrubs. There was no place to beach the raft – even if they could steer it towards shore. They were in something like a deep valley. They also noticed that they were moving faster and faster and that there were some very large rocks strewn throughout the river.

"I almost liked it better when we couldn't see," said Summer, staring in shock at the obstacle course ahead of them.

Even so, Solveig threw another bolt of light into the sky, but, like the first one, it faded much too quickly and most of the light was blocked out by the large overhanging trees.

She continued to throw bolts of light skyward, hoping to find a clearing of some kind. All they saw, though, were more and more boulders littered throughout the water and their raft heading for and hitting most of them.

The echoes from thunder-like crashes that accompanied the bolts of light Solveig created were initially distant and barely audible. That changed in the next few minutes. Soon the sounds were much closer and louder as they echoed off the sides of what was becoming more and more like a canyon. They all noticed that the wind seemed to have picked up.

With the next flash they could see more clearly that the sides of the canyon were beginning to close in and the overhanging trees were becoming sparser. That was when they realized that it wasn't the wind that had picked up. The river had gotten considerably narrower, and the current was now much stronger. They were moving very fast. Summer noticed something else. As the echoes from the thunder diminished she detected a low rumbling sound that was getting louder.

"Do you hear that?" she asked.

"Hear what," said Liam who had been covering his ears to block out the loud thunder crashes.

Summer flew up and pulled his hand away from his ear. "Listen," she told him.

At that same instant Solveig released another light flash and everyone looked ahead of them to see a wide open sky. A wide open sky and no river. The sound no longer echoed off the sides of the canyon. The sides had disappeared as well. As this realization sunk in, the nose of the raft began to dip, the back end rose into the air, and the whole thing quickly dropped over the edge of a huge waterfall. Summer still had Liam's sleeve in her hand as he dropped to the floor of the raft, jerking her with him.

"Hold on to something," he shouted as he reached up and pulled Solveig close.

They worked their fingers into the vines tied around the raft logs and held on tightly. They both reached one arm over to hold on to Quinn, who had started slipping forward. As the raft plummeted down the falls, Summer let go of Liam's sleeve and took flight, hovering at a safe distance above the raft, watching it disappear into the crashing water at the bottom of the falls.

It seemed to be under the churning white water forever, but the raft finally bobbed back to the surface and she flew down to make sure everyone was all right. Liam and Solveig were drenched and sputtering, but seemed fine. Their hands were still tightly wrapped around the vine lashing, but they had lost their grip on Quinn. Quinn was nowhere to be seen, and the raft was in a deep channel of rapids. She flew up again to get a better view, but in the darkness it was hard to distinguish anything. All she could see was black water and the white foam of the rapids.

She flew up and down the stream frantically searching for Quinn while trying to keep the raft in sight. Then she saw him. He was floating like a large log about fifteen or twenty feet behind the raft, coming down the current headfirst. She shot a blast of faerie dust at him to raise him up out of the water, but missed as his body dropped with the current. Quinn bobbed up just as quickly and then bounced off one large rock after another. Summer winced with each hit, thinking, "It's a good thing he's already unconscious, otherwise that would probably knock him out." And then she remembered having said that not long ago.

She got a little closer to him and shot another blast of faerie dust. This time her aim was true and Quinn rose up out of the water, but not quite high enough. He hit another large boulder and ricocheted nearly straight up, hung motionlessly in the air for a second or two and then dropped like an arrow right back under the water. He bobbed up several yards downstream, again bouncing off rock after rock.

"Oh, nuts," said Summer, "that wasn't such a good idea. His poor head! It's going to be like mush."

She tried once more. This time, instead of lifting him up, she changed his direction, spinning him in and around the rocks. In the meantime, Solveig and Liam were hanging on for dear life, as the raft seemed to hit every obstacle that Quinn was now missing. They were tossed from side to side. With each twist and turn, their bodies slid from one edge of the raft to the other, pulling at the vines.

The damage was taking its toll on them and on the raft. The vines holding the raft together began to tear one by one as the logs crashed against the rocks, and as Liam and Solveig pulled at them trying to stay on top. Before long, the vines unraveled, and the logs separated from each other, adding to the debris crashing through the rapids. Liam and Solveig pulled themselves up and rode the same log like a bucking bronco, trying to keep it from rolling over and dunking them under the water.

Summer could faintly make out what looked like a clearing ahead, so she shot another blast of faerie dust at the raft to point it in that direction, only to find out that it had broken apart. All she did was direct the various pieces of the ruined ship in the same direction as Liam and Solveig. She tried again, this time aiming for the one log that they were hugging onto. She spun back and then did the same thing to Quinn.

One more blast pushed the log with Liam and Solveig past the last obstacle to the shore. The rest of the raft logs skittered past them and continued to tumble through the rapids. The log on which Liam and Solveig were clinging ran aground with such a sudden stop that the two riders flew off. They landed with a splat, rolling and tumbling, and skidded to a stop on the beach. Quinn slid in sideways almost immediately behind them and rolled several times across the small shore before coming to a stop. However, instead of a sandy beach, the shore was a soupy mud covered with a thick coating of scum.

"Really? This was the best you could do," sputtered Solveig as she wiped the stinking, slimy goo from her face.

"I can always put you back in the water," answered Summer.

"Thanks, but I will do that myself," said Solveig.

She started to stand so that she could move to the edge of the river and wash some of the mud off, but the tension of the last several minutes had wrung her out.

"Maybe in a minute or two," she added as she flopped down where she was and allowed herself a brief rest. Besides, she thought, isn't mud supposed to be good for one's complexion?

Liam had started to pull himself further ashore, hoping to find more solid ground. He was covered head to toe in muck. When he at last reached drier, harder land, he rolled over onto his back and sat up. He was exhausted. The mud covering him felt like it weighted a ton. He reached up to clear it away from his mouth and nose, but could barely move his arm. He started to stand up, and found he couldn't move. He teetered back and forth and then fell straight back. A sense of panic began to overwhelm him. The slime was hardening.

Chapter eleven

Stella had awakened to find Princess Natalie's amulet around her neck. She reached up and held it in her hand. As soon as she grasped it, she knew that Natalie had left it with her as a means of communicating her location. She sat up in her bed, fully awake. She could sense that Princess Natalie had left with a messenger and traveled to Eastern Outpost Five where she met with a Dryad who left the Outpost with Natalie, but she could discern nothing more than that.

She jumped from her bed and staggered, light headed for a second or two and then, regaining her balance, returned to the Sanctorum where she could better clear her mind. Images almost immediately began to appear on the walls in random flashes as soon as she walked in. They were all mixed up and she couldn't seem to focus on any one in particular or put them into any kind of order. They were swirling together, overlapping and blurring, each one seemed to be fighting for dominance – competing for her attention.

She saw Lochen racing across the sky in some kind of runaway vessel. He was clearly out of control, but didn't seem to be overly concerned. The look on his face was almost cartoon-like. This image dissolved into another. She saw Natalie searching for a place to hide, but the image was wavy and distorted as if obscured by a waxy glass. Underneath the images she sensed, but couldn't see, Summer in extreme distress. She could feel the exertion of her fluttering rapidly back and forth.

Another vision pushed forward, blocking out the others. Sean seemed to be falling or careening from one side to another in a sea of blackness. He was shouting but no sound could be heard. His image transformed into another. Solveig seemed to be running, but she wasn't moving. Her legs seemed to be weighted down. In fact, her whole body seemed to be weighted down.

Within that same vision, Liam appeared to be slumped on a beach, but he wasn't relaxing. Just the opposite - his level of panic was rising. Interspersed through each of these images was one of Quinn, floating peacefully through the air, playing a narwhal bone horn. It was that last image, in such complete contrast to the others that she found most perplexing.

There were other images that were jumbled in with those of her friends. As much sense as those images didn't make, these made less. Tiny, mole-like creatures were scurrying in fear - hundreds of them; others, larger, pig-like creatures, were chasing the smaller ones, and hitting them with sticks. They were running through what looked like tunnels. All around them was fire. She had never seen these creatures before, nor had she ever seen images like these – all intertwined.

"Okay," she said to herself. "One thing at a time."

She moved to the center of the Sanctorum and sat on the floor. She closed her eyes and the images on the walls around her disappeared. Clearing her mind, she took several deep breaths and released them slowly. She relaxed her body and forced herself to picture only Princess

Natalie. She slowly opened her eyes. The other images, especially the mole-like creatures fought her efforts. She persisted in controlling the visions, and slowly the other images faded into the background. They didn't disappear, but they were less intrusive.

The walls and ceiling of the Santorum came alive with a single image. There was water everywhere. She was deep beneath the surface of the Cerulean Sea. That explained the waxy glass appearance, she thought. It was the water. There was a vast canyons that filled her vision in every direction. No – it wasn't a canyon. She was at the mouth of a cave. Before her was a single mountain, and that mountain was shaking. The Sea was bubbling. She looked around but she didn't see signs of any of the many creatures that lived in the Sea. It was deserted except for Natalie and another figure.

As if someone had turned a switch, the Sanctorum was filled with a roaring sound that was nearly ear splitting. Stella jumped at the sudden noise, but kept concentrating. She could sense a gradual transition. She was no longer seeing this vision as an outsider. She was seeing things through Natalie's eyes but in slow motion. She had managed to make a strong connection. She knew she was now exactly where her Princess was. She could see, feel and hear exactly what Natalie was experiencing.

The sides of the cave were filling more of the image. She saw Natalie – she saw through Natalie's eyes that she was backing into the cave. No –Natalie was being pulled into the cave. Who was pulling her? She turned, straining to see. It was a Dryad. I'm not alone, she thought – Natalie's not alone. Why was she being pulled into a cave by a Dryad? She didn't sense that Natalie felt danger from the inside of the cave, but rather from something outside the cave. There were so many distractions. Stella fought harder not to break the vision.

She was becoming uncomfortably hot. The temperature in the Sanctorum never changed, she thought. Her mind started to drift as she asked herself, why am I feeling hot? Thinking about the increasing heat was drawing her attention away from the vision and it started to fade. The image began to shift and she could see Natalie, instead of seeing through Natalie's eyes. Stay focused, she told herself. She ignored her discomfort and willed herself to keep the connection with her Princess. The image blurred slightly and then became Natalie's vision again.

The intensity of the images increased, becoming extremely vivid now. She saw every detail; she could feel the water around her. It was the water that was getting hot. She looked up, from side to side, and then behind her. The images in the Sanctorum were exactly like Natalie's surroundings – front, back, sides and top. As Stella looked around, she could see everything that was surrounding Natalie. It was all getting darker and darker. She was being drawn further and further into the cave. Her field of vision was narrowing as the opening to the cave narrowed and drew away from her.

She shifted her focus to what remained visible to her – to what Natalie was watching with great intensity - the distant mountain that still could be seen through the opening to the cave. Suddenly, there was a great gush of air that escaped from a crevice near the base of the mountain. The rush of air blew out of what looked like a hole and immediately flew to the surface. The air was an odd looking grayish white. Within seconds after the bubble of air rose to the surface, she could feel the temperature of the water rise dramatically and wash over her. It was as if someone had dumped scalding water into a cool pond.

Just as suddenly, she saw movement where the hole had appeared. It was a blur, but she was certain she had seen half a dozen small objects appear in the space where the air had escaped. They scurried with incredible speed. Even with the slow motion sensation of the Sanctorum image, it was difficult to see what was happening. And then the objects and the opening were gone. It happened so fast, Stella wasn't sure what she had seen, or that she had seen anything at all.

The sudden and unexpected activity caused her to lose focus. In spite of the amount of sleep she had, she was still not fully recovered from her back-to-back resurrection of the memories. The images projected on the walls and ceiling of the Sanctorum vanished in an instant, as if someone had turned out the lights. In the same instant, the roaring noise ended with a loud clap, like someone slamming a door. Before she even realized what had happened, the walls and ceiling of the Sanctorum went blank. It wasn't just the image of Natalie that was gone. All of them had disappeared. Stella slumped her shoulders, exhausted and confused.

---------------- *** ----------------

"Summer," shouted Liam, spitting the muck away from his mouth and blowing air out of his nose, "don't touch the mud, but make sure it's cleared away from Solveig's and Quinn's mouths. It's hardening."

"I'm fine," muttered Solveig as she coughed. "I got a mouthful when we landed. It tastes as bad as it smells. Fortunately I was able to spit it out. I thought it was just heavy, but it's hardening on me, too."

"Quinn's all right," answered Summer. "He seems to be blowing bubbles or something. What should I do?"

"I can't move," answered Liam. "Can you use some of that faeries stuff and get us further up the bank and out of this muck? The stuff that's covering us seems to be blending into the ground. If we don't move soon, I'm afraid we'll be buried here."

"Oh, yeah, sure." She swirled some around Liam as she fluttered above him.

His encased body creaked and cracked, as it pulled free from the mud. Then it rose into the air and floated over the ground to a place that looked a bit more solid. He was heavier than she thought he'd be – probably because of the mud. She moved him away from the mire and into a thicket of ground cover. When Summer released him he dropped to the ground like a lead weight.

"Oops," she said, "sorry. I let go too soon or maybe I didn't use enough faerie dust. You must weigh a ton."

"That's all right," he assured her. "I didn't feel a thing. It's like there's some kind of padding or cushion inside this stuff that absorbed the hit to the ground. Go get Solveig and Quinn, and bring them here. We need to figure out what to do and how we get this stuff off."

Summer flew back to Solveig and Quinn and one by one hoisted them into the air and deposited them near Liam – this time a bit more gently. She moved Quinn first because she knew he'd be much heavier than Solveig. She was afraid that if he got too stuck in the ground, she'd never be able to free him. She gave him a double dose of faerie dust, worried that one might not be enough.

"I'm sorry," she told Solveig when she flew past her to get to Quinn. "I'll do this as fast as I can. I promise,"

"Don't worry," said Solveig, "I don't think I'm going anywhere."

She was trying to be patient, but was becoming anxious. She could feel the mud hardening around her body and sensed she was sinking deeper into the mire. I really don't want to become part of the scenery, she said to herself.

Once Summer had them all grouped together, the already dark sky started to rumble and rain began to fall in torrents. The water beat down on Summer, shoving her face forward into the ground. She jumped back up and fluttered her wings to lift her off the ground. She was afraid the goo from the shore might have reached this far inland. She spit the mud out of her mouth and frantically wiped it clear of her face. It was a struggle for her to fly, the rain was so strong. She ducked under some large leaves in a feeble attempt to stay dry.

"Wait," shouted Solveig, coughing and choking. "Turn us over. This rain is collecting in pools over my mouth. I can't keep spitting it out and I can't keep it from going up my nose. I'm having a hard time breathing. This is awful."

Summer tried to shoot her faerie dust and turn them over from the shelter of the leaves, but she wasn't quite able to do so. Instead, she was only able to turn them half way, and they just kept rocking back and forth, bumping into each other. With each loud knock as one hardening shell struck another, she shouted out an embarrassed, "Sorry."

"Oh, poop," she said as she finally came to the conclusion that she couldn't avoid getting soaked.

She gritted her teeth and flew out from under the leaves. She hovered above the trio and quickly – and ungracefully – flipped them all over, much like pancakes; yet again causing them to collide into each other and once again shouting "sorry" over the loud drumming of the rain.

"Solveig," Liam shouted, "can you flash or bang or do whatever you did to shoot those flares into the sky and maybe break up this stuff?"

Having been flipped over, he was staring straight ahead at the ground. The only thing keeping his mouth out of the grass and water was the hardened shell on his nose. If this water gets any higher, he thought, I'm going to start wishing I had a bigger nose.

"No" Solveig answered. "I can't move my hands at all. I've tried concentrating but that doesn't seem to have any effect. My fingers tingle. That's all."

Then she had an idea.

"Summer, see if you can find a rock – a big one, or at least the biggest one you can lift - and drop it on one of us."

"A rock?" asked Liam. "Are you serious? Do you really want her to drop a rock on one of us? And who do you suggest she drop it on?"

Summer was not very happy about the thought of coming out from under the leaves again. Even under the leaf, the water was splashing up from the ground and she was getting soaked.

"A rock?" she echoed. "Now? You want me to do this now? Can't it wait? I mean, you said yourself - you're not going any place."

"Well, I didn't expect her to drop it on our heads," Solveig responded to Liam. "I just thought she might be able to crack the casing before it gets any harder. And yes, now," she answered Summer, growing increasingly frustrated and worried. "It's not like you've got anything better to do."

Grumbling, Summer flew out from under the leaves. Another torrent pushed her flat on her face into the mud once again. She bolted up immediately, scrubbing the mud from her face. Fortunately this mud didn't harden; it was just regular mud, but she wasn't taking any chances. She straightened up and forced her wings to lift her into the air while she grumbled even more and finished wiping the mud from her face.

She was soaked to the skin, her wings were heavy with water, and her hair kept washing over her eyes. She pulled her hair back with one hand, but still couldn't see clearly more than a few feet in front of her. She fluttered futilely for several seconds, and then she swirled faerie dust with the hand that wasn't holding her hair out of her face to produce enough light for her to see what she was doing. She flitted back and forth for a minute or two before she finally found a rock she thought would be of suitable size. She waved her hand, sprinkling faerie dust on it and moved the large rock over Liam's body.

"I've got one," she shouted over the noise of the storm and struggling with the weight. "Are you ready, Liam? I'm going to drop it on you."

"Me? Wait," he shouted in near panic. "No, not on me. This was Solveig's idea. Drop it on her."

"Fine," shouted Solveig until Summer spun it around and it hung over her head. "Wait," she shouted, "Where are you dropping it?"

"On your head," she answered, trying to hold the rock steady with one hand while she wiped the rainwater off her face. "I figured that since there was already an opening on the other side, you know – where your mouth is – it might be easier to crack by dropping it on your head."

"I said NOT over the head," protested Solveig. "Move it down a little."

"Fine," sputtered Summer.

She pushed another wad of soaking hair out of her eyes as the rock fluttered back and forth and up and down over Solveig's head. She flicked her wrist and the rock moved erratically down a little and higher into the air.

"Wait," shouted Solveig once again. "Watch out for my hands. If you break my hands I won't be able to cast spells. You don't have it over my hands, do you?"

"No!" Summer shouted back. "I don't have it over your hands. I have it over your butt. Is it all right if I break your butt? Make up your mind. This thing is getting heavy."

"I have a better idea," Solveig shouted. "Drop it on Quinn."

"What?" shouted Summer and Liam in unison.

"He's already unconscious," said Solveig. "He doesn't know it's coming and he won't remember it happening. Besides, he's got so many bumps and bruises already, one more won't matter."

"Whatever," answered Summer.

She flicked her wrist once more and sent the rock on path to land on Quinn's back. She released it just a bit before she intended and it landed on his head. It hit the hardened mud, made a hollow thump and rolled off without putting a dent or a scratch into the coating, and no evident bump or bruise – not that she or anyone else would have been able to tell.

"OK," shouted Summer, as she darted back and sought refuge under the leaves. "That worked well. Can any other bright ideas either of you come up with wait until it stops raining?"

She didn't wait for an answer. As the rain continued to fall, the ground surrounding the three petrified travelers began to get flooded. The puddles of water were beginning to combine and get deeper. Liam could see that even a bigger nose wouldn't solve this problem.

"Summer," sputtered Liam, blowing bubbles in the pool around his mouth. "Turn us over again. The water's covering our mouths."

She pulled her soaked hair out of her eyes and flew out from under the leaves. She immediately flipped them over, but as soon as she did, she saw that the rain was still pouring into their mouths and noses.

"This isn't going to work," she announced.

She looked around and then moved Quinn, turning him on his side, and leaning him against a tree stump. She then flipped Solveig over in the same manner and leaned her up against Quinn, and then moved Liam to complete the stacking process. She rolled the rock over to hold Liam in place. Satisfied that they were planted solidly and that the water wouldn't reach their mouths, she ducked back under the shrubs.

"You're welcome," she shouted over her shoulder sarcastically as she nestled between several large leaves, covering herself completely.

The rain was coming down so hard now and beating down on the leaves Summer had covered herself with. All she could hear was the rumbling of the drops all around her. She hadn't noticed that where she had stacked Liam, Solveig, and Quinn there was in a slight depression in the ground.

As the rain kept up and she pulled one leaf after another around and over her, trying not to get any wetter than she already was, the depression began to fill. As it did, the rock slid loose and Liam, Solveig and Quinn slowly rolled over onto their backs. Instead of sinking to the bottom of the puddles that had formed, they bobbed and floated. It was all they could do to breathe.

They sputtered and gasped, trying to keep the water out of their mouths. Every time they opened them wide enough to call for help, they filled immediately, cutting off the sound, except for Quinn, who was still blowing air, dreaming he was playing his horn. Any sounds they could make, were muffled by the falling rain and the water accumulating in pools around their mouths and noses. In a few minutes, the puddles collected to join each   other and became a small stream, which emptied into the nearby river, carrying the three statues with it.

- - - - - - - - - - - - - - - - - *** - - - - - - - - - - - - - - - - -

"Your Highness, please," pleaded the Dryad as she pulled on Natalie's sleeve.

They had backed up to a small cave not far from the volcano. As the rumbling began and the water heated, the Dryad seemed to sense a greater danger than her Princess. She knew it was highly improper for her to grab the Princess's clothes, but she was concerned for Natalie's safety.

"That mountain is not safe," she cautioned. "Please come into the cave."

Natalie couldn't take her eyes off the undersea mountain that had begun only seconds before to shake. She allowed herself to be pulled back into the cave in the event the mountain – what? She thought. What's it going to do? Explode? Cave in? She wasn't sure, which was why she wanted to watch. She could also feel the heat emanating from the mountain. But this is a long inactive volcano, she thought. How can it be erupting now after thousands of years?

She slowly backed into the cave, but not so far that she would lose sight of the mountain. Then she felt something different in the water – more than just the heat. She opened her mouth slightly and tasted. It was very bitter. She wasn't sure what it was exactly. The first thing that came to her mind was that the water was being infused with sulfur. She spun her hand around, casting a small spell and created a tiny bubble around her head so she could smell the water. She was right. It was sulfur.

She turned back to the Dryad and spun her hand again, encasing her head in a similar bubble of air.

"Do you smell that?" she asked the Dryad.

"Yes, your Highness. We have smelled the same foul odor wherever the water has become hot and the sea life has died."

She turned her attention back to the mountain. Suddenly Natalie spied movement near the base of the mountain. It happened so fast that after it was over, she wasn't really sure she had seen it in the first place.

"Did you see that?" she demanded of the Dryad.

The Dryad hesitated before answering. She was supposed to be observant, but the movement happened so fast, she was concerned about giving her Princess false or inaccurate information.

"I'm not sure what I saw," the Dryad answered.

"You can't give me a wrong answer. Tell me what you saw or what you think you saw. You may only be confirming my own perceptions."

"For just a second I thought I saw an opening appear at the base of the mountain. It almost looked like a door opening. Something escaped from the opening and then it closed."

"A door?" Natalie asked.

"I must be mistaken," said the Dryad.

"No. I saw it, too; but why did you think it was a door and not just a break in the side of the mountain?"

The Dryad thought for a minute, "Because it was too uniform to be a break in the mountain; because it appeared to swing outward; and because it then seemed to close – just like a door."

"I agree," said Natalie, having her own vision confirmed. "What else did you see?"

"I'm not sure, Your Highness. Do you mean the strange white bubble that escaped from the opening?"

"No. I saw that too, and you are right. There was something different about it, but that difference didn't mean anything to me until you said the bubble was white. I don't think it was just escaping air. It looked like more than that."

"Then what, Your Highness?"

"Steam," Natalie answered. "It wasn't a solid white; it was like a cloud – wispy. It looked like a bubble of steam. But that's not what I meant. Did you see something else that was out of place?"

The Dryad was not sure she should say any more. She wasn't sure what she had seen and didn't want to mislead her Princess. Natalie sensed her hesitance.

"Speak freely. I know you're a scout and I trust your instincts. Trust them yourself."

"A flurry of small creatures," said the Dryad. "I've never seen anything like them before, but I believe I saw about six of them. They moved very fast and they were very small. I'm not certain that's what it was, though. The distortion from the bubble could have just created such an illusion."

Natalie knew that the Dryads who were chosen as scouts had some unusual powers. What they lacked in other areas they made up for in their extraordinary vision. It was almost as if they had telescopic vision and that they could slow down time. She herself had greater visual acuity than most of her people, but nothing like the scouts. This time, though, she had seen the movement – a blur of white: almost like ghosts that appeared to have opened a large passage into the mountain, released something that looked like steam and then shut the door.

"Well done, Marcella," Natalie said to the Dryad. "Your eyes are very sharp, and they were not deceiving you."

The rumbling had stopped and the smell and feel of sulfur had disappeared as quickly as it had appeared.

"I've seen enough. It's time to get you back to your daughter."

They mounted the sea horses and returned to the Outpost.

Chapter twelve

t was more the lack of sound than the noise that woke Summer up. That and the small bird that was poking its beak into the water, which had accumulated in a pool in the leaves in which she was sitting. As she pulled back the large leaf she had used to cover her head, she startled the bird, which in turn startled her.

"Yeah?" she grumbled. "And good morning to you, too, you mangy old crow!"

The rain had finally stopped and the suns had come out. She was still cold, wet, a bit crabby and very hungry. With the sun out, she thought as she rubbed her arms, at least she would be able to warm up and dry out. Not being hungry would be another matter. She thought she might be able to find some berries or nuts if she scrounged around a little.

"I probably ought to see if the others are all right," she mumbled as she rubbed the sleep from her eyes.

She tried to stand up and found herself wrapped like a cocoon in the leaves under which she had taken shelter. She slowly unwound herself. The water from the rain had seeped into the folds of the leaves, and she was soaked to her skin. Once free of the wrappings, she stretched and shook herself trying to warm up. She flapped her wings to dry them off and straighten them out.

"The others must be sound asleep," she thought. "At least they stopped complaining. 'Flip me over, Summer; not that way, Summer; move me over there, Summer; drop a rock on me, Summer – oh, wait, not me, Summer, drop it on Quinn.' What a bunch of babies."

She flew from her perch on the leaves and went over to look at her friends. They were gone. What the what, she thought. I thought I put them over here. She flew around to some of the other tree stumps, but returned to the first one.

"No," she said out loud. "This is where I put them last night. I'm sure of it."

She saw the rock she had used to keep them stacked on their sides, but she could see that it had washed away from the spot where she had originally placed it. That was when she noticed that there was a small puddle that trickled down the embankment where she had last left them. Her eyes followed the trickle down the embankment and into the river.

"Hey," she shouted. "Where are you guys? This isn't funny. You can come out any time now."

Maybe they had finally gotten free from the hardened mud, she thought. But why would they leave me behind? They're probably playing a trick on me. And after all I did for them? What a bunch of ingrates.

She flew through the branches to a higher position so she could get a wider view of her surroundings. There was still no sign of them. This was carrying a prank a bit too far, she thought. She started to circle the area, going wider and wider to cover more ground. She swooped down and darted under branches and in the trees She looked behind logs and around rocks. Nothing.

There was a thick verge that surrounded the clearing in which they had landed. She examined it closely and could see that there was no sign it had been disturbed or beaten down. They couldn't have gone that way, she concluded, looking further into the woods. She turned back towards the water. The only option left was the river. Now she started to feel angry and panicky – both at the same time.

"Okay," she said to herself. "Get a grip and think about this. Think logically – like Stella, or maybe Lochen. No, not Lochen. No one thinks like him. Ok. Think like Stella. If they had broken the mud they were encased in or chipped it away, there would be pieces of it around, or at least some sign that they had been broken. They couldn't get rid of all of it. There isn't any sign of chips of mud, so that didn't happen.

"Could someone have come in the night and carried them away? I suppose, but it would take someone really big or a whole bunch of someones to carry Quinn off. And there are no footprints anywhere. I suppose they could have been lifted into the air, but somehow, I don't think so."

She looked up into the trees above, and hoped she was right about them not being carried off from above by some big bird or something. After some consideration, she dismissed that thought.

"That stuff got hard and stayed hard during the rain, so it didn't just dissolve. That means they're probably still covered with it. They couldn't walk – they couldn't even turn over, so they didn't wander off by themselves still covered. Could they have floated in that stuff?"

She thought for a few minutes, trying to look at things rationally. What did she know about things that could float? She recalled the ship that Liam had in the Venomous Swamp. It was hollow, but it could be filled with all sorts of things. She thought about the stories Quinn told about sailing in his kayak. That was another thing that was hollow, but could carry a person. She realized that was all she knew about things that could float.

"I need to get out more," she said to herself, disappointed that she could run through all she knew about things that float in such a short time.

She reasoned that it was possible that almost anything could float, especially if it wasn't solid. She remembered Liam saying that it didn't hurt when she had dropped him to the ground; that it was like there was some kind of buffer or cushion inside. Could it be possible that they were able to float? She thought hard and remembered seeing the puddle of water where she had last seen them. It was a lot deeper than it was right after the rain had started, and it was still trickling into the river.

"That's got to be what happened," she shouted. "The rain washed them into the river and they floated downstream."

At least she hoped that they had floated downstream. If not, they would be at the bottom of the river, unless they had been carried off by someone or something, which had floated them downstream. She didn't want to think what either of those options could mean.

She decided she had to determine if they had sunk into the water. She flew out over the river and hovered over the surface, flitting like a dragonfly where the stream from the puddle met the river. It was too murky to see very deeply into the water. Oh poop, she thought. She didn't have much choice, so she didn't think about it. She took a deep breath and shot like an arrow into the water. It was so muddy, that she couldn't see her hands stretched out in front of her. She skidded into the mud in the river bottom and immediately came back up to the surface.

"Oh," she sputtered, coughed and spit. "That wasn't as deep as I thought it would be. I need to be more careful."

She raced across the top of the water to clear the mud from her hands, arms and face. There was no sign that this mud was hardening. It must be different than the mud on the bank, she realized. She dove back into the water, this time a little more cautiously, and felt around as long as she could hold her breath. She conducted several more searches, coming up only long enough to fill her lungs with fresh air and dive down again. After almost an hour of doing this she concluded that the threesome hadn't sunk. They must have floated, she thought with relief.

She flew back up and over the river, and followed its current. The water wasn't as rough as it had been immediately following the falls and the rapids, but there were still a lot of obstacles along the way. She thought about flying high so she could see more of the river, but then thought that if they were stuck on a log or a rock near the shore, she might miss them.

Instead, she soared from one side to the other, looking in every niche and run-off and along any open area of shoreline. Soon she was approaching a large delta and dozens of tributaries began to appear. Oh, no, she thought. There was no way she could search each one of them. It would take forever. She soared higher into the sky to see where these various tributaries led. She could see that as each one broke off, it, too, divided further into several more run-offs. It stretched for miles in a web-like patter, as far as she could see.

"There has GOT to be a way to narrow down the possible choices," she shouted in frustration.

She was hovering over the river delta trying to think of what to do. A sense of dread nearly overwhelmed her. This was impossible, was all she could think. She was so distraught, that she was on the verge of tears, unable to make a decision.

"This is all my fault," she wailed in despair. "I should have stayed awake. I should have looked after them. I should have been nicer to them."

She went on and on berating herself. She could do nothing else but watch the water flow below her as it carried branches and leaves from the storm. Try as she might, she was unable to come up with an idea. She was just about to give up and start down one of the offshoots at random when an odd looking log enmeshed in a large clump of branches came down the river. Her first reaction was that it was one of her friends, but as it got closer she could see that it wasn't. She watched it as it swirled around in a small eddy at the beginning of the delta and then spun off down one of the tributaries to her right — not the one she had been considering.

That caused her to pause. She stopped her motion down the left tributary and reconsidered. She wondered if that was just a chance happening or if it meant that the main current of the river went down that channel. She waited a few more minutes. Her impatience was gnawing at her, and she almost decided to go with her first instinct, disregarding what had made her doubt that choice. Eventually, though, another large branch came down the river, swirled in the same eddy and spun off down the same waterway.

"OK. I'll take that as a sign. Besides, I suppose that's as good a choice as any," she said and flew down to follow that channel, hoping dearly that some higher power had actually sent her a sign.

------------------ *** ------------------

Stella knew she needed to rest and that she hadn't really recovered from her efforts at the resurrection of the memories; but the abruptly lost connection with Natalie troubled her. She wasn't sure how long she had been asleep on the floor of the Sanctorum. She sat up, rubbing her eyes, and then waived her hand in the air towards the walls. Like sparks of light or static electricity, bits and pieces of the previous images reappeared. She tried as hard as she could to conjure the images she had last seen of Natalie, but nothing happened. She was just too exhausted to make it return. However, the blur of the small white creatures flashed before her once more.

"All right," she finally thought, exasperated, "the Princess will have to fend for herself. Let's see if I can make some sense of this."

She shifted her vision to the mountain. She focused her thoughts and entered once more into a trance like-state. She willed herself to recall the images she had seen earlier and to concentrate in particular on the spot she had last seen those creatures and replayed the vision as slowly as she could. Since she was seeing this from the same vantage point as Natalie, it was in no greater detail or clarity, in spite of Natalie's heightened visual acuity. But she could slow things down. Eventually the moment came when the hole in the side of the mountain reappeared and the rush of the smoky air gushed out.

"No," she whispered, "it's not just air. There's something in it. And the break in the mountain - the hole. It's more like a door."

She was able to replay the image, back and forth, slowing it down to study it more clearly. The opening followed the shapes and contours of the base of the mountain, which hid it from detection. But it clearly swung out, very much like a door on a vault. The opening was quickly followed by the gush of air. Stella looked more closely this time. It was air, but it was also not air. It had a hazy quality to it. It wasn't clear. It was more like steam, she concluded. At the same time the rush of steam burst through the doorway and towards the surface of the sea, she could feel the surrounding water quickly heat up. It was like a blast from a furnace.

She replayed the image until she was sure she could learn nothing more from it. She almost turned away, breaking the connection, but something told her to keep focused on the opening. And then it happened – the flurry of movement that seemed out of place the first time she had seen it. She played it again, even slower. Six small mole-like creatures appeared. They seemed to be doing something to the exterior of the door, but she couldn't tell what, exactly. Even in the slowed motion their movements were extremely quick. Then they pulled the door shut and the opening blended seamlessly with the rest of the mountainside and was not the least bit visible.

"How curious," she thought. "There are creatures of some kind inside that volcano and opened a door to do what? Release steam?"

She made a mental note to search the archives for any references to these creatures. The vision of the mountain remained the same, but nothing more happened. And she could not regain her connection with Natalie.

"All right," she said. "Let's see if I can figure out some of those other images. I think I'll start with Lochen. I've always enjoyed a challenge."

She turned her thoughts to Lochen. She had always had an unusual telepathic connection with him and knew that when she provided him that very large transporter stone, he had done something to enhance that connection. She started with the day he asked about the stone. By going back that far, it would help her to transition to the puzzling impressions. She closed her eyes and recalled images of him and the last time he was with her. He had asked about the transporter stone and wanted to know if there were larger ones to be found. She had taken him to a giant sinkhole on a nearby island and they had transported to the bottom – several miles down.

As her concentration pinpointed on that day, her vision began to expand and the walls and ceiling of the Sanctorum came back to life. She slowly began to transfer her mind's eye to see through Lochen's eyes, as she had done earlier with Natalie. Her telepathic connection to him made this vision a little easier to raise. As the transformation completed, she was able to fast-forward.

She caught glimpses of a forest, and then of Sean. She saw the bubble covered stone. Then the Sanctorum walls were no longer blank, but the vision was entirely black. She waited patiently, and slowly stars began to appear. However, the stars wouldn't remain fixed in the vision. Instead, they spun and whirled first one way and then another. It was making her dizzy.

"This is not good; he's lost control somehow," she thought. "Something terrible is happening."

She remained in a trance-like position for several minutes, but the vision never changed. It just kept spinning, or twisting and turning. Her head was throbbing with pain. She finally had to end the connection, and like lights being turned off, the dome of the Santorum again went blank.

She wanted to try to establish a connection with Summer, but she was too exhausted to initiate another trance. She knew she would never be able to maintain the level of concentration necessary. She had a sense from the earlier images that Summer was in the same place or at least nearby to Solveig, Liam, and Quinn.

Unfortunately, the last connection had revealed nothing that told her where they were or what was happening to them. The same sense that told her these four were together also told her they were in danger. Stella was frustrated that she could not discover anything more that would help them. She decided to try something different.

She grasped with both hands the amulet Natalie had given her, and began chanting an ancient incantation. She had learned this spell from an older Enchantress, but had never tried it herself. All that was needed was an object from someone held dear, even if that was not the person whose image was being summoned.

In a few seconds light from the amulet began to glow. Rays of light beams like threads of color shot out from between her fingers and washed over the walls surrounding her. Each beam painted a separate piece to the picture. These images would not be as clear as those that were generated by her own thoughts. She would only have one chance at this, and would not have the same control over the speed as she did the other images, but the incanted pictures would at least tell her something, and this method was less taxing on her – mentally and physically.

One beam splashed an outline of Summer. It was like a drawing made with light. She was racing down towards a body of swiftly moving water. The image – drawing of Summer - splashed between white and dazzling yellow and seemed to disappear and then reappear. It danced across –

no, not across, but over - lines of gray and white that moved in a somewhat straight line beneath. She's flying over something, thought Stella. Looking closer at the patterns and movement of the gray and white lines, her first thought was that it looked like water. Go with your first reactions – trust your instincts, she thought. She's flying over water.

Another beam splashed an outline of Solveig. This one was drawn in vivid purple. She was immobile, but was tumbling in multiple directions, clearly separated and far away from the image of Summer. She seemed to move evenly over the same lines of gray and white. The image often made sudden stops and starts, twisting and turning. When it did, the lines of water over which she was suspended scattered and flared in intensity. Water was all around her. Unlike the image of Summer, this one was plainly in contact with the water, but she wasn't wet. She's floating somehow, thought Stella. In some kind of small boat?

A third beam – bright green - splashed an outline of Liam. He, too, was immobile, but tumbling in the same manner as Solveig and not far from her. His image was in the same proximity to the lines of water as Solveig. He's floating, too, thought Stella. But he seemed to be crashing into shapes in black and brown lines. Could those be rocks and trees, wondered Stella. But she sensed he felt no pain. They must be in or on a river, Stella concluded.

A final beam of blue splashed an outline of Quinn. He was separated from each of the others, but was also floating on the water. But his image didn't seem to be moving as turbulently as Solveig's and Liam's. Instead, he was rocking gently. At times, his drawing changed direction or he spun around in circles. Regardless of what direction he was heading, tiny splashes of different colors rose from the area of his mouth, floated into the sky above him and disappeared. This part of the image remained a complete mystery to Stella. She would never be able to know that Quinn was still playing an imaginary narwhal bone horn.

"What are these people doing?" asked Stella. More specifically, she wondered what, exactly, was Quinn doing?

These images were not making any sense at all. She knew she was exhausted and needed to rest and to get something to eat. Part of her wondered if maybe she wasn't hallucinating – just a bit – these last images were just too weird. She needed to restore her strength. It had been two days, or more, since she had last eaten and the resurrections were still taking their toll. With all the competing visions, she knew, too, that she needed to be at her best mentally and physically to sort things out. As curious as she was, she forced herself to stop pursuing the visions, at least for the time being.

She left the Sanctorum and headed for the kitchen. She never made it to the kitchen, though. Along the way there, she decided to take a short detour to the archives. Something about those small white creatures was nagging at her.

--------------------- *** ---------------------

During the night, the rain had fallen in torrents. The noise of the water beating down without a break had drowned out Liam's calls to Summer. The water pooling around their encased bodies had risen higher and higher.

"Solveig," he shouted. "Is the water rising around you, too?"

"I don't know," she shouted back in frustration. "I can't see anything but your back. I have no peripheral vision, either. It's all blocked by this...this...stuff."

Struggling as much as he could, he could not free himself in the least from the shell that had hardened around him. He was further frustrated in that he could only see as far as his peripheral vision allowed. He tried rocking his body back and forth. At first nothing happened, then he felt like he as sliding somehow.

"Solveig," he called. "Can you move at all?"

"No, but I feel like something is happening. It feels like I'm being moved." She had to shout to be heard, even though Liam was right next to her.

"Me, too. I tried rocking back and forth and thought that I was making some progress, but now I don't think that's what's happening. I think the rain is pooling around us and lifting us off the ground."

"Oh, no," Solveig cried. "What if it covers us?"

"I don't think it will. I think we're able to float. I just hope that we're able to roll over on our backs. I can't raise my head, and if I'm face down I won't be able to breathe."

"Thanks for giving me something new to worry about," she muttered under her breath.

The rain continued to fall and the puddle continued to rise. Before long the three statues began to lift slightly and move, knocking against each other and the rock and tree stump between which they were stacked. A few seconds later, a larger puddle that had formed a few feet above them on the slope crested and a sudden surge of water rushed down towards the river. Along its path, it swept across the pooling around Liam, Solveig and Quinn.

The rush of water separated them from one another and pushed away the rock that had kept them stacked against the tree trunk. With nothing holding him in place any longer, Liam slid sideways and dropped beneath the surface of the water for an instant, getting a face full of water, but then bobbed up, slowly rolling over to face the sky. He floated head first down the embankment and into the river, trying to keep the rain from filling his mouth and nose. As a result, he was unable to call for help, regardless of the fact that Summer would never have been able to hear him.

A few seconds later, Solveig followed suit. She had been stacked against Quinn at a sufficient angle so that she, too, slid under the water and quickly bobbed up facing the sky. As she moved slowly down the rivulet, head first like Liam, she collided with the rock that had washed away from its position of holding them secure. It was just enough to alter her direction, and then she continued on down the embankment feet first and into the river.

The ground under Quinn had been softened by the weight of both Liam and Solveig. He had been the first in the stack and was, therefore, positioned more perpendicular to the ground. When the water level rose high enough to dislodge him, there was no room behind him against the tree stump to rock back and forth. As a result, he simply rolled over face down, over the embankment head first and into the water. As he entered the river, though, a large branch that had been swept into the current further upstream barreled into Quinn's shoulder. It was pushed by the force of the water under one side of his body, and then glanced off, spinning him over to face the sky on its journey down the river with the other wreckage from the storm.

For what seemed like hours, but was in reality only about 30 or 40 minutes, Solveig, Liam and Quinn floated down the river in complete darkness with the rain falling in their faces. Their inability to see what was happening or where they were going was frightening, especially when they ran into a rock or a clump of branches. They could feel the vibrations as they struck these obstacles, but were unprepared each time it happened. Finally, the downpour abated to a light mist and then stopped altogether. The sun began to rise and lighten the sky.

"Liam," Solveig called out. "Where are you?"

"I'm here. I'm here," he shouted.

Her fear subsided at the sound of a friendly voice.

"Can you see me?" she called to him. "I'm over here."

"No, I can't see you," Liam answered. "I'm still trapped in this rock hard mud. From the sound of your voice, I'm about fifteen or twenty feet in front of you. Are you able to see anything?

"Only the night sky until just a few minutes ago. Now it's just the sky and the treetops, and only when I'm right under them. I've tried to rock back and forth, and every once in a while I can see a little more, but I'm afraid to rock too much. I may flip over."

"I tried that, too," said Liam. "You have to be careful that you don't get any water into the space between the shell and your face. I'm not sure how much space there is between our skin and this coating, probably not much. Whatever this stuff is, though, it may get filled with water and then I'm not sure we'd float anymore."

"Oh, no," said Solveig. "I hadn't thought about that." Great, she thought. One more thing to worry about.

"Do you know if Quinn followed us?" Liam asked.

"I can't see him – Oh, I guess that was stupid, since neither one of us can see anything. I thought I could hear him through the rain every once in a while. He was still making that odd noise. But the last time I heard anything was more than a few minutes ago. And now...I can't even hear that anymore."

For most of the time they had been washing down stream, the distance between Liam and Solveig had varied little. However, as Liam and Solveig were pulled by the current, Quinn was bounced from bank to bank by some of the rocks and debris that the other two missed. He was ricocheting from one side of the waterway to the other, and the gap between him and the other two had gradually increased.

As he moved diagonally across the current, he was often spun around and traveled feet first and then head first. Every once in a while he was rolled over face down, but almost immediately bobbed back face up. Overall, though, his progress down the river was slowed, and the distance between him and Liam and Solveig continued to grow.

By the time Summer woke up and discovered they were gone, they had already come upon the delta and its many tributaries. She would spend much time before she decided where they must have gone and started after them. By that time, they were well passed the beginning of the delta.

As they approached it, though, Liam was snagged on a branch that had fallen from the shore and was stuck in the current. He wavered back and forth between the main artery and a major run off, until Solveig came down the river. Unimpeded, she crashed into him. For a few seconds they both swirled in the eddies, nearly going off into separate streams. When she struck Liam she dislodged him.

As he spun away from the branch on which he had been stuck, he knocked into her side and pushed her away from the main artery. He spun once more and then drifted along next to her. Almost side-by-side, they drifted into the nearest run-off. The branch that had snagged Liam as well as several other smaller branches was slowly pulled from the ground and stretched almost three quarters of the way across the river's main flow. It nearly cut off access to the run-off down which Liam and Solveig were floating.

Several minutes after Liam and Solveig had been carried down one tributary, Quinn arrived at the same junction. By now smaller clumps of leaves and brush had been added to the dislodged branch and it had formed a small levee. As Quinn floated slowly along, he made contact with that same branch. His movement down the river had been slowed by his repeated collisions with rocks and branches, so he hit the blockage with much less force than that with which Solveig had struck and dislodged Liam.

Instead of getting caught up, or barging through it, he slid along the length of the cluster of branches as if being guided. At the end of the cluster he made contact head on with a large rock imbedded in the ground beneath the riverbed. He teetered for an instant as the current swept along either side of him. Just as he was about to tip towards the run-off after his friends, a large log came rushing down the river. It hit the strung out branches and leaves near the shore, jarring it loose. The entire chain of rubble came loose with it and jack-knifed like a train wreck, pushing Quinn down the main artery, away from Liam and Solveig.

As Quinn and the mass of debris drifted off several hundred yards, they ran into a number of smaller channels, where they were eventually separated. The debris split off to the right and left hand channels and Quinn was drawn into one of the center ones. By the time Summer came to the spot where she had to guess what direction her friends had possibly gone, Liam and Solveig were four miles downstream to the right, and Quinn was more than twelve miles away to the left.

Chapter thirteen

Summer raced down the narrow channel scanning the water as well as the shoreline. She moved with lightning speed into every niche and pool. There were so many cut offs, dead ends, loops, swamps and marshes, that she worried she would fly right past her friends. She needed to check every possibility, since she had no idea which way they could have gone.

"I should have stayed awake," she continued to berate herself. "I didn't take care of them. This is all my fault."

She swooped down on every object that bore even a remote resemblance to any one of the three. She had been traveling nearly an hour, inching her way down the river, sometimes backtracking, or reacting to some sound she thought might be one of them calling out to her. So far, she hadn't seen any sign at all that she had chosen the right path.

"Liam," she shouted. "Solveig. Quinn. Where are you? Someone, please! Answer me."

Whenever she came to another fork in the river, she drew on what had happened when she first faced this dilemma, and waited for a random branch or log to see what the natural direction of the current was. Sometimes it seemed to take forever for something to come along and provide her with a clue. Each time she followed the same path that the object took, and each time she hoped she was guessing right.

"What kind of place is this?" she moaned. "Why can't there be just one river? Who ever heard of so many streams? There are hundreds of them. This is insane." She was getting frantic.

Each time she came to another runoff, her confidence in her choice eroded further and further. By midday she was sure she had chosen the wrong direction. She was torn between continuing and possibly losing them forever and doubling back to take one of the other tributaries...and what, she asked herself. Losing them forever? It was not much of a choice.

After what felt like the hundredth divergence, she entertained this debate one more time. The question now was how far back should she go and what cutoff should she follow. She had shouted out names until she was hoarse. On the verge of tears she scolded herself and told herself to stay strong. Her friends needed her and she vowed to find them.

"Pull yourself together," she chastised herself. "You're a Princess of the faeries. You've faced hard decisions before and you will again."

She flew down to the water level and landed on a large leaf. All the time she had spent searching, and the anxiety she was feeling at her repeated failure to find even the remotest clue had taken its toll. She needed to rest and to take some time to think. In spite of her pep talk, a wave of desperation flooded over her, and she screamed, "Noooo!" Her voice was muffled by the foliage on either side of the channel, but was carried forward downstream. It echoed back to her.

Wait, she thought. I just heard an echo. There was nothing to cause an echo. She looked to either side of the river — nothing but vegetation. There were no rocks or walls to have created an echo.

"Hello," she shouted.

She held her breath and waited for a response. She was too close to the water. The sound of the river flowing in and around the rocks was making too much noise. She bolted up and shot forward like an arrow, shouting for Liam, Solveig and Quinn. Then she heard it again.

"That's no echo," she said as a jolt of energy shot through her.

She shouted again and again she got an answer. This time she clearly heard her name being called, but she still couldn't see the source. It sounded like Solveig. She screamed her friend's name and waited for a response. This time it was closer. She flew like a madwoman calling out Solveig's name every few seconds.

She came up to another split in the current. She was about to take the right fork again, but shouted once more. The response was down the right channel. She immediately took off and kept to the right. This time when she shouted Solveig's name, she heard Liam call back to her instead, but it seemed a little further away than she had expected it. Solveig must have gone down the other stream. She continued to call for Liam and finally caught up with him. In fact she flew right over his head and had to turn back when he called after her.

"Back here," he shouted as he saw her fly past. "I'm back here. Look down."

"I'm sorry, I'm sorry, I'm sorry," she pleaded, as she spun around, hovering over his face only inches above him.

At the same time he shouted with joy, "You found us, you found us, you found us. I thought for sure no one would ever find us. You can't imagine how good it is to see you."

They were talking over one another until she realized he was alone. Her head popped up and spun to the left and right.

"Where's Solveig," she demanded.

"I don't know. We could hear each other, but we couldn't see each other. Sometimes she was close by, but other times she seemed to fall behind. She must be close by. She was just here. I was just talking to her. Can't you see her? What about Quinn? Have you seen Quinn?"

"No," Summer answered. "I've only seen you, but I heard Solveig a few minutes ago. I'm sure of it. I don't see her, though. Quinn either. I don't see Quinn. Are you sure he was with you?"

"No. He was still unconscious. We were never sure he was anywhere near us. We need to stop going any further. Is there any way you can push me to the bank? Just park me so you can find Solveig." he said.

"I think so," she answered. "Let me find a good spot. Wait, I think I see one not too much further."

As soon as she saw a clearing up ahead, she maneuvered him over to it. Before she moved him toward the shore, she made sure it wasn't the same kind of mud in which he had been encased. When she determined it was just sand, and safe sand, she raised him with some faerie dust and beached him on dry land.

"Now what?" she asked.

"Leave me here and go back to find Solveig. She can't be too far away. We were talking to each other until just a little while ago. We must have gotten separated not too far back. Hurry."

"Are you sure?"

"Yes, I'm sure. Just go. I'm not going anywhere. I'll be all right for a little while. And, besides, you know exactly where to find me."

Before he had even finished his sentence, Summer raced back the way she had come until she reached the last cutoff. She skidded to a stop in midair. She looked around to see how many separate run-offs there were. Seeing only one, she turned in that direction and charged down the other waterway, shouting Solveig's name.

"I hope she didn't get separated farther back than this," she muttered. "Liam said he could hear her up until just a little while ago. This just has to be the fork she went down."

She shouted Solveig's name every few seconds. She was racing now, not taking any time to examine every possible inlet or cluster of overhanging branches. In a few minutes she heard Solveig calling back to her and in short order she caught up with her. Using a bit more faerie magic, she reversed Solveig's course and steered her back up the stream around the turn-off and into the same clearing where Liam was parked. She was so excited she was nearly in tears.

"I can't believe you found us," Solveig said, her voice shaking. "I was certain we'd never see you again. And when I got separated from Liam..." She was choked with emotion. She swallowed, took a deep breath, and asked, her voice still cracking, "Did you see Quinn?"

"No," answered Summer, "but now that you two are safe, I'll go back to try and find him."

"No," said Liam.

Summer and Solveig were shocked. What was he saying? How could he not want to help find his friend?

"What do you mean?" demanded Summer. "Now that I've found both of you, and you're safe on land, I can go back and search for Quinn. I know I can find him. We can't just leave him out there."

"Solveig and I can't stay here. We're too exposed and we can't protect ourselves. Even if you hide us some place or cover us over, there would be nothing we could to if someone or some thing found us. If you leave us behind we won't last through the night. If you put us back in the water, you'll never find us again. Your finding us this time was pure luck."

"What are we supposed to do, then? Just leave him?" Summer asked, unable to believe he was asking her to do that.

"Yes," Liam answered. "For now. Once we get to the Sea Sprites' island, Stella may be able to find him much faster, and Natalie can send out an army to find him. I understand how hard this is. He's my friend, too. But think about it, Summer. It was a miracle you found us."

They knew he was right, but it pained them to admit it. They also knew it was breaking his heart to tell Summer that she should not make an attempt to find Quinn and that they had to leave him behind.

"We need to find a way to get free from these casings," he continued. "And we need to find help. Until we do both of these things we can't have any hope of finding or helping Quinn."

"He's right, Summer," Solveig finally admitted. Tears were running down her cheeks.

"All right. I don't like it, but all right," Summer finally said. "Just tell me. What do we do next?"

"See if you can find some vines to tie us together. Look for ones that are thin and green. You'll have an easier time braiding them together to make them strong. You can make a kind of raft out of us by tying us together. That should also keep us from getting separated again."

She was about to fly off and look for suitable vines, when he stopped her.

"Two more things. See if you can find a branch – one that you could handle but is wide and maybe a bit flat at one end. We'll not make the same mistake I made with the first raft. We're going to have a rudder on this one. You'll be able to steer us. And then see if you could find two other branches – a long one and another one about half as long. Oh, and some large leaves. I guess that's more than two things. Oh, and see if you can find some food. Anything."

Summer and Solveig had no idea what Liam had in mind, but Summer flew off in search of the items he described. Along the way she came across some nuts and berries, which she brought back and gave to them to eat.

"Oh, thank you so much," Solveig said. "I hadn't realized how hungry I was."

Summer had to feed them individually, like a pair of babies.

"I'm starving," Liam said, munching on some nuts, "but this can wait. Find the vines – oh, but be careful. There may be some plants that are poisonous. Honeysuckle vines would be best."

Liam explained to her how to tell the difference between the poisonous plants and the ones that were safe. As she sought out the vines, she hoped she hadn't given her friends any berries that would knock them out – or worse. She found a grove of honeysuckle vines and brought back several of them. Liam told her how to intertwine them, like braids, to make them stronger. When she described how much rope she had made, he told her that was a good start, and had her find some more.

When she had enough, and had constructed several lengths of braided ropes, she lashed them together, side-by-side.

"At least I won't have to shout to have you hear me," he said to Solveig, whose head was now right next to his.

"I just hope you don't snore," she joked.

When Summer brought back the shorter limb, Liam had her tie it with more vines between his and Solveig's ankles. It took several attempts for her to get the knots right. Liam told her it had to be knotted in such a way that the rudder could be moved up and down – in and out of the water. He couldn't see the branch she had selected, but from her description, it sounded perfect. The part that stuck out over the water was only an inch or two high – just the right size for Summer to be able to maneuver. It twisted almost a full ninety degrees and fanned out to make a suitable rudder.

"At least now you'll be able to steer us," he told her.

She found some Banchu leaves, which by her standards were enormous. They were also very strong leaves. She brought back as many as she could find and he had her lace them together with the thinnest lengths of honeysuckle vines in the shape of a large triangle. He told her to hold on to the ones left over. They'd probably come in handy for something later on.

"What's this supposed to be," she asked, "a blanket? It's a pretty strange looking blanket."

"A sail," he corrected. "Now take the long, narrow branch, and tie it between our arms. Tie the shorter branch near the top. Now, attach the sail. Put the point at the bottom of the sail and run the base of the triangle across the top branch. It's not the best, but it should do just fine."

When all of this was done, Summer had fashioned a very serviceable raft out of her friends, complete with a rudder, a mast and a sail. She then launched them into the water She dropped the rudder into the water and steered them down the river following the current.

"I'm sure this is going to empty out into a larger body of water," Liam told her. "That's when the sail will be needed."

For the time being she just steered them along the river, trying to avoid rocks and logs, but not being too successful. Never having sailed a raft before, it took her a little bit of practice to get the hang of it. As large rocks appeared in the stream, she pointed the tiller in the direction she thought she should steer the raft, only to find that it went in the opposite direction.

"Oh, sorry," she said, cringing as she steered Solveig's head right into a huge boulder, nearly stopping the raft completely.

"That's all right," Solveig answered, thankful that she hadn't bitten her tongue off. "It didn't hurt that much. I mean it was a bit jarring, and my teeth seemed to rattle, but my head is all right. This stuff seems to be really hard."

"I don't know what happened," Summer added, still apologetic. "I pointed this handle thing to the right to steer it away from that rock, but you all just turned left. Did you do that or did I?"

Liam explained how the tiller – that handle thing – worked; how it moved the rudder; and how the rudder steered the raft. It still took a few more cracks on a number of rocks before she adapted. She ran into things equally, bashing Liam almost as often as she did Solveig.

As the sun began to set, Liam's prediction came true. The river emptied out into a larger body of water. In fact, the current of the river, as it exited the delta, was so strong, that they seemed to be racing. Once they passed the mouth of the delta, the sea spread out before them in all directions as far as the eye could see. Summer had never seen so much water before. She had seen the Cerulean Sea before, but always from the shore. Now the shore had disappeared behind her and there was only water.

"Oh, my uncle's elbow," she said, repeating an ancient faerie saying. She had no idea what it meant or referred to but her mother had said it whenever she didn't know what else to say, which seemed to Summer to be all of the time. It seemed the only appropriate thing she could think of.

"There's no land – anywhere," she said more than a bit apprehensively. "How are we...what are we...how...how..."

"Relax," Liam told her. "Just put up the sail and keep steering."

"Yeah, sail...up...and steer," she said, nearly too stunned to do anything but stammer, "But steer where."

"I'll tell you," Liam said.

"Oh, great. This coming from someone who can't see where we're going. Why am I not filled with confidence?"

And on they sailed into the night. A light breeze filled the sail of leaves, which held quite nicely. The storm of the previous night had cleared out completely and the night sky was filled with millions of brilliant stars. The moon was nearly full and soon rose high in the sky. Since this was all Solveig could see from her vantage point, it made her think about Lochen.

"Where are you when I need you," she thought. "I hope you're in a safer place than this."

A gentle breeze remained constant and the odd-looking vessel move easily across the sea. Periodically Liam would tell Summer to steer to the left or right. She looked up to the stars, wondering if he was using them as a guide. They all just looked like random pinholes of light. She had no idea how he was reading the stars, if he really knew where to go, or if he was just making this up to make her feel safe, but she didn't question him and steered as he directed.

The next morning the lead sun rose early and was shining brightly in the sky by the time the second sun rose. Summer looked behind her to where the delta had been the evening before. With no landmarks whatsoever, she wasn't even sure which way the delta had been. She began to feel a sense of panic. To control herself, she stared straight ahead, past the sail and hugged the rudder handle. By midmorning Solveig and Liam were getting hot and were very thirsty.

"Gee, I'm sorry," Summer said, "I should have thought of that. Next time, just let me know."

She started to scoop up some of the water that surrounded them in one of the leaves left over from making the sail.

"No," said Liam. "That's salt water. It will only make us very sick. In fact, it could kill us. It's like poison."

"Really?" asked Summer. "I thought this was the Cerulean Sea."

"It is," said Liam. "The Cerulean Sea is salt water."

"I don't understand," said Summer. "We drink that all the time. It's our main source of water. No one ever gets sick."

"Yes," Liam pointed out, "and you're faeries. You can drink salt water. We can't."

That night the sea wasn't quite as calm as it was the night before. There was no storm, but the swells rose and fell several feet. The tiny raft would shoot to the top of a large wave, hang there for a second or two, and then drop like a rock to the valley where it would stop suddenly before rocketing to the top of the next wave.

The motion made Summer sick and dizzy. The first few times this happened, she was seized with fear. She wasn't able to fly above it all. She held tightly to the tiller and stared straight ahead. Focusing on the drastically changing horizon only seemed to make it worse. She tried squeezing her eyes shut, but the anticipation just exaggerated the sensation even more. Finally, she just focused on her feet as she sat on Liam's legs and stretched her legs out in front of her.

When the motion became extreme, she slumped over the rudder handle and every once in a while threw up over the side. It seemed to her like she was throwing up every five minutes. This went on throughout the night until the Sea finally settled down just before dawn. By morning she was drained. She needed to rest. Solveig and Liam were equally drained. Their lips were drying out and cracking and their throats were swelling, making swallowing painful.

On the afternoon of the third day Summer was aroused from a fitful sleep when the sunlight beating down on her flickered. She could sense a fluttering motion that blocked out the sun. The sudden motion set off alarm bells in her head. She shielded her eyes as she looked into the sky to see what was causing it.

"Oh, poop," she whispered, afraid to alarm Liam and Solveig.

She came immediately fully awake when she spotted three Blue Falcons circling high above them. She quickly looked around to see if they were near land; hoping it was within sight. But all she saw was the ever-present water – not even a hint of dry land. She knew Blue Falcons could fly for days, but she had hoped they might have been closer to shore.

She curled up into a ball to make herself as small as possible. The Falcons had extremely sharp eyesight, and she knew she made a tempting and tasty target. She carefully slid between Liam's ankles and lowered herself into the water alongside the rudder. She debated about calling out to Solveig and Liam, but knew there was nothing they could do. They had fallen asleep shortly after she gave them the last of the berries she had gathered. She had then placed some leaves over their faces early that morning to help them sleep and to protect them from the sun. She hoped the leaves would keep the Falcons from attacking Liam and Solveig.

With just her head above the water, Summer tried to stay as motionless as possible. She was able to do that until she felt something touch her feet. At first she thought it might have been a piece of seaweed. Then it happened again, and this time it felt more like she be being nibbled on.

"Oh, faerie momma," she gasped, involuntarily.

The Blue Falcons were alerted to the sound. They altered their circling pattern and swooped down towards the raft. She took in a deep breath and plunked her head under water to take a look. She came face to face with a large grouper, apparently out looking for an afternoon snack. She thrust her arm forward angrily, and, shoving with all her might, poked the fish in the eye. It immediately swam out of sight, deciding wisely not to tangle with an irate faerie.

The sudden movement of Summer ducking underwater altered the Falcons and told them that the object floating below them was a potential prey. The lead bird moved quickly into attack mode and dive-bombed straight downward. The other two followed closely behind. Its razor sharp beak was open and ready to scoop up a tasty morsel and struck Liam head on.

The Falcon, assuming the leaves covered dirt or rock, headed instead for the location of the movement it had spotted out of the corner of its eye. It aimed for a spot next to the tiller near Liam's foot. The beak struck with such force that it would have been able to pierce something even as hard as a turtle's shell. The hardened mud, however, was more like granite.

The Falcon's beak snapped, cracking in half up the middle. The intense pain sent it off screeching. The second one had started its attack immediately behind the first one. It, too, assumed that the leaves covered dirt or rock. It focused on the shimmering of some drops of water that had collected over Solveig's stomach.

It heard the crack and screech of its partner too late to pull out of its attack. It ran its beak into the center of Solveig's body with a similar result. Having turned its head just slightly at the sound of agony coming from the first bird, it hit the hardened mud at a slight angle. The point of its beak shattered and its body smashed down on top of Solveig.

The third one thought it saw Summer's head pop out of the water right next to the point of attack of the first bird, but decided that it was either a trick of the light, or, that the tiny morsel wasn't worth the risk. In either case, it joined the other two, immediately pulling up and aborting it attack. It flew off to the right trying to catch up to its wailing partners, and took a last look over its shoulder, positive it could see something in the water staring back at them.

Summer poked her head out of the water, no longer concerned about the grouper, and watched the birds fly off. I'll bet they're headed for their nest, she thought. And I'll bet that nest is on land. She immediately altered her course for that direction. Blue Falcons or not, she thought, there just has to be land in that direction. Right about now, she felt her chances with a whole nest of nasty Blue Falcons was much preferable to more time on the water.

The thump on Solveig brought Liam out of his fog. When he opened his eyes, everything was dark – not black like the night, but a deep shade of green.

"What's happening?" he rasped. "What's on my face?"

"Don't worry," said Summer as she climbed up out of the water. "I did that. It's just a leaf. I put it on your face to protect you from the sun."

She lifted it from his face, but didn't take it off completely. She held it up so he could see her, but still kept the sun out of his eyes. Even so, he blinked and squinted at the sudden change in light.

"I thought I heard a screech. Was it a Blue Falcon?" he asked.

His voice croaked painfully. He was so thirsty it hurt to talk. It almost hurt to breathe. It was painful for Summer just to listen to him.

"Yes," Summer answered, "but it's gone now. Everything is fine. Don't talk. Save your strength."

"Summer," he said, his voice barely above a whisper, "I don't know how much longer I can last."

"You'll be fine," she said with false bravado. "We have to be close to land. Just hang on a little longer. I changed course to follow the Falcons. Don't worry," she told him when she saw that he was about to object. "After the damage the two of them did to themselves, I don't think we're going to be a target. Besides, if they lead us to land, I'll be willing to take that chance."

He seemed to either agree or he just didn't have the energy to argue. He didn't say a word. As he closed his eyes, she covered his face once more with the leaf. She lifted the one on Solveig's face and looked at her closely. She was more worried about Solveig than Liam. Solveig hadn't spoken or even stirred since early this morning. Summer knew that if they didn't reach land soon, none of them would survive.

Chapter fourteen

Stella had spent several hours in the archives, in spite of her rumbling stomach and her seemingly endless state of fatigue. She had found a few vague references to the creatures she thought she had seen in her last vision, but nothing that provided her with clear answers. She had found some information about creatures that lived beneath the earth, but some of it reflected them as guardians of the balance of nature, and other references indicated that they were minions of some evil lord.

So much of the ancient writings were based on myths and oral traditions, it was hard to tell what was accurate and what was just folklore developed to scare the little ones into behaving. She needed to discuss her findings with Princess Natalie, but the Princess had not yet returned from her hasty departure to Eastern Outpost Five.

Not knowing what else to do, Stella got something to eat, and then took a short rest before she returned to the Sanctorum. Once there, she tried casting a number of different spells. One thing she had discovered in the archives quite by accident was a reference book to spells and incantations she had long forgotten and a few she didn't even know. She took a few minutes trying to bring up visions using her traditional methods.

First, she focused on Natalie. The images she was able to bring forth were inconsistent, fading in an out. Whenever they stabilized, they were mostly a blur and didn't tell her anything more than they had before. She wasn't sure if the problem was with her, or if something was interfering with her connection to the Princess.

She cleared her mind and turned her thoughts to Lochen. This time the visions were even more confusing than the last time. The swirling stars had been replaced by flashes of light, and the black of space had been replaced by ghost-like colors. Her first reaction was to dismiss what she was seeing, but then she recalled some discussions she had with him about space clouds. He had described these formations that were of unimaginable size and were the home of complete solar systems, as well as such things as black holes and something to do with worms. It had quickly become more complicated than she could follow, but she recalled the references to the clouds.

"He must be in the heart of a gaseous…what did he call it…a nebula?" Stella thought out loud. "Why would he even get close to such a thing? I was certain he said those could be dangerous."

At that very instant the image she had of Lochen changed radically. It became greatly distorted – as if someone was pulling on the corner of a picture. His face and body were stretched beyond recognition. All the colors blended together and were dragged to one corner only to disappear altogether.

"This is useless," Stella thought. "I have no idea if that is reality or some other kind of transmission distortion. Let me see if I can find the others."

She again cleared her mind and focused on Summer, Solveig, Liam and Quinn. Her prior visions had given her no reason to imagine them together. However, that same vision seemed to somehow link them. As she concentrated, all she could see was Summer floating on some kind of odd looking raft. There was water all around, whereas before, it appeared that she had been on or near a river. There was no sign of Quinn, Liam or Solveig. This confused Stella. She was sure they had been together before, or at least in near proximity to one another. What could have happened to cause them to separate? What was going on?

"This is not working," she said to herself, highly frustrated.

She left the Sanctorum and headed for her laboratory. If she couldn't raise any understandable images, she could at least put her time to good use.   She then went about gathering the ingredients needed in conjunction with some of the incantations and spells she recently discovered. It was an unusual assortment of herbs and magical powders and liquids.

It had taken only her one reading of the different formulas to commit them to memory. Even so, she didn't want to rely solely on her memory. She waved her hand and a copy of the exact recipes appeared suspended in the air in front of her. She had to be very careful in mixing them together, since even the smallest amounts could alter the result dramatically. The amounts, proportions and the order in which they should be mixed were very precise.

She worked quickly and steadily, paying close attention to what she was doing. She mixed several different elixirs. As she finished with one, before moving on to the next, she put them into tiny vials, and placed them in the pockets of her gown. She didn't expect she would need all of them, or any of them, for that matter, but just wanted to be prepared for any event.

When she finished, she thought she would try to reestablish the visual connections with Natalie and the others. She was hurrying back to the Sanctorum when she was approached by a messenger. The Princess had returned and had summoned the Enchantress, she was informed by the messenger. Stella was a bit puzzled at first. She couldn't understand why she had been unable to reestablish her vision of Natalie when, in fact, she had been so close.

Have I been in the laboratory that long, she wondered. She never consulted timepieces of any kind. Time was usually irrelevant to her. However, she was too glad to hear of Natalie's return to give it much more attention. She left all thought of returning to the Sanctorum and headed for the Princess's antechamber.

"Your Highness," she said immediately upon seeing Natalie. Her excitement was cut short when she saw the look of concern on the Princess's face.

"Is something wrong?" she asked.

Natalie didn't answer right away. Even in the privacy of the antechamber, there was too much of a chance of being overheard. The palace had few doors, and voices often carried – even whispered voices. Natalie didn't want to keep information from her subjects, but she didn't want to create panic unnecessarily, and for now, she herself just didn't have enough information.

"I'm not sure," she eventually responded to Stella. "Please accompany me. I'd like to walk along the shore."

This had long been a code between them, even when they had lived in the bubble at the bottom of the sea. It meant that the Princess had a problem or needed to sort things out, and she needed the Enchantress' help and guidance. It also meant that the matter was serious or personal, and that they needed to have their discussion in complete privacy. They long ago discovered that the best place for a private conversation was in plain sight. They could stroll along the beach, far enough away from anyone to hear, but clearly visible to anyone who looked their way.

The island they had moved their community to was shaped like a large tear drop with the tail end of the drop stretched out and down. The main part of the island was parallel to the shore of the main body of land, not far from the edge of the woods where the forest creatures lived and just north of the village of the faeries. A channel of less than a mile separated the island from the shore. The extended tail curved out into the Cerulean Sea, nearly perpendicular to the main island and the shore. It was a very private area, but it was also one of the most beautiful places on the island. The Princess and the Enchantress headed that way now.

- - - - - - - - - - - - - - - - - *** - - - - - - - - - - - - - - - - - -

Summer felt like the entire faerie army was marching inside her head and that everyone was out of step. She was hot and uncomfortable and very, very tired. There had been a light rain the night before and she had used some of the leaves from the sail to make small funnels so that Liam and Solveig could get some water.

Both of them were only partially conscious. By the time she had been able to tend to herself, the brief rain had stopped. The respite from the beating heat of the twin suns lasted only a few minutes. Although she had plenty of water, since she could drink the sea's salt water, she couldn't recall the last time any of them had anything to eat. And she couldn't recall the last time she had been able to rest for more than a few minutes at a time.

The Blue Falcons hadn't returned, but she really didn't care much if they did. She was sure that there wasn't enough left of her or her friends to make much of a meal for the birds. The air temperature changed only slightly between the night and the day, but without any shade or clouds in the sky, the suns beating down on her were also becoming unbearable. She had lost track of how long they had been sailing. One day just blended into the next.

In the late afternoon of whatever day it was, she thought she saw land off to her right. At first she thought her eyes were just playing tricks on her. It was there one minute and gone the next. She was so worn out, that she didn't realize that it was obscured by the gentle waves. She shielded her eyes the next time it appeared, and then summoned the energy to fly to the top of the mast to get a better look.

"It's land," she said.

She knew she should have been excited, and a part of her was. She even smiled briefly. But she didn't know if this was good or bad, considering the last time she and her friends set foot on the ground. It didn't make any difference, though. She couldn't do anything to get to the land. There was no breeze, so the sail was hanging limp and she was too exhausted and too small to steer the rudder. Because of her exhaustion, she hadn't been able to regenerate faerie dust. All she could do was to hold on to the tiller, sway with it as the water moved it, and follow the current.

Over the next few hours, the mass of land seemed to grow, but not get much closer. The sandy, barren coastline was gradually replaced with hills and vegetation and then by cliffs, rocks and trees. She was half daydreaming and remembering when she first met Sean. She had been chasing something, but she couldn't remember what, when he suddenly appeared.

"It was a grasshopper," she mumbled. She had been talking to herself aloud for the last few days. "Or maybe it was a dragonfly. I really don't remember."

She had never seen a forest creature before, and he was nothing like she had expected. He had been so open and so inquisitive, that it was hard to be afraid of him. Their friendship had quickly developed and they began to meet secretly, since their respective people had a long history of distrust and conflict. Finally they had decided to meet in a cave in the cliffs along the shore of the Cerulean Sea.

She opened one bleary eye and looked towards the distant shore.

"It was a cave in a cliff, just like that one," she said out loud to no one in particular, pointing toward the shore.

She kept thinking about her clandestine meetings with Sean in the cave in the cliffs as she kept staring at the distant shoreline. It moved in and out of focus. She opened her other bleary eye to get a clearer look. The horizon slowly came into focus. She then sat bolt upright to look at it head on.

"I know this place," she said. As her awareness sharpened, she stood up on her tip toes.

"I know this place," she shouted and began to jump up and down repeating the statement.

She flew over Liam's face and tapped his nose, again shouting, "I know this place."

She pealed back one eyelid with no result. She lowered herself closer to his ear and shouted, "Hey. I said I know this place."

When she still didn't get any reaction she flew over to Solveig and did the same thing.

"Come on, you guys," she pleaded. "Don't give up on me now. I know where we are."

She flew up a few feet above the raft and shouted at the top of her lungs, "I know this place!!!"

For the first time luck seemed to be going her way. The tide was now headed in towards shore and had gradually picked up. The raft moved closer to land on an inward wave, and then backed away as the wave returned to the sea. As the trio floated past the cliffs, the islands and sand bars that dotted the shoreline began to appear. Summer's excitement abated, but only for an instant.

"Oh, no," she said, still talking to herself, "we can't get stuck on one of these sand bars now. I can't believe this. If it wasn't for bad luck, we wouldn't have any luck at all!"

With renewed energy, and feeling a slight breeze, she put all her strength into maneuvering the rudder and steering them back out into the sea. She didn't want to get too far away, but she had to make sure they didn't get beached on a sand bar – not this close to safety. The wind picked up just enough for her to clear the smaller islets. Before long one of the larger islands off the shore came into view. Another wave of excitement shot through her.

"I know this place, too," she shouted. "Solveig! Liam! We're going to make it. I know this place, too!"

This was the island the Sea Sprites had made their new home. She was sure of it. She could see the peninsula that curved out to sea and behind it the main island rose up. She remembered the channel that ran between the shore of the main land and the island. It was a deep trough that was deceivingly mild. At high tide, which is what had just started, the undertow in this channel created all sorts of mixed currents and eddies. There were a number of large rocks that were visible at low tide, but just beneath the surface at high tide. They made this channel extremely treacherous. If she got drawn in there she wouldn't be able to handle the makeshift craft and all three of them could end up sucked into the channel or would crash on the shore or on the hidden rocks.

She used all the strength that remained in her to push the rudder against the current. The long peninsula at the end of the island that formed the beginning of the channel was fast approaching. She needed to be to the left of that peninsula, but the breeze and the current had more strength than she did. They were pushing her to the right. With each wave that hit the rudder, the tiller was jerked from her hand. She was losing the battle. They were headed straight for the channel.

Even before Natalie and Stella reached their destination, they both started talking – sharing their recent experiences and information.

"Something's not right," said Natalie. "I can't exactly describe it, but I noticed it first when I went back to the bubble. I saw the same thing when I visited the Eastern Outpost Five. But you probably already know that."

"No, your Highness. My connection with you was lost or distorted. I couldn't get any clear visions."

Natalie stopped short and turned to Stella. This had never happened before and it only added to Natalie's sense of foreboding. She was upset that Stella had been back to the Sanctorum so soon after her efforts at resurrecting the memories of the ancient Enchantresses, but she was reluctant to scold her.

"I had disturbing visions of Lochen and Sean as well," Stella continued. "I know that they are traveling to distant places, but Lochen and I had cast spells on the transporting stone he was using. We should have been able to keep in contact with each other. I'm concerned that they are in danger, but I'm helpless to do anything."

Natalie could feel the anxiety in Stella's voice and her mood darkened. She looked back the way they had come and saw that they were still too close to populated areas.

"Come. We need to be more private," and she led the Enchantress further along the shoreline. "Let's go out to the promontory."

When they were a safer distance, Natalie continued their talk as they moved further along the beach and out to the end of the peninsula.

"What about Solveig and Summer?" she asked. "Weren't they traveling together? Had they gone too far for you to have made contact with them?"

"Yes, Your Highness, they were together – on the north side of the forest – still within reach. And at some point it appears that they met with Liam and Quinn."

"Quinn?" Natalie asked. "What would bring him so far from the Ice Kingdom? Could you discern anything?"

"No. In fact in my vision it seemed like they were all together – at least for a while. Then things became...I'm not sure how to explain it...strange is the only word I can come up with."

Stella proceeded to fill Natalie in on the turmoil she had envisioned. She described the disjointed visions of Lochen and Sean, and the extreme distortion at the end of the last vision. She explained how Summer, Solveig, Liam and Quinn appeared to be together and then they were not. Finally, she told her about the other images that had appeared – the small white creatures.

Natalie answered excitedly, "I saw them, too – well only a glimpse of them. They moved so fast they were only a blur."

"What should we do, Your Highness?" Stella asked as they reached the end of the shoreline.

"I'm not sure," she answered. "I need some time to think. I need to sort all this out."

This had always been a good place for her to think, so that's what she did as she looked out over the sea.

Summer was pushing the rudder with every ounce of strength, but she knew she was fighting against the inevitable. She had been pulling on it previously, but quickly saw that she didn't have the strength to fight the sea, so she changed her position. She had dug her toes into the vines wrapped around Solveig's and Liam's feet and was standing at nearly a 45 degree angle, extending her body its full 3 inches, arms outstretched to add another half inch, pushing against the tiny handle of the rudder. For the last several minutes she had held this position until her arms, back and legs were screaming with pain, when suddenly the resistance she had been fighting so hard against disappeared.

It happened so fast and so unexpectedly that the rudder swung completely around in its restraints. As a result, Summer flew out over the back end of the raft and hung by her fingertips from the tiller, dangling over the sea, which seemed to be dropping from under her. The shock of the change and her position, made her forget that she could let go and fly. Instead, she swung her legs up and wrapped them around the rudder handle, pulled herself tightly to it, hugging it to her body, and hung on for dear life. She closed her eyes and held her breath waiting for the crash.

Her first thought was that the bindings had come undone and the tide had carried Liam and Solveig off in different directions and thrown her high into the air. When she didn't feel the anticipated drop, she opened one eye to take a peek. She looked down, expecting to see the sea come rushing up at her. It wasn't close at all. In fact, it was several feet below her.

"What the what?" she muttered in complete astonishment.

Something had lifted the three of them up out of the sea, Solveig and Liam still tied together, and was gently floating them through the air to the stretch of sand near the end tip of the peninsula. The craft was lowered to the sand in the shallow waters along the shore of a long sand bar. Once they were safely down, the rudder swung back into place, carrying Summer back over Liam's ankles. As she put one foot down tentatively, Summer could hear her name being called. She dared to open the other eye and saw two familiar figures running towards her.

"Summer," shouted Natalie and Stella, as they ran up. "Are you all right? What are you doing here? What happened to Solveig and Liam? How did you get here? Where's Quinn?"

They were both talking at the same time. Summer was overwhelmed to see them and to finally be safe. She was too stunned to answer their questions and instead taking in her surroundings, could only ask, "What just happened?"

"Stella and I often come out here when we need a private place to talk and to think," answered Natalie.

"Yes," interjected Stella, "And then we started to watch what we thought were old tree trunks headed into the channel and thought how odd they looked. Then we saw you pushing...whatever that thing is."

"Stella was the one who recognized you," said Natalie.

"Oh, you're too kind, your Highness," interrupted Stella, "I'm certain you saw them first."

"Yes, I think I did, but I said, 'what is that odd looking thing in the water? It looks like it's headed right for the channel. But I think it was you who identified Summer."

"I don't like to correct Your Highness, but I really believe..."

"OK, OK," Summer cut in. "Who cares who saw what first? What happened?"

"Oh," said Natalie.

"Once we could see that it was you, the Princess cast a spell and raised you out of the water and placed you on the shore," Stella finally answered. "But how did you get here and what happened to Solveig and Liam?"

Summer filled them in briefly and described the slime that had engulfed and encased her two companions and everything that happened from that point until now.

"Ah, of course," said Stella. "I've seen this before."

And she placed one hand on the amulet around her neck and the other on Liam's head. She mumbled a few words that were incomprehensible to

Summer and the casing around Liam dissolved into the sand beneath him. It was gone completely. She did the same thing to Solveig and in a few seconds she, too, was finally released. Stella then took one of the vials from her pocket and poured a few drops into each of their mouths and slowly but surely, they returned to consciousness.

"They should be all right once we get them some food and water," announced Stella, whose comments were barely heard by any of them.

As Liam and Solveig sat up, everyone began talking at once, each as excited as the other to be together and to be safe. They exchanged hugs and held each other closely. Natalie and Stella were helping Liam and Solveig to their feet, and were preparing to take them back to the palace. Their conversations were suddenly interrupted by a blinding flash of light, an ear splitting clap of thunder, and a loud splash. They all turned as one to look out behind them.

On a tiny spit of a sand bar just a few inches below the surface of the water and about twenty feet off the shore of the peninsula sat a peculiar looking object. It was about ten feet long and a little more than three feet high. Once the surprise of its sudden appearance wore off, the five standing on the shore could see that it was a large bubble on an even larger flat stone. Inside the bubble were two totally bewildered travelers.

"Well," said Lochen, "that wasn't exactly where I expected to land, but I suppose it will have to do. I can see I'm going to have to make some adjustments to my control panel. It needs some slight re-calibration."

Sean popped his head up, having landed flat on the floor of their craft.

"We're safe?" he shouted as he asked the question.

Not waiting for an answer, he jumped up, danced in tiny circles and shouted, "We made it; we made it; we're home safe. I'm never ever getting in this thing again. It's been fun, but never again. Never! Not ever!"

He kissed Lochen on the top of his head and jumped out of the pod running to the shore of the peninsula. The sandbar that they had landed on, however, was on a shelf at the very tip of a narrow pinnacle. It did not extend as far out as Sean had jumped. Consequently, he landed in water that was more than twenty feet deep. Since forest creatures are not particularly fond of water, and since they usually can't swim very well, Sean panicked.

As soon as he popped up for air, he shouted, "Help. Someone save me. I hate water."

His head dropped under the water momentarily. When it broke the surface again, Lochen calmly reached over the side, grabbed a handful of Sean's hair and yanked him back into the pod.

"Ouch," shouted Sean, sputtering and spitting out water. "That hurt."

Lochen just stared at him as Sean gasped for air. Realizing he was back in the pod he again panicked and started to back away. He backed out of the pod tripping into the water on the other side, again sinking into water well over his head. Lochen moved to reach out to him and grab another handful of hair, but reconsidered. This time he decided to let Sean figure his own way out. He turned back to his console and with some minor adjustments and movements, steered the transporter stone and bubble to the shore, joining Stella, Natalie, Summer, Liam and Solveig.

"Welcome back," Stella said giving him a big hug. "I thought for a while we had lost you."

"For a while you did," he replied.

"Hey," said Liam. "Is anybody going to help Sean out?"

Sean's head was bobbing in and out of the water, his arms flailing until he reached out and grabbed a piece of driftwood that was floating nearby. He pulled his head up out of the water and gulped in the air.

"No," responded Lochen. "He'll be all right. Besides, I've been listening to him complain for far too long. I'm actually quite fine with his declaration that he never wants to travel again. He's not at all a satisfactory traveling companion."

Sean wrapped his arms around the driftwood and started kicking towards shore, all the time mumbling loud enough for all to hear, "I heard that. Wait until they hear what I had to put up with. I hate water. I hate water."

Before long he stumbled onto the shore, still clutching the driftwood, which was considerably larger than he was – almost twice his size. He struggled as he dragged it in the sand, refusing to let it go. He staggered with it held tightly in his arms, up to the group who was watching his arrival and then finally let it go to drop into the sand.

"Well, don't I get a hug?" he complained when no one moved to greet him.

Everyone's eyes were riveted on the large piece of driftwood he had hauled ashore with him. Any welcoming he expected was cut short when everyone but Sean got a good look at the driftwood. It wasn't driftwood after all. It was Quinn, still encased in the same hardened slime that had held Solveig and Liam, and still playing his imaginary narwhal whale bone horn.

Stella ran past Sean who watched her in stunned silence as she moved around him and over to Quinn. She quickly released him from the casing and gave him the same potion she had the other two. When it didn't immediately revive him, she gave him a few more drops. That did the trick and he immediately sat up, fully alert.

"Hey, Stella" he said. "How nice of you to visit." He then looked past her to the others who were all just staring at him. "What are all of you doing here? How did you get here?"

They all just looked at him in wonder as he rubbed his head and said, "Hey. Why am I all lumpy?"

Chapter fifteen

Stella suggested that the group return to the Princess's palace, knowing that the potions she had given to Solveig, Liam, and Quinn wouldn't last very long and they would need real food and drinks. She had to break off the discussions and exchanges to move everyone in that direction.

Along the way Quinn told of the discoveries he had made which was the reason for his journey to meet up with Liam. He omitted the details of his journey to the Swamp, as well as his experiences with the plants and animals. Liam described their trek to the point they met up with Summer and Solveig. He provided some of the details that Quinn left out, especially regarding how he got into the stated of unconsciousness from which he had only recently recovered.

Solveig related the adventures from the point at which she and Summer discovered Liam and Quinn up until she and Liam and Quinn were encased in slime. Summer filled in the rest of their story, apologizing again and again for having allowed the three of them to disappear from her watch.

Sean jumped, wiggled and gyrated the whole time, unsuccessfully trying to interrupt and tell everyone about his harrowing experiences with asteroids and worm holes and such. Lochen cut him off and just said, "It wasn't really that bad. He's exaggerating," every time Sean started talking.

Stella wanted to hear more from Sean and told him she would catch up with him later. Because of her telepathic connection with Lochen for at least part of the time, she knew that Lochen and Sean had been in much greater danger than Lochen let on. And probably much greater danger than Sean had been aware of. The encounter with the wormhole could have been disastrous.

When they reached the palace, they were greeted by several attendants. Natalie suggested they all get some rest and meet in the morning to exchange information and plan the next steps. They agreed and were shown to their rooms where baths, fresh clothing, food and drink, and most important of all, beds awaited them. As the group broke up, Natalie held Lochen and Stella back. When they were alone she led them to her antechamber.

"Lochen, I would not want to deprive you of some much needed rest, but I seem to recall that you only need to sleep about every week or so," she said.

"Your recollection is correct, Princess Natalie," he answered. "I was actually going to ask you if I could take advantage of your library. I thought I would use the time before our meeting tomorrow to jot down some thoughts I had on my recent expedition. I'd like to draft a dissertation on the impact of atmospheric pressures on bubbles and transporter stones in deep space and their relationship to memory implants, telekinesis, and wormholes. But if you need me for something else, I'm sure that can wait, and I am gladly at your disposal."

Natalie stared blankly at him for a second or two waiting to see if he was joking or not. She looked towards Stella, who had the same blank expression on her face. When she decided that he was serious, she continued.

"Stella has had some unusual visions over the last few days, and I, personally, have observed something first hand I believe is equally unusual. These events seem to have some degree of importance. I think they may also be connected with the problems Quinn discovered in the Ice Kingdom."

"Please, tell me how I can help," answered Lochen eagerly. "What do you propose?"

"I'd like for the three of us to visit the Sanctorum to see if Stella can summon the visions she had earlier."

"That seems like a logical starting place," agreed Lochen, and the three of them made their way to the Sanctorum.

When they arrived, Stella took a position in the center of the room. She sat on the floor and began to meditate. Lochen sat next to her until Natalie took his arm and lead him to some seats off to the side where she motioned for him to sit in silence. Stella drew on the energy of the friends who had recently arrived and were now safe from harm.

The room darkened slightly and then the walls of the Sanctorum began to glow; blurred images began to take shape. Lochen studied the shapes intently, standing up to move closer, until Natalie tugged on his sleeve and motioned for him to remain seated. But nothing looked familiar to any of the three of them. There were impressions of long tunnels that opened into immense caverns. Sensations of extreme heat alternated with the calm coolness of shimmering streams and rivers. All of this was underscored with an unshakable air of oppression.

Explosions of other images burst to the forefront and then just as quickly disappeared. Pictures of grotesque sculptures and idols intermingled with nightmarish, snarling faces. Stella was nearly overwhelmed with fear and anxiety. Lochen shared her sense of unease and started to move next to her. He quickly glanced back at Natalie and then decided he should stay put. As the projections on the walls of the Sanctorum began to fade, faint glimpses of the scurrying small white creatures appeared once again. And then everything was gone.

Stella slumped slowly to the ground and curled up into a deep post-trance sleep. Natalie summoned aides to have Stella moved to her room. All the while Lochen remained seated and silent. When they were alone again, Natalie turned to him asked what he thought.

"I can think much better when I am able to walk around. I am at a loss as to why you insisted that I remain seated."

Natalie furrowed her brow before answering, "Because the Enchantress is in a very fragile state when she is bringing forth images. Any physical contact or disruption during that time can not only affect the connection, it can do her harm. But that's not what I meant. What did you think of the images?"

"Ah, yes, the images," he said. He started to stand and half way up looked at Natalie. Not seeing any objection, he finished rising from his seat. "As I recall, Your Highness, you have quite an extensive library in your archives."

"Yes, that's correct," replied Natalie. She couldn't quite understand what this had to do with Stella's visions.

"And you still have the ancient scrolls of the earliest Enchantresses?" he asked, still providing no explanation.

"Yes, of course."

"Then I'll need to see them. I have some research to do before I share any hypothesis. I'm sure you understand. It will probably take some considerable time, so I'll take my leave and will rejoin you in the morning with the others. Now, if you'll be so kind as to show me to the library."

Natalie was nearly speechless. She felt like a child being dismissed by a parent, but she knew better than to question Lochen. She personally escorted him to the library. Once she provided him with the scrolls, he immediately focused all his attention in translating the writings.

"Well, ok," she said to him, although it was as if she had already left. She could see that he had shifted his thoughts and probably didn't even know if she was still there. He hadn't even bothered to thank her.

"I guess I'll see you tomorrow," she murmured as she left him to his studies, walking out of the library, uncertain as to what to do next.

------------------ *** ------------------

The next morning most everyone had congregated in the Princess's sunroom. It was an intimate atrium that overlooked the gardens and a small forest below. It was pleasantly warm in the atrium and a wonderful place for breakfast. When Quinn arrived, he was bundled up in layers of clothing and had wrapped a blanket around him.

"What's wrong with you?" asked Solveig.

"I'm freezing," he said. "Aren't the rest of you cold? Can we build a fire in here somewhere?"

They all looked at each other in puzzlement.

"Are you nuts?" asked Sean. "It's like the middle of the hot season. Besides, don't you live on a bunch of ice? Shouldn't you be used to being cold all the time. I'd think this would be too hot for you."

"It's an Ice Kingdom," answered Quinn, a bit testily. "It's not a bunch of ice. And, yes, I live there, but I've never been this cold before. Maybe I'm sick, although I don't feel sick. I'm just cold."

Stella ministered to him, feeling his wrist, and pulling him down so she could reach his head, standing on the tips of her toes.

"No, you're not sick," she pronounced. "The potion I gave you shouldn't have given you this reaction, either. Unless it was contaminated, which it wasn't. I just concocted it yesterday."

She thought about her potion for a few minutes, and then said, "The three of you who were locked in the slime – all of you were unconscious when we found you. Why? I thought you said only Quinn had been unconscious."

Liam answered, "Solveig and I got that way because we didn't have anything to eat or drink for such a long time. It was probably more like a deep sleep. Quinn was unconscious long before we fell into the muck."

"Why was he already unconscious," she demanded.

"He tangled with some dragon spadix. It spit some poison on his hand, and I had to make a poultice for him," Liam said. "I told him not to unwrap the bandages, but he did and got a strong dose of the vapors from it. Before I could do anything, he was out like a dead fish."

Quinn pulled the blankets up higher around his head and face, slightly embarrassed. "Well, I <u>didn't</u> unwrap the bandage. It smelled really bad, and he didn't tell me not to smell it," he said defensively.

"What was in the poultice," Stella asked.

Liam described the ingredients and the proportions of each. Then, when she asked him, he told her how long it had been wrapped on Quinn's hand before he inhaled the odor from it.

"Oh, wonderful," said Stella. "That poultice is reacting with my potion. I hadn't expected that to happen."

"Can you fix it?" asked Quinn, hopefully.

"No," said Stella. "Well, yes. Probably. I'm not sure. I think it would be best – safest – to just let it wear off by itself."

"Blubber on a biscuit" said Quinn. "How long will that take?"

"Not long," answered Stella, with a sly smile on her face. "Since I had to give you double the dose of the potion, you should be back to normal in about a year or two. Three at the most."

"WHAT?" shouted Quinn.

"Relax. I'm only joking. It should wear off in a few days."

Everyone's laughter was cut short as Lochen walked into the room and announced, "I think we have a problem."

"What kind of problem?" they asked almost in unison.

"And where have you been," asked Solveig.

Before he could explain Natalie interjected, "Let me explain a few other things first. Yesterday after you all went to rest, I asked Lochen to observe some of the visions Stella had been having. I, myself, had done some reconnaissance after receiving some unusual reports of sea creatures that appeared to have been boiled to death. In examining this situation, I discovered what might have been the source, but I also came across something inexplicable. When I returned I learned that what I saw also appeared in Stella's visions. Neither of us could decipher what we had seen. I thought Lochen might have some insights."

Knowing the others might feel left out, she added, "After all that each of you has been through, I didn't want to add to your burdens with mere speculation. If the visions meant nothing, then they could just be dismissed. I felt it was better to have something more specific to share with you."

"So," asked Quinn through chattering teeth, "now we have another problem – besides the one that's poisoning my waters?"

"Not exactly," answered Lochen. "After observing Stella's visions in the Sanctorum yesterday, I was struck immediately by the same single item that was in common with what Natalie had seen and which was of equal puzzlement to her; that is, the small white creatures. I then recalled having read something when I was studying the prehistoric canals on the planet Ares. I was much younger then, and the impact of what was discussed was not fully appreciated at the time. The treatise, however, was extremely fascinating, but based primarily on speculation and hypotheses, since there was no recorded history of the civilizations that may have..."

"Yeah, yeah, yeah" interrupted Quinn. "Is there a point to all this?"

"No kidding," Sean whispered to Quinn. "He did this to me all the time, and I was stuck all by myself in that bubble thing."

"Yes, of course," continued Lochen. "I had to research the ancient scrolls of the early Enchantresses of the Sea Sprites to confirm my suspicions. And even those reference materials were not as specific as I had hoped. I could find no reference to the treatise on the prehistoric..."

He sensed he was going to be interrupted again.

"To make a long story short," he said.

"Too late," quipped Liam.

"I believe the small white creatures visualized by Stella and observed beneath the sea by Natalie are Trepans."

He made the announcement as if everyone knew what he was talking about and no further explanation was needed. He sat down at the table to help himself to something to eat. He looked up when he realized no one was speaking. When he saw everyone just staring blankly at him, he concluded that he needed to expand a bit.

"The Trepans are believed to live far below the surface of the planet. They are very sensitive to light – even the light of our moon; the light from the suns would probably be fatal to them – so they never come up from underground. The lack of sunlight explains their white coloring. Actually, it's not so much a coloring as it is an absence of coloring. I know that sounds counterintuitive, since above the surface the absence of color results in black, but their color is not a true white. It's a very rare condition. I read about it once in a digest on…"

Once more he could see the impatience of his audience. He decided they didn't really need to know where he read about all of this.

"Yes," he continued quickly. "Anyway, they live underground, which is why they are white. Oh, and they have a tremendous tolerance for heat." Then, as an afterthought he added, "And cold, I suppose. That only makes sense. I guess they would then have a tremendous tolerance for any temperature variation."

"So what do they do, and why do we have a problem?" asked Solveig. She was used to these kinds of dialogues, but even she was getting frustrated.

"Ah, right. They…ah…well mostly… they dig tunnels. Their tunneling allows for the movement of molten lava as well as underground rivers and streams. They have an uncanny ability to know where these elements are needed and create passageways or close existing passageways to direct and redirect both the hot and cold.   They keep the polar caps from melting, maintain a balance in the temperatures in the seas and oceans, and divert any harmful lava flows. By doing so, they maintain a near perfect balance in the environment on our planet. And whenever the surface conditions create an imbalance, they compensate for it – almost intuitively. They're like a giant heating and air conditioning system. They are actually quite marvelous little creatures. We really can't do without them. And they've been around for centuries, completely out of sight and, for the most part unknown by those of us who live on the surface…"

"Arggghhh!" shouted Summer, who could take no more, as she flew right up to his face. Hovering just over his nose, she gave it a flick. "And how is this a problem?" she demanded, her patience at an end.

"Oh, yes. The problem. Well, it's rather serious, to say the least. Something or someone has caused them to start doing more damage than good. I'm not sure what, exactly, but it seems that the tunnels they are digging are releasing far too much magma. It's not clear if they're digging in the wrong direction, or if they're too many of them, or what. But as a result of whatever they're doing, large pockets of lava, which is very acidic, are forming and breaking through the normal barriers. That's probably what has been poisoning the water in the Ice Kingdom. It also explains the curious sulfur smell Princess Natalie reported."

"I've smelled that, too," said Liam.

"So have I" said Quinn.

"Of course you would," Lochen continued. "Their digging, for some reason, has run completely amok. If the balance isn't maintained, excess lava seeping through the planet's crust or other barriers that they have previously been responsible for maintaining, would release a number of different toxins and gases into the water supplies, and the smell would be sulfuric in nature."

"Would that explain the underwater mountain I saw?" asked Natalie.

"Yes, that, too, would make sense," Lochen answered. "If the pockets continue to build unchecked, even small breaks that are repeated will form volcanoes. Undersea eruptions are serious enough, but if those mountains keep growing and extend above the water level, the eruptions that will follow will spew lava and volcanic ash into the air. It's possible that what you saw was a vent of some sort. It diverted pressure from below to avoid an eruption of the volcano. That's just a guess, you understand, but it would seem to make sense, as I said."

"Won't the wind just blow that stuff away?" asked Sean.

"It might if there was only one volcano and it was small. But judging from the number of reports, just from Quinn, Liam and Natalie, I would expect there are several volcanoes and not small ones. At least for now, those eruptions are under the sea. That's bad enough, mind you. If the buildup continues, however, and the imbalance that has been created is not reversed, not only will the entire sea become polluted and toxic, but the air will, too. As those volcanoes continue to build, they will extend above the level of the sea, and the eruptions that follow will then begin to poison the air."

Everyone was just staring at him in silence. The magnitude of what he had just discussed as if he were merely giving a hypothetical lecture had not been digested by any of them. As he looked from one to the next, he was certain that they didn't fully understand the seriousness of the situation.

"We're running out of time, don't you see? They have to be stopped. The entire planet is in jeopardy."

Chapter sixteen

Everyone started talking at once, but no one had any idea what to do or where to start. Finally, when everyone calmed down, Stella said she had an idea.

"I agree with Lochen that it seems apparent that these Trepan creatures are somehow connected to the overheating of the seas, the dying off of the sea life, and the lava eruptions."

"And that smell," interjected Quinn wiggling his head and moving the blankets, "don't forget that smell."

"Yes," said Stella, "and the smell of sulfur."

"And how the water burned," Quinn interrupted again. "Remember? I told you how it burned my fingers."

Stella looked at him for a minute then asked sarcastically, "Anything else?"

"No," said Quinn, "not that I can think of." And he buried himself, shivering, back under the pile of blankets, pulling them tightly around his head.

"As I was saying," continued Stella, "all of these things seem to be interconnected. I think the logical starting place would be to try to locate the Trepans. If we find them, then we can learn what to do to fix this problem. We already know where to look. Princess Natalie has seen them."

"What about the Alchemist?" mumbled Quinn from under the blankets, mentioning this person for the first time.

"The Alchemist?" gasped Natalie.

And Stella, turning to face Natalie, said, "From my vision when I resurrected the memories of the ancient Enchantresses. The message for me to search for the Alchemist."

"What Alchemist?" Lochen and Sean asked.

Quinn pushed his mouth towards an opening in his coverings and quickly told them about his encounter with the Sage and her advice to find the Alchemist.

"That was the whole purpose of my journey to find Liam," he concluded. "I'm sure I mentioned this before."

He then curled into a ball, readjusted the blankets, and again asked if someone could please light a fire.

"Not to any of us," answered Solveig. "If you recall, you were asleep for most of your trip here."

"Unconscious," he corrected her, his voice muffled by the layers of blanket. "I wasn't asleep. And I'm sure I mentioned it."

"If we start looking for this Alchemist, that puts us back to square one," said Stella. "We have a general idea where the Trepans are, but we have no clue at all where this Alchemist is, if he even exits."

"I think you're right," said Lochen to Stella. "We need to find the Trepans. They are the key to all of this, I believe."

Quinn started to shed his cocoon again, struggling to make as small an opening as he could in order to object.

Lochen didn't give him the chance, and quickly continued, "I think we may still need to search for this Alchemist, but not right now. We don't know where to begin to look for him or her. And taking the time to conduct such a search may not be the best use of our limited time."

"We thought you'd know where to find him," said Liam, "or her. That's why Quinn and I set out to find you."

"I'm sorry to disappoint you," Lochen replied. "I haven't the slightest clue as to where to find the Alchemist. Furthermore, I don't recall ever having heard of such a person. Of course, I don't recall ever looking for such a person. I'm sure if I had been looking for him – or her – I would recall, but be that as it may, I can't emphasize enough that the time I would have to spend researching ancient tomes to learn more about an Alchemist could be better spent in our efforts to locate the Trepans and attempt to stem the tide of the damage being caused by them."

"Won't it be just as hard to find the Trepans as it would the Alchemist?" asked Solveig. "I mean, even if we know they live underground, we don't really know <u>where</u> underground, do we?"

"I think we do, or at least I do," Natalie answered. "I've seen them below the sea. They opened a doorway into the side of a volcano. I'm sure we can find a way to reach them much more quickly than we can the Alchemist."

For the next few minutes there was heated debate about who they should look for first – the Trepans or the Alchemist. Quinn and Liam argued in favor of finding the Alchemist. Natalie and Stella opted for the Trepans. The others seemed undecided. At one point someone suggested splitting up and having half of them search for the Alchemist and the other half search for the Trepans. In the end, Sean pointed out something that made the decision about splitting up easier for them to reach.

"We can't split up," he insisted. "We need each other too much. Just look at what we had to go through just to get here. Besides, if we split up, what happens if half of us find the Alchemist and the other half find the Trepans? The half that finds the Alchemist won't know where the other half is and the half that finds the Trepans won't know where the half that found the Alchemist is. Or worse than that. What happens if the half looking for the Alchemist never finds him, but the other half finds the Trepans? Or the other way around? What happens then? Or later? Or whenever? Right?"

It took a while for everyone to understand what he said, but when they did, they all had to agree. And then they all started talking at once again. Each of them had their own thoughts about who they should look for first and where to start.

"And there's one other thing," Sean continued. "I think I know a way we can find the Trepans."

That brought all the conversations to a halt, as all eyes turned to him, knowing how he felt about going in the water.

"Yes," said Natalie, "and so do I. I saw them at the opening near the base of the underwater mountain. There seemed to be a doorway. We might be able to get in that way. But I can't believe that you'd be suggesting that approach, Sean."

"But what about the Alchemist?" pleaded Quinn from deep underneath his blankets. "The Sage said I had to find the Alchemist. And she knows everything – well just about everything. I can't just ignore her."

Liam chimed in with Quinn, "I agree. We need to find the Alchemist. This problem is more than we can handle. We need help. Even if we find the Trepans, it sounds like there are too many of them for us to fight."

"But the images I've received," said Stella, "all point to the Trepans. Who knows how long it will take to find the Alchemist or where in the world he is. Besides, I don't think we have to fight the Trepans. I didn't get that sense. I think the Trepans need help – our help."

The debate carried on for several minutes, until Solveig noticed the Lochen was being uncharacteristically quiet. She turned to him and asked why.

"I've actually been considering two things. First, I've been weighing the facts and the information we have available to us right now," he said. "And second, I recalled something that I recently read. It was a series of articles on decision-making process in small groups. I've been applying those principles in this specific setting in conjunction with the facts that are presently known. It's really quite interesting. There are a number of processes that can be applied, such as pair-wise ranking, which is probably the simplest. There's a more complicated process, which in this situation is more likely to be applicable. You assign point values to the various issues in relation to a set of neutral factors, such as the amount of time it would take to accomplish a given task..."

"Is there an abridged version of this," interrupted Summer.

Lochen thought for a second or two and then said, "Abridged version? Certainly. We should seek out the Trepans first."

Everyone started talking at once again. Finally Stella called for silence and then asked, "That's it? I mean I agree with your position in this, but I was expecting more of an explanation."

"Oh, it's not my position," answered Lochen. "It's the logical place to start."

"OK," grumbled Summer. "How about something between the abridged version and the one that's so long we all grow beards waiting for the end?"

"Yes, I see. Something a bit more detailed without all the supporting analysis?" Lochen asked. Taking their silence for agreement, he continued.

"Fact one. We know there is a problem. There is clear evidence of that in the poisons in the water and the spikes in heat that have affected the fish and other sea life. OK so far?"

Hearing no objections, he stood up and moved on, pacing back and forth around the atrium and gesturing as if he was giving a lecture.

"Fact two. We know that the Trepans are involved in some manner. Again, there is evidence of that. Natalie and Stella have actually seen them, and there is research that speaks not only to their existence, but also to their role in the environment. Unknown number one: What we don't know is what the exact problem is, that is, the specific relation between the Trepans and the issue of the excessive volcanic activity that is apparently creating the environmental imbalance. Specifically, and I suppose these would be subcategories under unknown number one – are they aware of the consequences of what they are doing; are they doing this on purpose; or are they being forced to do this. Which leads us to unknown number two: what exactly is the solution we're seeking?

"And finally, the conclusion: even if we found the Alchemist, what would we ask him or her to do? We don't know. Therefore, the only logical path forward is to find the Trepans, learn as much as we can about their connection with the problems and identify what needs to be done, which may or may not include finding the Alchemist. And if it did include finding the Alchemist, we'd have a better understanding of what to ask him – or her."

Once more everyone was quiet, trying to understand everything that Lochen had outlined. And then Sean spoke up.

"And like I said, I think I know how to find the Trepans – without having to go underwater to that volcano thing," he quickly added with a slight shudder at the mention of the word "water."

Before Natalie could argue the point, Lochen once again interjected.

"I think we need to let Sean explain. I don't mean to say that his way is better. Without knowing what he proposes, that can't be determined. However, in light of your description of the doorway, as you referred to it, I doubt that we would be able to gain access. You said it seemed to blend into the mountainside, so I can assume there were no handles or other mechanism to open it. Furthermore, since it appears to have been a release portal for the heat inside the mountain, it seems unwise to me that we should try to open that portal without knowing what's on the other side."

"I have to agree, too, your Highness," said Stella. "I'm concerned that the most obvious way in may be the most dangerous. There must be another alternative."

They all looked at Sean, and Natalie, resigning herself to a different approach said, "OK, Sean. Tell us what you know."

Suddenly Sean was not as confident as he had been when he first made his pronouncement.

"Well I don't exactly know; I mean I <u>know</u> - sort of, you know? But I don't – like – know, know," he stammered.

Summer flew over to him and bonked him on the nose the same way she had bonked Lochen. "What is it with you two? Out with it," she shouted.

"All right, all right," he went on. "There's this giant sinkhole kind of thing deep in the forest. All of us know about it, but not very many of us have actually seen it. It's taboo for anyone to go near it, and the punishment for braking that taboo is…well, it's not really pleasant."

He thought for a minute and then added quickly, "but I didn't know it was taboo when I found it. Well I knew it was taboo, but I didn't know that what I found was that thing that was taboo, or I would NEVER have gone near it, and I would NEVER, NEVER, not ever, have climbed down inside it."

"What makes you think this will lead us to the Trepans?" asked Lochen.

"I think they made it," he answered immediately; glad to have the discovery of his misbehavior diverted. "One of the ancient myths of the forest creatures tells of the beginnings of creation. When the land was first formed, it was all covered in darkness. The Great Dozor, who created everything, slept after making the land. While he slept, and before the suns were added to the sky, the people that lived in the forest were called the Bradawls. They dug canals to move water, which created the rivers and the streams. The dirt they moved to make these waterways created the mountains.

"Then they started to argue and fight about where the rivers should go and where the mountains should be placed. Their fighting disturbed the Great Dozor's sleep. When he woke up, and opened both his eyes, they lit up the sky. His eyes are the twin suns that look down on us each day, but it was too bright for the Bradawls, so they burrowed deep underground. They made the sinkhole and kept it open, waiting for the time when the Great Dozor would once again sleep and the suns would stop shining. When that happened, they could return to the forest."

He looked at all the faces staring at him.

"Well it's only a myth," he said.

"And you've actually seen this sinkhole?" asked Summer.

"Yes," answered Sean a bit sheepishly, quickly restating his innocence, "but I didn't know it was THE sinkhole. Honest. I had no idea this was the thing that was taboo."

"So where is this sinkhole?" asked Liam.

"It's on the far northern side of the forest – probably a week's journey from here."

"Not necessarily," said Lochen, turning to the others. "We still have the transporter pod that I used to take Sean to Capurnica. I'm sure I can make some adjustments to the control mechanism."

"Ohhhh, noooo," wailed Sean. "Not that thing. I'd almost rather try to swim there. Besides we all won't fit."

"Nonsense," said Lochen. "You can't swim there. First of all, I'm sure the waterways don't reach this sinkhole. Even though I've never seen it, I'm certain that it is far inland and not anywhere near major rivers or streams. Second, you don't like to be in the water, so I find your assertion that you'd rather swim there to be highly suspect. Third, even if you did like the water, the indirect route of any waterways, even assuming they reached the sinkhole, would..."

"He's not serious," cut in Solveig. "He just doesn't want to get in that thing with you again."

"Oh," replied Lochen. "I see. Yes, of course."

"Wait a minute," objected Quinn, whose muffled voice rose through the blankets. Only his nose poked through. "Are we decided then that we're going to find the Trepans? We're not looking for the Alchemist?"

"Quinn," Natalie said as she put her arm around his shoulder. "I think all of us want to do whatever it takes to make things right in the Ice Kingdom. And maybe that means finding the Alchemist, but maybe not. I don't think any of us are giving up. Right now, though, we think the best next step is to find the Trepans. Are you all right with that?"

He considered this for a few seconds and then stuck his nose out of the blankets once more and said, "Oh, I suppose. Do you think it will be warmer there?"

"It looks like we're heading for the sinkhole," said Liam. "But I've seen that transporter pod. It barely fit Lochen and Sean. It's never going to fit all of us." He looked back at Quinn and added, "Especially him."

"I can shrink us down so we all fit," she continued. "And I'm sorry, Sean, but I think this is the best way. Do you know exactly where this sinkhole is?"

"Oh, poop. Why couldn't they live in the trees," Sean mumbled. "Yeah, I'm pretty sure I can remember where it is."

"Pretty sure may not be accurate enough," said Lochen.

"I think I can help with that," said Stella. "I'll take him and Liam to the Sanctorum. If I can project Sean's memories on the walls, we should be able to get a better fix on the general setting. Liam can then get a mental image of the exact location, which should help guide the transporter pod."

"Yes," said Lochen. "That should work."

Stella took Sean and Liam to the Sanctorum. Lochen made arrangements to move the pod from its last position on the sand bar in the water to a place on the beach nearer to the palace. Quinn went in search of more blankets and the others made their own preparations for the journey. When the necessary information had been transferred to Liam, they all reconvened to the beach where Lochen had moved the pod.

"Ooooh! We're never going to fit in there," whined Sean. "Even if Solveig can shrink us down, Quinn has so many blankets on him, he'll take up more than half the room all by himself."

"I'm sorry," chattered Quinn, "but I'm still freezing. I can't understand why none of you is cold."

"Can't you fix him?" Solveig asked Stella.

"I'm afraid to give him an antidote," she said. "The combination of potions still active in him makes anything else just as unpredictable."

"Couldn't you just guess at something?" asked Summer. "He's shaking so much, he's going to make the pod vibrate."

"And his teeth are chattering so much it sounds like castanets," added Natalie.

"Hey," objected Quinn, stammering, "I'm r-r-r-right here. And I'm not some science p-p-p-p-project."

Stella thought a minute and then, against her better judgment, she reached into one of her pockets and pulled out a tiny object. She looked at it for a second, then at Quinn. Then she tore the object in half and held out a small blue leaf in his direction.

"Take this," she said. "Just put it under your tongue. But don't chew it," she admonished him. "And above all, don't swallow it."

Quinn took the leaf, gave it an uncertain look and took a sniff of it. Reluctantly he slipped it into his mouth and under his tongue.

"Nothing's happening," he said.

"Give it time," answered Stella.

"All right," Solveig said. "Is everyone ready?"

And without waiting for an answer, she waved her hands and cast a quick spell. In the blink of an eye all but Summer were miniaturized. Even with this spell, Quinn was a bit on the large size, especially with all the coverings in which he was still wrapped. He had shrunk, but they blankets hadn't. He looked like a walking pile of coverlets as they dragged in the sand behind him.

They all climbed into the pod, filling it to capacity. Quinn pushed himself up against the back side of bubble, but not hard enough for him to fall out the other side. If he stood up straight, the top of his head poked out of the bubble's ceiling.

"Can't you make him any smaller?" Liam asked Solveig.

"No," she said. "Sorry, but that's as far as I can get him to go. We're just going to have to adjust."

Grumbling as he pulled at the blankets that everyone else was now stepping on, he bent over the others who crowded in front of him. Lochen stood next to him on his right, with Sean on the left side. Liam was in the middle of the pod, immediately in front of Lochen, and Stella. Natalie and Solveig were on the side opposite facing Quinn, while Summer fluttered in the back of the pod. When everybody was situated, and Quinn had stopped readjusting his blankets, Lochen placed Liam's right hand on the control panel to fix the transporter stone's directions. With a flash and a loud bang, they were gone. Almost immediately they reappeared deep in the forest.

They landed with a thud and a sudden stop on a slight ridge, rocking slightly. As soon as they arrived, Quinn stood up to look at the strange surroundings. His head popped above the top edge of the bubble, just below his eyes. He turned around to look behind him and was face to face with a near perfectly circular opening nearly twenty feet across. He pulled his head back into the bubble and bent over just a bit. He teetered backwards as the pod shifted on the dirt ridge.

Trying to keep his balance, his head popped out of the bubble and he looked straight down. He was staring at the sides of the sinkhole. The suns' rays bounced off the edges, making long grey shafts of light disappearing into a well of blackness. A wave of vertigo passed through him and he had the sensation of falling forward. He immediately flailed his arms, flapping the multitude of blankets and arched upright. He took a short step backwards, pushing those opposite him out of the pod.

Natalie and Solveig flew forward, nudged unceremoniously out of the pod and onto the ground. Surprised by the sudden movement, they reflexively reached back to grab on to something or someone. Natalie's hands flew to Stella and Solveig reached out for Liam, hoping for a steady hand; but to no avail. All they managed to do was to pull them out as well.   The four of them tumbled out of the pod, tripping off the transporter stone and onto the ground of the forest.

The pod had landed on the rim of the sinkhole. One side of it – the side with Quinn staring into the black - teetered over the edge. When four of its passengers abruptly left, the balance shifted as if in slow motion, and the pod dropped over the side. Summer flew out of the bubble as it changed position.   She hovered over the pod with the gaping hole behind it, watching Quinn, Sean and Lochen drop into the abyss.

Chapter seventeen

"What's happening," shouted Sean, panic rising with each question. "Where are we? Who turned out the lights? I knew I didn't want to get back in this thing."

He felt the pod turn somewhat sideways and the floor dropped out from under him. He would have flown out of it altogether, but he had been pushing one of Quinn's blankets out of the way at the time and now had it clutched tightly in his grip. The light of the opening was shrinking quickly above their heads. Darkness was rapidly enveloping them.

"Quinn," shouted Lochen, who was holding onto the control panel, trying to avoid flying outside of the bubble, "please get your head back inside the bubble. I can't get the controls to work while you're busy sightseeing."

When the pod dropped over the side, Quinn had straightened up again and his head had poked through the top of the bubble. Half of his head –

from his nose upward - was on the outside while the rest of him was on the inside. As a result, the transporter mechanism was locked.

Lochen was gripping the control panel with one hand, just to keep from being thrown out of the pod, while trying to regain control with the other. Quinn was waving his arms to keep his balance. One part or another of his body kept passing out of the bubble, continuing to block the transporter mechanism. Sean was flattened on the floor of the pod, struggling to unwrap himself from the blankets while trying to avoid being repeatedly stepped on by Quinn. All the while, the pod was dropping steadily, crashing against the sides of the shaft and spinning wildly.

Back at the opening, Summer stared in disbelief as the pod disappeared from sight. She had been drawn downward with the initial movement, but after spinning this way and that, had managed to fly free and was now hanging in the near darkness, just below the mouth of the sinkhole. The tossing around before she broke away from the pod had made her dizzy. She narrowly escaped colliding with the wall as she cleared her head and pulled to a stop.

"What happened," shouted Solveig, as she lifted herself up off the ground. "Where did they go?"

"I don't know," answered Natalie. "I felt something push me and I just grabbed whatever was nearest."

"That was me," said Stella, as she stood up and brushed herself off. "You grabbed me, your Highness, and pulled me out with you."

Liam rolled over and sat up. He looked back at the ridge around the top of the sinkhole. "Where did the pod go?" he asked. "Where are the others?"

"Did they transport to some other position?" asked Solveig, moving over to where Liam was sitting.

"No," said Stella. "We would have heard the shift – that noise those transporter stones make when they...transport."

"They went down here," called Summer, who was still out of sight, just below the rim of the opening.

They all rushed to the edge and saw Summer still floating over the gaping mouth of the sinkhole. They nearly tripped over one another as the skidded to a stop on the rim, overlooking the spot where Summer was hovering.

"They went down there," she said as she pointed to the large black hole. "They just dropped. And hit the side. I saw them go down. I don't know what happened. Why aren't they coming back up?"

She started to fly down after them but was stopped.

"No, Summer. Stop," Natalie called to her. "You don't know what's down there, or how far it is to the bottom."

"We have to DO something," Summer cried in frustration fluttering back and forth. "We can't just sit here doing nothing."

"We will do something, but until we know what to do, nothing is exactly what we have to do for the time being," said Stella.

Summer reluctantly flew out of the black hole and joined the others. Everyone was as stunned as she was. They listened for a few seconds to see if there was any sign that their friends were on their way back or had crashed on the bottom. The silence only lasted briefly when they began to all discuss the issue at the same time and offer a multitude of options to consider.

Their chaotic exchange stopped abruptly when the pod suddenly reappeared. With its usual flash and bang, it materialized before their eyes. This time it landed a safer distance away from the rim of the sinkhole. Lochen was off to one side, still clutching the control panel, and Quinn was sitting almost directly in the center, hugging his knees underneath his layers of covering. He was sitting right on top of Sean whose shouts and objections were muffled under Quinn's blankets.

"You can stand up now, Quinn," advised Lochen. He sat down on the edge of the pod with his hand on his knee, and added with a sigh, "I'm sure Sean would like to be able to breathe again."

Quinn struggled to his feet and climbed out of the pod, tripping over the blankets as he pulled them behind him. Sean spun around as the covers were ripped away from him and he sat up gasping for breath. He nervously opened one eye and then the other, taking in his surroundings. As soon as he saw that he was back on solid ground, he jumped from the pod.

"That's it!" he shouted, turning from Lochen to the others and back again. "I don't care where we have to go or how long it takes. That's it. I'm never, not ever, not in a million years, never, ever getting in that thing again."

He stomped off away from the pod in a huff, and sat heavily on the ground. The others stared at him with their mouths open and then looked back at Lochen and the transporter pod.

"What took you so long to reposition the transporter stone?" Stella asked Lochen once she had collected herself.

He glanced at Quinn, who looked away sheepishly, and answered, "We had some minor technical difficulty."

"How far down did you go?" asked Solveig.

"Not all the way," he answered. "I was able to regain control of the pod and redirect it before we came to any sudden stop."

"And how far was that?" asked Natalie.

Lochen thought for a minute before answering.

"Well, I can only speculate, you understand." He looked skyward as he did the mental calculations, making invisible notations in the air with his finger. "Considering an average rate of velocity of about fifteen feet per second, increasing exponentially over time, of course, and estimating the time that lapsed during our descent at somewhere around twenty seconds, maybe a bit more, but staying on the conservative side, I would estimate about three miles, give or take a standard deviation."

"Three miles?" repeated Solveig.

"Give or take a standard deviation," added Lochen.

His assessment was met with silence and despair. Each of them was trying to grasp the idea of a hole that dropped three miles into the earth and still didn't touch bottom, and the apparent impossibility of getting down there.

"How are we going to get down that hole?" asked Solveig. "There's no way we can climb down."

"In spite of Sean's declaration about never getting in that pod again," whispered Liam so that Sean couldn't hear, "I don't see an alternative. Why couldn't we use the transporter stone? It seems to be the best choice."

"You would think so, but, no. It would be too unpredictable...too dangerous," said Stella, "The transporter stone needs to have a specific place to land or stop; otherwise it doesn't have a point of reference and could reform either too high above the bottom or deep below it."

"Not exactly," Lochen thought out loud. "I mean, you're correct, of course. It needs a point of reference. However, I have an idea as to how we may solve that problem. First we need to know the precise depth and what is at the bottom. Solveig, I need you to flash light into the hole."

"But the light won't last long – only a few seconds," she said. "And judging from what you said, it will fade before it reaches the bottom. That's assuming there is a bottom. Are you even sure of that?"

"I know the flash won't last long; and yes, I'm sure there's a bottom. Would you like an explanation? No," he said when he saw her shake her head. "Right now, I want you to flash your bolts of lights, and I need Summer to fly down immediately behind them. Led by those light flashes, I believe she will be able to locate the bottom. She'll have to be careful, though. One flash will not be enough and she'll have to stop when the light diminishes."

"No," several of them shouted. "That's too dangerous. It's too much to ask of her. You can't ask her to fly alone."

"Well, I'd suggest that someone fly with her," Lochen argued, "but seeing that none of us here can fly, it seems she must do this alone."

"Hey," she said stifling the objections, "I'm all right doing this."

She turned to Lochen and added, "But I don't know what good it will do. I can't calculate or even estimate distances. I won't be able to tell how far down it is. Even if I fly straight back up, I don't know how fast I fly, and I never fly at just one speed, so you won't be able to do any of your fancy calculations."

"Leave that part to me," Lochen replied, smiling. "Just allow one of Solveig's light flashes to illuminate the walls and then go as far as you can until it darkens again. When the light fades out, stay as close to the side as you can, so she can send another one down. Don't look at the light. It will obliterate any night vision you have. Keep doing this as far as you can go. Once you've reached the bottom, come back up using the same process, and tell us what you've found."

She raised her eyebrows and blew out a long breath. "OK. Whatever you say," she answered.

Solveig moved hesitantly to the edge of the hole, sticking one foot far out in front of her body. She was right up to the edge, her heart pounding. Before she clapped her hands and threw the first bolt of light, she made the mistake of looking down into the gaping chasm. The extreme absence of any light or shadows or reflection gave her an overwhelming sense of vertigo. She felt a wave of dizziness rush over her, and she quickly sat down so she could catch her breath. Everybody rushed to grab her, but stopped when Lochen motioned them back.

"Oh, yes," Lochen said as he helped her up. "I forgot to tell you to not look down. Without a frame of reference...well, you saw what happened."

"Thanks," she said. "And you expect Summer to just fly down that? Won't she have the same reaction?"

"She'll be fine," he assured her. "She has no sense or fear of falling. She can fly. Remember?"

Solveig inched forward once again, and as she got close to the edge, she squatted down. With her head turned away from the opening, she clapped her hands and threw her fist forward wildly. The bolt of light struck the opposite side of the hole only a few feet from the top. It bounced back and forth, ricocheting from side to side, and dissipating almost immediately.

"Sorry," she said, slightly embarrassed. "I'm still a bit dizzy. I'll get it right. Don't worry."

"That's all right," said Lochen. "It's perfectly understandable. Just relax. Are you ready, Summer?"

"Let's get this going," she said with more bravado than she felt. She floated out over the center of the sinkhole and waited for Solveig to do her thing.

This time Solveig's aim was far more accurate. The bolt of light shot down the center of the fissure nearly perfectly. It illuminated the nooks and crannies along the jagged sides for several hundred yards. Before anyone could offer words of encouragement, or before she could give too much thought to what she was doing, Summer shot like a small rocket into the opening and after the flash of light.

A few seconds later the light had vanished and the hole had returned to blackness. Inside, Summer's vision faded as quickly as the light in front of her. In spite of Lochen's admonition, she had focused directly on the ball of light Solveig had sent down the shaft. As soon as it disappeared, Summer's vision went totally black. The light from the top of the opening was still visible, but shrinking and fading rapidly. She used this light to guide her a bit further until she came to a slight bend, which reduced the light from the opening by almost half.

"Holy jumping bean sprouts," she said to herself as the darkness enveloped her. She could see nothing ahead of her and little if anything immediately next to her. The imprint of the ball of light was still blazing on her retina. She stopped and reached out her arms, feeling for the side of the shaft. When she reached it, she looked up and could still see the opening above her. But it had shrunk to the size of a beach ball and didn't provide any illumination at all.

Summer was uncertain as to what she was supposed to do next, or how long to wait for Solveig's next flash. She looked down, but still could see nothing. This time, don't look at the light, she told herself. She hung suspended in mid air, face up against the wall, waiting for the next bolt of light from Solveig.

It was difficult for Solveig to judge when the light had extinguished, since the bolt dropped so quickly out of sight. She dared a quick peek over the edge. Any remnants of her first flash were long gone. She turned back to Lochen.

"How long should I wait before doing another one?" she asked.

"Send one every ten seconds," Lochen told her. "Don't worry whether the previous light is gone or not. Keep them regularly spaced. I'm sure Summer will soon figure out the pattern. I suppose we should have thought about this earlier."

"Yes, WE should have," Solveig replied and did as he instructed.

She clapped her hands, threw another bolt of light down the hole, counted to ten and sent another. In the near total darkness, it felt like it was taking forever for the next flash of light. Summer didn't know what else to do, but wait. And then it came. She could see the walls starting to lighten. This time she kept her focus on the sides of the shaft, instead of the flash of light.

It shot much too close over her head. The force of the light pulled her along with it, and she tumbled head over heels. Careening down the opening, she stuck out her arms for balance and started flapping her wings. It took a second or two, although it seemed much longer, and she stabilized herself. And then came the crash.

Summer had forgotten that these bolts were just like lightening in the sky. They were followed by a crash of thunder. These shock waves were stronger than the force of the light. This one flipped her upside down and slammed her against the side of the sinkhole. She now understood what Natalie had said one time before about running into a brick wall. The collision knocked the breath out of her and her wings flattened behind her. She began to drop, sliding downward, face first, against the rough wall.

To make matters worse, as she spun over, her eyes were wide open in fright and were drawn instantly to the light from the flash. Once again, she was temporarily blinded. She squeezed her eyes shut tightly trying to clear the image burned into her retinas on top of the last one. She was free falling, scraping along the wall and blind. Could this get much worse, she asked herself.

She pushed out her arms and spread her wings, floating towards the center of the hole. In a few seconds, she took control of her descent. Once her flying was back to normal, she slowed down to a stop. Feeling along the wall, she found a small gouge with enough of a protrusion for her to sit on the edge and catch her breath.

"OK," she thought out loud, "This is a lot worse than I thought it would be. I have to be ready for the next one – whenever that comes."

In a few seconds it did. This time she could hear a whooshing sound coming from above. She dug her heels into the perch on which she was sitting, pressed her back against the side, closed her eyes and waited for the shock wave to pass her. As soon as it did, she opened one eye at a time to find the extreme brightness of the flash safely ahead of her and the walls glowing. She waited another second for the blast and then dived out into the chasm like a skydiver. This time she forced herself to focus on the walls and not the light. She hoped that Solveig would be sending these flashes at regular intervals and began to count.

By the time she was up to eight, she could hear another blast approaching. She pressed herself against the side, closed her eyes and let it pass. The same thing happened about ten seconds later and Summer assumed that from that point on, she could expect another flash every ten seconds. That will help a lot, she said to herself. We should have thought of that before.

Before too long, the walls of the hole had narrowed considerably and the bolts of light were bouncing off the sides at this depth. She had to be more careful. She spent a little more time finding niches in the sides to hide, and hoped that the bolts didn't bounce off her.

Summer estimated she had been flying downward for nearly twenty minutes. Finally, she noticed a different kind of sound. She thought she heard something echoing off the bottom. It took five more flashes before she emerged from the hole into a larger cavern. She moved away from the opening she had come down and hovered along the ceiling of the cave.

"Oh, my momma's bunions," she said when she saw what the sinkhole opened up to.

The next flash of light revealed an underground dome-shaped canyon with several tunnels going in various directions and a wide lagoon at the center. It was like spokes emanating from the hub of a wheel. The walls curved up and blended into the ceiling, which was solid, except for the opening to the shaft she had just descended. The walls of the dome sparkled like it was filled with tiny stars. If she didn't know better, she would have thought she was looking up at a clear night sky on the surface.

She noticed a definite drop in the temperature in the canyon, which surprised her. She assumed it would get hotter this far down, especially since the Trepans were opening passages for lava. In fact, when another bolt made its way down, and there was enough light, she could see her breath. Quinn's going to love this, she thought. Maybe we won't tell him.

She floated down to the water to make sure it wasn't coated with ice. It was completely smooth, and black as night, but she couldn't tell if that was its natural color, or just because there was so little light in the cavern. She reached down and ran her fingers in it. The ripples floated silently across and disappeared in the darkness. It felt colder than anything she had ever felt before, but there was no sign of ice.

She let Solveig send three more bolts of light down, as she tried to capture mental images of all she could see. There were odd crystals of some kind in the walls that held the illumination from the flashes for a few minutes even after the flash itself had dissipated. With this additional light, she was able to get a good view of the entire cavern. After the third flash, she began her return. It took several more minutes, before she could again see the sunlight peeking through the opening at the top. The return trip was much easier than the one coming down.

"Cease fire," she shouted to Solveig, who, by now was nearly exhausted. "I'm coming up."

She was met with a round of applause. "Good job, Summer," Lochen told her. "What did you find? Tell us everything."

She relayed everything she could remember. She hesitated when she came to the part about the water, glancing as Sean, and she quickly glossed over the part about the drop in temperature, hoping Quinn was too buried under his blankets to clearly hear her. When she was done, Lochen announced that they would be taking the transporter pod to the bottom of the sinkhole.

"WHAT?" shouted Sean.

"Are you sure?" asked Natalie.

"I assume your question is rhetorical," Lochen replied to Sean, "and, yes, your Highness, I am sure. I can transfer the memory images from everything Summer observed into the transporter stone the same way we transferred the images that Liam received from Sean which brought us here."

"Oh, and that worked so well the last time, didn't it," said Sean, still shouting. "Did you forget already how close we came to landing on thin air?"

"A minor miscalculation," said Lochen, dismissing Sean's objections. "I'm confident I can make the necessary corrections."

"Of course," said Stella, with a sudden understanding. "That explains the modifications you made so that you could travel to Capurnica."

"And do I have to remind you, that didn't work out so well, either," said Sean, still shouting. "Did you forget about that worm house thing?"

"Wormhole," corrected Lochen. "And as I've already said, if you will recall, that wasn't entirely my fault."

"It's fine by me," said Quinn. "Anything to get moving, so I can warm up. It is warm down there, isn't it?"

"Well, sure it's fine with you," Sean continued to shout. "You had your head buried under blankets while we were dropping like a lead ball down that hole. And weren't you listening? Summer said it's COLDER down there."

"I have an idea for when we get to the bottom," Summer said. "I think I know a way we can get light down there."

"Hey," Sean kept shouting, "Can't anybody hear me? He's talking about getting in that pod thing again."

"Dude," said Liam. "We can hear you just fine. We're just not paying any attention to you."

"But, but," stammered Sean. Finally he gave up. "Whatever. Just remember who it was that said this isn't such a good idea."

"I'm sure you won't let us forget," said Natalie with a smile. "I knew there was a reason we kept you around."

Lochen placed Summer's tiny hand on the controls as everybody once again crowded into the pod.

"No," said Sean as he pushed himself as far away from Quinn as possible. "You're not sitting on me again. Move over to..."

He was cut off in mid sentence as the transporter pod vanished with a loud crack. It reappeared nearly six miles down in the middle of the lagoon a split second later. Somewhere in its journeys, the stone base had been splintered. The landing in the lagoon, which should have been relatively soft, was just jarring enough. It broke the stone in half and at the same time, broke the seal on the bubble as well.

The pod and its passengers rematerialized directly below the bottom of the shaft, nearly twenty feet from any land and in sub-zero degrees, but mysteriously unfrozen, water. The bubble vanished as soon as it touched the water, and the broken base of the pod sank immediately into the lake, pulling its passengers with it deeper and deeper.

Chapter eighteen

Natalie could feel the earth shaking. This must be an earthquake, she thought. She had heard about such things as earthquakes, but had never experienced one. Living her entire life in a giant bubble on the floor of the Cerulean Sea, she had managed to avoid such a catastrophe. She couldn't believe this was happening on their new island community.

The trembling seemed constant, and everything around her appeared to be moving. There was a roaring sound that seemed to fill her ears and settle in the middle of her head. Actually, it sounded more like a rattling then a roaring. Things were falling off tables, furniture was tumbling, glass was breaking, and the shaking didn't stop. She couldn't remember falling to the ground, but that's where she was. She struggled to get up but was restrained. She looked around but could see nothing that was holding her in place. She fought with all her strength to move.

"What's going on," she wondered. "Where is everybody?"

She looked from side to side, but couldn't see a single person, just the walls and windows of her palace. Wait, she thought. I wasn't in my palace. Where's Stella?

She filled her lungs and shouted, "Stella!"

"She's right here," a voice answered. "She's fine. You're all fine. Don't worry. Just relax."

She had been dreaming, but it seemed so real, she thought. She didn't understand what had happened or where she was. She shook her head to clear her thoughts, but it felt like it was filled with broken glass. The pain was nearly unbearable and she rested her head on the – what? Ground? She fought to open her eyes. When she finally did, she saw Quinn staring down at her through incredible darkness. It was so dark she could barely make out his features.

"Take it easy," he told her. "You've been out for a while."

"Out where?" she asked, more confused than ever. "Outside? Am I outside? Why am I outside? Why is it so dark?"

Quinn looked puzzled. "That's hard to answer. You're sort of outside, but you're also inside."

"What happened?" she asked as she tried to sit up, still feeling restrained, although Quinn was not holding her down.

The fog slowly began to clear and she remembered the transporter pod, the sudden blackness, and then a feeling of immediate and stabbing cold. She looked around her and saw that her restraints were, in fact, blankets. She was covered in blankets. They were the blankets Quinn had been wearing. The quaking had been her own shivering, and the roaring – rattling sound had been the chattering of her teeth. She was incredibly cold. She couldn't remember ever being so cold.

"Where are the others?" she asked, even before he could answer her other questions.

"Uh, I don't know what happened," he said, trying to address her concerns in the order she raised them. "We took off in that transporter pod deal and the next thing I knew, we were getting soaked in some really, really cold water, and we were sinking fast. So, I guess you're not really outside, since you're inside this cavern, or whatever it is. Uh, and it's dark...well, I guess it's dark...because it's dark in here. And the others are all right here, next to you. It's just too dark to see them very well; because, like I said...it's dark in here."

"How did we end up here?"

"Well, you know...uh...we transported here. Well not exactly here, here, but there," he pointed into the darkness.

"I guess you can't see it, but we landed in that lake or pond. I suppose it's kind of hard to steer that thing; you know – that transporter bubble thing. I have to agree with Sean. I'm not real crazy about that thing, either. It seems to land wherever it wants. Anyway, we landed in some water or something and we started to sink. I just grabbed whoever was closest to me and started swimming."

"You got all of us? At once?"

"Yes. No. Not exactly. Yes, I got all of us...all of you, but not all at once. I couldn't really see who was who. I think I was next to Lochen and Summer when we took off. He was still holding her hand when we misappeared, or whatever we did, and I think he just never let go. So when I grabbed him, she was attached. It's a good thing he never let her go. I don't think I would have been able to find her – you know, because she's so small? But he was holding on real tight, so when I grabbed him, she just came right along – kind of like a package deal.

"I think Solveig was behind me and I grabbed her in the other hand and just kicked until I got to the surface. I wasn't sure what direction to go in, since I couldn't really see too well, so I just guessed. Once I could feel the ground under me, I figured it was some kind of land, so I pulled them up and went back in to find the rest of you.

"I knew you and Stella could breathe underwater...well not exactly breathe, I know, but, you know, you can hold your breath for a really, really long time, so I tried to find Sean and Liam. I mean, it wasn't like I just skipped over you two. I would have pulled you out if I found you first, I mean next, but I didn't. It took a while to find the other two, but I did it. Then I came back and got you and Stella. It wasn't as hard to find you two, especially since she was holding your hand – ha, another package deal. I just thought about that."

"Well, you're right. We can't breathe underwater, but we can hold our breath for quite some time. You made the right decisions. Thank you. Thank you for saving us – all of us."

"Aw, you'd have done the same thing," he said. She thought he began to blush, but it was hard to see.

She could see the others nearby – shadows in the darkness. She noticed a mist rising in the air above them, and then saw that same mist coming from her own mouth. She focused on how cold she was.

"Why didn't you try to light a fire?" she asked, pulling the blanket closer around her shoulders, and shivering.

"I did." He pointed behind him into the blackness. "It's right over there, except it didn't work out too good."

That was when Natalie saw the minimal source of light. It was a small flame, but it was not moving. She looked closer at it. She could have sworn the flames were covered in ice.

"I got it started all right. But it froze solid as soon as it ignited," Quinn confirmed her suspicions. "I've never seen anything like it. Not even in the Ice Kingdom, and it can get pretty cold there. Weird, huh?"

That was when she realized he had covered each of them in the blankets he had been buried in for the last few days. She also noticed that they had all returned to their normal size. The spell that had shrunk them appeared to have died when they hit the water, or shortly thereafter.

"You must be frozen to the bone," she said, pulling to blankets off to give back to him. "Here, put this on."

"No, please. You keep it. You need it more than I do. And actually, I'm really not cold at all. That water was just like back home. Well – not exactly, but sort of. It was a lot colder than the water at home, but, even still, it didn't bother me too much. In fact, right now, I'm kind of hot."

He could faintly make out the look of disbelief on her face. "No, really. I feel fine. Honest."

Stella started coming around next. She was shivering almost uncontrollably. Natalie scooted over next to her and put her arms around her. She rubbed them vigorously to improve her circulation. In a few minutes, she seemed to warm up some and appeared to be fully alert.

"Do you have a potion or some kind of remedy in those pockets of yours that might revive the others?" Natalie asked her.

"Yes," she said, slowly getting to her feet and staring at the walls of the cavern. "I'm sure I do."

She refocused her attention on the question Natalie and asked, and thought for a minute. When she remembered what she was looking for she rummaged around inside her pockets. She pulled a small vial and went over to Solveig who was resting right next to her. Natalie and Quinn helped warm her up some, while Stella moved down the line and administered to the others.

"Can you provide us some more light?" Natalie asked Solveig, once she had recovered. "If you're up to it, that is."

"Oh, yeah, of course," she answered.

She clapped her hands and thrust her fist into the air. The bolt of light splashed against the rounded ceiling of the cavern, illuminating the thousands of crystals that were scattered in the rock. The clap of thunder that followed was magnified in the enclosed cave, and echoed off the walls. Even though she knew it was coming, the closeness of the sound made her wince and duck.

One by one, each of them woke up, shivering with the cold and holding their ears to block out the reverberating thunder. By the time they were all awake, the light reflected in the crystals had faded to nothing. It wasn't lasting very long. In fact, it faded much more quickly than it did when Solveig sent the bursts down the shaft.

"Summer," Lochen said through chattering teeth. "Before we transported down here, you said you had an idea how to generate light. Was that something more or different from what Solveig has been able to do?"

"Oh, yes. I remember," she said. "Solveig. Can you set off another bolt, just so I can see where I'm going?"

Solveig waited for everyone to cover their ears and then set off another bolt of light. The crystals glowed as they had before, and Summer flew up and around the grotto, sprinkling faerie dust at key points along the ceiling. She seemed to find larger deposits of the glowing crystal in several locations.

"OK," she said when she was done. "Solveig, if you would do your magic one more time."

Solveig set off another blast of light, and the crystals covered with faerie dust absorbed it and radiated it back. It was like dawn on a slightly foggy morning. The light stretched across the cavern from one end to the other in a soft diffused sort of glitter.

"Brilliant," announced Lochen.

"Thanks," said Summer, a little bit embarrassed by the praise.

"No, I meant the firmament above is brilliant with light, but not so bright as to be blinding," replied Lochen.

"Oh," said Summer, her ego slightly deflated. "Well, thanks anyway, I guess."

"But we must do something about the cold," he continued. "This is really intolerable. We won't last long at this temperature."

He looked at the frozen fire that Quinn had made. He stooped down to get a closer look and reached out to touch it. As he thought, the flame was covered in ice. The fire had been frozen immediately upon being ignited.

"What an odd phenomenon," he said. "This can't happen naturally. There must be some kind of spell on this place."

"Couldn't we just cast a different spell?" asked Solveig. "To counteract it?"

"No," he answered. "Without knowing the nature of the spell, we could make things worse."

"Oh, yeah," said Sean, "and we wouldn't want that to happen. We're soaked, in the dark and freezing our butts off. How can it get worse?"

No one paid any attention to him. All this time, each of them had kept the blankets Quinn had divided among them tightly wrapped. They offered only a little relief from the cold. Summer was the first to notice that she wasn't wrapped in a blanket. When she looked closer, she discovered that she was wrapped in the odd looking material that Liam always wore.

She jerked her head in his direction, thinking, why would he tear up his own clothes to for me to use. He was wrapped in a blanket like the others. If not Liam, she asked herself, then who? She turned her attention to Quinn. He had taken off all but his underwear. Quinn was the only one who seemed unaffected by the cold. In fact, he appeared to be sweating.

"Quinn," she nearly shouted in shock. "Where are your clothes? Why aren't you covered? Why aren't you freezing?"

"I'm fine," he assured her. "You need that stuff more than I do. Besides, I'm really hot. Maybe it was the excitement or the exertion of pulling all of you out of the water. Don't worry about it."

"It appears you'll be all right for the time being," observed Lochen. "But we really need to do something to warm up. Otherwise, even you will be affected."

He appeared to have an idea and turned to Liam to ask a question. Liam was gone.

"Where's Liam?" he asked.

"I think he went exploring," said Sean, who was squatting, curled up into a tight ball, wrapped several times over in his blanket.

"Liam," shouted Solveig.

Instead of her voice carrying or even echoing in the enormous cavern, it was dead and muffled. Everyone exchanged glances. The boom that followed her flashes of light had been amplified and bounced from side to side. The lack of an echo now was unnerving. She shouted again, with the same result.

"Just as I suspected," said Lochen. "That confirms my belief that there is a spell on this cave. We need to get out of here."

"I don't understand," said Solveig. "Why would my flashes echo, but my voice just disappear?"

"Because the noise associated with your flash is different. Whatever spell is on this cavern is directed at people, not natural phenomena, like from your flash. I could go into much more detail if you like, but not now. Now we need to get out of here."

"But which way do we go?" asked Sean.

"That passage over there," said Liam, who had just returned from his excursion. "The one with the narrowest opening."

"How can you tell?" asked Natalie. "I mean, I believe you, but...how can you tell?"

"I went around to each tunnel," he explained. "And in most of them, when I took a few steps in, I didn't notice anything unusual. In the ones that were on the opposite side, I could feel a little bit of warm air. In that one over there, I felt air even colder than in here."

"Why should we go into the tunnel that's even colder than we are now?" asked Natalie. "Shouldn't we choose one of the warmer ones?"

"No," said Sean. "Whoever put the spell on this cave is trying to keep people out. They must want to keep people away from something important. The best way to do that is to make the most appealing exit the wrong one to take. It makes perfect sense. I have to agree with Liam. If we want to get out of here, we need to go where it looks like the worst place to go."

Everyone just looked at Sean in silence.

"What?" he asked. "I can't have come up with a good idea?"

"I don't care either way," said Quinn. "I just need to get someplace cooler. If it means taking that cold tunnel, it's just fine with me."

He wiped the sweat from his brow, mopping at it with a piece of cloth as he pulled his tee shirt away from his chest and fanned himself. His hair was wet and stuck to his head. His body was covered with perspiration.

Liam led them to the opening. The inside was as black as the grotto had been before Summer and Solveig had illuminated it. There was a slow but steady frigid breeze coming from deep within, blowing into the cavern.

"This must be the source of the cold air for this cave," said Stella, shivering as the air blew her hair and chilled her even further. "I hope we don't have to go too far into this wind."

The breeze at the mouth of the opening had been fairly gentle, but the further they got into the tunnel, the stronger the wind became. In a matter of minutes, Summer could no longer fly. Without a word, Lochen scooped her up and dropped her into the hood behind his head. She burrowed into the folds of the hood on Lochen's robes, and settled in for a more comfortable ride. She was glad for the added warmth and that Lochen's head was blocking the cold air.

"Isn't there anything anyone can do about this temperature?" asked Solveig, who had been sending forth blasts of light. The wind was just too strong for Summer to sprinkle more faerie dust on the way ahead. "My hands are getting numb. It's harder and harder to create these light flashes."

"Yeah," said Quinn. "Is there any way to cool things off a bit? It's so hot in here, I'm really burning up."

"How can you be so hot when the rest of us are freezing?" asked Sean.

"I don't know," said Quinn. "Maybe it's my metabolism."

"No," said Stella. "It's probably that last potion I gave you. I was afraid that it would interact badly with what was already in your system. It seems I was right. It's still under your tongue, isn't it?"

"Uh...well..." Quinn tried to think of a way to avoid her question, but in the end realized he couldn't. "I think I swallowed it."

"What?" shouted Stella. "I specifically told you to NOT swallow it. Why would you do that?"

"Well, geez," he whined. "It's not like I did it on purpose. I guess when we got dropped in that lake, and I came up for air, I must have gotten some water in my mouth, so I just swallowed. I think that leaf thing was just there when I swallowed."

"You swallowed water from that lake?" Stella asked incredulously. "With the leaf? Together?"

"Well, sorry! I had to breathe," he shot back, defensively. "Next time I'll be sure to stick that lump of really rotten tasting leaf behind my ear before I gasp for air to save my life! Holy blubber on a biscuit!"

"I'm the one who's sorry," said Stella. "I should have been more explicit in my instructions. I probably shouldn't have given you that leaf in the first place. It's just that swallowing the leaf was bad enough, but the damage would be done in a few minutes. But now, with whatever spell was cast on that cave, as well as the water, I have no idea how long the results will last."

"That's OK," Quinn said. "So far this isn't really much worse than the heat in that Swamp of Liam's." He was lying and she knew it.

Quinn was sweating so much now that it was literally pouring off his body and pools of water were forming along the path. Although the wind seemed to have died down, but only slightly, the air was still extremely cold. As a result, the pools of sweat dripping from Quinn immediately froze into ice and everyone who was behind him in line started slipping and sliding. They had to keep looking from the path ahead and down at their feet, both at the same time.

Eventually the path began to narrow. They came upon a sharp curve on the other side of which the far wall split off away from them and opened over an expanse of inky black. Liam stopped walking until Solveig threw out another flash of light. The bolt of light revealed a huge chasm running parallel to the edge on which they had been walking.

The ledge they were on was about eighteen inches wide. Even though it was wide enough for them to walk, everyone turned sideways with their backs to the wall and inched along the path in single file. Liam was in the lead, followed by Lochen with Summer in his hood. She got crunched a few times when he arched his back and pressed the back of his head against the wall, but she didn't object. She had a peek at the chasm, and thought it was better that he not be distracted.

After Lochen came Quinn, who was huffing and puffing, drenched in sweat. Every few steps he had to stop to catch his breath. His internal body heat and the extreme loss of fluids were wearing him out. Each time he stopped, more water pooled into ice at this feet. A few feet behind him was Natalie, followed by Solveig and then Stella and Sean.

The path curved around sharply once again. Just as Quinn rounded out of sight, Natalie slipped on one of the patches of ice left in Quinn's wake, and went over the side. She flung her arms out as she tried to spin around, and grabbed onto some rocks along the edge. Solveig immediately leaned forward, realizing too late how narrow the ledge was, and nearly pitched over the side.

Stella quickly seized the edge of the blanket wrapped around Solveig, squatted low to the ground to drop her center of gravity and kept Solveig from toppling over. Sean grabbed on to Stella to keep her from going over the side with the others. With Stella and Sean holding tightly, Solveig regained her balance and leaned a little more and took Natalie's hand in hers, and pulled her back to the ledge.

None of the others noticed what had happened until the path had curved back the other way and Liam looked back to see where everyone was.

When he didn't see anyone behind Quinn, he had them all back up until they came into sight. Just as they rounded the curve, they saw Solveig pulling Natalie to safety.

"We need to do something about this," Liam said to Lochen, gesturing towards Quinn. "I know it's not his fault, but we're all in danger."

When they reached a small indentation in the side of the cliff wall, large enough for them all to gather, Liam announced that they would take a break. Lochen pulled Stella aside to speak with her.

"I understand your apprehension, Stella, and normally I would agree with your decision. However, in this case, I think it may be worth the gamble to give Quinn another potion. He's clearly in discomfort and he's creating a hazard."

As private as he intended his conversation to be, and in spite of the spell that had dampened their voices, everyone heard his comments.

"Hey," Quinn said, as he moved to join the two of them, "at this point I'm boiling up so much, I'll do anything. Remember what I said about not wanting to be someone's science experiment? Well, do me a favor and disremember it. I don't mind being the science experiment. Give me something. PLEASE!"

Stella looked closely at him. She pulled him down and stood on her tiptoes so she could feel his forehead. Then she pulled back one eyelid and then the other, holding his head in her hands to keep him from pulling away from her. When she was done, she wiped his sweat from her hands. Shaking her head, she pulled two vials from her pocket. In this light it was hard to see which one was which.

She held the largest one up so she could see better what exactly was in it. Quinn thought she was handing the vial to him. He grabbed it out of her hand, pulled off the top and emptied the contents into his mouth before she could protest. She stared at him with her mouth open in shock.

She started to say something, but then thought there really wasn't much point, and, besides, it might only cause him to worry. She didn't want his emotions to influence the potion – assuming he had taken the right one and had taken the right dosage: two very big assumptions. Almost immediately, he stopped perspiring.

"Ah. Thanks. That feels better already," he said.

He picked her up and gave her a big hug. He was still soaked with sweat. Stella pushed against him to not get soaked herself. Once he put her back down on the ground, she breathed a sigh of relief as she straightened her clothing. Maybe he'd be all right after all, she thought.

They moved on from the niche and continued. A few minutes later, the path took another sharp turn and ended in a small clearing before three tunnels. One seemed to be the source of the cold air and another seemed to be the source of the wind. The third one was calm and quiet.

"So, should we take the cold tunnel or the windy tunnel?" asked Solveig.

"Neither," said Liam. "We take the calm one."

"Why?" asked Summer. "The last time you told us that the easiest path was the trap. Why isn't that the same now?"

"Really? It's so obvious!" said Sean, smiling because he knew the answer and the others apparently did not. "Because, if anyone was smart enough in the first place to figure out that the worst choice out of the cave was the right one, then they'd most likely think that they should keep making that same kind of choice. But that would be the wrong choice. And if they thought they would be clever and NOT go down the cold tunnel, thinking that the windy tunnel is the right one, they'd be wrong. At this point, whoever set this up didn't want to make it harder for themselves, so now, the easiest looking path is the right one."

Again everyone looked at him in silence.

"What?" he asked.

"As strange as that sounds," said Liam, "it makes sense to me."

"Me, too, little buddy" said Quinn, and he bent over, took Sean's face in his hands and gave him a kiss on the top of his head.

"Let's boogie," he said to everyone as he elbowed his way past Lochen and Liam, and headed right into the tunnel of choice, humming an odd tune and wiggling his butt in time with whatever music was playing in his head. Everyone watched as Quinn seemed to dance off down the path.

Stella watched him nervously, thinking to herself, "Oh, no. Now what?"

Chapter nineteen

After going about another mile, they all noticed that the temperature had become more comfortable. With no wind, Summer was able to flit ahead and pepper the walls with faerie dust to capture and hold Solveig's light flashes. They seemed to be making better time, even though they still had no idea where they were going.

A little further along the path widened out and became flatter. It was becoming so much more normal that they all began to worry and became more cautious. There were no signs of any further spells or enchantments. The texture of the walls also seemed to be changing. While much of it was still rough, every once in a while a streak of cream colored luminous stone would appear.

Stella was wearing the amulet that held the stone from Sean's armband. She usually wore it in her headband, but more and more, lately, she only wore the headband when she was in the Sanctorum. Now, she was wearing the stone from a thin chain as a pendant around her neck. As she approached one of the larger veins of the cream colored stone, her amulet felt like it was vibrating or humming. The cream colored stone seemed to pulse slightly and even crackle.

The reaction of the pendant and the crackling of the veins of stone caught her attention. She stopped walking and moved closer to the wall. The vibrations of her pendant increased, and the streak of stone in the wall seemed to brighten. She reached out and touched the milky colored stone and noted that it felt warm. She got even closer, and a small spark flew from the stone in the pendant to the stone in the wall.

"Hey," she called out to the others. "Come over here and look at this. I'm not sure what to make of it."

They all gathered around to watch. She moved the amulet closer to the vein of stone. The humming was loud enough for each of them to hear. Once the amulet was close enough, the spark flew again, and the vein of stone started to glow.

"Oh, wow," said Sean. "I remember hearing about this stuff in the Lodges. Can you give me the amulet?"

"Sure. Here."

Stella removed it from around her neck and passed it over to Sean. He gently touched the stone in the amulet into the cream colored stone in the wall of the tunnel. It was like turning on a switch. There was a small popping sound, and then the streaks and veins of the cream colored stone produced a gentle glow approximately twenty feet in every direction radiating from the amulet.

Sean was grinning widely. "I remembered it right! And my lodge teacher thought I couldn't remember anything. Ha. I fooled her."

He turned to the others and explained, "Once this stone has touched those stones – actually, any one of those stones – a connection is made.

After that, they'll stay lit, but just for a while after you pass by, and at a lower level and not for long. All you have to do is wear that amulet."

"That's great. How do we turn it off?" asked Liam.

"Why would we want to turn it off?" asked Summer. "If we turn it off, then Solveig has to keep flashing lightning bolts and making that thunder noise."

"We may not be alone down here, and we may not want others to know we're here," answered Liam. "The flashes we can control. I know the thunder noise is a problem but it doesn't tell anyone where we are – just that we're here. Right now, I don't think it's a good idea to announce our presence any more than we have to."

"We may not be alone down here," Quinn started to sing.

Everyone's head slowly turned in his direction. Acting as if he was playing an invisible guitar, he continued to sing, "All alone are we...unless we're not," and he started to giggle. "I think we're alone now, boombidy boom boom, not a soul arou-ound!"

"What's up with you?" asked Solveig.

"Nothing," he said, regaining his composure. "I guess I'm just happy. I'm happy that I'm not real hot or real cold. Aren't you happy that I'm not real hot or real cold? You should be."

He reached over and poked her in the side, trying to tickle her.

"Stop it," she said, slapping his hand away.

"So," asked Liam, turning away from Quinn's odd behavior and directing his question to Sean again, "how do we turn it off?"

"Easy," said Sean. "She just needs to tuck the amulet under her clothes. The light will sort of fade away – not like closing your eyes; more like when the suns go down, but a little faster."

Stella did so, and the glowing faded away. She took it out again, and the glowing lights returned. "Neat," she said.

Continuing along the path they came upon an archway cut into the rock that curved to the right. The archway was roughly curved like a bridge over a small pond. However, this bridge extended out over a ravine. They all took a few tentative steps out onto the bridge to look over the side. Even before they got to the halfway point, they could feel the air wafting up from the ravine. It was exceedingly hot and had a smell familiar to several of the travelers: sulfur.

They had all crowded together a few feet from the edge, trying to crane their necks to see. The depth of the ravine was too great to see clearly to the bottom. The glowing lights from the veins of stone lit up both directions, but didn't extend downward. Solveig sent a bolt of light over the edge of the bridge. It briefly lit up a river of lava nearly a thousand feet below them before it vanished into the molten rock.

"Oh, oh," shouted Quinn. "Look at that! WOW!"

He elbowed the others aside and stepped up to the center of the bridge at it highest point and went right up to the very edge. Liam and Lochen reached out to grab him. With them holding onto the back of his shirt, he leaned forward even further and spit over the side.

"I guess no one's going to want to swim in that," he said, and again started giggling. "Swim away little dribble of spit. Swim to the sea."

He straightened up and shook off the hands holding his shirt. He turned back towards them as if he was ready to return to the path, and waited for them to move. Everyone slowly backed off the bridge. Instead of following them and before anyone could stop him, he turned back in the other direction and started hopping and singing, "Hopping down the bunny trail…" and he hopped on one leg over the archway and across to the other side.

"Are you insane," shouted Solveig. "What do you think you're doing?"

"Doing? I'm do-whack-a-doing," he shouted back, and started laughing. "I'm mil-doing! I'm...Wooo hooo! I'm...I'm...I'm cock-a-doodle-doing! Come on, you guys; follow me. What are you? Chicken?" And he laughed again. "Hey, Liam! What's a chicken? You keep telling me everything tastes like chicken. I don't even know what chicken is. Ah, ha, ha, ha."

"What on earth?" said Lochen, stunned by Quinn's behavior. "Something is most definitely not right with him."

"You've just discovered this?" asked Summer. "He's as nutty as a Bong Bug. We have to do something."

"Yes, you're right – and fast before he hurts himself. Stella," Lochen started to say, "can you..."

"NO!" she cut him off. "I can't. Don't you see? All these potions are mixing with one another. They're interacting, and the interaction is changing their properties and dynamics. If I give him anything more, there's no telling what will happen. He just needs to let this wear off. We need to keep a watch on him and just make sure he doesn't hurt himself – or us."

"And how long do you think that will be?" asked Lochen.

"I don't know," she said, clearly frustrated.

"How could you not have predicted this kind of reaction," Lochen pursued.

He wasn't blaming Stella or accusing her. His question was meant as more of a scientific inquiry. Stella however, didn't take it that way. A dark look passed over her face as she glared back at him.

"I don't know," she said again, seething. "There are far too many variables, most of which I have no control over or of which I am not even aware. First of all, I don't know how much of an exposure he received to the poultice Liam gave him. I probably should have just let the cold sensation he was feeling wear off, but I didn't. Sorry!

"Second, he's bigger than most people for whom I've prepared potions. If I were administering medication, I'd normally need more to have a greater effect on bigger people. But I didn't administer medication. I administered a potion, and that's not the case with potions. With potions, the less taken, the greater the effect. I thought I took this into consideration, but apparently not. Sorry!

"Third, he had been shrunk, so, even though he was still bigger than what I'm normally used to dealing with, he wasn't his normal size – until we got down here. And then he wasn't shrunk and who knows what that did to the potion I gave him when he was shrunk. I don't see how I could have anticipated that, but maybe I should have borrowed someone's crystal ball. Sorry!

"Fourth, he swallowed the leaf I gave him, instead of just keeping it under his tongue. That changed everything. Fourth, he's not a Sea Sprite. My potions are designed for their biological systems, not for whatever he is. And Fifth, I can't be certain what he took."

"What?" asked Natalie, in disbelief. "What was that last thing about not knowing what he took?"

"I was trying to look at the potion to see what it was, not give it to him. Then he just pulled it from my hand and drank it" she answered defensively. "All of it. Without any hesitation. I'm sorry I couldn't stop him in time and I'm sorry I didn't say anything at the time, but I didn't see any point in raising this after he had already drunk it. By then any damage was already done."

"No one is blaming you," said Solveig. "Even when he's not under the spell of some kind of potion, he can act a bit rashly."

"Well, I vote that we don't do anything," said Sean, "I kind of like him this way and I don't want to change him back – at least not too soon."

"Why?" asked Natalie.

"Because," he answered, "now I'm not the only one doing goofy stuff. And all of you aren't looking at me the way you're looking at him right now."

They all laughed at Sean's comment, which broke the tension. Even Stella had to laugh, although she still felt responsible.

"So," shouted Quinn from the other side of the ravine, where he had been waiting and wiggling to some imaginary tune throughout the discussion. "What are you waiting for? Do I have to come back over there and carry you across?"

"NO!" they all shouted back in unison and one by one inched their way over the arch to the other side.

Once they were all across, Liam asked him, "So did you see something over on this side? Is there a better way forward?"

"I don't know," answered Quinn, "I just thought it would be nice to hop on over. Hop on over to the other side!" He had broken into song again.

And he started laughing again. Everyone stared at him in shocked disbelief.

"See what I mean?" asked Sean, smiling widely.

And on they went; in spite of the fact that they were being led by someone they had declared was not right in the head. Liam had no strong feelings about this course compared to the one they left, so they proceeded deeper and deeper through the winding tunnel.

After nearly an hour had gone by, Liam slowed down until Lochen caught up with him. Quinn was still singing and dancing ahead of them, and Liam used the added noise as a distraction to cover his comment to Lochen. As they walked slowly side by side, he whispered out of the side of his mouth, without moving his head, "Something or someone is following us."

"I sensed that, too," said Lochen, displaying no reaction. "Do you have any thoughts on what or who?"

"Not exactly," he answered. "I think it's no more than one or two – whatever it is; most likely only one. What I don't know is if we're being just observed, scouted, or hunted. I'd hate to think we're walking into a trap or some kind of ambush. I don't have a sense of that, but I can't say for sure."

"Do you think we could capture whatever is following us? I don't want to harm it, you understand. I just want to see if we can determine what it is and what its intentions towards us are."

"We can certainly try," Liam answered. He thought a bit and then whispered to Lochen, "I have an idea."

He slowly changed his position and waited for Summer to drop back into the group. She had been shuttling back and forth. In part to scout ahead, but in part to keep an eye on Quinn. Liam motioned to her to sit on his shoulder while he shared his plan. Then she floated back to Sean and filled him in.

At the next turn in the path, Summer flew to the top of the tunnel, pressed herself against the ceiling, and faded into the surrounding colors. A few seconds later, Sean crawled into a nearby cranny in the side of the wall, armed with his sling shot. They disappeared from sight as stealthily as they could. However, they didn't really have to do anything to divert attention, since Quinn was making enough noise to raise the dead.

Liam slowed his pace somewhat so they wouldn't get too far ahead of Sean and Summer. He and Lochen had decided not to tell the others what they were doing, since they didn't want them to act any differently.

Natalie, Stella and Solveig barely noticed the slower pace or the disappearance of two of their group.

They had moved nearly a hundred yards ahead of Sean and Summer in just a few minutes. Liam was worried that they were getting too far ahead of the other two. He thought that maybe they were walking into a trap after all. He was worried about leaving Sean and Summer so far behind them. He was having second thoughts and was about to share them with Lochen. The distance between them was increasing too fast, and this was taking too long.

As the rest of the group slowly moved out of sight, Summer remained silent and motionless against the ceiling of the cave. From her vantage point, she would normally have had a clear view of everything below her, but as Stella moved further away, taking the amulet with her, the glowing lights that lined the cave were fading away. She was not yet in total darkness, but it wouldn't be long before that changed. In any case, she could no longer see Sean, but she thought that might just be because he was so well hidden. After several minutes passed, she was beginning to get nervous. The tunnel was getting very dark.

Sean had smeared himself with dirt and curled up into as small a ball as he could, and then wedged himself into a small crack in the wall along the path. He had learned to make himself invisible by using materials from the scenery around him, since just after he learned to walk. As a young boy he had learned to hunt and to scout, and had also learned the importance of keeping silent and still. But those lessons had been learned in the forest; not deep underground in a near black tunnel.

He could normally stay in this position indefinitely, but without the normal indicators of the passage of time, he was less certain of how long he could maintain his secrecy. Fortunately, his hearing was even more acute than normal when he was in this mode. Even though the others were far ahead of him, he could still hear their footsteps, and, of course, Quinn singing.

"I think we need to go back," Liam whispered to Lochen. "We're getting too far ahead of them."

"Not yet," he replied. "I agree that I don't want to allow too much of a gap between us to develop, especially with the visibility diminishing so greatly. However, our trap has to be as clever as one we may be walking into, and certainly more clever than whoever is leading us into it."

"What do you mean?" asked Liam.

"If we're wrong about just being observed, and we are in fact being scouted – or hunted, I would assume that we are headed into an area where we will have no way out. Any ambush has a better chance of success if the quarry has limited escape routes. That might be why we're being followed. If that's the case, then I also assume any trap will be sprung shortly."

"You seem to be convinced that we're heading into a trap. Why?"

"Not so much convinced as just being cautious. But think about what's happened. If you assume that whatever is following us has purposely let it be known that we are being followed, then its design must be to either cause a diversion to allow the trap to be sprung, or to cause us to attempt to flee and seek escape directly into the trap. In either case, whatever is going to happen should happen soon."

Liam thought this over, and then said, "OK. I see what you're thinking. So, if you're right about the trap, then it would be to our advantage to have our only avenue of retreat protected by Sean and Summer. I hope they're able to cover our backs or that we don't really need them for that."

Lochen looked over at him. "So do I."

Behind them, both Summer and Sean had closed their eyes until they could barely hear the others as they faded away up ahead. They were adjusting their eyes to see better in the shadows. By the time they opened their eyes, the pathway was in near total darkness. The veins of lighted stone were only blurs. They could barely make out the shape of the wall and the terrain of the path. As the minutes passed, the concentration needed to keep this still for this long was wearing on them.

Just as Summer was at the end of her patience, she caught a faint movement out of the corner of her eye. It wasn't much, but she was sure she had seen a smoky white figure move very slightly along the path. She forced herself not to move her head and only shift her eyes in the direction of the movement. It was so small and so quick, that at first she wasn't sure she had actually seen anything.

Then she saw it again. It almost looked like a wisp of smoke. Once it passed in front of her, she released herself from the ceiling. Without flapping her wings or making any sound whatsoever, she glided gently downward, making minute adjustments with her wings to control her descent. As she floated closer to the path, she saw it again and more clearly. This time she was certain. It was a small white creature moving stealthily along the path.

Inside his hidey-hole, Sean couldn't see much at all. His eyelids were closed halfway down, but his ears were on the alert. He heard movement from behind him several seconds before he saw anything. He opened his mouth to quiet his breathing and slowed it down as much as he could. He strained to listen more closely. He thought that maybe his imagination was playing tricks on him.

There it was again. It was as soft as someone moving on air, but it was enough for him to pick up. Something was definitely moving. He still couldn't see what, and had no idea how close the object was. He then held his breath to keep his body from moving at all, and closed his eyelids to tiny slits – enough to still see; to the extent he could see anything at all, but also enough to hide the whites of his eyes.

Summer glided easily downward, floating like a falling leaf, until she realized she was coming down too fast and was getting too close to the target. She could see it more clearly now. She still couldn't tell what it was, but the shape of the object was more evident. She was within a few feet of landing right on top of it, and needed to do something fast.

Before she knew it, she was so close that she was afraid that a flap of her wings would be heard. She was also afraid of colliding into whatever it was and losing whatever advantage she had. She was holding her breath, willing herself to slow down. The creatures' back was growing larger and larger. She felt like she was dive-bombing it and couldn't slow her progress.

At the very last moment, she heard a peal of laughter from Quinn far up ahead. It was enough to disguise the little bit of noise that a quick flap of her wings would make. She knew she'd never have another opportunity as good as this one. She had to make the decision in a split second. She gave one enormous push with all her might. She was able to raise herself a few feet higher, and allowed herself to begin once more to float downward.

All of a sudden, the target stopped. She was sure she had made no noise at all with the flap of her wings. She watched the creature closely. Its head moved to the right and left. She was right. It hadn't heard her wings flap, but it had felt a minute change in the air pressure. It detected another presence close by in the tunnel and all its senses were on alert.

Sean felt the creature pass him. He was certain he hadn't been noticed, but kept his eyes to slits and kept his breath held. He could actually see it now, not far in front of him. He wanted to let it get a little further before he moved. It was literally crawling forward. Sean forced himself to be patient.

Then he heard Quinn laugh. The sound echoed down the tunnel. The target stopped. Sean wasn't sure if it had stopped because of the noise Quinn had made, or if something else had alerted it. He couldn't see or hear any sign of Summer, but assumed she was right overhead. He also thought he felt a very slight movement in the air. What was that, he wondered. Did the creature notice it too?

It did. He could tell. The creature was looking around, but Sean wasn't sure if it was reacting to the noise from ahead or something else. He debated over stepping into the path and blocking the creature's exit. The problem was he didn't know what the creature was. Even though it was clearly smaller than him, it could be extremely vicious. Even if it wasn't normally dangerous, it could react very unpredictably if it thought it was trapped.

"Why are we stopping?" asked Natalie, as Solveig came to a sudden stop and looked up at the ceiling, back to the end of the line and then up towards the front.

"Is Summer still with you, Lochen?" asked Solveig.

That prompted both Natalie and Stella to look for her. Not seeing her, they looked more closely behind them and saw that Sean was missing.

"Where's Sean?" asked Stella.

Now all three of them had stopped. Lochen only glanced over his shoulder and motioned to them to keep moving. Quinn was getting further ahead of the group, and Liam was trying not to let him get too far away, as the rest of the party was slowing down.

"Don't be alarmed," said Lochen in a low voice, which only had the effect of alarming them.

"Don't slow down and don't turn around," whispered Liam, who had sidled back to the stalled members. "We're being followed."

In spite of his admonition not to turn around, Natalie, Solveig and Stella, who had already stopped, suddenly and quite deliberately turned around and looked behind them. Quinn had overheard Liam's comment and skipped back with the rest of them.

"We're being followed?" he asked much too loudly. "Oh, no!" he added, and he started laughing uncontrollably. "Ah, ha, ha, ha, ha. We'll probably be eaten by some horrible monster. Hee, hee, hee. Or torn apart limb from limb. Ha, ha, ha, ha. I guess we'll be torn limb from limb first and then eaten. Ah, ha, ha, ha, ha. It wouldn't make sense for it to happen the other way."

He had nearly doubled over with laughter before Lochen and Liam pounced on him, pulling him to the ground and muffling his noise. Liam pressed his hand across Quinn's mouth, and wrapped his arms around Quinn's head, while Lochen pulled him to the ground and then sat on him. In their efforts to quiet him, they were only making more noise. The others watched this reaction with wide eyes.

"What are you two doing?" demanded Solveig. "Have you both lost your minds? Get off of him. Hasn't he been through enough?"

The three women ran over to the fracas and began pulling Liam and Lochen off of Quinn, adding further to the level of noise and confusion.

Summer could hear muffled voices ahead, and then she quite clearly heard Quinn's voice and laughter. What's going on up there, she asked herself. Then she heard other noises and was at a loss as to what was going on up ahead. At that same moment, the figure before her, which had already stopped, slowly began to back up. Although it was difficult to make out clearly, it appeared to be looking around, as if searching to see who or what was nearby.

She tensed up, not knowing what to do. The creature obviously had been startled by the noise up ahead, but what was it doing now? Does it sense the trap they had tried to set? Is it planning to run? Is it planning to attack? Is it looking for help? Are there others following behind it, she wondered. Are we being trapped? She was overwhelmed with questions and indecision. What should she do next?

As the echoes of Quinn's laughter ricocheted down the cavern, Sean saw the white figure move past him and stop about two yards ahead. He had no idea where Summer was or what she could see. As the noise from ahead reached him, his eyes fully popped open, and he saw the creature stop and start looking around.

It was backing up slowly. It knows something's not right, thought Sean. He wasn't sure what to do. They hadn't discussed this as part of their plan. Actually, aside from laying in wait for whatever it was, he realized they didn't have a plan. Man, he thought, we really need to get better at this kind of stuff.

The creature turned almost halfway around to its right, and seemed to be looking directly toward where Sean was hiding. It was just standing there, waiting for something. Assuming he had been spotted, Sean decided to go on the offensive. He jumped from his hiding place, pulled his slingshot up and started shooting small stones at the creature's feet. He was careful not to hit it, only wanting to create confusion.

"Get him!" he shouted at the top of his lungs. "Quick. Move in from the left, he's trapped," he continued to shout, changing his voice, and hoping his bluff would encourage the creature to surrender. Instead, it seemed to stand upright, turn around and then bolted in the opposite direction towards the sound of Quinn's laughter.

Chapter twenty

"What is he doing?" Summer asked herself, stunned at Sean's sudden appearance and shouting. She backed off, fluttering a little higher in the air. At this point, with all the noise Sean was making, any sounds from her would be completely lost.

"Who is he talking to? Has he gone completely mental?"

And then it dawned on her. "He's trying to get that person or thing or whatever it is to think there are a whole bunch of us."

Thinking about what she could do to help, she dive-bombed right towards the creature, darted to its left side and began to shout in her deepest and most threatening voice, which actually was not very deep and not at all threatening.

"I've got him," she said as rumbly as she could.

She then zipped around behind him to the other side and, and. trying to change her voice, shouted, "No, he's mine."

All the while Sean kept firing stones at the figure, which Summer could see, were purposely aimed towards the ground. She understood that Sean was trying not to hit the figure, but to intimidate it. All of a sudden, and much to her surprise, instead of giving up, or even attacking, their target turned around and headed towards the others, scrambling as fast as it could.

At the sound of Sean's raised and oddly changing voice, Natalie, Solveig and Stella halted their rescue of Quinn and looked back down the tunnel. Lochen and Liam released Quinn and struggled to their feet. They pushed past the ladies, and started running back down the path.

"Quickly now," Lochen said to Liam as they moved carefully down the darkening passageway, "we must capture it before it can summon assistance."

Liam pulled a long dagger from a side pocket and handed it to Lochen, and then pulled two more for himself as they were running towards Sean's shouts. Lochen held the dagger up to the nearby glowing rocks to examine it, dangling it awkwardly between his thumb and index finger as if it was something disgusting.

"I certainly hope this won't be necessary," he said, huffing and puffing. "I'm sure we don't intend to do it any harm. After all, it's quite likely that it has no intention to harm us. At least not by itself."

"I don't want to inflict any harm either," said Liam, "but I've learned that it's better to be safe than sorry."

In a few seconds they both saw the white creature headed towards them. It seemed to be waddling more than running, but it was clear from its movements that it was frightened. Lochen skidded to a stop and thrust out the arm without the weapon, gesturing for the creature to halt, waving the dagger wildly in the air above his head. He positioned himself between the creature and Liam.

"Halt," he shouted. "Come no further. That's far enough. We are well armed and quite numerous, so it would be in your best interests to desist."

"What?" asked Liam, peering over Lochen's shoulder.

He felt like they were threatening a bunny rabbit. They both towered over the cowering figure, who was evidently in no real danger whatsoever, other than being in danger of laughing to death at Lochen's attempt to be menacing.

Lochen was crouched in a kind of fencing stance with one arm extended outward and the other waving the dagger in the air. He cast a sideways glance at Liam, trying to keep his focus on the strange creature in front of him.

"I was issuing a warning," he said to Liam. "I thought it only proper. Should I not have done so?"

"A warning," said Liam, trying not to let Lochen see the smile on his face. "No, that's fine. It was a...ah...just fine."

As the others came running up behind them, they had not expected the two guys to be stopped in the middle of the path. Stella was behind Natalie, who was behind Solveig. One by one they collided into each other, like an accordion being squeezed shut. They couldn't stop their momentum, and abruptly ran into Liam, pushing him forward into Lochen.

Lochen, feeling increasing pressure on his back, stiffened his knees, braced his legs and dug in his feet to keep from being pushed any closer to the creature. However, by locking his knees, his upper body took the brunt of the weight behind him, causing him to bend severely at the waist. He became completely unstable and flew forward, sprawling at the feet of the frightened figure.

Flat on his face with the one empty hand still outstretched and the other limply waving the dagger, he mumbled, "Don't be deceived by my demeanor, and don't do anything rash, now. We...ah...all of us, that are...you are...uh...we have you surrounded...uh...and...ah...you are at our mercy."

"Smooth," was all Liam could say.

Liam pulled Lochen to his feet, and took the dagger from his hand, thinking, he's likely to do more harm to himself with this than to anyone else. Sean and Summer appeared, running up immediately behind the figure. The veins in the walls came to life again with the close proximity of the stone in Stella's pendant. They were all looking at the threat that had been following them.

Huddled between them was a mole-like person with large, protruding eyes, who was about a foot tall. He was covered in a short dull white fur from head to toe. He had large feet with claw like nails. His shoulders were slumped in an air of defeat, and he was wringing his hands, which were disproportionately large.

"Please," he said in a quavering voice, "I'll come peacefully. I promise to return to the mine. Just don't hurt me, I beg of you."

Everyone was staring at him in silence. Natalie finally pushed her way in front of Liam and Lochen and approached the creature.

"We mean you no harm," she said, looking over to see that Lochen had been dispossessed of the dagger. "Honest! Please don't be frightened."

She bent down slightly and reached towards him, offering her hand. "I am Natalie, Princess of the Sea Sprites."

When the figure just looked at her unmoving, she asked, "What's your name?"

The creature stared at Natalie and blinked a few times. He looked around at the others staring at him, clearly frightened and uncertain. He turned back to Natalie who still had her hand extended. His eyes moved slowly from her face to her hand and back again. Not sure what was expected of him, he tentatively reached forward and touched her hand, completely engulfing it in his own enormous hand, and said in a voice still quavering, "Exa Tor Va."

She startled him even further by grasping his hand and shaking it. He started to pull it away, but she covered it with her other hand and shook it even more. He looked from her to his hand and back, as if expecting something to happen.

She smiled broadly and said, "It's very nice to meet you. Is Exa your first name, Mr. Va?"

He was obviously in a state of shock. His mouth opened wordlessly; his eyes were riveted on his hand being raised up and down. Finally, he realized he had been asked a question. He straightened up, but was still much shorter than Natalie. He cleared his throat.

"Ah, my first name?" he asked. "I'm not sure what you mean."

Still shaking his hand vigorously, equally as nervous as he was, she explained, "Well, where I'm from, our first name is what our friends call us. As I said, my name – my first name – is Natalie. That is usually followed by our family name, which would be the same as everybody in our immediate family – well most of the time, anyway. Oh, unless, of course, you have a title. Do you have a title? You know? Like mine? Princess? Princess Natalie? I mean, you are more than welcome to just call me Natalie, if you like."

She knew she was rambling, but she thought the more she talked, the sooner he would relax. In spite of her best efforts, it was not yet working. Still uncomfortable with his large hand being shaken by this strange young lady, he took a deep, but unsteady breath, and tried to understand. A look of puzzlement caused the very bushy eyebrows above his enormous eyes to wrinkle together. Finally, he answered.

"Well, I suppose my first name would be Exa, but we put our family name in the middle, not at the end. So mine would be Tor, not Va."

"That's certainly interesting," said Natalie, finally releasing his hand. "In our worlds your name would be Exa Va Tor

"I suppose so," he answered, starting to feel more at ease, especially since he had his hand back, "but no one calls me Mr. Va. Or Mr. Tor for that matter. Certainly not the invaders."

"Invaders?" they all asked at once.

Exa shrunk into himself, startled by the sudden reaction. He seemed to actually shrink to half his size and covered his head with both his overly large hands, covering it nearly completely.

"Please," he pleaded, "I meant no offense. Don't strike me, please! I'll do as you order. Don't hurt me."

Natalie knelt down, to look directly into his eyes, and put her hand gently on his shoulder.

"It's all right, Exa. No one's going to hurt you. I promise," she said as soothingly as possible. "Can I call you Exa?" When he nodded, she went on. "You didn't offend anyone. We were just a bit surprised when you mentioned invaders. Who are these invaders, and who are you, exactly? Take your time, and begin at the beginning."

Her voice was so calm and caring, he began to relax. He was still wary, but slowly straightened up, much like a turtle poking its head from its shell. Looking from one to the next, and seeing the looks of compassion on their faces, he decided to take a chance, and began to explain.

He was a Trepan. His people had inhabited this underworld for centuries. Their civilization was responsible for guiding the elements of water and fire wherever needed to ensure a balance above and below the surface of the earth. Everything they did was carefully planned, and had an intended consequence – to keep all the elements of the world in harmony.

Many of them were miners and engineers, but there were hundreds of other occupations his people undertook. He was one of the miners. For as long as their history had been recorded, they had dug tunnels, redirected magma from deep in the planets' core, shifted waterways and made sure the polar caps stayed cold. Recently, though, that had changed.

Not long ago an explorer from the upperworld – the word the Trepans used to describe the surface of the planet – discovered one of the enclaves (a village, interjected Lochen). At first he seemed friendly, but they soon discovered that he was a scout, and his friendly demeanor was just an act.

At first he came alone and befriended the Trepans. Later they realized he was only doing reconnaissance. Before long, others just like him followed. These people, though, were not as nice. In fact, they were not nice at all. They forced the Trepans from their enclaves, drove them deep into the channels (tunnels and caverns, Lochen once more explained), and made them dig for lambentite.

"What's lambentite?" asked Solveig.

He looked at her with uncertainty.

"Why it's the stone that lit your way along this path," he said pointing to the veins of glowing rock.

Everyone looked around them.

"What do they use if for?" asked Summer. "I mean, I know how we've used it, but we didn't dig it out of the walls. What could they use it for?"

"They take it to the upperworld. There they carve it and make palaces and monuments," he answered.

"So what happens to the walls they take it from or the other tunnels down here?" asked Solveig.

"They're destroyed," he said. "Most of the tunnels have to be widened to allow for transport. It's been disastrous."

"So, if all the digging they've forced you to do has been without regard for anything but finding lambentite, and has resulted in total chaos regarding the channels for controlling the fire and water," concluded Lochen, "then nothing is balancing the escape of the magma, which is now making its way to the surface and poisoning the waters. Is that a correct assumption?"

"Yes," said Exa who was beginning to feel more and more comfortable with these strangers. "It's been horrible. They've caused so much damage, that we may never be able to correct it. And there's no end in sight. I suppose it won't stop until they have stripped all the lambentite from the earth. But by then...oh, I don't know what to expect. I'm afraid to think about it."

He was instantly worried that he had said too much. The one called Natalie had been far too kind. He was suspicious and frightened again.

"Why are you here," he ventured to ask, directing the question to Natalie, who was still kneeling before him.

They all looked at each other thinking about where to start. They turned back to Quinn, who, although he had been quiet for a while, still had a silly grin on his face. None of them was sure he was the right person to explain.

"It all started with him," Liam said, pointing to Quinn. "He discovered water near his home had been poisoned. He came looking for me to..." He tried to think of a way to explain Quinn's search for the Alchemist without making the explanation seem farfetched and unduly long.

"All of us are close friends," interjected Solveig. "We rely on each other when any one of us needs help. Quinn – that's his name – came to find us to help him."

"One thing led to another," added Lochen, "and we realized that there must have been some connection between your people and what was happening on the surface, as you've just confirmed."

One by one, they each told a piece of the story as to how they came to be there, and who they were. For a few seconds they all just stood there in silence trying to fully understand the situation – theirs and the Trepan's.

"So," asked Sean, refocusing everyone's attention. "What are you doing here all by yourself? I thought you said something about coming peacefully, that you'd return. Return where?"

"I escaped," answered Exa, looking at them closely; once more uncertain of their intentions. "I slipped away some time ago and have been hiding ever since."

"All by yourself?" asked Stella. "How long have you been hiding? Are there others like you?"

Exa was still not sure he could trust these strangers. He was hesitant to share too much information. No one pressed him for an answer. He began to waiver, but he had to know more about these people, who, so far, were so greatly different from the invaders.

"How did you come to be here?" he asked, avoiding Stella's questions. "It seems you did not come in the same way as the invaders."

Without hesitation, they shared their respective stories, Liam filling in the parts for Quinn, who was humming some tuneless song. They explained how they had all first met each other and what they had gone through to get this far. They were so open and appeared to be completely honest with the Trepan. Eventually, he decided he had to take a chance, and tell them more. When they were done, he turned back to Stella.

"I didn't forget your question," he said. "No. I'm not alone. There are others. We are part of an underground."

Quinn, who had been quiet up until now, broke out laughing, "Wow. That's a good one. The underground underground." He doubled over laughing. "Get it? They're under the ground and they're the underground." See? Underground under the ground. The underground underground. Down in the ground. Ground down. Ground round and round. You know if you keep saying ground, it doesn't mean anything anymore. Ground. Ground. Ground. Ground. Grrrroooouuuunnnnddd! Ground, ground, ground, ground. See what I mean?"

"Just ignore him," said Solveig, not knowing how she could even begin to explain what happened to him. "He's not right in the head."

"We are here to help," said Liam, becoming more insistent. "We need to find the others like you."

Exa immediately grew suspicious. He tried to take a step back, but realized he was surrounded, and trapped. He immediately feared he had said too much.

"That's what the first explorer said," he mumbled, his head down and his voice barely a whisper. "He told us he wanted to be friends; that he wanted to help us."

"Actually," said Lochen, "it is we who need your help. As we've explained to you, we are all from the upperworld." He saw Exa begin to shrink again, and he hurried on, "but a different part of the upperworld. We have no use for or interest in lambentite. In fact, our villages – our enclaves – are suffering from the results of the rampant digging that has been going on. Our enclaves are in jeopardy of being destroyed – lost forever. We need your help to stop this and to return the balance. That is our sole purpose in being here. We are asking for your help."

Exa looked at each of them again. In spite of his apprehension, he had to admit to himself that he didn't feel threatened by these people. He looked them all over once again. He seemed to focus on Natalie, since she was the first to offer her friendship. He was still wary, but it was clear to him that these people were all from different kinds of enclaves – villages as they called them – and were much different than the invaders. Still, he vacillated.

"I sense you're still unsure," said Natalie, looking directly into his eyes. "What can we do to earn your trust?"

Exa thought for a minute, his eyes darting around the tunnel, and then said, "There must be more of you. Where are they?"

"More?" asked Natalie. "No, this is all of us that are down here. We've told you about others like us in our villages, but we're the only ones here. Why would you think there were more?"

"There must have been several of you behind me. I was attacked by several adversaries trying to pelt me with stones," he said slightly indignantly. He thought he had caught them in a lie.

"Ha," said Sean, proudly. "That was me. I was the only one shooting at you. I was the one using different voices. Oh, and Summer, too."

"Impossible," said Exa. "I detected the false voices, but there were certainly more than just one of you shooting stones at me. They were fired much too fast for a single person."

"No," said Summer. "He's really fast with that slingshot of his."

"Then I suppose it was my good fortune," said Exa, not fully believing her, "that he has such poor aim."

"Poor aim?" asked Sean. "Poor aim? I hit exactly what I aim for. I wasn't trying to hit you. I was trying to scare you. It seemed to work pretty good, too."

Afraid that he had offended Sean, and may be subjected to some kind of retribution, Exa quickly apologized. "In that case, I suppose it is my good fortune that you are so accurate."

"So," said Lochen, trying to get back to the issue at hand, "is there anything else we can do to earn your trust?"

He saw Exa eying the dagger Liam had taken from Lochen's hand. He had not yet put it back in a scabbard. Without being asked, he reached over to take it from Liam's hand, and then reversed the blade and offered the handle to Exa.

Exa took the dagger in both hands and brought it closer to his large eyes. He waved it around as if feeling the balance of the weapon. He then looked at the strangers and saw that none of them had reacted to his possession of the knife. No one backed away; no one appeared threatened; no one took a defensive stand. It was clear that they trusted him to do them no harm. They are either crazy, he thought, except for the large one, who clearly <u>was</u> crazy and really didn't count, or their story is true.

"No," decided Exa. "Your story is sufficient. If I took this weapon from you, I would be no different than the invaders."

He handed the blade back to Lochen in the same manner it had been handed to him. Liam reached over and took it from Lochen's hand and returned it to the scabbard on his belt.

"You're right, of course," said Lochen. "That actually belongs to Liam," he added referring to the dagger. "I am not entirely comfortable with such armament. There are, however, many threats in his homeland, and such a weapon is, unfortunately, necessary. It is really quite useless in my hand, as you most probably realized."

"We have all faced evil," added Solveig. "If you remember, that's how we all came together. We know what it's like to be threatened, to have your home invaded and to be forced to flee."

That seemed to be enough for Exa. He took a deep breath and made his decision. He agreed to take them to meet the others in the underground.

"You've convinced me," he told them. "I'll take you to one of our hideouts. It's not far from here. We noticed you even before you crossed the bridge. I was sent to follow you, observe you, and if possible, determine your intentions. We were particularly amazed that the largest one of you actually hopped across that bridge. And sang while doing so. Of course, we assumed that you must have known that it was unstable."

"No," said Stella, "we didn't know that at all. How is it unstable?"

"No, not is. Was," he corrected. "It <u>was</u> unstable. It collapsed not long after you passed over it."

Everyone turned to look at Quinn, who just grinned at them and again started laughing.

"Oh, wow!" he said between fits of laughter. "That would have been a real downer. Get it? A downer? We would have fallen down into that ravine. Downer, see?"

They all turned back to look at him and then slowly turned towards Stella.

"Don't ask," she said, irritated each time he opened his mouth, "I have no idea how long before it wears off."

"You have made several references to these invaders," said Lochen, quickly changing the subject and inserting himself between Exa and Quinn. "What can you tell us about them? You said they have forced you to mine this lambentite. Who are they, exactly, and where do they come from?"

"We don't know much," Exa answered. "They are a vicious and treacherous people. They can't be trusted. That much is certain. They call themselves Rebbercands…"

"Rebbercands?" Sean stopped in the middle of the path and gasped. "This is worse than you can imagine."

Chapter twenty-one

"You know something about them, don't you," said Solveig.

Sean had stopped so suddenly, she had to catch herself from running into him.

"Yes," said Sean, his head lowered and shaking in dismay.

"What is it?" asked Stella. Sensing his reluctance to dredge up old and painful memories, she added, "You must tell us. We need to know as much about these invaders – the Rebbercands – as we can."

He looked at each of them, finding the courage to explain. It was evident from the tremendous sadness in his eyes, that this was not an easy task for him. He took a deep breath and then began.

"The history between the forest creatures and the Rebbercands goes back a long way. And it's not one of peace and harmony."

Sean's comment piqued Exa's interest and he listened closely as he lead them along the trail. He was taking them back to the others like him who formed the resistance movement of the Trepans, and took a few unnecessary diversions along the way. He wanted to hear what this forest creature had to say about the invaders.

"After the wars between the forest creatures and the faeries," Sean started, "the forest creatures moved further into the wooded lands that had originally been shared by both of our people. We had fought the faeries and drove them to the shores of the Cerulean Sea, before both sides agreed to a truce. They had always accused us of lurking on the edge of their village and stealing their small ones – their children. We had always accused them of placing spells on us.

"As it turns out, though, the forest creatures were just as afraid of the faeries. So we agreed to move as far away as we could. We went all the way to the other side of the forest where it meets the Viridian Ocean. The faeries agreed to stay on the shores of the Cerulean Sea. As things happened, though, we were forced to move back – closer to where we started. We just did everything we could to avoid the faeries.

"It wasn't until I met Summer and got to know her that I learned about the stories they told their small ones about us. They were a lot like the stories we told about them. I think all the stories our people told about each other were just that – stories. I'm beginning to wonder, now, if someone else was responsible for taking the faerie children and for putting the hexes and jinxes on the forest creatures that started the wars in the first place. But that's another matter."

Having a natural aversion to water, the forest creatures settled in just out of sight of the Ocean. They were still hundreds if not thousands of miles from the faerie village, and, so, felt safe. For quite a while things were good. They were able to rebuild their Lodge, and seemed to be free of the tormenting from the faeries. Then one day a stranger appeared.

He was clearly not from the faeries, as he was much larger and heavier. He was shaped like a barrel: rounded and thicker in the middle. Atop his stocky body was a large head with bristling hair. He had small beady eyes, a large round upturned snout and a wide mouth with two large fangs rising up from his lower jaw nearly to the outside edges of his snout.

He wore a leather vest-like, armless tunic that added to his large frame. To assume he was merely overweight would be a mistake. His arms were large and muscular and ended in thick stubby fingers. In spite of his threatening appearance, he did not seem to be hunting or doing anything that was even remotely hostile. He just seemed to be walking in the woods and admiring the scenery.

He was first spotted by a scout, who immediately reported his presence to the Lodge. The Lodge requested some of the Dozors to look into the matter. The Dozors initially kept a close eye on him as he walked along the shoreline and made short day trips into the forest. He appeared to be taking notes, but doing nothing more. After a few days, deciding he was alone and was clearly not trying to conceal his presence, one of the Dozors made contact.

The stranger smiled broadly when he met the Dozor. With most people a broad smile makes them appear friendlier. With the stranger, however, it looked more like a sneer. His head dropped slightly and protruded forward; his brow furrowed making his tiny eyes bulge outward, while his grin spread across his face. It was unsettling to the Dozor, who was summoning all his courage to appear confident. He greeted the Dozor openly, with a booming voice.

At first the Dozor thought the stranger's open manner might be a trap. But the stranger did nothing to harm or distress the Dozor. In fact, he invited the Dozor to share his camp with him and offered him some food. The Dozor was smart, though, and didn't let on that he and the stranger were being watched by several other Dozors, all of whom were well armed and experienced hunters. The stranger chatted amiably throughout the evening and then went to sleep shortly after dinner.

The Dozor stayed awake all night, anticipating some treachery on the part of the stranger. However, when it was evident by the next morning that the stranger presented no apparent danger to the forest creatures, the other Dozors made their presence known. If the stranger thought it odd that these other Dozors appeared from nowhere, he didn't reveal it, and welcomed them to his camp.

The stranger told them all that he was an explorer, which explained why he wasn't armed. When the Dozors commented on this, he admitted that being unarmed may be foolish on his part, but his mission was only one of research. His name was B'nair. He was a Rebbercand. His people had sent him on a journey and he was mapping out the terrain for educational purposes. He had traveled the coast for weeks, coming from distant lands far to the south. He hoped to create a map of all his travels across the many different lands he had visited. He said he planned to reproduce the map and make it available to all travelers.

The forest creatures were unfamiliar with the lands to the south, but had no reason to doubt his claim. They thought it was very generous of him to offer his maps to other travelers, although they had no idea what maps were and who would need them. Once the Dozors got past his intimidating looks, they found the stranger to be very engaging and a pleasure to talk to. He laughed easily and offered to share his food and drink. Eventually, he suggested the idea of establishing trade between his people and the forest creatures.

The Dozors said they would have to consult their Lodge, since they could not decide on such things, but wanted to know what the stranger proposed. He told them that there were no trees in his land, so their homes and other structures were dug into the ground. They were much like caves, and not very safe or clean. He suggested that, if his people could cut just a few of the trees – or just remove the ones that had already fallen - and perhaps transplant a few saplings, they would be very grateful and would be a strong ally to the forest creatures.

In return, the stranger offered, his people could provide food from the sea and teach them spells and provide potions that would defend them against the hexes cast by the faeries. The Dozors agreed that this sounded reasonable. They were especially intrigued by anything that would ward off the mystical powers of the faeries. They said they would recommend to the Lodge to agree with the stranger's proposal, but the decision would be up to the Lodge. They arranged to meet in the same place in three weeks. It never dawned on any of them that no one had ever mentioned hexes cast by the faeries. No one ever questioned how the stranger knew of this.

When the Dozors returned and reported to the Lodge members, many of the members still had memories of their battles with the faeries and how those had started. The faeries had once been allies, they pointed out, and look how that turned out. They were reluctant to open up to any new alliances. Others, though, were intrigued by the offer of the spells to combat the faeries' powers.

The debate continued for nearly the full three weeks by when the Dozors were expected to return to meet with the stranger. In the end, it was agreed to explore this offer of trade a bit more. The Lodge members suggested that before agreeing to the trade, the stranger should take one or two of the Dozors back to his village so they could get a better idea of whom they would be dealing with. They would wait until these Dozors returned before deciding on any trade agreement.

When the three weeks had passed, the party of Dozors returned to the meeting place. B'nair was there waiting for them. But this time he was not alone. He had brought more than twenty others with him. The Dozors were shocked to see that they had already started cutting trees and taking more than just those that had fallen of their own accord. They had cleared a very large area adjacent to the shore. The trees were being loaded onto a large ship that was anchored near the shore.

When the Dozors confronted him, he was very apologetic and said he assumed that there would be no problems with the trade agreement. He thought they wouldn't mind if his people got started with just a few trees. He had been so sure that the proposal would be accepted that he had brought the items he offered in trade. He presented them with three large containers that were filled with sea creatures.

"Here," he said, as the containers were handed over to the Dozors, "these are for you as a sign of good faith," and he grinned widely.

He never mentioned the spells or potions to counteract the mystical powers of the faeries, and these were quickly forgotten by the Dozors. The Dozors conferred with one another, and then decided that they at least had to convey one of the conditions the Lodge had given them. They told the stranger of the request from the Lodge members that he escort one or two of them back to his village. They used his own term, "as a sign of good faith."

He grinned even more widely and said, "Why of course. What an excellent idea. I should have offered that in the first place. It would be my pleasure. In fact, I'll do even better than that. Instead of inviting just one or two of you, all of you can come for a visit."

Before any of them could respond to his offer, he turned and called one of the other strangers to join them. This second stranger had been hacking the limbs off a fallen tree trunk nearby. Unlike B'nair, this stranger was armed, carrying a large double-headed axe, the edge of which gleamed in the sunlight. When B'nair noticed the Dozors eying the axe, he quickly said, "This is Sapin. She's our head cutter."

"She?" thought the Dozors. How could they tell the difference between the men and the women? They looked identical. In fact, Sapin looked bigger and meaner, and, each of the Dozors thought, but never voiced, uglier.

"Sapin," said B'nair in a gruff voice, still grinning widely and waving his arm in an expansive gesture towards the group of Dozors, "take our guest to the transport and escort them to our village."

"But we thought you would be our escort," said one of the Dozors, as Sapin came over, carrying the axe menacingly in one hand.

B'nair turned abruptly and for a second sneered and glared at the Dozor who had spoken. It was as if he resented being challenged or even questioned. But then his grin returned slowly and he said, "Oh, no. I have too much to do here. I need to make sure these cutters don't take too much. Have to keep an eye on them." He winked and gave a deep, guttural chuckle that was anything but humorous or inviting.

"Besides," he continued, "Sapin knows exactly how to handle visitors. Never had any complaints. Go with her," he said dismissively. It almost seemed more like an order than a request.

The Dozors looked from Sapin to B'nair and back again, unsure of what else they could do. They marched off tentatively. Six Dozors followed Sapin, who led them to the large ship. Their dislike of the water was quickly overwhelmed by other feelings. Six Dozors left the forest that day. Those six Dozors were never seen nor heard from again. Sean's great grandfather was one of them.

Nearly a week went by before the Lodge realized that the Dozors had not returned. The Lodge debated once again; this time about what they should do. Eventually they decided, and another party was sent to learn what had happened to the first party. This party, though, was larger and better armed. When this group arrived, what they found astounded them.

More than twenty others had joined B'nair, and their operation was in full swing. They were leveling the forest, cutting trees down to the very ground. The Dozors were stunned by the number of trees that had been removed. The expanse of stumps was incredible. As soon as he saw them, B'nair approached them, grinning and waving his arms in greeting.

"Hello, my friends," he snorted. "How good of you to come. Welcome to our small camp. I'm glad you could join us. I have gifts for you."

He presented the containers of sea creatures that he had offered the first group of Dozors before their unexpected departure, lifting the lid of one and displaying the so-called gift. By now the contents were rotting and beginning to smell. The foul odor didn't seem to bother B'nair in the least, but the Dozors stepped back as a wave of rancid decay wafted their way.

"Where are the other Dozors that came before us," demanded the leader, ignoring the offered gift and its offending stench.

"Oh, yes," responded B'nair, nearly slamming the lid of the container shut. "Well, they argued for a while and couldn't agree on which ones were going to visit my village, so I solved the problem for them and offered to send them all." His smile widened. "And they eagerly agreed. Would you like to join them?"

"No, we would not," said the leader, wisely. "What we would like is for you to stop what you are doing."

"Stop what we are doing? I don't understand," said B'nair, feigning ignorance and confusion. "Your predecessors – the other, what do you call them? Dozors? Well, they said everything had been agreed to. They said everything was cleared. I took them at their word."

He looked back at the other invaders as they continued to cut down trees, and then returned his gaze to the Dozors, and continued, "My people have gone to great lengths and at much expense to bring these cutters here and to transport these trees, based on the word of those Dozors. If they weren't telling me the truth I just don't know what to do. What do you suggest we do to resolve this dilemma? My people value the friendship and good will of the forest creatures. We want to be your allies. We don't want to do anything to jeopardize that. "

B'nair's response caught them completely off guard. They had expected him to be belligerent and argumentative instead of conciliatory. Could it have been possible that the previous Dozors had made a commitment, they wondered. Since they were nowhere to be found, there was no way to ask them. They excused themselves and stepped away to confer with one another.

Once they were out of earshot, they debated about what to do with this turn of events. One of them suggested taking B'nair up on his offer of joining the other Dozors, but this idea was dismissed. They found it highly unlikely that all six of them had ignored the Lodge's directions to send only one or two. Without knowing exactly where they went or what happened to them, it was not a sound idea to send more after them. They discussed whether or not it was possible that the other Dozors could have left the impression that this so-called agreement had been approved. They dismissed that as well. Besides, one of them pointed out, that didn't explain where they had gone.

All the time they were huddled together in this discussion, B'nair just sat on a tree stump and watched them. His arms were folded and he just smiled in their direction. And all the time they were huddled in discussion, B'nair's woodcutters were hacking down tree after tree. The other strangers were working with machine-like efficiency as they destroyed the forest. Finally, they decided they would have to return to the Lodge for more specific guidance. The leader left the group and walked up to B'nair.

"We do not think that an agreement was reached, as you have claimed," said the leader to B'nair. "You are to stop removing trees until we return."

B'nair grinned widely at the leader and slowly looked from one to the next, eventually returning his smiling face back to the speaker. He rose just as slowly from the stump on which he was sitting and stood. He faced the Dozor leader, but towered nearly two heads taller. He was uncomfortably close with his round midsection protruding outward, but the Dozor stood his ground.

"I'm sorry you feel that way," B'nair finally said. "I assure you, your predecessors raised no objections to the terms of our agreement, and we fully believed that they spoke for your leadership. I was left with the clear impression, in spite of your thoughts to the contrary, that our arrangement had been approved. Now, if there's some dispute about that agreement, or if you want to renegotiate it, then perhaps you're right in seeking guidance from your masters."

"They are not our masters," interrupted the lead Dozor. "They are the elders of our Lodge. No one is master to any forest creature."

The grin on B'nair's face faltered for only a second, but the anger that filled his eyes was unmistakable and lingered. He leaned in closely to the leader, forcing the leader to lean his head back at an awkward angle to maintain eye contact. In spite of this he maintained his stand, showing that he would not be intimidated by this stranger. B'nair was close enough that the Dozor could smell his putrid breath, his head boring down, but the Dozor refused to back away.

"My apologies," murmured B'Nair, glaring at the Dozor, "I meant no offense."

The tone of his voice, however, did not match his words. He kept his face close to the Dozor. His breath was hot and stale. He continued in a slow and deliberate response.

"I only meant that it would be a wise decision on your part to seek counsel from your - from whoever you chose. I will be here when you come back, and will await your answer."

He gave no indication that the cutting of the trees would stop, and the Dozors knew this. They also knew they were far out-numbered to press the matter any further. They slowly backed away and melted back into the forest. B'nair's eyes never left them until they were finally out of sight.

Once they were out of sight of the invaders' camp, they broke into a run and didn't stop until they were back at the Lodge. When the Dozors returned, they reported their encounter to the Lodge. Some of the Lodge members were still weary after the long war with the faeries and were slowly recovering from the suffering of that encounter. They were reluctant to take a stand that could result in renewed hostilities. They argued for just ignoring the invaders or, if necessary, moving to another part of the forest.

Others, however, disagreed. They were certain that the first party of Dozors had come to harm and should be avenged. Further, they argued, if the destruction of the forest was not stopped here and now, when and where would it end? Their home was once again being threatened. This time they had to draw a line in the sand. No further action by the invaders would be tolerated.

"We need to act fast," insisted one of the debaters. "In just a week, they brought in more than twenty cutters and have done much damage. If we wait much longer, they are sure to bring in more. Their numbers may grow to a level that we cannot defeat them."

"I agree," said another, "we need to attack while they are least prepared and push them into the Ocean. We need to force them from our land once and for all."

"That's the kind of talk that got us into the last war," responded one of the elders. "There is nothing good than can come from a war."

And the debate went on. It was three days later before a decision was reached, and not without some difficulty and rancor. Another group would be sent to inform the strangers that there never had been, nor is there now, any agreement to trade. The delegation would thank the strangers for their offer, but decline in no uncertain terms. They could have the trees that had already been taken, but the cutting would end. The group would remain at the site of the cutting to ensure no further destruction occurred, and the trees that had already been cut were removed.

They decided that this group would have to be large enough to ensure that these strangers understood the message and would not be inclined to argue. Fifty warriors, veterans of the wars with the faeries, would make up the heavily armed delegation; but they were instructed to use force only as a last resort.

When the delegation arrived, their leader, who was the same Dozor who led the last group, could not believe his eyes. The number of invaders had more than doubled and the devastation was unimaginable. Tree stumps were visible several hundred yards in from the shore and stretched more than twice as far in both directions. There were large ships in the water onto which the cut trees were being loaded. There seemed to be no end in sight.

"Ah," said B'nair, when the delegation arrived, "back so soon? And I see you've brought more people with you. Wonderful. The more the merrier. Have you changed your mind about joining your friends? I have an escort ready to take you to see them any time you're ready."

"No," said the leader. "We will not be going with you. Instead, we have come to tell you that there is no trade agreement, there has never been an agreement, and we do not wish to have such an agreement."

"Really? Do you mean to say that you don't want anything at all in exchange for all these trees?"

B'nair pretended to look surprised. He spread his arms out in the direction of the forest, indicating all the trees that had not been cut down, instead of the wreckage behind him that his people had already caused.

"That is not what we mean at all," said the leader, who refused to be tricked by B'nair's words. "You may take what has already been cut, but you may cut no more."

B'nair seemed to ponder this for a few seconds. He eyed the leader and then looked over the delegation that had been brought along.

"I believe you are trying to intimidate me," he said pointing at the delegation. "You are not being at all hospitable. We have come here in peace. We have made a fair and honest offer of friendship. We offered gifts, which you have spurned. We have initiated no hostilities. You, however, have renounced an agreement made by your predecessors and now you appear to have brought an army to settle a dispute that we had nothing to do with starting. I am appalled."

B'nair had begun to raise his voice, and his gestures were becoming exaggerated. The Dozor knew B'nair was twisting the facts to cloud the issue, and would not let himself be diverted.

"There was never any such agreement. We will take you at your word that you misunderstood this point. However, you have come to our land uninvited and have been destroying our home. We have asked you to stop, but you have not. We have asked you to leave peacefully, but instead you bring more of your people, who are also uninvited. We will ask no more."

B'nair stood up and strode over to the leader. He leaned over him as before, and puffed out his chest. He again looked down at the Dozor and said in a low, rumbling voice, "Are you threatening me?"

The Dozor stared right back into B'nair's eyes and responded, "Consider it a point of clarification."

For the next few seconds it was as if time stood still. The delegation had been closely watching the exchange B'nair and their leader. They had remained passive throughout, hoping for the invaders to leave peacefully. They seemed to be unaware that the cutting and dropping of trees and the loading onto the ships had stopped. B'nair slowly backed away.

"All right," he said as he turned and moved towards the shore. He waved his hand in the air as if he was bidding the delegation a farewell. "Have it your way."

With that he quickly dropped his arm and a swarm of cutters wielding their large double headed axes attacked the delegation from their left side. No one had seen them take this position. Almost as soon as the forest people turned to meet the attack, head on, the cutters dropped to the ground. The forest creatures had focused their attention on the advance of the axe-wielding cutters. They failed to notice that another group had taken position behind the forest creatures, hidden in the trees.

An assault of arrows fired from crossbows showered the delegation from behind. Nearly half of them dropped to the ground, injured or worse. When the survivors turned to face that attack, the archers took shelter behind the trees, and at that same moment, the cutters jumped up and continued their assault on the turned backs of the few remaining forest people. A second assault from the crossbows was not necessary. The siege was over in less than a minute. The cutters made sure there was no one left to tell the tale.

B'nair looked over the carnage and turned to the leader of the attack.

"Kant're," he commanded. "Take some of your warriors and haul this rabble far out to sea and give the sharks a nice dinner. Stay there long enough to make sure they are disposed of as well as the first ones were, and then get back here to finish the cutting. The next time these creatures come, they'll be better prepared than this group."

His attention was diverted. He spun his head around and looked into the forest in the direction from which the delegation had come. A sound from deep into the forest caught his attention and he looked for its source. His beady eyes scoured the trees and bushes. He jerked the axe from Kant're's hand and walked in the direction from which he thought the sound had come. He hacked at the bushes and undergrowth, trying to root out the source.

He stopped every few seconds and listened again. After a few minutes, he dismissed the sound, assuming it was nothing or had just been his imagination. He marched back to the waiting cutter and tossed the axe back to him. He then returned his attention to the removal of the fallen forest creatures and the continued removal of the trees.

He was wrong, though. The sound had not been his imagination. Although there were no survivors, there had been one observer: a small boy who had idolized the leader of the Dozors. The leader had been a mentor to this boy, and the boy followed him everywhere he went. As the delegation left the Lodge, the leader had stopped the boy and told him that he had to stay in the Lodge. Just this once, he had promised.

This boy had disregarded the leaders' instruction, and had secretly followed them. He poked his head above the bushes under which he was hidden and watched the exchange between his hero and this stranger. His heart filled with pride when he heard and saw his hero stand up and defy this stranger. And then he watched on in horror as the events unfolded.

A gasp of shock escaped as B'nair referred to his fallen idol as rabble. He ducked his head and squeezed himself as tightly as possible into the smallest ball he could, when B'nair had heard him. He held his breath and forced himself to stop shaking with fear as B'nair moved in his direction. He clamped his eyes shut, waiting for the axe to fall as B'nair chopped at the bushes and undergrowth.

When he heard the chopping stop, and heard B'nair move back to the scene of the devastation, he slowly released the air from his lungs, as quietly as he could. Even after B'nair had turned back to the cutting of the forest, he remained in his hiding place. He stayed there motionless until nightfall and then, as quietly as possible, he crept away and as soon as he could, ran for his life back to the Lodge.

Chapter twenty-two

"That boy was you, wasn't it?" asked Solveig.

"Yes," said Sean. "It was worse than you can imagine – what they did to all of...I've never forgotten that image. I've never forgotten that this was our introduction to the Rebbercands."

"What happened when you got back to the Lodge?" asked Summer, somewhat surprised that, in all their time since they had become friends, he had never mentioned any of this before.

"I reported everything I had seen. Those images are burned into my memory even to this day and so is the look on the faces of the Lodge members when I told them all what had happened. Normally I wouldn't have been allowed to stay – you know, not being a Dozor. But I think what I told them had shocked them so much, that they forgot I was still there.

"After some debate and a lot of arguing, we – they – finally agreed that we would not be able to defeat them in battle. They were just too powerful for us and well armed, even though we outnumbered them. We realized that the only way to be rid of them was to make them want to leave. We had to eliminate the reason for them coming to our land in the first place."

"You destroyed the trees," said Stella, knowing how drastic such a measure would have been for the people of the forest to have even considered.

"Yes," said Sean, looking up at her; tears forming in his eyes. "We cut a swathe about a mile away from where they were. It was deep enough to serve as a firewall to keep the fire from jumping to our side. We cut a long arc from one part of the shore to another that circled them. We had them trapped. Their only way out was by sea. And then we set the forest ablaze.

"It took several days for the fire to burn itself out. When the fire had consumed everything between the firewall and the ocean, and was safe to pass through, we sent a scouting party. There was no sign of the Rebbercands – nothing at all. We had achieved our goal, but at a terrible price. The land that we had burned became a desert. Nothing ever grew in that area again, and it's still that way today.

"We knew we could no longer stay that close to the wasteland. We moved our Lodge away from the firewall and ended up nearly back where we had started – not far from the faeries. We still post sentries on the edge of the desert to watch for any sign that the Rebbercands are returning. We've been more worried about them than the faeries. I had hoped never to see or hear of them again."

Everyone had stopped walking and was in complete silence as Sean described his people's history with the Rebbercands. Even Exa had been listening intently, learning much more about these strangers than he had expected. When Sean had finished, Exa walked up to him and touched his shoulder.

"Then you understand fully what tyranny my people have endured," he said. "Will you help?"

"Yes," said Sean with more determination in his voice than his friends had ever heard before, "whatever it takes."

"We all will," joined in the others almost in complete unison, and without a moment's hesitation.

"When will we reach the place where your underground is located?" asked Solveig. "Is it much further?"

"We're there now," said Exa.

"Well where is everyone?"

"All around you," Exa said.

As he made this pronouncement and as if on cue, dozens of people just like him slowly began to appear, coming out from behind almost every crack and opening in the walls, from around rocks, and from fissures in the ceiling. There were dozens of them, all just like Exa.

"These people are here to help," Exa announced.

"How do you know we can trust them?" one of them asked, after a few moments of silence had passed.

"They did not harm me when they had the chance," he answered. "They had me surrounded and could have easily disposed of me, but they didn't."

He could see that this alone was not sufficient to convince the others. Before he could be challenged further, he gestured towards Sean.

"And this one has fought the Rebbercands," he added. "He met them face-to-face and drove them from his people's land. He pushed them back into the sea. He's a true warrior."

"No. Wait," said Sean. "That's not the way it happened. I didn't do that. I'm not a warrior."

Even more of the Trepans emerged from hiding places when they heard this piece of news. They crowded in closer so they could see this small hero. Some boldly came closer and looked at Sean in awe.

"You fought the Rebbercands?" one of them asked. "All by yourself? Weren't you frightened?"

"I didn't exactly fight them," Sean tried to clarify. "I was actually just hiding in the forest."

"The forest," shouted Exa. "Yes. He's a forest creature," he said, announcing it proudly as if he and Sean had been long time friends. "He and his people expelled the Rebbercands from their land. They burned them alive, forcing them to flee. He's going to help us defeat them."

"Uh, wait a minute," said Sean. "I didn't do that. I was just a little boy when that happened."

"You defeated them when you were a little boy?" another Trepan asked loudly enough for several others to hear.

And like the ripples that emanate from a stone thrown into the water, the word of Sean's accomplishment spread through the Trepan underground, gaining in magnitude as it went. All his protests were dismissed as if they were merely signs of humility from a valiant hero. Before long, the account had taken a life of its own, growing and distorting, and soon it no longer bore any resemblance to the truth. The Trepans had a new savior, as reluctant a hero as he may have been.

"Sean, the Rebbercand Slayer. It has a nice ring to it, but it is going to be a hard image to live up to," Lochen whispered in Sean's ear.

"But that's not what happened," he objected, "I never said anything like that. You have to make them stop."

"OOOh, Sean, my hero! Can I have your autograph," Liam teased him, poking his finger at him.

"Oh, Sean, you're such a he-man. You make me swoon," joked Summer.

Fluttering over his head, just out of reach of the hand he attempted to swat her with, she raised her wrist to her forehead and pretended to faint. Liam caught her in his arms and fanned her with his hand.

"Come on, you guys," pleaded Sean. "I told you what happened. I'm no hero. I didn't do anything. Please, make them stop."

They all laughed, especially Quinn who finally said, "That's a real hoot. But I don't get it. What's so funny?"

"You've certainly set a high standard for us all," said Lochen.

Before Sean could make any further objections, he quickly continued, "and we will all have to work on the plan to meet those expectations."

"What plan? What do you have in mind?" asked Natalie. "I can tell you're already thinking of something. What is it?"

"Patience," he told her. "We first need to find out what the strength of the underground is, how they are organized, who is in charge, what they've done already to rid themselves of these invaders, and what they know about the Rebbercands. At least that will get us started."

When the general excitement settled down, Lochen pulled Exa aside and asked if he could lead them to whoever was in charge of the resistance. Exa apologized, and led them through another tunnel, leaving Sean's admirers reveling in their imminent salvation. Along the way, Lochen asked several questions, and Exa was more than happy to explain the social structure of the Trepans.

Exa told them that there were many different tribes within the enclave. Each tribe was trained in and skilled at different tasks. His tribe, for example, was comprised of miners. They had been miners for centuries and knew all about digging, whether it was for something small or on an epic scale. He proudly announced that it was his ancestors who had dug the initial sink hole.

Not long after they started walking, their conversation was interrupted by the appearance of another Trepan walking towards them, studying some large pieces of parchment. They stopped and Exa introduced them.

"This is Ar tek kaht," he told them. "She is the master designer of all of the passageways. The members of Ar's tribe are all designers and planners."

She looked almost exactly the same as Exa, and Solveig was wondering how they could tell one another apart. On closer examination, though, she could see that Ar was slightly shorter than Exa, and her hands were much smaller. Her coloring was a bit different, too, although in this light, Solveig thought, it was hard to be certain.

She was the leader of her tribe, which was why Exa had referred to her as the master designer of all the passageways. The masters were not leaders in the sense that they had any authority or control over their tribes. They were just the most experienced and skilled members. A tribe could have several masters, or, sometimes, just one. Ar didn't design the passageways all by herself. The members of her tribe did, but she was their leader and made sure that every member of the tribe learned their skills to the best of their ability.

She had been walking and speaking with another Trepan when Exa introduced her to the newcomers. This one was named In Ir Jin. In was the master of the tribe of builders. Many of the channels that Lochen had led his group through were not just holes in the ground. The walls, ceilings and the footpaths had almost certainly been constructed by In's tribe, following the designs and specifications of the people from Ar's tribe. In every instance the building used materials that blended in with the environment. They also worked in coordination with Exa's tribe to ensure the balance was maintained in everything they did. Materials that were dug during mining operations were transported and used for building operations. Everything had to be properly coordinated. There was a tribe for that, too.

There were tribes for everything, he told them all. There was a tribe responsible for growing and distributing food, another one for making tools, another for providing medical care, and so on. Each aspect of their civilization was addressed by tribes of Trepans dedicated to those needs. As they were talking, other Trepans joined them. Lochen began to engage some of them in a lengthy discussion about inter-tribal relations, divisions of labor and the impact on the growth of their society. He was quickly pulled away from this conversation by Liam.

"We need to focus," he told Lochen, pulling him by his elbow. "I'm sure all that stuff is interesting, but it doesn't get us to where we need to be. Can you save this for another time?"

"Yes, of course," agreed Lochen, reluctantly. "My apologies. Exa, this is all very fascinating, and I would certainly enjoy exploring this further, but as has been pointed out to me..."

"Get to the point," murmured Summer."

"We need to talk with whomever would have firsthand knowledge about the Rebbercands," he rushed on.

"Oh, yes," Exa answered.

The very thought of the Rebbercands made Exa shudder. He tried to put them out of his mind and continued taking his guests to the leader of the underground. They were led further through the tunnel until they came to a fairly large alcove. There they saw the leader of the resistance. He was sitting on a rocky ledge talking to one of the other Trepans. He looked quite a bit different than any of them had expected. He appeared much older than the others in the underground. His demeanor seemed different, as did some other physical characteristics.

He had long white hair that blended into the same kind of fur that covered the Trepans. In his case, though it seemed more like a cloak than his own skin. Even though he was sitting, he seemed taller than most and other features were clearly different. His face and hands were very pale – almost like parchment. He was devoid of hair, except for a long white beard. The most noticeable difference from the Trepans was his eyes. Unlike those of the other Trepans, which were large and protruding, his seemed to be more of a normal size. They were, however, milky white.

His name was Hal Mest Kim, Exa said, as they got closer. Upon their approach, he stood and turned towards them.

"I've been expecting you," he said when Exa presented the newcomers to him.

The person he had been speaking with silently backed away, leaving the leader with the newcomers. With no other words, Exa did the same.

"How could that be?" asked Stella. "Until recently we didn't even know we were coming here."

He turned towards her with a slight smile on his face, and said, "I have known for some time, my dear Enchantress. The chroniclers have foretold for centuries of the enslavement as well as the deliverance of the Trepans. We have been waiting patiently for your arrival. And before you ask, yes, I am blind. However, I have had a mental image of you all for a very long time."

"This is starting to sound strangely familiar," said Lochen, without any further explanation; and no one asked.

"I'm sure it is, Sorcerer," Hal replied, as he turned towards Lochen.

Stunned, Lochen asked, "How did you know which of us spoke and how do you know I'm a Sorcerer?"

"As I said, we have known for quite some time of your arrival, and although my eyes have long ago failed me, my mental images have not. And now that you're here, we have no time to lose. You know, of course, that your worlds as well as ours are in great peril. I think you used the term 'mortal peril,' Princess Solveig, if I'm not mistaken. Unfortunately, that term is most appropriate. We are besieged by a common enemy – one that has no regard for the well being of any other society, including its own, or for the planet on which it lives."

With that, he turned away from them and headed off down a narrow path. It was hard to believe he was blind, he moved with such certainty, ducking to avoid small outcroppings from the wall or ceiling. Once they got over their initial shock and stopped looking at one another, everyone hurried to catch up to him and follow.

"Where are we going?" shouted Stella, who was near the end of the entourage.

"You must observe firsthand the pestilence that has been wrought by the vile and sinister Rebbercands, my dear Enchantress, if you expect to be of any help," he called back to her.

Natalie looked over to Stella, shrugging her shoulders, and mouthing the question, "How does he do that? And who talks that way?"

Stella silently mouthed back to her, "I have no idea."

As if those questions had been asked out loud, he said over his shoulder, "As Princess of the Sea Sprites, Natalie, surely you have seen for yourself things that defy explanation. As has your friend Summer, the faerie Princess. And, I apologize for my arcane speech. I am ancient and far too set in my ways to adapt easily to change. However, I am sure you are able to clearly understand me."

"Are you taking us to where the Rebbercands are?" asked Liam.

"Come now, Pathfinder. You know that would be foolhardy. Though whatever magical skills I have are still quite acute, a blind man is clearly not the most appropriate person to lead you into the jaws of danger."

"This really is the blind leading the blind," said Quinn, and he began laughing.

It started as a low chuckle, but the more he thought about it – a blind man leading a bunch of people who had no idea where they were going, through a dimly lit cave – the chuckles quickly evolved into giggles.

"If you think about it," he continued through fits of laughter, "It's really the blind leading the blind, leading the blind, leading the blind…"

"Enough," shouted Sean, a bit embarrassed by Quinn's repeated references to the blind. "We get it. Once was plenty."

"Yeah," said Quinn, "but there are eight of us, so the blind is leading the blind, leading the blind eight times."

The more he giggled, the harder it was to control himself. Soon he was nearly in tears with laughter. Hal stopped abruptly and turned around. Those in the front of the group nearly ran into him. He walked through them parting them with his hand, and approached Quinn. He turned his head to the left, and then to the right, and sniffed the air.

"It appears that you may have had a nasty encounter with a rather unpleasant plant. I detect the signs of a poultice to counteract the effects of dragon spadix," he said, thoughtfully. "A very good remedy – very good, indeed. You have my admiration, Pathfinder, especially considering the limited ingredients that were available to you in the middle of no place."

He leaned in closer to Quinn and continued, "And your curiosity got the better of you, so you took a huge whiff of it and passed out. Afterwards, you experienced extreme cold. No matter what you did, you couldn't get warm. You could have walked through fire, but nothing would have made you shake the cold. You were frozen to your core.

"Holy blubber on a biscuit," said Quinn, and he launched into another fit of laughter.

"And then," Hal continued, "the Enchantress gave you a leaf from a hackberry bush, and told you to put it under your tongue. I'm sure she gave you explicit instructions not to swallow it."

He couldn't see, but sensed that the others were nodding their heads in agreement.

"But you did, in fact, swallow it. And then, you began to get warm until your body was so hot, nothing would cool you down. They could have encased you in ice, and you would not have been any cooler."

"Holy blubber on a biscuit," said Quinn again, and once more he launched into fit of laughter.

"By now you were in danger of becoming dehydrated, and against her better judgment, the Enchantress was prevailed upon to give you something to counteract the heat. I would have to guess that she gave you dose of the Bloodwort bile..."

"Ewww, yuk," interjected Solveig.

"...probably by mistake. But given your size and the amount the Sorcerer shrunk you, and your sudden return to your normal size, the dosage was inaccurate – not really your fault, Enchantress: I'm sure he acted before you could administer the correct potion. At this point he was acting even more rashly than he does otherwise. I imagine you had intended to give him a half dose of Sarnanock's elixir, but he grabbed the wrong bottle. Regardless, though, the temperature changes stopped immediately. That was the good part. The bad part though, was that you haven't been able to stop laughing. In fact, the more perilous the situation, the funnier it seems to you."

"Oh, poop," said Quinn. "Does that mean we're in even more trouble?" And he laughed even harder.

"Oh, no," said Hal. "For the time being, I imagine this is about as bad as it can get. But enough."

He waved a thin, pale hand across Quinn's face as he said those last two words, and the laughing stopped immediately.

"Thanks," said Sean. "That laughing all the time was driving me nuts. Now is something else going to happen to him?"

"A lot is going to happen to him, my young Dozor friend," Hal answered mysteriously. "But not as a result of any of the recent spells and potions. Of those he's cured. Let's keep going." He turned back the way he had been walking and continued.

"How did he do that?" Natalie whispered to Stella.

"I don't know," Stella whispered back, "But I'd sure like that recipe."

"Of course," Hal said.

He stopped walking and turned toward Stella. He raised one hand in the air, mumbled something none of them could make out and then pointed his finger at her.

"There," he said. "Now you have it."

He turned back the way he had been headed and started walking again.

"I do," announced Stella, with a look of surprise on her face.

Who is this person, Lochen asked himself, as they all followed.

Chapter twenty-three

"This is Dee Derr Fenn," said Hal, pointing out someone who seemed to be giving directions to other members of a small group that was gathered in another deep recess off the main path. "He's the strategist in charge of our resistance effort."

He walked directly up to the resistance leader and without any introduction or explanation said, "Please share with our friends all that you know about the Rebbercands. They are here to help us."

The group the leader was addressing dispersed, apparently off to follow the directions he had provided. With no hesitation at all, he began.

"The Rebbercands all seem to stay close to wherever the mining is being done. Our reconnaissance indicates that they don't seem to have a very good sense of direction, and probably fear getting lost in the tunnels and caverns that run all through this area. A few of them are part of exploration parties, but they never venture anywhere by themselves. They make prisoners lead the way and actually conduct the searches for the lambentite. It's almost like most of them don't know what it looks like when it's staring them in the face.

"Anyway, as long as there's a supply that can be extracted, they pretty much stay in that one place. They only move when that supply is depleted and they have to move on. Then they relocate their entire operation. The lambentite is really easy to find, at least for us; because it glows."

He looked around at the increase in light being emitted from the veins in the recess, and then at Stella.

"Although it doesn't glow as much as it does around you people," he added. "Even with the lambentite lighting the caverns, though, they can't see well, which had enabled us to spy on them and set traps for them. But don't think that our ability to see better than they do is much of an advantage. They are very quick and very vicious. They react before they think."

"Our Dozor friend here knows very well how vicious they are," said Hal, gesturing towards Sean.

Dee looked at Sean and nodded in silent understanding, and continued. It wasn't clear if word of Sean's exploits from the other Trepans had reached Dee before Sean did, or if he had some other kind of premonition.

"There are nearly a hundred of them, including the handful that make up their scouting parties. That overall number doesn't seem to change. They divide them up over different shifts supervising the mining. At any one time, there are only about thirty of them in the mines, except during a shift change when that number nearly doubles. Other than that, it almost always stays the same.

"They don't view any of us as a threat, and, in truth, we aren't. So they never bother to go looking for any of us who have escaped. They keep a close eye on the workers, but it's not really in our nature to be confrontational, so escape attempts are rare. And they don't feel the need to search for any signs of an attack. In all our history, we've never had to do battle with anyone, so we just aren't prepared, skilled or even inclined to do this. At the first signs of war in the upperworld, our ancestors dug the Great Portal. Ever since then, we've lived in this world. There's never been anyone who waged war on us or invaded our world."

"Until now," said Sean.

"Yes," agreed the leader. "Until now. And our resistance effort is still in its infancy. We're learning fast, but we're still learning. Warfare doesn't come easy to us, nor is it natural, as it seems to be with the Rebbercands."

"Can you take us to where they are now?" asked Lochen.

"What are you thinking?" asked Natalie.

"I don't have any ideas, yet," he answered, "but I think we need to see how they're set up, how they operate, what in their surroundings might be of advantage to us, and more importantly how heavily armed they are."

"Yes, I can take you there now if you like," said Dee. "They've just discovered a new vein, and have just relocated their operation, so they won't be moving from that soon. Unless, of course, it breaks another seal."

"What do you mean, break another seal?" asked Lochen. "What kind of seal?"

"The channels we dig and the walls we build are done so very carefully and after much study and planning. The placement must maintain a balance between the sources of water that comes from the seas as well as from underground aquifers, rivers, and reservoirs; and the sources of heat, which comes from the lava and volcanoes. If the walls are not built properly or the channels are dug randomly, seals that ensure the balanced flow of water and heat may be broken. Repairing them is extremely difficult and dangerous."

"What happens then?" asked Summer. "If one of the seals breaks?"

"Channels can become flooded. Any people working in those channels would have no warning and would be washed away and drown. That's if the seal is to a water flow. If the seal to a lava flow is broken, it's much worse. An eruption, much like a volcano, could occur. The fire and gases from this almost always affect other channels, even those far away from the eruption.

"The eruptions could infect fresh water supplies and poison the rivers; they could burn through to other channels and destroy our living areas; or the lava could burst through under the sea, which would poison the salt water around it and make the beginnings of an underwater volcano. Or it could do all of this. Those seals are the hardest to repair and control."

"That's what I saw under the Cerulean Sea," said Natalie. "There was an underwater volcano. That's where I saw some of your people. But this one had what looked like a door. What was that?"

"The door – what we call a portal – that you saw was probably a release gate. The worst kind of seal break is where the channels that divide waterways from lava flows are breached, and the two mix together."

"Of course," said Lochen. "Especially if the water is cold, as it would be deep in the Cerulean Sea. The result would be a poisonous steam with immeasurable pressure. Without a quick release, the consequence of the mixing of the two elements would be an immense explosion."

"Immense is one word for it," said Dee, shaking his head. "Cataclysmic would be more accurate."

"What do you mean?" asked Natalie.

"Yes. Cataclysmic is more accurate. It would be akin to a thermo-nuclear explosion," answered Lochen. "Several factors would come into play that would determine the extent of the impact. Depending on the size of the breach, the temperature of the water, the amounts of water and lava that are intermixed, and the degree to which the resulting steam is compressed…"

"Blah, blah, blah," said Summer, waving her hand in a circular motion indicating he should hurry up. "Bottom line?"

"Oh, yes. I'm sorry; bottom line," said Lochen. "It could be severe enough of an explosion, or, actually a series of explosions, along the lines of a chain reaction – sufficient enough to shift the planet from its axis."

Everyone looked at him blankly.

"Which means…what?" asked Summer.

"Which means," answered Hal, who had been listening quietly to the entire exchange, "that our world – the entire world, not just the worlds we know – could quite possibly be thrown out of its orbit. Depending on when and where the explosion occurred, we could be thrown into a direct path with one of our suns – it really matters not which one - in which case the planet would burn to nothing in a matter of seconds. It would literally evaporate to nothing.

"Alternatively, we could collide with our moon. We wouldn't burn up in such a collision, but the result would be equally devastating. Regardless of the precise point of impact, again, the entire world would be destroyed. Or we could be hurled deep into space, so far from our suns that our atmosphere would cease to exist. It would collapse in on us and we'd suffocate if we didn't freeze to death first. None of these options seem particularly pleasing."

The silence that greeted this statement was nearly deafening.

"Oh, poop," as expressed by Quinn was all any of them could say. "This is worse than I thought it was. I kind of wish you hadn't cured me of that laughing spell. Things didn't seem so bad then."

"Has anyone explained this to the Rebbercands?" asked Solveig. "Surely, if they knew this, they would stop what they're doing."

"Of course," said Hal. "This was discussed in detail to the one who first discovered one of our enclaves. He said he was just exploring and developing maps. I knew that was a lie, and that he had ulterior motives."

"He didn't believe us," said Dee. "He asked for proof. There is no proof, because we've been careful about maintaining a balance. How do you prove something that's never happened? If it had happened before, there would be no one here to tell about it. We know what we're doing. We know what the consequences are. We've been very careful to avoid these kinds of breaches."

"What did he say to all that?" asked Natalie. "Obviously he disregarded what you told him; otherwise he and his people wouldn't be here now. But how could he just ignore all your warnings?"

"He just dismissed our concerns," Dee said. "Besides, he said his people would only need small amounts of lambentite. He even offered to establish some kind of agreement to trade for what they removed."

This last statement made Sean's ears tingle and his skin began to feel like it was crawling.

"That was how it started," continued Dee. "The Trepans he first met told him that they would need to obtain approval from our leaders before any trade agreement would be reached. That group came back to discuss the offer with the leaders of the enclave and to make their own recommendations."

Summer, Solveig, Stella and Natalie all took deep breaths at the same time. Their eyes grew wide and their heartbeats quickened.

"The leaders decided to send a delegation to carry back their message. The message they sent was to respectfully decline the trade offer," Dee said. "But we never saw or heard from them again."

Lochen, Liam and Sean gulped loudly. The palms of their hands began to sweat, and they looked from one to the other.

"When we received no word from the first delegation we sent a party to find out where they went. At the same time we sent a second delegation to the Rebbercands. This one was larger and intended to make sure the stranger left the enclave. Instead, they discovered that he had been joined by many, many more Rebbercands. They had captured and enslaved the search party that had been sent out, as well as one entire enclave.

"They had put them to work and had already started digging out the lambentite. Only later, when the second delegation failed to return and we sent out scouts did we discover that they were heavily armed. They had easily defeated our delegation before enslaving them. And the digging they started was done without regard to any forethought at all, and has gone on unchecked and recklessly ever since."

"What is this stranger's name?" asked Sean. His voice was barely above a whisper and the blood had drained from his face.

Dee looked directly at Sean and said, "B'nair."

"Oh, poop," said Quinn. "That's bad. That's really, really bad. That's the same guy, isn't it Sean? That's the same guy!"

Sean didn't answer. He really didn't need to. The silence that followed Quinn's question was broken by Hal.

"So you see why we need to act swiftly and decisively. We also need to have a careful plan. The Trepans, as willing as they may be, are completely unprepared and unable to address this matter themselves. The underground movement for the most part has been gathering information only, with the exceptions of a few relatively successful acts of sabotage. This is why you were brought to this place."

"Then I think it's important for us to see them as closely as possible," said Lochen. "Now would be good."

Dee led them through a veritable labyrinth until they came upon a very wide and very deep cavern. He motioned to them to be as quiet as possible as the approached the rim of the canyon. They dropped down to the ground and inched their way forward to the edge and looked down. Beneath them they could see a number of Rebbercands and several dozen Trepans under their careful eyes. The Trepans were digging with shovels and picks into the sides of the cavern.

On one side of the vault, scaffolding had been erected along parts of the wall so that the veins at higher elevations could be extracted. Some workers hacked out large pieces of the wall, and others dug out the luminous stone. Once the stone was separated it was passed to others who lowered it down from the scaffolding to other Trepans who loaded it into carts. The carts were hauled out of sight – pushed, actually - down one of the channels.

On the other side of the vault the upper layers had already been stripped away, and miners were digging at the lower sections. Along the far edge of the cavern was a ravine. Another team of workers was moving the unusable rock and dumping it into the ravine. It was apparent that this opening was very deep and at the bottom was a river of lava. As the rocks were dumped, the Trepans scuttled back from the edge and in a few seconds a wave of heat would rush up from the fissure and flood over the entire cave.

The Rebbercands were all over the place. They were carrying what looked like sticks, overseeing each step of the operation, and beating any Trepans who weren't working fast enough. Some of them had whips. When the beatings with the sticks weren't enough to get the desired results, the whips were used. Overlooking it all was B'nair. Although only Sean knew what he looked like, everyone could see that he was in charge.

"What do they do with all this stone," whispered Natalie. "The lambentite, I mean. What do they do with that?"

"As far as we can tell, they have established a city somewhere on the surface not far from here. They take the lambentite back to this city where they cut it into blocks and build something they call the Desideratum," Dee whispered back. "From what we can tell, it's some kind of monument to their heroes or something. I've overheard bits and pieces of conversations among the Rebbercands, and others who have escaped have shared what they've heard, which seems to be along the same lines."

"A monument? You mean they're not using this for something essential to their lives?" Summer asked incredulously.

"Not that we can tell. We've heard no mention of any critical need for this stone. It all seems to be for this monument."

In the distance they heard a snort. It seemed to bounce from wall to wall to ceiling and down. They all ducked down closer to the ground and then slowly inched their way back to the edge. They peeked down to see that something appeared to have caught B'nair's attention. His head was jutting forward and moving side to side. He was squinting his beady eyes and examining every inch of the cavern walls across from where he was standing. Dee motioned everyone to slowly and quietly back away from the edge. He was concerned that their voices had been carrying.

"In this dim light, their eyesight is poor, but their hearing is extremely keen," he told them. "I'm worried that our voices may be carrying. If you've seen enough, we should get back to a safer place."

They all agreed they had seen all they needed or wanted to see. They very carefully and quietly turned around, and started back the way they had come. After a few yards, Dee turned back to count heads and to make sure everyone was staying close.

"Wait," he said, a bit of urgency in his voice as he searched in the darkness behind them. "Where's the faerie?"

They all looked around, but Summer was not with them.

At the mention of B'nair's name, Summer had become incensed that the person who had done so much harm to her best friend and his people was still around and still hurting even more people. When she finally saw him from their perch high above on the ledge, she just had to get a closer look. She stayed behind, and once the others had disappeared down the tunnel, she blended herself into the background of the cavern ceiling and floated down directly towards B'nair.

"Everyone stay right here and remain completely quiet," Dee told them.

He was furious that someone would do something so foolish. He made his way back to the overlook as quickly and quietly as he could. When he returned to the ledge, he carefully poked his head over and looked down. Even though his eyes were well adapted to the dim lighting, he didn't immediately spot her. He scanned the cavern in every direction. He was becoming impatient and concerned that he could find no sign whatsoever of Summer. He was momentarily startled when he felt something crawl up next to him. It was Sean.

"She's probably made herself invisible," he whispered in Dee's ear. "If so, you'll never spot her."

"Invisible?" asked Dee.

"Well, not exactly invisible," Sean answered. "More like – I don't know – clear. You know? Like water. If you know what to look for you can see her, but mostly, you can't. She blends into the background."

Dee was growing very annoyed to see that Sean had disregarded his instructions to stay put. He was also worried that this conversation was too long and too loud. He was about to order him back when he noticed that all the others had reappeared. He was speechless. Had they no understanding of the danger, he asked himself.

"We don't leave anyone behind," whispered Stella as she wiggled on her stomach closer to the edge.

"That's right," whispered Natalie, as she crouched down behind Stella and next to Dee. "We stick together, no matter what. That's how we roll. You need to know that."

"All for one and one for all," whispered Solveig, as she settled in on the other side of Sean. "Just like the Three Musketeers, except there are eight of us."

"Yeah," agreed Quinn. "What's a Musketeer? Is it anything like chicken?"

Solveig thought a minute and said, "I'm not sure. I just read that someplace. But I don't think it has anything to do with chicken."

They all turned their attention into the cavern, each trying to get a glimpse of Summer, but she was well hidden from sight. Dee could only stare at them, from one to the other, thinking they must be mad.

In a few seconds Sean caught a slight ripple in the air – like a small heat wave rising from a hot surface. It was very small, and in mid-air, a few yards above B'nair's head. He had spotted Summer. He quietly pointed her out to the others.

Summer glided slowly downward in the same silent, floating drop that she used to come up behind Exa. She kept herself aimed straight for B'nair. Then just a few yards above him, something caught her eye and she modified her descent, changing direction with a gentle tilt of one wing.

She saw a long tunnel running behind where B'nair was standing. It seemed to incline slightly upward and disappear deep into the darkness. Another Rebbercand was overseeing a team of Trepans moving carts towards this tunnel. The carts were loaded with lambentite. Each cart was being pushed by a pair of struggling Trepans through this tunnel.

This must be the way they're getting the lambentite to the surface, Summer thought. She was half tempted to follow the line of carts through the tunnel to see where they ended up. But then she thought that might not be such a good idea. I might get lost, she realized. And then what good would that do? She didn't have Liam's ability to know where to go. However, she decided to get just a little bit closer look, so she could share what she saw with Dee. He would probably be better able to use this information and tell where it was all going.

She continued to float in a downward spiral – like a leaf falling from a tree - trying not to get too close to B'nair. She could see that Dee had been right. There were about thirty of the Rebbercands in different stations around the cavern. They all looked just as Sean had described them, and her recollection of his story gave her a chill.

A small number of the Rebbercands were carrying large double-headed axes. Even in the low light, the blades glistened. These looked more like soldiers and seemed to be guards rather than supervisors. Several others were armed with short whips and clubs. They were spread out in and around the Trepans. They were snapping the whips over the Trepans to scare them and make them work harder or faster. They used the clubs to beat or poke at them. Hal was right, she thought, we need to help kick these rotten Rebbercands out.

She had seen enough, and what she had seen sickened her. It was time to get back to her friends. She was about to give herself a couple of good strong flaps of her wings to get out of this place, when she remembered what Dee had said about the Rebbercand's hearing. Then she remembered how Exa had detected the shift in the air when she did that before. With this in mind, she made slower, longer movements of her wings and gradually began to lift higher.

As she was gaining altitude and was about twenty feet above B'nair's head, she looked back at the scene she had surveyed. Just then, one of the Trepans' pushing a cart lost his footing and fell. The Rebbercand overseer swung his club down hard, cracking it on the fallen Trepan's back. The Rebbercand grunted with the force, and the Trepan cried out. The action was so violent and so unexpected, Summer let out a slight gasp.

Before she knew what happened, she saw out of the corner of her eye, B'nair move with frightening speed. In one lightning fast motion, he pulled a large whip from his side and snapped it in her direction. The tip made a very loud crack, just inches away from her face. The shock waves in the air caused her to tumble backwards. She dropped several feet before she righted herself and regained altitude.

"What is it, my lord?" asked one of the Rebbercands standing near B'nair.

"Mind your business, Kahn-L," he barked, without taking his eye off the spot where his whip had cracked.

Kahn-L was a complete suck-up. B'nair couldn't stand to be around him. He knew Kahn-L wanted desperately to discredit him and take his position. He had close alliances with another Rebbercand — one named Bacham — who also had challenged B'nair for leadership. He knew they were both conspiring. B'nair despised Kahn-L, but knew he needed to keep his enemies close. There was nothing he could to about Bacham — at least for the time being — but he had to put up with Kahn-L just to be able to keep an eye on him.

"Of course, my lord," said Kahn-L in an almost syrupy voice. "I was only concerned that you would strike out at nothing, my lord. Have the strains of this command weakened you? It would be my honor to take your place — only temporarily, of course."

B'nair continued to stare at the spot his whip had struck, certain there was something there, but unsure of what it might have been. He cursed his weak beady eyes that they couldn't see clearly inside this wretched cavern. He was sure, though that he had heard some kind of flapping noise. His ears had detected the sound, but his eyes could only see a blur — much like a wave of heat, which occurred everywhere in this pit.

Ignoring Kahn-L's barb about becoming weak or taking his place, he said, "It was just some miserable bug or pest. It displeased me - as do you on occasion. Go back to work, or I'll have you hauling rock."

"Yes, my lord," said Kahn-L as he slithered away, looking in vain for whatever B'nair claimed to have seen. Safely out of their line of sight, Summer finally let out her breath and rejoined her friends.

Chapter twenty-four

"That was stupid," Dee chastised Summer, once they had moved far enough away from the site of the mining.

"But informative," she answered. Before he could argue the point, she continued, "There's a long tunnel on the far side of the cavern. It seems to lead upward. There were several filled carts being pushed in that direction. Could that be where they're taking the stone?"

"It's possible," said Dee. "No one who has been forced to transport those carts has ever escaped. It's too hard. They're closely watched and there aren't any opportunities once they disappear into that tunnel."

He was still upset with her, but had to admit to himself that the information she had gathered in that short amount of time was more than most of his scouts could gather in weeks. Of course, it helped that she was so small – and could make herself virtually invisible. Still, what she did was more dangerous than he would normally allow.

"It must come out on the surface someplace," said Liam. "Is there another sinkhole?"

"A what?" asked Dee.

"A portal. You know. The way the Trepans got down here in the first place," Liam explained.

"No," answered Dee, realizing what he meant by a sinkhole. "Not that any of us are aware of."

"What about Hal?" asked Lochen. "Would he know?"

Dee thought a minute. "Hal has been here as long as anyone can remember, although no one seems to know where he came from. That aside, though, I suppose if anyone knew about another portal he would. But he's never mentioned it. If one existed, why wouldn't he have said anything?"

"I know that look," Solveig said to Lochen. "What are you thinking?"

"I'm not sure, myself," Lochen answered. "But I agree that we need to speak with Hal. I think at least part of our solution rests with him."

Dee led them back to the hiding place of the underground and took them directly to Hal.

"Yes, in fact there is," he told them when they asked about another portal. "The Rebbercands forced the Trepans to create one so they could haul the lambentite to the surface and to their village – well, their current village at any rate."

"Wait a minute. What do you mean, their current village?" asked Natalie. "Do they have more than one?"

"They only have one at a time," explained Hal. "A very long time ago, they became engaged in a…how can I explain? A bit of unpleasantness. Let's just leave it at that. They were duped by someone rather powerful and influential. However, that does not excuse what they did. As punishment, they were transformed into the rather less than pleasing appearance they presently display, and in addition they were cursed."

"You mean being butt ugly with a really nasty disposition wasn't the curse?" asked Sean. "What about being a bunch of murdering thieves? Was that part of the curse?"

"No, my young friend," answered Hal. "Their appearance was...how would you say? A bonus? As for being murdering thieves, that was a matter of their own choice, not due to anyone else's control. No, the curse was that they would never have a real home. Consequently, they establish a village in a certain area and stay there for a while – sometimes years, sometimes much less, but never for long. And then they move. They have no roots; no real home."

Everyone thought about what Hal had told them, but still couldn't get the pictures of what they had done to the forest creatures out of their minds – or what they were doing now to the Trepans. They deserved no sympathy. They had created their own future by their past. When Hal thought they had spent enough time considering the fate of the Rebbercands, he asked Summer about her little foray. Summer described what she had seen – the tunnel into which the Trepans were moving the carts loaded with stone.

"But it didn't look like it led to the surface," she added when she was finished. "Of course, I didn't go into the tunnel to see where it led. It was too dark and on the other side of the cavern.

"No, the tunnel itself wouldn't go to the surface, " said Hal. "They'll most likely have a storage area at the end of that tunnel which I imagine would be at the bottom of their portal. They must have some system of hoists or some other method to bring the carts to the top."

"We need to see what that is. It may be their weak point," said Lochen. "Summer, do you think you could go back and observe a little more?"

"Sure," she said immediately.

"Hold on a minute," objected Dee. "This isn't some picnic. You just can't walk in there..."

"I'll fly," interrupted Summer.

"Walk, fly, swim or dance. I don't care," snapped Dee. "It's too dangerous. If the Rebbercands even think some kind of attack or resistance is in the making, they're liable to take it out on the Trepans they have captive. We can't put them at risk."

"They are already at risk," said Lochen. "If you think they will just release your people when they are done, you are sadly mistaken. Sean can tell you exactly what to expect from them, and it's not compromise or mercy. We need to act and we need to act quickly. You know better than we do the damage they are doing. If it continues much longer, more than just the captive Trepans will be in danger. We all will."

"Besides," said Summer. "I'll be careful. It's not like I enjoy facing mortal peril, you know."

"And I'll go with her," volunteered Liam. "She won't be alone, and I can find my way there and back."

"I'll go, too," said Sean. "I have some old scores to settle."

Hal put his hand on Sean's shoulder. "No," he said. "Not this time. That opportunity will become available soon enough, but not now. There are other things you can do for now. If too many of you are included in this scouting venture, the greater the chance of discovery."

Begrudgingly, Sean agreed to stay behind. He and others watched with trepidation as Liam and Summer made their way back towards the cavern. Sean stayed in the alcove until he could no longer see either of them. The last image he had of Summer was her looking back at him over her shoulder and waving. He fought the overriding desire he had to go with her.

As they neared the edge, Summer told Liam to wait there for her. From this point forward, she would have to go alone. She didn't want to risk any noise that might draw attention to them. Besides, she said to him, if something happened to him, she'd never be able to find her way back. She told him to stay out of sight and be careful, and then quietly floated to the top of the cavern, far above the activity below and well out of sight and range of the Rebbercands.

She moved stealthily, inching her way across the ceiling of the cave to the narrow tunnel. She checked out where all the guards and overseers were, and in which direction their attention was focused. No one was looking up, thankfully. When everything seemed to be right, she lowered herself on top of one of the carts of lambentite. She found a space near the edge of the cart, and just under a large irregularly shaped piece of the stone. From this vantage point, she could see her surroundings and remain fairly hidden.

Once she settled in, she quickly changed her chameleon-like camouflage and blended in with the iridescent slabs of stone. She rode along completely unobserved, but in plain sight as the cart trundled deep into the tunnel. She cringed each time she heard a whip crack and each time one of the Rebbercands yelled at or struck a Trepan. More than once she wished she had the magical powers to turn them all into blood slugs or even worse.

Finally the cart she was in came to a large open area. It was another cavern but the ceiling was much lower. It was barely high enough for the Rebbercands to stand and move around. The carts were moved four at a time onto a large platform strung with several cables that rose straight upward into an opening just wide enough for the platform to squeeze through.

It seemed to take forever, but finally, the cart she was in was rolled onto the platform. With a jerk, the platform lifted and began to rise through the shaft. The sudden motion jiggled the rocks and she nearly got caught beneath the one under which she was hiding. She shifted slightly and poked her nose over the top of the cart. All she could see were the black walls of the shaft.

After several minutes, the platform finally arrived at the top of the opening. Summer had been underground for so long, she had lost track of time. It was nearly sunset. The first sun had already dropped below the horizon and the second one was close behind. The sky above her was turning a deep purple. The last rays of the second sun broke through the clouds and shone brightly against the lambentite, causing it to begin to glow. Unlike the gentle soft white that emanated from the rock deep underground, the sunlight had a much different effect. The stone glittered with all the colors of the rainbow and shifted depending on the direction one looked at it.

The cart Summer was hiding in rolled off the platform and down a gentle slope to a large conveyor belt. She dropped down at the movement, and then peeked over the top of the cart when she didn't hear anyone nearby. Her heart nearly stopped. She saw hundreds of Rebbercands. They were everywhere.

"Oh, poop," she whispered. "There are a lot more than we thought. They're like mosquitoes, or something."

The shaft through which the carts were raised was at the top of a long incline. Near the bottom, they were dumped out and then diverted to another path where they returned to the platform to be lowered back into the mine. At the dumping site, several teams moved the stone into different directions and onto smaller rolling platforms. Along the way, the stones were prepared.

Many of the Rebbercands at the dumping site were wielding large hammers, breaking debris away from the lambentite. Large pieces were sent one way and the smaller pieces were sent another way. Some of the Rebbercands were chiseling the large pieces into evenly square blocks, while some of the other chiselers were cutting designs or shapes into the smaller pieces.

As her cart continued to trundle down the incline, her focus was drawn further ahead. Behind all of the workers and at the end of the line, Summer saw an enormous fortress. There were heavily armed Rebbercands patrolling the tops of the fortress walls. There were more armed Rebbercands in towers at various intervals along the wall. And even more armed Rebbercands were patrolling the grounds surrounding the fortress.

And then, through the large gate in the center wall, she saw where all the lambentite was going. It was being sorted and stacked at the base of an enormous structure. There was a gigantic statue being built in a central atrium. It was a statue of some Rebbercand. Summer was stunned. This couldn't be the reason the Trepans had been enslaved: to mine a stone for making a statue. She couldn't believe that the Rebbercands would destroy the balance in the planet for such ridiculous self-adoration. As her cart got close to the point where its contents were to be dumped out, she was just close enough to see through the gate and could read the inscription at the base of the still unfinished monument: "To the great and all powerful Reng'n – destroyer of the weak, oracle of the stars, and emperor of war – we commit our souls."

Unbelievable, Summer thought. She was getting more and more irritated at the self-centered arrogance of these people. She thought back to Sean's account of how they invaded the forest and just stripped it of the trees. She looked around and saw that a few of the trees had been used as scaffolding for the construction of the statue. A few others were used for the platform and supports for hauling the stone. From Sean's description, the trees she could see were far fewer than they had taken from the forest creatures. And these didn't look like the ones that grew in the forest with which she was familiar.

Then she remembered what Hal had told them about the Rebbercands moving their village after a while. It dawned on her that the trees taken from Sean's forest had been left behind at some other now-deserted village. The trees in this place had been taken from some other victims of their selfishness. Her blood was really beginning to boil. What made her most angry was that there were piles of cut trees scattered around the fortress that were rotting. They hadn't even used all the trees they had taken. Their wastefulness and their selfishness and their disrespect for everything around them infuriated her.

Without thinking she shot up in the air, hovering above the cart in which she had hidden and yelled, "You pigs!"

As soon as the words were out of her mouth, she knew she had made a serious mistake. She clamped her hands over her mouth as if that could take them back. She looked all around her as she fluttered a few yards above the cart. All the noise nearby had stopped. Dozens of beady eyes turned in her direction. Her reaction had made her lose her focus and her camouflage disappeared. She was completely visible, even in the waning light. An arrow whizzed past her head before she regained her focus. It had come so close that the air from its feathers spun her around.

"A faerie," shouted one of the Rebbercands. "Quick! Kill it before it escapes."

The one closest to her snapped his bullwhip. The tip missed her wings by no more than the width of a hair. Her first thought was to retreat down the portal and return to her friends. She swooped down towards the ground, dive-bombing towards the one with the whip. She was too close for him to use it on her, and he became a much larger target for the next arrow, which shot past her and buried in his right shoulder.

"Yeooow!" he yelled. "Shoot at it you booger eating morons! Not me!"

She darted in and about, keeping low to the ground where there was much more cover and the Rebbercands were forced to stop firing at her for fear of hitting each other. She was headed straight for the mouth of the opening.

No, she said to herself, reconsidering the potential danger that would follow her. Instead, doubled back and soared high into the sky, dodging spears and arrows that were coming much too fast and getting much too close. As she swerved to avoid two razor sharp missiles, she veered to the left. She concentrated on her appearance and once again blended into the sky behind her, disappearing from sight.

"Where did it go?" shouted one of the attackers.

"Spread your aim," shouted another. "Keep your eyes sharp. Just don't shoot one another."

The flurry of arrows aimed at her widened to a larger circle. Fortunately, immediately after veering left, she pinned her wings back and pressed her arms to the sides of her body and shot like an arrow herself down towards the ground in the direction of the fortress. She circled behind one of the leaders and, hovering just behind his shoulder, made herself visible.

"There it is," shouted one of the archers, and he and several others let loose a volley of arrows, most of which hit the leader. As he fell to the ground looking like a porcupine, Summer again blended into the background and darted in another direction. She reappeared behind another one of the leaders. She made herself visible just behind his head. When no one seemed to spot her, she shouted, "There it is!" Before the Rebbercand leader could get out of the way, he was peppered with more arrows. Finally, someone shouted for everyone to stop shooting. By then they were in a mass of confusion with everyone spinning and jerking in every direction, taking aim at anything that moved or even appeared to move.

"My work here is done," Summer thought to herself proudly, and then she easily disappeared back down the portal and out of sight.

A few minutes later, she reappeared right behind Liam, who had not left the spot from which she had initially departed. Her sudden and unexpected appearance was so startling that it was all he could do to keep from jumping up and shouting. She smiled mischievously and motioned for him to lead them back to the others. He quietly and carefully got up from his position, and made his way through the tunnels to the rest of the group where she filled them in on what she had learned.

"A statue," shouted Sean. "A stinking statue? You can't be serious."

"I'm sorry to say I _am_ serious. That was all that I could see," she answered. "It's in the center of this large fortress. You can see it through the main gates."

"That really makes me mad," he said. "All right then. When do we attack?"

"We don't," answered Hal. "Their force is too great and they are too well armed. A frontal assault would be ineffectual."

"We have to do something, though," pleaded Sean. "We can't just let them keep doing this."

"Hal's right," said Lochen. "Any attack would be futile. We have to think of something else — something they wouldn't expect, and, at the same time, something that wouldn't result in retaliation against the Trepans."

He started walking back and forth, mumbling to himself as the others watched him. Hal sat patiently; Dee looked from Hal to Lochen and back, sensing that one or the other was hatching some kind of plan. Sean was much too agitated to think, but Solveig pulled him aside.

"Just give him a few minutes," she said to Sean. "When he gets like that he's thinking. He'll figure something out. Trust him." Sean sat down with a thump and watched as Lochen paced around in what seemed to be no particular pattern. He squirmed and fidgeted as Lochen mumbled to himself and the others just watched silently. He looked over towards Hal, expecting the resistance leader to do something, but even he just sat by quietly watching — listening, actually, since he couldn't see.

Lochen walked over to a small vein of lambentite and stared at it for several seconds. As if seeing it for the first time, he reached forward and rubbed the dirt off. He stared at it for a few minutes, still saying nothing; just studying it intently. The continued silence was met with huge and loud sighs from Sean. Lochen rubbed more of the dirt away from the glowing stone, and then, wetting his finger, he rubbed it again.

He turned to Stella and asked, "Your amulet. It contains the stone that had been the centerpiece of the armband that Sean wore. Is that correct?"

"Yes," she answered. "And it seems to make this stone glow more brightly and for longer periods of time – at least when the stone is close by. You know all this, though."

Stella looked at Sean almost apologetically. "I never returned it to you. I never really thought about it. I apologize. You should have said something."

Stella began to remove the chain on which it hung from around her neck.

"No," Sean said, motioning to Stella to keep the necklace. "I meant for you to keep it. If I wanted it back I would have asked for it."

Lochen turned to Summer. "But the stone in the band originally came from you, as I recall. What exactly is that stone?" he asked.

"Who cares?" Sean snapped; frustrated at the inactivity.

"I don't know," said Summer, ignoring Sean's outburst. "It was handed down from one generation in my family to the next. I never knew it had any magical capabilities until you put it in Sean's armband and until Stella wore the band. But other than that, I haven't seen that it does anything really special. It makes this lousy stone glow. What does that have to do with anything?"

She was beginning to share Sean's impatience.

"I'm sure this is really interesting, but I don't understand what we're waiting for. I thought you were coming up with some kind of plan; not developing an interest in geology."

Lochen ignored Summer's comment. He turned to Hal.

"What precisely in the lambentite makes it glow?" he asked.

"Scylla scales," he said as a smile crept across his face.

"I don't understand," said Stella. "Scylla serpents are a myth."

"What are Scylla serpents?" asked Quinn. "Are they anything like chickens?"

Natalie interjected, "I can answer that. The story is that the Scylla were sea nymphs, much like the Sea Sprites who are my people. They were all very beautiful, but, as the myth goes, they offended a powerful witch. In retaliation for the offense, the witch prepared a powerful poison and poured it into the waters where the Scylla lived. In making the poison, the witch added a potion that was extracted from her own nightmares.

"They were all turned into horrible monsters as a result of the potion, and their form was taken from the images of the witch's nightmare. They turned into giant serpents with five heads at the end of five very long necks; each head with three rows of razor sharp teeth and fangs. It also had two pairs of legs on which it could run upright, like a person, as well as another pair that acted more as arms with very sharp talons. It resembled a lizard more than a serpent, except for the forked tongues and large venomous fangs in each of the five heads.

"They were horrified by the transformation and vowed to take revenge. They searched for several years, and eventually found the witch hiding in a cavern deep underground. They cornered the witch and in spite of her pleas for mercy, they killed her. But the witch had expected they would show her no mercy if they ever found her, and she had cast a spell on herself. Whoever killed her would turn to stone. As a result, the Scylla disappeared from the land and the seas, and were buried deep beneath the ground. But it's only a myth."

Sean gaped at Natalie and then turned to Lochen.

"What a nice bedtime story. So, can somebody PLEASE, tell me what this has to do with anything?"

Continuing to ignore him, Hal spoke up, "Ah, but there's more to the story – the myth, as you call it, Your Highness. Every time a witch makes a potion or a spell, she always makes an antidote as well. This instance was no different. The witch had cast a counter-spell on a small substance she buried on the other side of the world. That substance was called Nostrumite. When the witch was killed, all of her powers were transferred into this substance, making it even more than just an antidote. As I recall, this Nostrumite was compressed into a stone of unusual color. As the "myth" says, with the right incantation and the right force, the Nostrumite can break the spell that turned the Scylla into stone. It will not, however, reverse the potion that turned them into serpents."

"AARRGGGGHHH!" shouted Sean. "What does all this mean? Wait a minute. Let me find someone who cares."

"You said it was an unusual color. What does the Nostrumite look like?" asked Solveig, ignoring Sean.

"It's a golden brown in color," said Hal. "The original stone was part of a pendant that was broken apart in a...let's just say in a disagreement. The various parts were scattered to places unknown. One of you is wearing an amulet that seems to make the lambentite glow. Is that correct?"

"Yes," answered Stella. "I am."

Hal reached out his hand and asked, "If I may?"

Stella took off the amulet and handed it to him. He felt the stone by rubbing it between his thumb and forefinger.

"How did you come by this?" he asked as he raised the necklace.

"It was given to me by Sean," said Stella.

"Actually," said Summer, "I gave it to him. It fit into an impression in his armband. I don't know where it came from originally. It had been handed down from one generation to another, although I think the faeries may have…" she looked guiltily at Sean, "borrowed it from the forest creatures."

Sean just looked at her, stunned and then turned back towards Lochen and Hal.

"This is all very interesting, but I don't see what any of this has to do with the Rebbercands and getting them out of here."

"Oh, I forgot to mention," added Hal. "The witch who cast the spell on the Scyllas was a Rebbercand."

All eyes turned to Sean.

"Oh," he said. "I see."

Chapter twenty-five

"Not really," he said, after reconsidering everything that had been said. "I still don't get it. I already touched the stone from the armband to the lambchop…"

"Lambentite," corrected Solveig.

"Lambentite, lumpenite, bump in the night…whatever," he replied, his frustration at having to wait continued to grow. "I already rubbed that stuff…that LAMBENTITE… with the nosey bite…"

"Nostrumite," corrected Natalie.

"Nostrumite…" he nearly shouted, having no other mispronunciations to string together. "Whatever – again. All this yakking is fine, but we need to do something. I'm tired of just sitting around."

"And we will," said Lochen. "But I believe we've already concluded that attacking a force much greater and more heavily armed than ours is not the answer, nor is doing something that will result in retaliatory action against the Trepans."

"Then what is the answer? Having a blab-fest about some ancient stories?" Sean snapped; his exasperation becoming more and more difficult to control.

"No. Those ancient stories you're complaining about are only a part of the solution. What we're looking for is something similar to what your people did to the Rebbercands to expel them from the forest," answered Lochen. "The answer rests in all of these events."

"We're going to set the tunnels on fire?" asked Sean. "That doesn't make any sense at all. Rock doesn't burn."

"No," said Solveig, suddenly understanding the plan that was being formulated. As the pieces fell into place she became more animated. She jumped into the discussion, waving her arms.

"We make it so that they don't want the lambentite anymore. In fact, we make it so that it's the last stuff on earth that they want."

"Exactly," said Lochen, smiling at her. He knew she was an excellent tactician and that the plan was becoming clear to her.

"How are we going to do that?" asked Quinn. "Like Sean said, we already rubbed the armband stone against it, and all it did was glow."

"But that's because the lambentite that came in contact with the Nostrumite was still imbedded in dirt," interjected Hal. All eyes turned to him as he explained. "The spell that changed the Scylla into stone also compressed them. And as that stone was covered in dirt, the imprisonment was more intact. In order for the antidote to work and for the spell to be broken, there has to be room enough for the Scylla, so that when it is released it can expand to its natural size."

"Its natural size?" asked Quinn. "How big is that?"

Hal was silent for a second or two, "Hmmm. Quite large, I'm afraid. In their original form as sea nymphs they were no larger than you," he motioned to Natalie and Stella. "But as serpents they grew to an intimidating size; nearly fifteen feet in length or larger, and often six to eight feet wide – nearly as big as dragons – and, I might add, just as fierce and dangerous."

"Holy blubber on a biscuit," said Quinn. "That's big enough to swallow all of us – whole."

"There's just enough room for them to fit through that tunnel to the top," said Summer, recalling the width of the shaft through which the carts were moved and then hoisted to the surface.

"We should only need to release one. Releasing more might put all of us in jeopardy – more than we are in now. One should be quite sufficient. Oh, and we have to somehow make sure that the Scylla we release is on the surface," said Lochen. "Releasing it in the cavern would be too unpredictable. If we can get the stone in contact with the lambentite in one of the carts near the surface opening to the shaft, that might be the optimal location – certainly the safest for us. It will be difficult, though, to do this without being observed."

"We'll need a diversion, then," said Liam. "We have to make sure that whatever diversion we come up with is timed just right to allow all the mined stone to get to the top, and leave whatever is left below still encased in dirt."

"I believe you have summarized the situation correctly, my friends," said Hal. "As to the timing, I believe there may be an opportune time for such a diversion. The Rebbercands are very precise in their daily activities. They do not cope well with change and are very much creatures of habit. That makes them very efficient – almost machine-like at times, but it also makes them very predictable. Without fail, the mining slows down considerably when there's a change in the guards and overseers. Previously that had always been a mystery to us – why the need to slow down and actually stop their operation. Now, thanks to the Faerie Princess, we know why the mining slows to a near halt."

"We do?" asked Summer. "Because of me? Really? I didn't see anything that would lead to that conclusion."

"Of course you did," said Lochen. "They have only one hoist to take the stone to the surface. They need that same hoist to bring down the replacements and then to take up the guards that are getting off duty. That's why the mining slows down. It has to stop to transfer one team for another. From what you described, there's not enough room on the platform to bring all the carts and the complete change of shift up or down at the same time."

"Exactly," smiled Hal. "Consistency is the hobgoblin of small minds. And in this instance, their efficiency will be their undoing."

"So, I assume you have finalized a plan," Liam said to Lochen. "I've been watching the wheels turn for the last several minutes."

"One is coming together," he answered, motioning for him to be patient. "Hal, do you know when they next change the guard? Oh, and do you know approximately how much time that change requires?"

"Dee will know the answers to both of those questions, and probably any others you may have. He's studied them for some time and has recorded all their movements and locations. One other matter to consider is that of the small search teams the Rebbercands have deployed. They usually only have one or two about, and they are independent of the mining teams, so they don't arrive and depart on the same schedule. I'm sure Dee's underground fighters can dispose of them, given enough advance notice. His fighters will ensure that the search team members will be away from the central cavern and fully occupied. That should leave all the rest of them in one central location at the time of the transfer."

"We should plan the attack for just before the shift going off duty leaves," offered Solveig. "They'll be more tired than the ones coming on duty and more vulnerable to an attack."

"Actually," said Lochen, "I would normally defer to your judgment when it comes to combat strategies, knowing how much you've studied them, but in this instance I have to disagree. We should attack immediately upon the arrival of the replacements before the departing team begins its ascent on the platform."

"Are you crazy?" asked Sean. "That's when their number will be double. Why would we want to fight twice the number when we don't have to?"

"Yes," said Lochen, "I mean, no. I'm not crazy, but yes, their number will be doubled. Keep in mind though, that this will be the time they will least expect any trouble and when their leadership is most likely to be issuing contradictory orders, creating the most confusion. There will be so many of them in a confined space that their doubled size, like their efficiency, will work against them instead of for them."

"I suppose, if you say so," said Sean, still not sure of the logic and still not happy about the delay in immediately confronting the Rebbercands.

Lochen shared the rest of his plan with the group while Hal conferred with Dee about the questions Lochen had asked, and about the timing of a separate attack on the Rebbercand search parties.

"Summer," said Lochen when their discussion had concluded. "I'm afraid we have to ask you to once again sneak to the surface."

"I can do it," she said confidently.

"It won't be as easy as you think," he cautioned. "This time you have to carry with you the stone from the armband. We'll take it out of its setting, but it's still going to be heavy."

"I don't understand," she said. "I used to wear that stone from a thread around my neck. Why would it be heavier?"

"It's larger now than when you wore it," answered Lochen. "If you recall, it grew in size when it was placed in Sean's armband and the band expanded when it was worn by Stella."

"And it's gotten heavier," added Stella. "I'm not sure why, but it seems as if every time I've worn the headband to conjure images, the weight of those images is absorbed by the stone."

Lochen removed it from the headband and handed it to Summer. She was stunned by the change in the weight and size. For any of the rest of them, even with the changes to the stone, it would be as simple as carrying a pebble in their pocket. But for Summer, this was something entirely different. Since Summer was only three inches tall, it would be more like carrying a lead weight on her back; and a weight that would not blend into the background as she did. In addition, she could not let the stone touch any of the lambentite before she reached the surface. It was important that the Scylla that was freed from its prison be on the surface so the Rebbercands would know that it came out of the Lambentite.

If the Scylla was freed below the surface, the Rebbercands could just cave in the shaft and move the mining operation. If it was freed in the shaft leading to the surface, it may get stuck or it may drop to the cavern. In either instance, the impact would not be the same.

"You're right," she said, looking up at Lochen. "It was much smaller and lighter when I wore it as a pendant – before you put it in Sean's armband. Couldn't someone just shrink it down again?"

"Or I can cast a small spell on it to make it weigh less," said Stella. "If you think we aren't able to shrink it."

"I'm afraid that either option might lessen its power," said Hal. "It's one thing for the stone itself to effect the changes, but quite another for those changes to be the result of a spell. It's just not a chance we can afford to take. I'm sorry, Princess Summer. I don't see an alternative. I fear you will have to bear the full weight."

"Well, it was just a thought. I'm still sure I can do it," she repeated, although with a little bit less confidence.

Solveig had the idea of creating a harness that held the stone in place on Summer's back, nestled between her wings. Dee provided her with some very thin cord and helped with the harness as well as a simple release mechanism. It was still heavy, but she would be able to maneuver better this way than if she had to carry it in her arms or had it dangling from her neck, swaying every which way.

"You only have to place it or merely drop it on the nearest cart of stone," Hal told her. "No need for heroics, please. Just make sure it comes in contact with a clean section of stone – devoid of any dirt."

She thought a minute, and answered as an impish smile broke across her face, "Oh, I know exactly where to drop it."

Dee coordinated that attack with his plans for the diversion, and then left with his team as the others headed back to the cavern. They had little in the way of weapons. Liam, of course, had the arsenal of knives and daggers that he always carried with him, but no one was anxious to get close enough to any of the Rebbercands to need a weapon of that nature. They agreed that Sean would be the primary point of the attack. There was a nearly limitless supply of small stones with which he could arm his slingshot. Lochen and Quinn would take up positions on one side of him with Liam on the other side, and they would hurl larger rocks. Solveig would provide flashes of near blinding light and Stella and Natalie could generate clouds of smoke. Given the Rebbercands' poor eyesight in the limited light in the caves and tunnels, it wouldn't take much to blind them totally.

When everyone was ready, Summer crept to the edge of the cavern and looked down. B'nair was well below them at the far end directing the final load of lambentite to be taken to the surface prior to the shift exchange. She took a deep breath and leaped over the edge. She spread her wings and tried to float down to the cavern floor. She misjudged the weight of the stone she carried and began dropping like a load of bricks. It was much heavier than she had expected and certainly a lot different than the feel of it when she wore it in a smaller, lighter size around her neck. It was driving her straight to the ground.

"What on earth?" she thought. "Exactly how many images has Stella conjured with this stone? It weighs a ton."

Struggling, she flapped her wings to keep from crashing into the floor, and floated a few inches from the surface. The sound caught B'nair's attention and he quickly turned around. Summer managed to slip behind the far side of the nearest cart just as his eyes scanned the place she had been only seconds before. Fortunately, he had looked first where he had expected her to be – higher in the air. By the time he shifted his gaze lower, she was hidden from his view.

In spite of her effort to stay afloat, she hit the ground with more speed than she had intended and the rock on her back knocked the wind out of her. The cloud of dust that sprung up around her was contained underneath the cart she slid beneath. That was a lucky break, but as the dust settled, it covered her completely and filled her mouth and nose. She fought back the urge to cough and sneeze and was just barely able to push herself upright as the cart began moving forward.

For a few brief seconds, she was exposed. She picked herself up and ran to catch up, squatting to get beneath the bottom of the cart. The base was only about two and a half inches above the ground, so she was bent over and waddling like a duck. Finally, the cart was loaded to the hoist platform and began its ascent to the surface. The wooden platform creaked with the weight of the carts as it was hauled up through the shaft. Summer sat down and used the time to catch her breath and regain her strength. The hardest part was yet to come.

Her friends had watched her flight with trepidation. One by one they each peeked over the rim of the ledge, and nearly gasped aloud collectively when she landed unceremoniously in the dust behind the last cart to be loaded to the hoist. They ducked down the instant B'nair made a sudden move, at the sound of her flapping her wings. When they thought it was safe, they poked their noses up. The cart under which Summer had hidden was out of sight being pushed down the tunnel to the hoist.

They all slid back away from the rim and mentally prepared for the next step. For the time being, though, there was nothing to do but wait for the hoist to reach the surface, and for the replacements to arrive on the return trip. They could only hope that Summer made it to the surface, would be able to place the stone on one of the carts of lambentite and release one of the Scyllas. The wait was excruciating.

The hoist lumbered upward and upward until it finally came to the surface. By now the sky was dark. The only light came from the torches that lined the way from the hoist landing down the path into the fortress and to the monument. It was clear that work continued on this monstrosity day and night. Summer kept hidden under the cart, waiting for the signal that had been arranged by Lochen to signify the start of the diversion. As the cart was moved off the hoist to make room for the replacements to be transported downward, she resumed her duck waddle underneath and kept out of sight. When the cart finally stopped, she crept out from under it and looked for her target.

Back underground, the diversion team heard the sound of the lowering hoist as it echoed through the tunnel. They watched and waited as the hoist made its return trip down the shaft. After what seemed like an eternity, it finally landed, complete with a full team of replacements. While the Rebbercands were overly efficient in everything else they did, this exchange of guards seemed to be the exception. There was no order to it at all. The arriving guards dispersed in multiple directions, and the departing guards jostled to get past the arrivals and make their way down the narrow tunnel that was still lined with filled carts to get on the hoist.

They bumped and shoved each other, shouting and complaining the entire time.

Sean had inched his way around the rim of the cavern to a position closer to the entryway of the tunnel that led to the hoist. Liam and Quinn changed their original positions, and moved higher up the rim and armed themselves with the largest rocks they could find and hurl. Lochen moved to the opposite side and did the same. At the highpoint of the transition below, Solveig clapped her hands, threw her fist forward and downward and released a brilliant flash of light.

The Rebbercands reacted with stunned surprise, looking up directly into the bright light, temporarily blinding themselves. At the same instant Sean began rapid firing his slingshot and Lochen, Liam and Quinn began hurling rocks. As predicted, the leaders of the Rebbercands gave contradictory orders. The commander of the arrivals was shouting to take cover and to return fire. The commander of the departing squad was ordering them to get on the hoist and leave. The bumping and shoving increased as each party got in the way of the other.

And to make things even more chaotic, no one knew which orders were directed to which group, so nobody was getting out of anyone's way. Furthermore, they had no idea where the attack was coming from, since they had been blinded by the light. Their shouting and screaming drowned out the orders given by their commanders, and brawls broke out all over the place. Those who attempted to return fire had no idea in which direction to aim. Several of them just began shooting, and aimed their crossbows indiscriminately. More often than not, their arrows bounced off the ceiling and ricocheted downward, shooting their own soldiers instead of their unseen enemy.

At the sound of the chaos below and the flash of light that preceded it, Summer knew the diversion had begun, and she moved from her hiding place. The Rebbercands that remained near the cart above ground were alerted by the light and noise and crept to the edge of the hoist opening.

Their attention to anything above the opening was drawn down the shaft. That gave Summer enough time to take flight and move to her target.

She decided to ignore the advice she had been given to drop the stone on the nearest cart. Instead she headed straight for the monstrosity being constructed in the center of the fortress. If she had one shot at releasing a Scylla, she was going for broke. She hoped the graven image would be destroyed beyond recognition and repair.

Hauling the piece of Nostrumite and walking in such an awkward position had sapped her strength. It took longer for her to lift off the ground and soar into the air, and it took all her reserve to gain enough altitude to rise above the top of the statue. Fortunately none of the Rebbercands had spotted her. The shouting and the light and other noise from the shaft had not only drawn the attention of the nearby Rebbercands, the guards in the watchtowers and along the ramparts were equally distracted.

They were too occupied by what was going on underground to pay any attention to her. Finally, she was high enough and slowed to a hover directly over the incomplete monument. Trying to maintain her balance and her altitude, she reached behind her to a drawstring. Giving it a yank, the harness that held the stone unraveled and the small triskelion-shaped gem dropped downward.

Summer watched intently, praying that no wind came up and move it off its course. As if in slow motion, the stone maintained its course, spinning around and around, until it struck the top of the statue, where it shattered into dozens of tiny pieces. She was shocked and instantly saddened to see the stone she had worn most of her life break apart.

"Oh," she gasped, and then thought to herself, "I really liked that charm. And I'll bet Stella won't be happy it's gone, either."

She watched, expecting a dramatic change in the statue; expecting the transformation into a giant reptile; but nothing happened. She began to despair. Did she do something wrong? She fluttered lower to get a closer look. Moving closer and closer, she eventually was at eye level to the top of the sculpture. Her attention to the statue was momentarily distracted as she saw the bits and pieces of the triskelion that were scattered and sparkling on the ground, one by one, rise up into the air. It was as if they were being gently lifted.

Within seconds they had joined together like the pieces of a jigsaw puzzle – fitting neatly into the original shape. The pieces fused themselves to one another. The only sign that the piece had even been broken apart was the lines that now resembled veins where the breaks had occurred. The triskelion hovered in the air inches in front of Summer's face.

"Oh, man. That's weird," she whispered.

Before it could slip away, she reached out and pulled on one of the arms of the shape, moving it closer to her. She grabbed the cord that was wrapped as a harness around her body and from which the stone had originally been released, and tied the end of it to the arm of the stone. Once the amulet was secured, it dropped and hung from her neck, pulling her down, weighing as much, if not more than it did before. She fluttered her wings and brought herself back up to eye level with the statue.

Almost at the exact same time as the triskelion reformed, a small crack appeared near the top. Summer jerked her head up from looking at the amulet to the sound of the fracture. The crack started slowly and then spread in an upward arc until an eye deep within the stone itself popped open. This was followed by a great shudder as one reptilian head and then another emerged. Pieces of the luminescent stone began to break and fall away and the beast beneath emerged, just as a chick hatching from an egg, except this chick was fully-grown. Summer was so intent on watching the change she failed to consider the danger she was in.

"Whoa," she said out loud to no one in particular. "This is much bigger than they said it would be."

The creature continued to break away from its stone prison. Pieces of the lambentite peeled off and dropped to the ground in large chunks, crashing as they hit. In spite of the noise, the guards in their towers and on the ramparts were still transfixed on the sounds and the light emanating from the shaft. Summer had forgotten all about them, transfixed herself on the beast emerging before her.

The Scylla reared up on its hindmost legs and extended a full forty feet into the air before settling down with a crash. It shook its five heads, each at the end of its own long neck, shaking off the remnants of the glowing stone, like a dog shaking off water from its coat. The head in the center was the largest. Oblivious to Summer's efforts at blending into the background, the Scylla thrust its center head directly at her. She was frozen, suspended less than a foot from the tip of the creature's nose.

The Scylla fixed its center head on Summer while the other heads examined their surroundings, taking in the remnants of the lambentite prison, the fortress and the Rebbercands. The creature stared at her with its deep green eyes; blood red slits running from the top of each eye to the bottom. Its head moved from side to side; its forked tongue slithered back and forth.

The Scylla opened its mouth wide, revealing rows of razor sharp teeth and baring its enormous fangs. Just when Summer was sure she was going to be swallowed or impaled on one of the fangs, the Scylla hissed. Its eye caught the glimmer of the triskelion dangling from Summer's neck and its head jerked, zeroing in on the stone. Its vision shifted from the stone to Summer's eyes.

"You are the one who has released me from my prison," it hissed.

It was more of a statement than a question. Once Summer got over the shock that the beast was addressing the statement to her, she felt compelled to answer.

"Y-y-y-yes," she stammered. "I did."

She was so frightened she couldn't move and could hardly speak. Her mouth and throat were like cotton.

"Then I will spare you this one time," it hissed; its forked tongue darting back and forth on either side of her, but never coming close enough to touch her. "But make sure our paths do not cross again. Now leave me while I free my sisters."

Sisters, she thought, but Summer didn't wait to ask questions. She shot like an arrow to the hoist opening, zooming past a mob of surprised Rebbercands. By the time they realized the faerie had reappeared, she was well on her way down the hole. In spite of the fact that she had vanished down the hole, several of them threw spears at her or shot arrows from bows and crossbows. The missiles clattered against the side of the shaft, none of them even coming close to her, as they dropped to the bottom.

They turned to see from where she had come, and their eyes fell on the beast that had appeared from nowhere. A few of them had the wherewithal to fire arrows at the Scylla, but they were as ineffectual as those that had been fired at Summer. They merely bounced off the armored scales and only served to further enrage it. As they stared in horror, pieces of lambentite flew from the several carts and from storage areas surrounding both the hoist opening and the construction site. As if magnetized, they collided in the same manner as the triskelion had transformed. They coalesced into several larger shapeless objects and, one by one, cracked open like giant hatching eggs to be replaced by nearly a dozen more Scyllas.

Chapter twenty-six

Meanwhile, as Summer was making her way back down the portal, the Rebbercands were being pelted with stones and rock, blinded by repeated flashes of light, choked with smoke, and shot by their own arrows. Stella and Natalie filled the cavern with smoke that clung to the floor instead of rising to the ceiling. It was like looking at thick cloud coverage from high above it in the sky.

Solveig was hurling bolts of light deep into the cloud cover, adding to the confusion. She had told the others that she would send out the flashes at pre-arranged intervals. This way, her fellow attackers could shield their eyes at the right moments and not be blinded like their enemies were. Even under the cover of the clouds, the flashes were exceedingly bright. As the cloud of smoke dissipated, Lochen told Stella and Natalie to hold off on creating another one. They all needed to be able to see what was going on below them.

He instructed Solveig to keep up the flashes of light, but still at the pre-arranged signal. The general confusion below them was reaching panic level, but they needed to be careful that the Trepans caught in the middle weren't harmed. Solveig's precise pattern of delivery was disrupted when she noticed that the carts filled with lambentite that were lined up waiting for the relief exchange to be completed had started moving.

"Look" she whispered to Lochen. "The carts are moving. You don't think they're trying to load them on the platform, do you?"

They were rocking back and forth, and this motion was increasing. At first she thought they were being moved towards the hoist and the shaft. But then she could see that they weren't moving forward; they were being jostled. She then thought it was being caused by the Rebbercands running for cover and bumping into them. In some cases it was, but for the most part, the carts seemed to be moving all on their own.

"Maybe the Trepans down there are pushing them," suggested Stella.

"That's possible," answered Lochen. "Dee said his fighters would not only be attacking the Rebbercand search parties, but when the Scylla was being released, his team would try to reach the Trepans in the cavern and guide them out."

Suddenly, like dominos, the carts all fell over, one after the other, all in the same direction with their contents spilling out to the side. At first the rocks just tumbled out haphazardly. Then, as if by magic, they pulled themselves together into separate and distinct piles.

The lack of the expected flashes of light drew the attention of Sean, Liam and Quinn from what they were doing. They looked from the chaos below over to where Solveig and the others were. The remaining Rebbercands down below also noticed that the flashes had stopped, and then also noticed that the attacks had stopped.

"Stop shouting and stop firing," shouted one of the Rebbercand commanders. "Form up by the nearest squad leader."

Within seconds the remaining Rebbercands clustered around available leaders and established a defensive posture. Once their shuffling around came to a halt, the only sound that remained in the cavern was the rumbling of the stones that had dumped out of the carts.

Everyone's eyes were drawn to the piles of lambentite that were rocking back and forth on the ground, sliding across the dirt and attaching to other, larger pieces. The bizarre movement of these luminous stones had everyone's attention. Only B'nair sensed something dangerous was happening. He used the lull in the attack as an opportunity to try to get to a safer and higher location. He scrambled up the nearest scaffolding and onto a protruding ledge. The other Rebbercands gazed in wonder at the moving rocks. Some of them approached the piles to either touch them or to push them over.

That was a major error in judgment. It was like poking a beehive. Just like their counterparts on the surface, these piles of lambentite began to crack open like more eggshells, and six more Scyllas emerged. The first thing the newly released Scyllas saw were the Rebbercands armed with axes, crossbows, spears and whips. Sean drew back on his slingshot, but was stopped when Liam put his hand on Sean's arm. Everything stopped; but for just a few seconds. And then the Scyllas attacked. In very short order, they had done to the Rebbercands what the Rebbercands had done to the forest people and many other victims just like them.

Sean pulled back away from the edge of the overhang and pressed himself against the wall. Liam and Quinn immediately did the same thing, hugging the wall. Solveig, Stella and Natalie quickly ducked down, and covered their heads. Then Solveig looked and saw Lochen standing there. She reached up to yank on Lochen's robe and pulled him down next to her. His curiosity had gotten the better of him, and he had stretched even further over the rim to get a better look at these unusual creatures.

"Are you nuts?" Solveig whispered as he dropped down beside her. "Those things aren't going to take the time to find out whose side you're on."

"This is an amazing opportunity," he started to protest, but then continued, "but you're probably right. Now is not the time for close observation."

The Trepans that were still in the cavern had crawled under the fallen carts. They dug into the dirt beneath the carts, creating tiny shelters, and escaping the attention of the Scyllas. The giant reptiles, having totally decimated the Rebbercands, looked around for any other threats. Seeing none, they let loose ear piercing screeches that echoed off the walls of the cavern, and turned to the tunnel and the shaft to the surface. One by one they squeezed into the opening. It was a narrow fit for them as they clawed their way to the top – straight for Summer – digging their talons into the sides of the shaft. She was more than halfway down when she heard the shrieks from below. The sound made her stop dead in her flight, her blood chilling. She could still hear screeches and screams from above and debated about which direction would be worse to take. Then she heard the clawing advance from below. She was out of options.

She found a chink in the side of the wall and took refuge there. Standing on the lip of the depression, she pressed herself into the small niche and blended herself as much as she could to the surroundings. The sound of the talons digging into the sides of the portal was getting closer and closer. She could hear the razor sharp nails scraping against the rock and the dirt. The sound made her shiver.

The hissing and shrieking was nerve-wracking. Beads of sweat broke out on Summer's forehead, in spite of the cool night air that was filling the shaft. Her heart was pounding so hard, it nearly blocked out the sound of everything else. She was certain the Scyllas would be able to hear it. Finally, the lead Scylla crawled up to her position. Its claws gouged the sides of the shaft, tearing bits of dirt and rock loose, sending them to the bottom. She held her breath as the talons sunk into the wall just inches from her. She thought it was about to pass her by when it unexpectedly stopped.

She squeezed her eyes shut and concentrated with all her might on being invisible, but there was nothing she could do about the triskelion dangling from her neck. The Scylla slowly inched back down the shaft until its heads were level with her hiding place. Its multiple heads moved side to side and up and down. The forked tongue of each head shot out its mouth and danced eerily in the air.

Abruptly the larger central head turned directly toward her. She slowly opened one eye and then the next. Still holding her breath, she found herself staring into the piercing red slits centered in the deep green eyes. Every muscle in her body was rigid. Twice in a very short span of time, she had come eye to eye with these creatures. She was certain her luck had run out. The Scylla turned its head slightly and moved in closer. It sniffed the triskelion.

"It's discovered me," she thought. Her stomach flipped with anxiety.

And then in a hissing voice beast said, "Fear not, faerie princess. You have been granted safe passage for your bravery in freeing us. We will not harm you." And then it continued on.

Summer let her breath out, feeling weak in the knees as the Scylla climbed past her to the surface. She wished she could sit down; she was so drained. She took a second or two to regain what little composure remained and waited for the last Scylla to pass her, remaining glued to the wall. Only when the last tail slithered past her did she move from her spot and continue her flight downward.

After the Scyllas had left the cavern, an uneasy quiet settled in. Liam, Quinn and Sean had not renewed their attack. There was no one left to attack. The scene below them was one of carnage. The army of Rebbercands that had tormented and enslaved the Trepans had been fully vanquished. Everyone was momentarily startled when Summer made her sudden reappearance. Afraid that her friends were still in danger and needed her help, she sped as fast as she could down the portal, through the tunnel and into the cavern without any regard for her own safety. She was nearly in the center of the chamber when she came to a full stop.

"Wow," she announced. "You guys really know how to throw a party."

She flew over to her friends who relieved her of the burden of the necklace.

"I thought it was lost for a while back there," Summer said, explaining how the stone had broken into pieces when it struck the lambentite statue.

"The statue?" asked Lochen. "You were supposed to drop it on the nearest cart, not the statue."

"Oh, yeah," she said a bit innocently. "I forgot."

Before Lochen could interject, she added, "I know. I didn't forget. I did it on purpose. If you had seen that travesty, that false idol, that...that...mockery of everything honest, you would have done the same thing."

"Why don't you tell us how you really feel?" joked Sean.

Once the necklace was removed from Summer, Stella asked her if she wanted it back. She was sure she could return it to its former size.

"No," she said. "Don't get me wrong. It was a gift that I really treasured, but I think you can make better use of it. And I think Hal is right. Putting a spell on it might just reduce the power. You keep it. I know it's in good hands."

The sound of voices from near the top of the cavern echoed to the floor below. The Trepans who had been trapped in the middle of the conflict, and had all burrowed into tiny openings or dugouts underneath the fallen carts took the voices as a sign that it was safe. They all slowly came forward as they sensed the conflict was over and that they were free at long last.

"We should report back to Hal," said Natalie. "He needs to know that his underground is out of a job."

A great sense of relief washed over everyone. They all started smiling; some laughing.

"I'm sure that's one job all of them will be glad to be out of," added Natalie to even more laughter.

The Trepans began talking excitedly and for the most part drifted off one by one, returning to their friends and families to begin the task of returning their lives and their world to normal. Up on the ridge, Liam announced that he could lead the others back to the underground, and they all fell in line behind him. Sean scampered over the narrow ledge on which he had been perched and caught up to his friends as they headed back.

As they wound their way through the labyrinth of trails and tunnels, and over makeshift bridges the stress of all the events since Quinn's initial discoveries in the Ice Kingdom began to take its toll. The animated chattering faded away as exhaustion set in. Each of them was exhausted and began to slacken their pace. Before long, the line they had formed began to stretch. Periodically Sean, who was at the end, had to shake off his fatigue and run a bit to catch up to Quinn. He was afraid of getting separated and lost. Most of the others were so far ahead of him they were out of sight completely, and the few sounds they made were muffled and barely audible.

Then Sean heard a noise behind him that electrified his senses. As quickly as a flash of lightning he became suddenly alert. His body was recharged by the sudden influx of adrenalin. He stopped and spun around, pulling his slingshot from his belt and scooping up a handful of nearby stones. He crouched down to make himself a smaller and less visible target, as he scanned the passageway behind him. He couldn't see anything out of the ordinary in the dim light, but he could sense a presence that had not been there before. Slowly he inched his way along the path, carefully walking backwards, searching the darkening space he and his friends had just left. The glow of the veins of lambentite in the walls grew dimmer and dimmer.

In only a few minutes, he knew he was cut off from everyone else. He could feel that something ominous was behind him, but he didn't want to alert whatever it was by calling out to the others. He also didn't want to put them in danger when he wasn't positive a danger really existed.

"It's probably just another one of those Trepans looking for his family," he whispered to himself.

He stood absolutely motionless, holding his breath and straining his ears to pick up any sound. He had positioned himself strategically on a narrow path that had just curved through a small round tunnel. If something was coming, this was the only way it could approach and he would see it before it could see him. He put a stone in his slingshot, moving very slowly and quietly. And then, like a ship materializing in a fog, out through the tunnel opening walked B'nair carrying his whip loosely in his hand.

"Well, if it isn't the little Dozor," he said in a low voice.

Sean was so stunned by his unexpected appearance, that he lost the advantage of his position. B'nair grinned widely that same sneer Sean remembered from the first time he had seen him. He let out a low rumbling chuckle that was anything but humorous.

"I like Dozors. I usually can't eat one all by myself, though." He snorted at his own joke. "But in your case I'll make an exception."

As he took a step forward, Sean let loose with his slingshot. B'nair immediately flicked his whip and struck the stone in mid-flight. His reactions were incredibly fast. The deflected stone caromed off the side of the tunnel and fell away harmlessly.

"You'll have to do better than that," he taunted Sean. "Or is that all you have?"

Sean quickly reloaded and shot again, instantly following with another shot. B'nair cracked his whip and brushed both shots aside in a single motion.

"How does he do that?" Sean asked himself.

Sean sent two more shots towards B'nair, but didn't wait to watch him deflect those as well. He turned and ran down the path. At every twist and turn, he scooped up more stones and took more shots. Many of these he didn't even really aim. He just needed to slow B'nair down, but he wasn't having any success. He was feeling his way along the wall when he came to a fork in the path. His senses told him that his friends went to the left. He dodged the crack of B'nair's whip and took the right fork into a darker tunnel. He needed to keep B'nair away from the others at all costs.

Sean ran as fast as he could while still firing stones. In a matter of seconds he was completely lost, but he knew he had drawn B'nair safely away from his friends – or at least he hoped he had. He could only trust that they would soon discover he wasn't with them and come after him. He desperately wished for this, but deep in his heart he knew that this wasn't going to happen; at least not in time. B'nair was gaining on him. He needed to find a way to defeat B'nair on his own. There was really no other alternative.

He came up to a deep ravine at the bottom of which was a river of lava. The fire below sent waves of heat and a little bit of light upward. He scooted across a very narrow bridge and slipped on the slick stone, nearly falling. The bridge was only inches wide and smooth as glass. As he regained his balance, he looked back. The bridge over which he had skidded was a shimmering milky color. It spanned a fissure so deep he could barely see the ribbon of molten rock at the bottom. He followed the narrow ledge on his side of the bridge as it curved around to the right.

And there it ended. He was up against a solid wall with no other avenue of escape.

"Oh poop," he said to himself. "This is the wrong way."

Panicked, he spun around and started to run back to the bridge only to see B'nair standing in the center, looking directly across the circular expanse that separated them. B'nair stood still on the thin strip of stone glaring at Sean.

"Suppertime," he said with that same rumbling chuckle.

He was inching sideways, his movement and the bulk of his weight causing some of the ground at one end of the bridge to shift. Stones and dirt at the end of the bridge were jarred loose and fell to the lava. As B'nair looked down to make sure of his footing, Sean took advantage of this momentary distraction and fired a stone with all his strength. The stabbing sensation in B'nair's left eye brought his attention back to Sean.

"I'll eat you slowly just for that," growled B'nair threateningly as he continued to side step along the bridge.

The stone had lodged itself in B'nair's eye socket. He held his hand over the wound as blood seeped through his fingers. The shock of the impact caused him to shift his weight. More ground shifted and debris slid down the side of the cliff to the abyss below as he regained his footing and continued to carefully sidestep. This time Sean sent two quick shots to B'nair's knee. The sting threw his balance off and he started slipping. His arms were flailing and it looked like he was about to fall when Sean stood up and fired again.

As the small stones found their target, Sean shouted, "That's for what you did to my people."

B'nair continued to flail his arms, compensating and then over compensating for his unbalanced weight. His feet began slipping more and more and the narrow bridge began to shift even more. He could no longer keep his balance. Just before he toppled over he snapped his whip in Sean's direction, wrapping the end tightly around Sean's ankle. Unable to stop his momentum, B'nair dropped off the bridge and down into the bubbling lava deep in the darkness below. The whip drew taught and yanked Sean off the ledge. He flew at the bridge and caught it in his arms. The whip tightened around his ankle with B'nair's weight pulling on the other end.

Frantically, Sean held the thin stone expanse close to his body, wrapping his arms around it as tightly as he could. He was hugging it close, but the weight pulling him down was too much for him. His palms began to sweat and his arms were beginning to cramp, further loosening his grip on the shimmering stone. He knew this was the end. Just as he resigned himself to his fate and readied himself to let go he heard someone call his name.

"Hold on, Sean. I'll get you," shouted Quinn who was running towards the bridge. "Don't let go."

Through the sweat pouring into Sean's eyes, he watched as his friend leaped from the path, across the ledge and dove onto the bridge. As the strength in his hands gave way and he started to fall away, Quinn landed with a grunt, slid along the narrow overpass and caught Sean's arm in a vise-like grip, his other arm wrapped around the stone bridge.

They hung there, suspended for several seconds. Quinn sprawled out, straddling the thin stone bridge holding on to Sean's arm for dear life, with the whip still wrapped around his ankle and B'nair dangling at the other end. The ground around the far end of the bridge gave way some more, and it was apparent that it would not hold for much longer. It was beginning to slant downward towards the bottom of the chasm. Quinn started to wiggle backwards off the bridge, but only managed to dislodge it even more. At the same time his grip on Sean was starting to weaken. The heat rising from below was making them all sweat.

Quinn knew something was about to give. He couldn't hold Sean much longer, especially with B'nair's added weight. And he knew the bridge was about to collapse. Then he heard a noise behind him. It was footsteps running in his direction.

"Careful," he shouted back to whoever was approaching. "There's a tiny bridge that's holding all of us and it's about to give."

He wasn't sure whom he was shouting to, but he figured there were two chances in three that it was someone coming to help instead of another runaway Rebbercand. Then he heard something whiz past his head and saw the flash of a blade as it sliced through the whip, cutting it cleanly. The sudden loss of the weight of B'nair as he dropped completely out of sight caused Quinn's arm to jerk up suddenly, rapidly changing the distribution of the weight on the bridge. This abrupt movement caused the ground at the far end of the bridge to dislodge even more, and before he could do anything, it slowly fell away and dropped into the abyss after B'nair.

Only minutes before Liam had felt something was wrong and stopped long enough to see that neither Quinn nor Sean were still with the group. He shouted to the others, and without knowing if they heard or not, he rushed back along the way they had come until he found traces of the direction they had taken. Racing as fast as he could, he arrived at the path to the bridge on which Quinn was straddled, holding Sean who seemed to be tied to some kind of rope.

As soon as he heard Quinn's caution, he drew a dagger from his belt, and without breaking stride or slowing down, he threw it with uncanny accuracy. The blade neatly sliced the whip, freeing Sean from its grip. What he hadn't expected was the resulting shift in weight and movement that weakened the abutment to the point of collapsing. He watched helplessly as Sean and Quinn dropped into the blackness below, clutching the narrow stone bridge tightly in his arms. The last words he heard were Quinn saying, "I wish I was home."

Completely distraught, he returned to the others. He was nearly in tears when he told them what had happened. They were devastated by his news. The excitement of their recent victory was instantly replaced by the deep sadness of their loss. They made the trek back to the underground encampment in total silence, too shocked to react any other way.

When they shared the news with Hal, he was oddly unmoved.

"Hmmm. I've learned in my many years that things are not always as they seem. Especially in a world rife with spells and hexes," he told them all.

"What do you mean?" asked Summer, fighting back tears.

"Just that," he said somewhat too nonchalantly, they all thought. And he didn't explain any further. When he saw that they were still confused, he added, "Don't give up hope is all I can say. I'm sure your friends wouldn't want that."

They were too dejected to argue with him. Instead, Natalie said, "At least you and your people can have your lives return to normal."

"Yes," said Hal. "The Trepans have much work to do in setting things right again. My time here, though, is done."

"What do you mean?" asked Stella. "You're not staying?"

"My dear Enchantress, I am not a Trepan. I am a mere wanderer in the pursuit of knowledge. Granted, I have spent many years with these interesting people, but then there was much to learn from them. Now, though, it is time for me to move on."

With that, he said no more and took his leave. Dee thanked them all for everything they had done and turned them over to guides who would escort them to waterways and passages that would take them all to their respective home lands. They were reluctant to leave one another, but they each knew that they had been gone from their homes far too long. There was nothing more for them to do here.

They all said their farewells to each other, but with a gnawing sense of emptiness. Each of them knew they would never forget their two fallen friends. Each returned home with a story of a bitter ending to their success.

------------------ *** ------------------

Far on the other side of the world, in the Ice Kingdom, Rover and Kelsey had positioned themselves outside the gateway to the Ice Hall. They had been there since he sent them away such a long time ago. Their heads rested on their paws; their sad eyes scanned the horizon. They had no concept of the passage of time, but were keenly aware of the extended absence of their master.

Both of the suns were low in the sky. Both of them would not set. At this time of year, one of them was always in the sky, but still, it was late in the day. Kelsey heaved a mournful sigh that was immediately followed by a similar sigh from Rover. Suddenly, there was a flash of light and a loud bang. The snow directly in front of them exploded as a long thin slab of transporter stone appeared miraculously before their very noses. They jumped up, their ears raised and their heads cocked. On top of the stone were their master in some very strange clothes, and a strange looking creature resembling a bush, held tightly in their master's hand.

"Holy blubber on a biscuit," shouted Quinn. "Where are we?"

He looked around and saw Rover and Kelsey staring at him in wonder, whimpering and wagging their tails.

"Hey! We're home!"

"Well, you're home," said Sean. "And where exactly is your home?"

"The Ice Kingdom," said Quinn, still shouting. "How did that happen? I thought for sure we were goners."

"Transporter stone," answered Sean. "I never thought I'd say I was glad to see that stuff again. Even if it meant taking me to Ice Cube Land."

They got up off the frozen ground and pushed past the dogs who, by now, had realized that their master was home and were barking, jumping and running around him in circles. They ran inside, shivering.

As soon as the giant doors closed behind them, they were met by the Sage. It was as if she had been waiting for them to arrive.

"Welcome home," she said to Quinn. "You were expected."

"How did you expect me?" he asked, rubbing his arms to warm up. "I didn't even know myself that I was coming."

And then he realized something else. "Our friends. They must think we're dead."

He turned to Sean, "We have to get word to them somehow."

"By now they know what really happened," said the Sage. "Don't worry. They know you are safe. A very wise old friend of mine has assured them of that."

"How? Who? What?" Quinn was too confused to know what questions to ask first.

"Trust me," was all the Sage would tell him.

And then he remembered the conversation he had with her at the beginning of his journey.

"You said I should find the Alchemist. I never did that. I'm not sure exactly what happened, but I failed. I never found the Alchemist."

"To be more precise, I never said you should <u>find</u> the Alchemist," she corrected. "I said you must <u>search</u> for the Alchemist, which you did. In spite of what you may think, you achieved your objective, and your search provided the answers to your problems."

He looked at her a bit skeptically. Sean was totally lost.

"I don't understand," he said.

"In time you will," she answered. "For now, see to your guest and get some rest. And then she left the two weary travelers.

"Hey," he said to Sean. "We need to get you back home. We could probably use that transporter stone."

Sean shuddered at the thought of another trip on a transporter stone. He looked around at the Ice Hall and then back at Quinn.

"Actually," he said, "I think I need a vacation, and this seems like as good a place as any to take one."

ABOUT THE AUTHOR

Richard Reda spent most of his life working for various agencies and Departments in the Federal Government. He believes this gave him a solid foundation for writing fantasy and fiction. He lives with his wife in Manassas, Virginia, where he retired – the first time.

The *Quest of Eight* series originated as bed time stories for his grandchildren. As the grandchildren got older and the bed time stories got longer, it was suggested to him that he write them down. So he did. One, however, was not enough. Follow the saga in *Part Three: The Flight of the Wedgamaroon.*

14243894R00225

Made in the USA
Lexington, KY
16 March 2012